Bitter Comes the Storm

HELEN ILES

A catalogue record for this book is available from the National Library of Australia

ISBN: 978-1-876922-34-4

Published by Linellen Press
265 Boomerang Road
Oldbury, Western Australia
Website: **www.linellenpress.com.au**
Email: linpress1@bigpond.com

DISCLAIMER

While based on a true event, the story, characters and places in this book are imaginary and bear no resemblance to any real or existing person or town.

CONTENTS

Acknowledgments   vii

Part One - The Gathering   1

Part Two – Town Under Siege   79

Part Three - Rebellion   177

Part Four – The Chase   341

Epilogue   461

ACKNOWLEDGMENTS

Sincerest thanks to my family for their patience while I penned this, my first novel. And to all who provided input with critiquing and support during the long yet enjoyable process of going on the adventure. I thank you all.

Part One

The Gathering

CHAPTER ONE

Sunday, March, 1976

In a stand of tall bamboo, Nick slept soundly, his tanned cheek resting on massive biceps, his muscular chest cushioned by feathery, green ferns. High overhead, the triple canopy of Vietnamese jungle obscured the moon, and the sun, and sent all below into a state of constant gloom. Nick lay within that darkness shrouded by a haze that hovered above the ground, and moistened by the perpetual mizzle steaming down from the trees.

Beneath the pungent layer of damp earth around him crawlers slimed, bugs clicked, and a million insatiable mosquitoes attacked his skin in droves. But Nick didn't care. In the depths of his sleep he felt nothing.

Somehow though, through his fatigue, he sensed the sun had risen, that beyond the leafy ceiling the sky had gilded. Soon the land would turn from black to gold, from brown to vivid green. Soon the magnificence of the landscape he longed for would be restored. But with the light would come the heat, its steamy bite promising another day of torture, a day where his flesh oozed sweat; where his hair hung wet and droplets fell from stringy tendrils; where muddy cammies would stick to his skin like a rain-soaked poncho.

Always the heat was swift, the sun's probing rays prising apart the chiffon mists that lay above the forest floor, steaming them to an airless haze that hampered breathing. He sucked in a lungful of its thickness and forced the breath out again.

As if on cue, way up high a sunburst prised its way through the jungle canopy, sent sparks of gold dancing over giant glossy leaves, their leathery skins glistening with diamond dewdrops that glinted in the shadows, further chasing away night's earthy gloom. But Nick didn't see this – nor did he care.

As the sun's fingers crept across the jungle floor, a bird took flight, its frantic wings whooshing through the tangled verdure. Its haste stirred the mists, sent them swirling into the thicket where Nick lay. He shuddered as the chill passed over, the movement of air touching his skin reminding him that at least he could still feel. But that was all. He was so depleted of strength he couldn't even raise his head to dispel the raindrops drenching his hair from the leaves above.

He heaved another breath and slightly stirred, remembering in the deepest recesses of his mind that he'd escaped; he remembered running – running till his adrenaline receded beyond his reach, then he'd staggered, shouldering his way through tangled vines and branches in the night, his boot snagging on a twisted tree root and throwing him to the ground. Yes … he'd stumbled … then tumbled headfirst into this bamboo grove.

Wincing at the scrapes across his torso, he'd slithered on his belly, crawling deeper into its blind, even his breath becoming painful hissing gasps. *Stay only long enough to ease your laboured breathing,* he'd told himself, *then go again, continue running,* as he'd run for days, ducking and diving through the jungle, splashing across muddy rice fields and brown rivers, hunkering down in paddies whenever he saw a soul. *Keep heading south,* for south was where he'd be safe.

He knew he only had a minute to rest for his enemies were close behind him – too close. But the minute turned to an hour, and the hour into time forgotten. When he'd urged himself to push on there was not a spark left in the tank– not a sniff of fuel to keep him moving. Cursing his weakness, he'd rolled over and surrendered to his need for sleep.

A long time passed. An insect buzzed. A bug clicked. A scurry of something long slithered through the leaves near his hand. His consciousness woke. He heard the whisper of wings whoosh over him, a movement of air. And somewhere farther on … *footsteps!*

His breath left him: the soft, sandaled scrunching of many feet padded across the damp jungle floor nearby. *They're coming!*

So soft … so very soft on the trail, but he could hear them; he could hear most sounds in the jungle, so well he had been trained. And as alert as he was to sound he could also pick the subtlest movement in the trees, decipher the shadows in the branches; he knew the manner and movement of men and the way they crept, or burrowed. He could pick the snick of a rifle bolt from two hundred metres, a stifled gasp in the dark, or the strike of a match. Anything abnormal red-flagged his senses.

The brag point of his Unit, they said he was exceptional, which was why he always walked the Point. Watching. Listening. Treading the path before the rest of them, his life, and those of his Section at risk if he misread or misjudged.

He tried to lift his head now to listen more astutely, but realised his memory was off – it should have been kicking in by now. He remembered he'd been separated from the troop; he just couldn't remember how or why. Hell, he didn't even know where they were or if they were still alive. All he knew right now was that he was alone, and despairingly so.

The soft soled scrunching ceased, ramping up his senses. Another bird flapped frantically away. The insects went to ground. His breath seeped out. If he remained quiet maybe they would miss him.

But he could feel their eyes burning on his back, their hatred scorching him. They'd found him, and by the amount of breaths and murmurs reaching his ears there were too many to fight his way out this time.

He could feel the slanty eyes scrutinising him as they pressed in, and cursed silently in that moment of acceptance that his time was up. Their revenge for the merry chase he'd led them on would be slow and excruciating.

He drew a deeper breath, his mouth drying at the thought of the next few moments; at his prospects. They were waiting for him to stir, to make a move for they knew he would do everything in his power to survive.

His pulse raced; charging his skin with resolve. He tried to calm his heartbeat; tried to fight back the cold sweat rising to his skin. *So this is it? This is how it will end?*

He could accept that: Death was inevitable, *and there's nothing you can do about it when your time is up.*

He breathed out. The snick of a rifle bolt pulling back filled his ears, sent a chill scudding through him. He almost shuddered.

Time's up, Nick.

Bracing for the impact, he enjoyed the cool sensations of the world in his last few moments – the cold damp mud against his now constricted chest – the determined rays of sunlight fingering across the broad bareness of his back – the thick, heavy scents he drew in for the last time.

It's a nice enough place to die, he nodded silently. He breathed in again – deep breath. Blew it out. *But you could have chosen better.*

His spine tingled at the thought, stirred his chest; his heart kicked sharply, started racing again, loud aggressive beats that thumped in his ears. A shiver coursed through him, adrenaline charging his pulse. *Do something!* he ordered. *Get up, you bastard, and fight!*

Blood heated in his veins, raising his aggression. His teeth clenched. No matter how futile it was he would fight to the end – he wouldn't let them take him alive, for he'd heard ... *seen* ... what the Cong did to prisoners, and he wasn't about to give them the pleasure.

Many hands reached for him – dozens it seemed. His heartbeat stopped. *Too many to fight off.*

Come on! Do something before it's too late!

His hand slipped from beneath his head; slid through the

layer of slime and bugs, inch by inch edging forward. Then he made a grab for his rifle ...

– groped for his rifle

– panicked

– grappled with the earth.

Say goodbye, Nick!

His finger on the cold metal trigger he dragged the rifle into his hand, braced for impact of the bullet that would soon tear through him. The snick of another rifle bolt clicked as he rolled.

"Nick?"

He froze. Frowned. Kept his finger off the trigger.

The familiar voice was coarse, husky, female; lacked the soft sing-song lilt of Vietnamese women.

He stayed primed lest his mind be playing tricks, and forced his dark eyes open.

Flopping back exhausted, he exhaled fully; blew the air out of his lungs. He was home! Safe.

Sprawled on his belly across the expanse of a double bed, his arms stretched above his head, he noted his right finger had curled around the cold metal handle of the brown bedside cabinet. He breathed in; exhaled deeper. Vietnam was a long way away.

In the next moment he realised he was not at home, but at a place he felt comfortable, a place as familiar to him as where he'd just been. The powder-blue walls and soft-beige curtains were a late night haven.

The cold sweat abated from his skin, expelled by the warmer glow of security, his waking mind having again effected his escape.

He lifted his head slightly, turned, blinked away the scenes that lingered behind his eyes, his heartbeat beginning to beat normally again. Only when the images fully faded would his knotted muscles unwind, and he realised again, for the hours of sleep he must have had the dream had robbed him of all benefit.

Yet, even as these thoughts rambled through his mind he could still feel the eyes piercing him. He turned further.

Sheila McKenzie stood at the end of the bed, wearing the pretty pink robe he'd bought her for Mother's Day a few years earlier, and he half smiled; pulled the crumpled blue sheets higher to cover his nakedness.

CHAPTER TWO

Sheila raised the coffee cup. "Thought I'd have to poke you with a long stick," she said, amused by his modesty. A smile hinted at her lips as an image of Nick's father being far less modest when he'd used that bed flicked to her mind – and while Franco Manetti had been a good-looking man, he'd been nowhere near as tall, well-structured or handsome as Nick. Then her lips thinned as the image warmed her. How she missed those days ... those nights ... in Franco's arms.

Almost sighing, she forced the thought away and focused back on Nick. At least the drawer hadn't flown across the room this time, nor had its contents been flung far and wide.

She'd learnt early in the peace when he'd first started staying not to touch him when he slept for he'd always come up fighting, fending off enemies who pursued him in his sleep. A frightening stigma to bear, she shook her head unconsciously, one Ken McKenzie had been spared ... for her Kennie hadn't come home from the war.

Her gaze lingered as Nick's taut muscles rippled beneath the golden sheen of his skin as he rolled to his side. The long hours he worked in the sun had sculpted and bronzed him to perfection, his skin tone even deeper than Franco's. The wavy mass of thick black hair though was the same, though Franco sported distinguished grey flecks at his temples. More than anything though, Sheila adored Nick's eyes. They were deep and peaty, almost depthless, and for many years they'd held a sadness she could not repair. In the rare times his eyes lit with a smile, her heart would melt, glad that somewhere in his soul still dwelt a spark of life.

She sighed openly then pushed the thought aside. There was no point dwelling on it. Nick was very much a gorgeous man going to waste.

"Eight o'clock," she warned, sliding the coffee cup onto the bedside cabinet within his easy reach.

He yawned and rolled to his back; stretched the stiffness from his muscles as she crossed to the window and pulled back the curtains to flood the room with light. A warm yellow glow cut a path across the bed, and across Nick.

He soaked in its warmth, noting from the sun's early heat another scorcher of a day was on its way. Yawning again, he pushed the annoying dark curls back from his brow, bones clicking at the base of his neck as he moved. Then he banked the pile of pillows higher behind him and reached for the cup.

Sheila clicked the door shut on her way out and padded in fluffy slippers back to the kitchen. Nick would rise and dress in his own time, usually when his fears subsided and he'd fully controlled the anger the dreams invoked. She shook her head. Vietnam had to be the cruelest place on earth, she thought, for it never let any of them leave it fully behind.

Then sadly she thought of Kennie.

A short while later Nick entered the kitchen and pulled a chair out from the table. Sheila slid a fresh brew in front of him as he sat – hot and strong, just as he liked it. He didn't make conversation this morning – he rarely did most mornings. Frank on the other hand had always prattled on, telling her his plans for the day, his plans for his life. She never featured in them much, but she'd let him stay regardless.

She noticed Nick glance up at her, thought for a moment he was going to smile, but he didn't. It was just that familiar realisation that he'd been there again. Even with their vast age difference, she liked his company and prompted him to stay longer and longer, sometimes just sitting watching a movie after the hotel closed, or talking until it was too late for him to drive home. She liked having someone in the house when she woke in the morning.

She'd never told Nick about his father though; that would be her and Franco's secret forever – it would ruin what she and Nick shared if he knew. She smiled inwardly then widened it to include Nick. But Nick looked away again, his own thoughts retreating deep behind his eyes, drawn back into his solitude. How she wanted to throw her arms around him and beg him to let out the pain of whatever tortured him so. But he wouldn't, for Nick never gave in to anything. Not in his bloody life!

Curling his hands round his coffee cup, Nick frowned inwardly. Sheila was too quiet this morning, and Sheila was rarely short on words. His nerves crinkled as he wondered if he'd drunk too much last night; had he maybe slipped up and confessed what he'd done? It would ruin everything if he did.

But she seemed content, sucking on her half-length cigarette, her grey eyes following the smoke's helical dance to the ceiling. Indeed, she seemed calm enough.

His worried glance however drew her attention, and she smiled at him fleetingly. No, he'd not said anything. She wouldn't be standing there so calm if he had, and he wouldn't still be sitting in her kitchen. He knew he must never let the words slip out; he must guard his secret forever or lose the only person that meant anything to him. If Sheila McKenzie ever found out what had happened she would hate him to eternity.

That familiar guilt riding within him, he drained his cup, pushed the chair back and rose. Sheila crushed out the cigarette as he slid the empty cup onto the sink. He turned to her. "Thanks for the company," he said.

She placed a hand on his chest and smiled thinly. "You know I'd be lost without you coming over," she said. "You know you're all I have." She patted his heart and her face brightened. "Just don't leave it so long till the next time, you hear?"

He nodded, his lips fighting a smile. He'd be there every night if she didn't work such long hours in the bar, and a woman her age could ill-afford to sit up half the night yakking to him about nothing in particular and still run two businesses next day. He stepped out onto the polished wooden verandah, the heels of his boots resounding on the boards as he flicked a glance up and down the roadway. *Definitely a Sunday*, he noted. *Not a soul in sight.* But Cullan on any day could rarely boast more than one or two people on the street at any time. He shrugged at the reality, noting that was exactly how he liked it.

Stepping down to the bitumen between the house and hotel verandah, he headed for the yellow pick-up truck parked in the lane; walked a few slow steps backwards, tossing the keys in his hand. "And thanks for the bed," he said with an embarrassed smile.

Sheila wrapped the gown closer to her, glanced up and down the path then stepped up onto the hotel verandah. "Any time, love," she smiled. "You know there's a bed for you here any time you want." *And how many women in town would like to say that to Nick Manetti?* she smirked.

She nodded as Nick hoisted himself into the cab of the F100. He fired the engine, released the handbrake and let the slight gradient roll the truck to the road.

Drawing level with her, he nodded goodbye and pulled out onto the main street, the motor roaring throatily as he accelerated towards the fork a short way down. There, the Northern Highway swung north-east towards the mining towns, the minor road branching west to run parallel with the railway all the way to the coast. Nick took the right hand fork and headed home.

CHAPTER THREE

To the right of the fork stood the bright green and gold roadhouse, its four modern petrol pumps paralleling the highway. A shapely figure strolled out from behind the pumps, the bum-hugging shorts and deep V neck top catching Nick's attention as he negotiated the turn. *Shit! Marilyn!* he propped.

He gave her a slight nod as she blatantly watched his departure but that was all she warranted – an acknowledgment that her presence had registered. And even then he wished he hadn't done that.

Too late now though, he huffed. She'd made her presence obvious and he couldn't just ignore her. *And of course, she knew you'd look. You always do.*

He blew out another tense breath, his disappointment brewing at what might have been between them, at the growing annoyance that those thoughts flowed every time she came into view. They'd been pleasant memories at first, memories of what they'd shared and how special she was to him; memories of what they'd planned, but those memories always turned to images he detested.

He killed the tight smile thinning his lips, refocused on the 'had been'; wiped the pleasant images away by recounting how special she'd been with a lot of guys while he'd been in Nam. He didn't know why she had, and now, after all this time, he didn't want to know. He just kept reminding himself that he'd made a long term commitment to her and she'd wrecked it – she'd damn well ruined everything.

His jaw tightened as he realised for the umpteenth million time that his father had been right. *Damn him!* He'd called her names from the start, names that ignited his fist —God he'd wanted to pummel him for it. He'd labelled her 'the un-marrying kind', a whore he didn't want in his family. "Women like that have a place in life," he'd hissed at Nick one night, jabbing him in the chest with a vicious finger, "and it has nothing to do with the marriage bed!"

Like all young striplings, he'd learnt the hard way, and hated him for being right. Hell, he damn well hated her for it! He saw her now for what she really was, and realised the purpose of those tight, tight shorts and skimpy breast-hugging tops which revealed just enough to tempt the mind and make you look further. *As you just did then!*

He realised his prolonged gaze in the side mirror, watching her watch him drive away, and placed his elbow over the door ledge to block the view. His jaw muscle flexed with the unwanted admission that she still turned him on, and God how he hated his weakness!

He dragged a broad hand across the back of his neck to pull away the tension, questions rolling as they usually did: *why can't I forget how close we'd been? Why can't I push her from my thoughts once and for all? Why can't I forget how smooth she'd felt against me ...*

His heartbeat doubled. *Damn this! Why can't I just stop missing her?*

He glanced at the rearview mirror again but the image was gone – too much distance between them, and he put his attention back to the road.

If you miss her that much, take her back! She still wants you.

He heaved another breath, his nostrils flaring as the idea dried his throat.

No way! You're too proud for that!

He dragged in another breath, huffed that out as well, his grip tightening on the wheel. *No, not proud ... smart! You're too damn smart! She hasn't changed at all.*

His jaw clenched further and he thumped his fist on the door sill. *Damn her!*

Forcing his thoughts back to the road he realised he was halfway home. Had he been thinking about her that long?

On his right was Tatem's farm, Ross Tatem checking his bore before the heat became intolerable. Richardson's farm on the left, its fence-line ending at Wolsley Road where, across the bitumen, was the start of Crestwood's southern boundary.

Sheep crammed noisily round the dam in Crestwood's lower pasture and he wondered if the new owners had checked their water-points yet. Sheep liked to drink when the water was cool, either early morning or late evening. They would stress quickly in this heat without a good supply. He reminded himself to check his own stock on his return for he was already late and the day was becoming unbearable.

He glanced at his wrist watch: nine o'clock.

Slowing the truck, he turned left onto Weldon Road. Several times he'd lost control of it on the loose gravel at the corner, and he didn't want to spend the day pulling it out of the deep ditches at the road's edge — it was far too hot for stupidity.

His attention drifted down the main driveway as he passed the northern gates though he didn't expect to see much. The house sat higher up the slope, concealed behind the scrubby curve of the tree belt. The driveway was, as he expected, devoid of life, and his attention went forward again.

Ahead, the road mottled, shaded by a canopy of tall trees whose branches fingered out and interlocked over the roadway, linking Northgate with Ellesmere opposite. He pressed his foot down and pushed the truck to top the hill, burst back into the brilliant light at the end of the living tunnel. Here, the land levelled out and Nick entered the farm through a wide swinging gate.

A cruel sun scorched the ground as he zipped around the rough upper pastures. After flushing the filters at two bores he skirted the boundary fence of Crestwood, stopping part way down the slope in the shade of the southern tree belt to gaze across the lower paddocks. The noisy kwaking of a large trail-bike disturbed the silence and he watched as it passed; returned the half-saluted wave thrown by young Jason Cooper who performed the same task on Crestwood. Nick eyed the cycle; hoped it was fitted with a spark-arrester – he would hate to be fighting fires on a day like this.

Satisfied that all looked calm, he climbed back into the truck and drove on.

The sheep at this time of day sheltered amongst the blue-gums in the north-east corner, within easy walking distance of the dam; he skirted round them, located another flock dotted through the tree belt on the rise and crowded around the concrete trough that now received a fresh flow of water. Satisfied further, he drove on; returned the tooting hello from John Sampson's station-wagon as it sped home along the highway. He warmed, for he liked living here in Cullan, more so now than he'd ever done in his youth. Ironically, Vietnam had taught him something totally surprising: it had quenched his desire for action and dangerous living – it had turned his recklessness into duty-bound responsibility – it had pelted him with enough noise, fighting and death to drive him nearly crazy. Cullan had been the only cure for his growing insanity. Cullan. It was a quiet town, its people friendly yet private. And that was how he liked it best.

CHAPTER FOUR

As Nick steered the truck in beside the machine shed opposite the house he noted Sam and Pete were home, their cars sheltered beneath the giant, spreading Pepper tree in the front yard. Languidly he panned the lower pastures behind them then surveyed the slope behind him.

Northgate. Northgate. Northgate, he sighed deeply, his hands propped on his hips. *Old MacFranco's farm* – which was now his responsibility to keep going. His grandfather, Giovanni, had left it to his father, and in good old family tradition Nick's father had passed it to him three years earlier – only Nick didn't want it. Northgate had been his father's dream, not his, for he had no dreams any more – he'd lost them somewhere in the war. That was something else Vietnam had taught him, he acknowledged silently – nothing was ever permanent – so don't make plans. Don't have dreams. And never get attached ... to anything. Just survive day to day because tomorrow might never happen.

That didn't only apply in Vietnam he'd realised on returning from his last tour. His father, Franco, who'd loved this dream to the exclusion of all else, had collapsed and died in his arms. Heart attack, they'd said. And Franco had never had a sick day in his life.

Nick forced his eyes from the paddocks – he could still see his father there, in fact the man lingered everywhere – by the new tractor in the machine shed, his father standing by its rear tyre smiling with unabashed pride the day it had arrived. "Hey, Nick! Get over here!" The gruffness of his voice was as loud in his ears as if it was yesterday. Never a kind word to go with it – no praise, no hint of affection. Just orders. Orders and more orders. 'Do this, Nick. I want it done by nightfall.' 'Do that, Nick. And I want it done before I go to town.' And he'd slogged his guts out day in, day out, sometimes working under a purple sky till only the moon lit his way. Regardless of the weather, he'd be out in the paddock completing tasks boys twice his age couldn't do. He sighed again; shrugged openly. It had paid off, he guessed, trying to find the positive slant: the stamina he'd developed had prepared him well for the Army, where nothing was any different. Drilled by power-crazy officers, he'd thanked his Dad some days for the strength he'd found to see things through. The gruelling years on the farm had prepared him for that living hell on earth as Nam had been aptly dubbed. And they hadn't been far wrong.

Nick focused on the sky now as more visions filled his mind, but he fought them, pushed them back – Vietnam had also taught him control. Instead, he centred his attention on a road-train rumbling along the highway beside the bottom paddock; pushed his thoughts to other things. The land was as good a place as any, and right now it shimmered with heat waves, the cropped paddocks blurring in the distance. It was as peaceful and quiet as an atheist's Sunday mass. Sheep milled about the trees on the hill; lay motionless, twitching only to disturb the irritating flies that settled on their faces. All lay idle waiting for the change of seasons.

Behind him, higher up the slope, two kangaroos rose on powerful hind legs and sniffed the air. They could see Nick, and Nick could see them. Arrogantly, they scratched their bellies and went back to their grazing. Nick smirked. *One day*, he promised them silently, *one day you'll get too cocky.*

He shook his head. *How long have you been saying that? Two … three years?* He guessed he didn't mind them being there. To be rid of them meant killing, and he'd had enough of that to last a life-time. And as much as he hated Northgate, this farm was his haven; his place to hide from the cruel, cruel world outside.

He poked his thumbs in his pockets as the chipped and

peeling paintwork on the house jabbed at his attention. His mother would be greatly annoyed that he'd let the house fall into a state of disrepair. *But it hasn't been easy this last three years,* he told her ... told himself. He was still learning how to make ends meet, and some things just had to wait. The house had been one of them. He'd fix it this year though, he promised her.

Further up the path, across the wide verandah, laughter drifted through the grey fly-wire screen door. The deep rolling laugh ... *undoubtedly Sam's.* The higher pitched giggle ... *Carla Richardson.* Then another familiar guffaw which creased his brow, the owner's face prodding his mind, he just couldn't come up with the name to attach to it. And Pete's voice, loud and excited. Obviously the morning's activity was providing some amusement.

He raked a hand through his hair, pushing back errant tendrils that fell across his brow; noted he needed a haircut, which he might get time for this week he decided without much commitment. Right now though he debated whether he really wanted company, not liking crowds at the best of times. And the quietness of the morning so far had been pleasant. On the other hand, his thirst had become noticeable.

Huffing a breath out, he gave in to his need and headed up the path. After all, he prepped himself, he didn't have to stay long if he didn't want to.

As he drew nearer the verandah two words drifted through the doorway: his name and 'Vietnam'. He stopped; tensed. *Not a day of old Army stories.* He had enough of those memories at night without remembering during the day as well.

He glanced back at the machine shed. *That injector on the tractor is long overdue for fixing ...*

He turned back as a shadow appeared behind the fly-wire door. "Come on, Nick! What's taking you so long?"

Sam.

His back tightening, he slapped an irritated hand against his thigh, puffing a dust cloud from his jeans. *Damn it!*

It wasn't that he didn't like his mates — he did — but sometimes they reminded him too much of the war — and so much he needed to forget. Like Ben Carter's head rolling past his boot, decapitated by a cleverly concealed trap, the blade hitting so suddenly that death occurred in silence. Like Dougie Simpson, his torso skewered by a dozen sharpened stakes at the bottom of a pit, each point dripping blood and sticky entrails. Or Ken McKenzie, standing there one minute, blown to oblivion the next, only a smoking combat boot reminding him that Kennie had been there at all.

And the screaming ...

Nausea gripped his guts; fried his nerve endings. The screaming filled his head day and night, from the unlucky ones who survived, for a while. The lucky ones died outright. He swallowed thickly as screams ripped through his mind: soldiers wanting to be put out of their misery. Begging. Pleading. One bullet. Just one bullet would do it. A chill touched his skin as the returning cries flooded through his soul; cries from mates who couldn't bear to see their agony yet who couldn't do what needed to be done.

His chest caught in a vice, he shot another glance at the shed. *Which way? Run fast.*

He looked back at Sam, everything telling him he should be forgiving for Pete and Sam had missed the horrors of war, having only served one tour, and only part of that 'in country'. About the worst they'd witnessed was when he'd copped it, the long scars on his left side a constant reminder of that luckless day. They'd saved him though, all of them; they'd kept him alive till the chopper came; provided covering fire while it made it out again. *Good mates?* His lips thinned. *Yeah, good mates,* he sighed with resignation. One or two stories wouldn't hurt. If it got on his nerves, he could always drive back to town and load the truck for Monday.

The wire door creaked as he entered, warning those inside of his presence. A huge ginger tom looked up from the bench where it sunned itself in a strip of golden light below the kitchen window. It made itself heavier, blinked big yellow eyes at Nick, and purred, but didn't move. Nick stroked it absently as he passed. It was a nice enough cat, for a cat.

Around the can strewn table sat Carla Richardson – he'd been right on that score – Sam and Pete, and John Casson, the unnamed guffaw. They were each three cans into the day, which meant they'd either started early or not yet finished from the night before.

He nodded but didn't say hello. Hello was such a superfluous word and by principle he rarely used it. And if there was one thing he hated more than anything else, it was superfluity.

Something silver hurtled at him from across the room, and his hand shot out and grabbed it before it touched his skin, its sudden onslaught leaving him reeling internally for he hated being caught off guard like that, the fear of what it was always bringing back bad memories. But he shrugged it off, and inwardly settled his nerves – the metal in his hand was nothing more than a tinnie.

Pulling out a chair from the table he parked himself, noting immediately one was missing from their midst. "Where's your other half?" he asked Sam.

Sam's lips pursed and a disappointed sigh slunk out. "She's got a family thing on – something about her kid sister coming home today." He played his can in the ring of moisture on the table, his aloneness obvious with the absence of Rosalind Cooper, the stunning Barbie-doll-type model from next door. "Apparently they're close and she wants to be there to welcome the kid home."

Nick nodded. It sounded a fair enough reason to miss the exciting gathering at Northgate. Some people had family. Some people cared.

❧

CHAPTER FIVE

Same day: same time.

Sitting beneath the shade of an ancient Norfolk Pine, my jeans-clad legs dangling from the Fairlane's sage green fender, I scoffed down a lukewarm burger and Coke, eager to be on the road again. Further across the car park the big red Semi I'd been tailing from the city, which had snaffled most of the shade of another tree when we'd pulled in, was preparing to pull out and I wanted to stay on his tail. It must have looked pretty suspicious, me following the truck all the way along the highway then both choosing Ginger's Roadhouse for a rest stop. I don't know why he stopped – I stopped because my eyeballs screamed at the sunlight and my lids were winning the fight to shut out the light.

The driver had flicked me a wave as he'd crossed the car park and disappeared inside the shop – he'd obviously noticed I'd been following him. I crossed the car park a short time later, not wanting him to think I was actually stalking him. *Who needs men anyway.* I grabbed the Coke and burger, knowing all too soon I'd be on move again. We'd done the best part of four hours driving up from the south, and still had about the same to go. I just prayed I'd make it. The heat however had increased the farther north we travelled, that largely contributing to my tiredness – that, of course and the extremely early hour I'd hit the road. I also needed this rest stop to clear my head: the distance had given me far too much time to think – set too many questions rolling around in my head. *Am I doing the right thing going home? Isn't going home just an easy way of solving my current dilemma? Do I have any other option? Will Tony's wife notice there's been a woman in her house?*

Damn it, there it goes again!

I wiped a tear; slid my sunglasses back down off my head to stop the burning. The counter girl in the roadhouse must have thought I was weird wearing them inside but I needed to hide my eyes. I didn't want any looks of sympathy, or anyone asking if I was okay. Maybe I wasn't okay right now, but I would be. In time I would be. No way would I let Tony destroy me that much – restoring myself just might take a while.

The truck driver slammed the cab door and cranked up the engine, which prompted me to do the same. It would be so easy following along in his slipstream for as long as he headed north – I'd decide what to do next when we separated. Right now I was much too tired to think of more than that and, with my whole life crammed into the back seat and trunk of the Fairlane, or poked into feed bins and buckets inside the horse float, taking the easy option was the sanest thing to do.

Sliding from the fender, I flipped the empty can into the big yellow bin, noting the red ants scurrying from a nest the truck had parked on. *That's right. Just when life is all bells and roses some bastard comes and stomps on your nest.*

Watching those ants flooding out of that tiny mound, I realised I had every right to be as angry as those ants – angry at Tony for destroying my home and sense of trust. Not angry at Madeleine. Tony was the one who'd left me without a hole to crawl into; left me without a purpose, or options. He'd taken our business. *Our* business! My money, the whole six months of competition winnings poured into *our* venture, which he now had for himself – a venture built on my skills and reputation. *Had this all been part of his plan, or did it just happen that way?*

"I've got something to tell you," he'd said after taking the late night phone call. He'd climbed out of bed, walked across the room, as if the news was best coming from a distance. *Right on that score, bucko!* His expression had instantly worried me. "My wife's coming home."

I said: "What? … Say that again … did you say 'wife'? You don't have a wife?" I grinned. He had to be joking

He gave me that 'oh-yes-I-dooo' look. "We've been separated for two years."

"No. You're kidding me!"

That look again purchased my belief. I shook my head; felt suddenly cold. "Why didn't you tell me? …" I'd flung the blankets back, climbed out of bed, my skin crawling at the thought of sleeping with a married man. "You bastard! I had a right to know if you were married, Tony." *God, what did that make me?* Disgust crawled all over me, followed by the raging pain of betrayal. I almost laughed, praying he was really kidding. But his eyes, those beautiful blue grey eyes, said otherwise. "Christ, I feel like a whore. I've been sleeping with a married man!" The heel of my hand slapped hard against my forehead. "Why didn't you tell me? Why didn't you tell me you were married? You utter bastard!"

He shrugged. "Would you have taken the chance on us? … come into the venture if you knew? I never thought for a minute she'd come back."

"And that makes it alright?" I looked for something to throw at him, but pillows seemed so insignificant. "So what now? What does she want?"

Tony scratched his head. "She wants to come home."

"And?" My thoughts blurred between packing my bags and running and wondering where I figured in all this. Just what did I mean to him? What did our love for each other mean at this awkward time? How would I cope without Tony? How would my days be without him?

He'd obviously already thought about that for his answer was immediate. "She owns half this property, and I don't intend to lose any of it in a divorce settlement. If she wants to come home, I have no choice, she comes home and we pick up the pieces. You can move into the vet's room and it can be business as usual. Nothing has to change between us, we just have to be careful."

I felt even more disgusted and a lump blocked my throat as he spoke. It was one thing to be a whore unknowingly, but for him to expect me to maintain that role when his wife returned churned my stomach. In that precise instant I grew up, and the silver lining blew off my Cloud 9. I realised my role in his plans. Living as business partners and lovers, I would put all my winnings back into the business, which I did, needing no nest egg for the future – we had each other – which is what I'd done for the past six months. I knew I'd been pushing Jerry too hard, hitting show after show, but being on the circuit meant I was seen, my skills noted – the stables were now full of horses sent for me to train. Becky Cooper, the youngest competitor on the show circuit, was now Showjump trainer to the rich and famous. Well, to the rich at least. *Yahoo! Becky Cooper, stupid bloody fool.* Tony needed me to be his rider. The rest was just convenient.

"So what about the horses?" I asked, coming to my knees on the bed and fighting back tears, fighting to hold some semblance of dignity where there was none. I felt raped. "What about our clients?"

"As I said, you can move into the barn – nothing will change. We'll still be together. You'll still have horses to train." It was stated so matter-of-factly, just another phase of his plan playing out, a plan thought out to the last detail in advance. I made a mental note to contact our clients, at least to advise them I was no longer training their horses. I was no longer involved in the business. How could I ever resurrect the dream that had just gone up in smoke.

That's when the first tear fell; I couldn't contain it. Barely an adult, my life-long dream had been achieved and lost, and he'd just ripped out my heart.

Battling to retain my pride, I'd tossed everything I owned into the cavernous car boot or the front of the horse trailer. At four in the morning I'd bandaged Jerry's legs, booted up Millstream's for the journey, not knowing what I would do or where I would go. I was just getting out.

Tony hovered for a while, acting contrite, but he had more sense than to ask if I wanted help. As dawn poured over the rolling hills and turned our fields to gold, throwing off the silhouette of my brand new set of show-jumps, tears rained down. My back turned to Tony, I loaded the boys as the sun touched the barn, crawled the Fairlane away down the long rutted lane to the highway.

"I'll get you your money," he promised as I climbed into the car, "it'll just take me some time."

"I need it straight away," I bit back, knowing there was very little cash in my purse, none in the bank, and I would need to buy horse feed at the first opportunity. "And you can take my name off the front sign. Take my name off the business. I want it done today!" It probably would be so his wife didn't see it.

After an hour of driving the pain and anger merged, having realised what I'd lost – I'd lost my livelihood – I'd lost my lover, who I thought was my best friend, and my dreams that one day our surnames would be the same I'd lost my reputation on the showjumping circuit. *Just how many of them knew he was married? Were they laughing at me because I didn't know? Why didn't anyone tell me?*

In the next hour I realised I was just driving, with absolutely no idea of where I was going; realised I had nowhere to go, and nowhere to bed the horses down come nightfall.

Thoughts poured into options. My first priority was to my boys, Jerry and Millstream; my second was to find some cash to support them. With no big circuit events scheduled in the near future and Jerry needing a spell, I had no other option than to return home. And that was the biggest fall of the axe I had to bear – Tony had chopped out every ounce of my pride and I had to go crawling home.

So here I was, halfway there, alone, stone broke, and with my two magnificent boys needing care.

Through the rear-vision mirror I glanced through the float window at the shadowy silhouettes of one great grey head and one fine brown one. A new trickle of tears wet my cheek. *Please don't let the stress of this journey set them back in training. And please don't let their legs blow up from the long travelling.* Another more poignant thought drilled through. *And please don't let them colic from the disruption. I simply can't afford a Vet bill right now.* And that would be all Dad would need to crank up again.

The horses watered, I pulled onto the highway, the rumbling V8 chewing up the distance as I chased down the red Semi. *Pops will have a field day when I get in, you watch, Jerry-boy,* I mused.

"We can't bear any more of this wasteful expense, girlie." I mimicked him perfectly. *"It's about time you grow up, Rebecca. Get a real job like other girls your age before that brute of a horse breaks your flamin' neck!"*

"He isn't a brute," I'd snap back at him. "He just doesn't like being bullied."

That had been the turning point in our relationship. With Grandpa no longer around to see, he'd stopped helping me completely. But with that Jerry had stopped reacting badly too and we'd started winning events. I guess Dad hated me for that, for being so right. And he probably hated Grandpa too because Grandpa had always had faith I'd make it to the top. Then Dad started pushing me to 'get a real job'. The problem was, I didn't have the brains other girls had – he'd told me that most of my life. Well, maybe I wasn't a brain, but I could ride a horse, and I'd earned more in the last three months than my friends earned in a year. I wondered if Dad would acknowledge that. Surely he would know the cost of the car and horse trailer I'd bought since leaving home, and of course I would wear them like a badge. At least I no longer had to worry that he'd suddenly refuse to drive me to a show, leaving it so late that I had no time to organise anything else. I was fully set up now, totally independent, and sooner or later he would have to accept that this is what I do.

My foot had pressed harder on the pedal, and I noted with the increase in speed the temperature gauge had climbed again. I eased my foot off; settled my breathing. *Don't let him get to you.* But the corners of my lips lifted at the thought: *Won't Millstream get on his goat.*

I glanced back at the brown head tossing in the breeze coming through the air vent above the float's front window. Jerry had caused so many arguments over the years he'd grown used to the shouting and no longer flinched when Dad was around. I could only hope my second in the string would follow his lead in the face of this adversity.

Then I wondered if Ros would be home, or if she was on some photo-shoot somewhere off the coast – the early hours of morning when I'd rung home had been an inappropriate time to ask. I prayed she was for I needed her shoulder right now and Suzie and Jason were so young we were planets apart, almost estranged. If I could just bite my tongue, avoid arguments, I would take the next few months to get back on my feet and work my way back to the circuit. This time though, I wouldn't rely on anyone. I didn't need Dad's help. I didn't need Tony's. Hell, I didn't need any goddamned man for that matter, for anything!

CHAPTER SIX

Same day, same time. Central Queensland.

By mid-morning the old Windeyer Pub was crowded, stout, sweaty men shouting jibes across the room or jostling each other for a space at the bar. Others slouched at tables, breathed in smoke, an occasional laugh overriding calls for another round as the chink of glass upon glass emptied another jug. Grey smoke hung from the ceiling where the slow rotation of overhead fans swirled it back to the floorboards, the oppressive layer doing little to improve the general air of despair infecting most of the drinkers.

Behind the bar, three young lasses dipped and darted, blocking out sexual innuendos as they kept a steady supply of liquor to the glasses. The Publican grinned widely, its spread in direct relation to the clink of coins dropping in the till. He hoped the flow continued much longer for grim times were coming. The last of the Semis had headed south that morning, their bellies filled with three thousand bleating sheep. Only those lucky enough to be worth carting found greener pastures – those less well-bred or old found the Pit – and any likelihood of future employment for shearers, shooters and rousties had just gone south with the flock. With the muster over, the town would soon return to its quiet, sleepy countenance. For now though, he alone would reap the benefits of this job's end.

He scanned the room from corner to corner. Tomorrow it would be empty, the lads dispersing in all directions looking for work, the bar once again left to the handful of station-hands living out of town. Not a happy prospect, he thought, but for now, business boomed. Tomorrow, the sad realisation would take place that outside was drought, and drought meant everyone suffered.

His interest lingered on the farthest corner where a group of tables had been dragged together by McCaig's rabbly bunch. Not a laugh had escaped the table since they'd arrived and that worried him. Huddled at their centre was McCaig, a mean, self-centred creature if ever there was one. If a fight broke out, the Publican predicted, his fingers drumming on the counter, it would come from that direction, and he would be ready.

Ignorant of the Publican's interest, Bill McCaig snubbed out his cigarette with fat stubby fingers, forced the filter deeper into the ashtray till butts spilled onto the table. Right now he felt real shitty for his livelihood had just been ripped away and there was no chance of another job in this dead hole of a town. How was he going to feed himself now; buy his beer? He'd be penniless in no time. And that, he considered, was good enough reason for his meanness.

To his immediate left sat his son, Ron, a tall, wiry thirty year old. Completely opposite to his father in looks, Ron mimicked his Dad in action, his brow wrinkling and his eyebrows dipping down – he too had a wife to support, and a baby on the way. What the hell were they going to do? What the hell were they all going to do?

Old Jim Sweeney emptied his glass in one long gulp and slapped it down on the table, his thin gnarled hand matching the rest of him. "Ah! stuff it!" he spat, pushing his trademark green peaked cap back off his weathered brow. "I'll just hafta go back shearin', that's all ... if me back'll hold out."

Indeed, his bones cracked and his fingers trembled when he worked the shears now, his withering frame barely lasting out his nearly sixty-two years. Most nights he popped pills for the pain of his deformities, but lately even the pills hadn't helped.

"There's no bloody sheep up here no more, you stupid git!" McCaig snarled. "We just sent the bastards south, remember?"

Jim touched a flame to his scantily rolled smoke, rekindling its life. "Then I'll just hafta follow the bastards, won't I!" he shot back, flicking out the burning match and tossing it into the mounded ashtray. He shot a glance at McCaig. "If you had any backbone you would too," he challenged, cringing that that was not quite as he'd intended it to come out. He wondered at his chances of surviving the remark and countered with another. "You used to be a crack shearer in your time, Bill."

Jim's watery grey eyes followed McCaig's slow rise from the table; he forced himself not to slink in his chair for nobody ever came off unscathed questioning Bill McCaig's backbone, not even a mate. But a smile inched over the fat man's face and he eased himself back down again at the compliment.

Jim breathed with relief.

McCaig watched his old friend across the table, realising 'Jimmy boy' had baited him. He gulped a mouthful of beer to cure the dry patch in his throat and nodded: indeed, he had been a 'gun' in his time – two hundred plus a day and everybody knew it. But he hadn't sheared in years – had given it up – and now too many young fellas were in the game to give it another go. Even Ron was as good as him, though he'd never tell him so.

He glanced round the table, wondering if they knew it was beyond him; wondering if they knew in his final season he'd busted his gut every day to keep ahead of blokes half his age, half his experience. It had nigh on killed him.

Nah! he shook his head. If he went back shearing now, he'd just be one of the team. He shook his head again. "Nah! The missus would have a screaming fit if I pulled up stakes now. I think she likes living up here." Of course, he could always use the old bitch for an excuse!

But Jim's point sparked Ron's interest. "Rosie wouldn't care, Dad! Why don't we? Kerry could move in with Rosie and we could head south. We gotta find work somewhere."

Another jug arrived on the table and tilted glasses chinked against glass; were filled to the brim again.

"We've got a team right here," he said, scanning those at the table. Steve Beattie, the slate-haired, green-eyed vagrant who, at twenty-four, was on the road picking up jobs wherever he could; had been rousting in sheds in the south before moving up to Queensland, and had also bragged one night after one too many drinks he'd been tossed out of home for groping his little sister. He'd been on the road ever since and had no intention of ever going back. Any job that came his way suited him just fine. Beattie had a mate, Pete Lacey – Lacey to his friends. Older than Steve, he was a bit more reliable. Auburn-haired and athletic, he worked like a Trojan in a fit. Ron wondered at times though if he was fully set up top for the coldness of his narrow eyes sometimes frightened him, and Lacey had an obsession, one rule he always brought to bear: nobody touched his stuff. He had two friends to enforce that rule: Beattie, and a small steel-bladed knife he always carried. Lacey had toured the sheds with Beattie, driving the only other thing that mattered to him – an old bus-cum-camper van and the few possessions in it.

Counting them, old Jim Sweeney, his Dad and himself, they pretty much had a team. His gaze drifted across the room to Alan Todd and Merv, the cook with no known last name. They also needed work.

McCaig scratched his beer belly through a slit in his shirt where a button had popped open; he didn't bother doing it up for it would only pop open again and he decided Rosie would hear of its errant ways in no uncertain terms. He burped loudly; wiped beer froth from his mouth onto the back of his hand. He said nothing.

Sweeney's gaze remained on the fat man. "Go on, Bill, what do ya say? You need a job just like the rest of us, and I really do need this season. Hell, no team's gonna take me on this close to startin'." He leant across the table. "Come on. You have the knack for making things happen."

Scowling, the fat man half shook his head.

"Shee-it! If you really don't want to shear, Bill," the man prodded, "go contractor. You can go get us all the jobs."

"Yeah, Dad, go contractor," Ron urged. "We've got a team already, and I know a wool-classer that'll tie in with us. We can work our way south then across the bottom. We could really make a killing if we move now."

McCaig's heavy jowls tightened and he stroked the heavy stubble on his chin, his eyes narrowing. True, there was good money in shearing, and the south now crawled with the sheep they would have done if the drought had broken. But it hadn't, and now there was nothing.

His lips pursed, and his squinting eyes settled on the only two at the table who were yet to say a word. He didn't miss the glance Dave Taylor threw his brother nor the subtle shake of his head.

Neither of the Taylor boys had worked much with sheep, not until the recent Pit slaughter. Yet being neither shearers nor rousties, Taylor's expression indicated he knew making money wasn't as easy as Ron made it sound, because Ron had forgotten about boundaries – team boundaries – and about gaining contracts. One team wouldn't take kindly to another intruding on their turf. He sensed Taylor was about to make a point.

"You lot have got to be fucking joking!" the older Taylor scoffed, lowering his glass to the table. "Will you take a look at yourselves ... take a good damn long look. Who the hell would hire an overweight..."; his cold green eyes pierced McCaig – "... over-aged ..."; his scrutiny fell on crippled Jim Sweeney – "... under-experienced bunch as you lot?"; he scanned the rest at the table and snorted a laugh. Before he could add more McCaig shot to his feet, his chair toppling over backwards as he reached across the table and locked a grip on Taylor's thick neck.

"Nobody belittles William T. McCaig, you fucking creep!" he bellowed. "Nobody!"

Taylor tensed his bull-like neck, locked mean green eyes with bright blue ones, his piercing stare warning McCaig of his error. He didn't retreat, and he didn't shift, the smirk on his lips showing the fat man that his grip lacked the strength to even make him wince. But McCaig had already sensed it, and Taylor could see it in his eyes. All he had to do was reach up and snap the fat man's wrist ... snap it quick and hard. But not this time. And Taylor was a master of timing.

For the moment he let it go, but his sneer grew, further alerting McCaig to his mistake. The concern in the fat man's eyes verified what Taylor already knew. He was however unprepared when the fat man hauled him up till they were nose to nose. Glasses toppled, and beer spilled over the table as the others grappled to restore order.

"... then we'll punch some fuckin' heads until they do!" the fat man hissed in his face. He tossed Taylor back to his chair, its legs clattering on the floor as the force almost knocked him over backwards. "Now it's your round!"

Taylor's smirk spread to a smile and he glanced at Ben, the slight grin and subtle tilt of his head telling his brother McCaig stood no chance of beating him. Ben's slow blink confirmed he understood as Dave picked up his glass and emptied the contents down his throat. That smile and hard gleaming eyes also told McCaig, and Ben, that if McCaig ever tried that again he'd be a dead man.

"Yeah? Well if I'm doing the buying," Taylor barked, "we're coming with you."

Silence.

Then McCaig's hearty laugh boomed around the room. In the space of a few moments he'd been duped into doing something he didn't want to do, and, as uncannily as it had been done, a team had been formed, and the team wanted him as Boss-man. Hell, if it was going to be that easy, he might as well go for the ride. All he had to do was work out the finer points, and tell Rosie he was going.

By the time they left the pub hours later he actually looked forward to going. The break would do him good, and it would be a great holiday away from Rosie. A nice, long holiday.

CHAPTER SEVEN

Pete Kennedy sat across the table from Nick, his smile spreading that Nick had joined them. It was no big secret Nick hated crowds and seldom suffered parties. Even in the Army he'd stayed to one side listening to the sparring but rarely joining in. It had caused Pete to note some time ago that even at home Nick worked too hard, worried too much, and kept to himself too often. This morning would give him a chance to relax.

To make the session really enjoyable however he'd have to get Nick talking and that wouldn't be so easy.

Flicking away the shaggy blonde fringe that tickled his eyebrows he smirked then pulled it back. He'd have to be careful for he didn't want to upset Nick seeing the man had taken him in and all. And he liked living at Northgate; liked it a lot. The quiet was bliss, the routine calming, and the isolation had given him time to put his life back in order. Living here had kept him away from the trouble he'd created after the Army had told him "Go back and pick up where you left off," literally abandoning him. But picking up his life again wasn't so easy. They'd thrust him into a war he didn't want any part of; they'd taught him how to kill till it was almost second nature then they'd just cut him loose. Life after the Army was dull, so he'd made his own fights, and he'd found more trouble than he could deal with. Finally to flee the city he'd jumped aboard a fast moving truck hauling north. Where it was headed he didn't care – anywhere was better than where he was. Somewhere along the highway, a road sign jogged a memory. Cullan. So he'd stopped off to look up a friend. He'd not yet gone looking for that truck hauling north.

His smile tightened as he flicked a glance at Nick. The man

was watching him, his dark eyes unobtrusively taking in every detail, undoubtedly suspecting he was up to something. Pete widened his grin and stared straight back.

Nick held Pete's stare a moment longer then diverted his gaze to his can, his eyes hardening as he thought of ways of escaping. They almost glinted when he remembered the truck down in Sheila's Supply Yard still needed loading for Monday's deliveries. But the mere thought of Sheila sent him to dark places too; welled up memories and hurled him back in time ...

After his release from the Army Hospital he'd headed straight to Cullan, the quietness of the town, the isolation of the farm a peculiar cure for his ills as its endless demands induced a depth of fatigue that sometimes blotted out the war. But only sometimes. When the chores on the farm were done, he'd head into town and do things for Sheila, taking care of the tasks Kennie would have done if Kennie had come home from the war. It was a war Kennie should never have gone to. For whatever stupid reason he'd enlisted, he'd ended up in Nick's Unit, totally unprepared for what he would encounter. *Hell,* Nick shook his head, *they were all so unprepared.* Kennie though had coped the worst, and the outcome was predictable. Tiring too quickly, affected by the intense humidity, carelessness often crept over him. Nick had watched him closely, more closely than the others, but even that hadn't saved him. Now he bore the guilt.

He heaved a sigh and shook his head. Had he not stopped for that ten seconds to examine tracks in the dirt, had he been more attentive that Ken had passed him on the trail, maybe Ken McKenzie would have come home and Sheila wouldn't be left without her son. Ten seconds, and it would have been him not coming home, and Sheila would still have something to live for.

He couldn't tell Sheila about the ten seconds, yet he remembered it every time he saw her, every time her name was spoken, and he looked for more work to blot out the guilt.

Coping like this, he hoped the visions would one day erase from his mind.

Occasionally, he waded through a day when he didn't think about the war at all, but those days were rare. And death was a constant reminder to him for it was everywhere. His father was gone, dying in his arms a few months after his return; his mother gone, passed away before he'd enlisted; and Marilyn ... well, she was off with anyone she could lock her legs around. Now he was on his own, and that was the way he liked it – nothing left to destroy him. He now lived day to day keeping alive his father's dream, locked into the daily routine of the farm.

He was happy enough with that existence. Then Pete had wandered up his drive one day, and Northgate proved good for them both, the quiet and hard work filling the gaps. In the autumn they would shear the sheep then sow a crop and watch it grow. In the spring they'd crutch the sheep, cut the crop, turn it, bale it, stack it and turn the sheep out onto the stubble. Then they'd shear the sheep, sow the crop, and so it went on. It was a good life – a disciplined life – disciplined maybe only by the seasons, but it was discipline just the same. Pete's visit had started two and a half years ago. For the past eighteen months, he'd added Carla Richardson to his plans.

He swept his gaze round the table.

Pete pulled the top back on his next can, leant forward and smirked – it was time to get Nick talking. "Did I tell you Nick was our Sergeant?" he said to Carla, his lips pursing as Nick glared at his can. The man's brown eyes darkened and narrowed, which they did when something bugged him. Sometimes Nick's eyes turned almost black, but that was dangerous territory, and he always made sure he never pushed Nick that far.

Carla's cheekbones lifted, and her blue eyes sparkled though she tried to conceal her pleasure that Nick had joined them. "Yeah, I knew that," she murmured, gazing across the table. As long as she could remember, which was her lifetime growing up in Cullan, she'd adored Nick Manetti. Even though he was always dark and broody, one glance from him made her heart skip double beats, robbing her of breath. He was bigger than most boys in town, which hadn't changed over the years, and even now her father sometimes called him 'that veritable powerhouse'. The only thing that dampened his tough exterior was a friendship he'd kept with young Ken McKenzie. Kennie, The Wimp, they'd all called him. But Nick's friendship changed that – it brought Kennie untold respect, for if anyone picked on Kennie Nick stood behind him, propping him up. She remembered the later years, Nick hanging about in Cullan with a few of the other boys, or sitting with the Carter brothers on farm-bikes behind McKenzie's Supply Yard. That was before Nick had gone to war. Her crush was giant-sized back then, along with most of the other girls in town. She still admired him now: those deep looks, those dark eyes, that rugged square jaw, and those incredible muscles. There was no denying he was the most desired man in the whole northern wheatbelt.

Her gaze drifted to his biceps. For years she'd longed to see if her fingers would touch if she locked a grip around them, and they were so close now she tried to estimate if they would. She looked back at his eyes, remembering that her mother had once said Nick was a little boy who needed a great big hug, and a smile flickered at how often she'd longed to give him that great big hug, even more so since he returned from the war. He'd returned so quiet, so serious, so awfully alone, maybe even looking a little dangerous now with all that army training. Then she'd heard what happened when he'd caught Marilyn Perry in bed with that creepy boy from Dayton, and the town now feared him. She wasn't afraid though. Not really afraid.

Her smile grew as she realised she still wanted to give him that great big hug. But Nick was so much older than she, and he hadn't noticed that she'd grown while he was away. Then Pete had come along ...

She shrugged inwardly, happy with things the way they were, but found she enjoyed Nick's presence at the table a little more than she really thought she should.

Smiling wider, she dragged her gaze from his biceps and chest, blushed on realising Nick was watching her, a wry smile on his beautiful well defined lips.

"I bet I could tell you a few things about him he'd rather you didn't know," he said. His delectable smile and mellow voice tumbled her heart, flipped it like a landlocked fish. She caught the devious glance he flicked at Pete, and her skin tingled that he'd included her in his ruse. His softer countenance in that moment burned deep into that place she stored her precious memories.

She caught Pete's 'you-wouldn't-dare' expression, and warmed that it amused Nick too. She smiled fully as Pete reacted with: "Oh no! ... she doesn't want to hear about that sort of thing! Just tell us about that time your Unit had that run in with the Yanks."

Carla's high pink cheekbones lifted further and she nodded to Nick. He shrugged and smiled back.

"Okay, but I'll tell you about him later."

Pete squeezed her hand as Nick began recounting, weaving one tale into another, exposing vivid pictures of the real war – from the antics of R & R in Saigon to the sprawling jungles and the ghost-like Viet Cong – to soldiers' reactions and how they would shoot at the slightest sound because they would never see the enemy – how they would move with gut-wrenching fear knowing the next step might be their last ...

Nick's first tour had been a heart-stopping experience; his second just a job to be done, but the fear in both was always present. It was fear that kept them alive. And while he told true accounts of what happened where, he kept the details guarded, oh-so very guarded. They didn't need to know how many body parts lay strewn around a smoking fox-hole in Long An; nor how quickly a razor wire severed a jugular vein; nor ...

He looked up from his can. Carla was perched on the edge of her seat, leaning forward, her white knuckles resting high on sun-kissed cheeks. Her jaw had dropped open and her blue eyes were wider than usual. Her face almost matched the blondeness of her hair. A bit more detail, he realised, and he could probably have her puking on the floor. But he wouldn't do that, he caught himself. That sort of detail no-one would hear. Those memories were his until he came to terms with them. But now, he sighed inwardly, he'd talked long enough. It was time to weasel out of this 'good' time.

Glancing at his wrist watch he rose, noting the cans he'd downed. *Four!* Had he been there that long? Drank that much? "Sorry people, but I've got work to do," he said, giving Carla a light smile. He pushed the chair back in. "I'll see you all later."

Heading for the door, he picked up the cat and dropped it on the floor where it belonged.

Carla's heart thudded as her gaze followed him. She was not queasy at all; awe-struck was more like it; totally entranced that Nick had seen, done and survived.

The room remained silent as the door creaked then banged behind him.

"Shee-it!" John Casson drawled when Nick was out of range. "Incredible." He heaved a breath to restore his normal breathing. Until that morning at Northgate he'd been jealous of those who'd gone to Nam. Now he thanked his lucky stars he hadn't.

His gaze shifted to Sam and Pete for they'd been there too. If Nick had seen and done ...

But Pete caught the look and shook his head. Sam's attention however remained on Nick, his eyes narrowing as he wondered if he'd heard the words correctly. He'd certainly felt the icy chill of fear as Nick brought it all back in wide-screen technicolour, stirring memories as vivid as yesterday of the times in the jungle.

He remembered when Nick had saved his life, risking his own in the balance though Nick had never mentioned it, not then and never since – he'd simply sailed over him, rolled to his feet in the one swift move, hurled the lobbed grenade away and gotten on with his job. But that was Nick. He only talked of less important things, as he had just then, reviving the tingle of excitement as he'd walked them down silent jungle paths, hidden them deep in the folds of beautiful valleys, meandered them along the banks of winding rivers. He'd seen again the smiles of friendly natives, and their wide grinning children, heard them calling "Soldier! Soldier. You American?"

- Nah, mate! We're Aussies!

His eyes narrowed more for he'd noted how Nick's deep voice had softened at those recollections. But there was something else mixed with it – something in the vocal inflections. He scanned the others and wondered if they'd heard it too. To him it had sounded like someone recalling a long lost friend; that quiet tone of familiarity tinged with a hint of longing. His frown deepened. Could it be that Nick actually missed those times?

His jaw crossed as he wondered what the 'other side' of Nick Manetti was like – the unshielded side. Maybe, just maybe, it had tried to break through that morning. His gaze returned to the door as he tried to imagine how anyone could possibly miss Vietnam.

Then Pete's fervent response broke through his contemplation: "No, no ...," he waved John off. "Nick did three years in Nam; he saw it all. We," he said, tipping his head to Sam, "... we came in at the end. Things were a lot calmer then as we backed out of the war. And thank God for that! What we saw was bad enough." His smile thinned and he gripped Carla's hand.

"So that's why Nick is like he is," John mused openly, maybe a little ruefully as if a bright light had suddenly flicked on.

"Like what?" Sam frowned. To him, Nick was Nick, unless of course John had detected what he just had.

"Silent. Broody," the man declared. He took a swig from his can. "You know, I've often been tempted to go up to Nick at the bar some days just to say hello, but I'm always afraid I'll catch him on a bad day and die for it."

Pete's guttural laugh ripped through the room. "Not many people would admit that," he said when he finally settled his mirth, "but I don't think you're the only one who feels that. Personally, you all couldn't be further from the truth. You're just scared of his size. You just need to take the time to know him."

Sam however shrugged. "I don't know so much," he muttered. "I've known Nick a long time and I think he's walking the edge." He drew a deep breath as images flashed through his mind. "... and I sure as hell don't want to be around when he tips over the other side.'

Pete's grin ebbed, and silence reigned for long moments. Then he said: "Nah!" though he didn't sound as cogent as before.

Sam nodded at his own statement. "You don't see the horrors he saw in Nam and stay totally sane," he apprised. "I think John's right. Get on the wrong side of Nick, push him a little too far while he's sitting on the brink and you just might die for it. Even in Nam, killing didn't seem to bother him much."

CHAPTER EIGHT

Propped against the green and gold petrol pump, Marilyn sighed deeply as a huge silver Semi geared down, made the turn at the fork and rumbled away to the north; she scrunched her eyes against the dust billowing across the intersection; kept them closed as another Semi approached heading south, their deep throaty horn blasts blurting Hello as they passed each other. She listened as the dark blue Semi disappeared behind the Hotel opposite, its loud grunt as it picked up speed and headed out of town drawing her thoughts – she wished she'd moved to the city when she'd had the chance; wished she had the nerve to hitch a ride on one of those south bound trucks. Maybe not moving from Cullan when her mother left was one of her biggest mistakes; maybe things would have been a whole lot different if she had.

Her second biggest mistake, and her throat tightened at the thought, was the only reason she stayed, and he'd headed down to the Supply Yard some time ago and hadn't come back yet.

Huffing a long breath out, she pushed herself away from the pump, wiped her hands on paper towels at the dispenser and glanced at her watch. It was three o'clock – time for her break. If she could catch Nick alone, maybe she could to turn things around.

Checking her image in the roadhouse window and signaling Kate it was her break time, she adjusted her low-cut blouse to sit a little lower and finger-smoothed her lipstick. If she really put her mind to it she could win Nick back. There was always hope, especially seeing even Ros Cooper hadn't turned his head and she'd thought when Ros had arrived in town that would have been the end of it. In fact, no girl had turned Nick's head since they'd split. She smiled, remembering that she had that very morning, the thought spurring her on.

Flicking her sun-gold hair over her shoulder, she headed for the Supply Yard. It was time to start de-bricking that very high wall he'd built around himself.

Backed up to the doors of the grey Farm Supply shed, the old red Atkins truck stood loaded with tight rolls of wire, tall cylindrical stands of fencing mesh and heavy bundles of black steel posts, the flat-top's tray filled to brimming. Nick's back and chest glistened from the effort expended loading it, his veins standing proud. He swung down from the tray, shook his arms to release the bunched up tension of his aching biceps – it was a good healthy ache, he noted; a good healthy sweat, and he'd enjoyed the time in oblivion creating it.

Picking up the orange rope and striding beside the tray, he noted the sharp sting of the sun on his skin and reached for the hose; flooded cold water over his head and neck. The chilly liquid pouring over his chest and shoulders made him flinch, yet it felt good. Shaking the moisture from his hair, he smoothed the black curling strands back with both hands and looked at the fruits of his labour, nodding that at least this part of the day had been productive; he hoped he had sweated out the alcohol he'd consumed the night before; maybe some of what he'd consumed that morning. Now that had been a rarity he didn't want to make a habit of, he smirked inwardly, glad that he didn't drink like he used to; more so, glad that he no longer needed it like he'd needed it in the Army. On his first tour, he'd drunk himself stupid just to find restful sleep, sleep so deep dreams couldn't break through. Somewhere though between that tour and the next, his sense of survival changed. He didn't know when – maybe he'd just realised that to stay alive he had to be aware.

The orange rope, now tied to the side-bar of the truck, arced up and over the load, unfurling on the bitumen on the truck's other side. He followed it round, wondering why he bothered to drink at all these days – like those four this morning. He didn't need them. Found no pleasure in the taste. No release. Certainly, they provided no escape. And the dreams that came with the liquor these days were worse, the memories more vivid … slower.

He whipped up a knot and hurled the rope again. This time the coils landed in the water still trickling from the hose. He turned the tap off tighter, watched the puddle fade away in the extreme heat of the day. Steamed into non-existence. A painless, fading death, his lips pursed. *Not a bad way to go.*

Pulling down hard on the rope, his back and arm muscles bulged as the load flattened, his mood bordering somewhere between enjoyment and nothing. Either way, it was bliss. He stepped from behind the truck, wound the nylon rope around the next side-bar, and caught a glimpse of movement near the front of the truck, his diverted attention killing his contentment.

Marilyn sat on the truck's front fender, and the muscle in his jaw flexed as his head rumbled with curses. He put his boot on the side bar, braced and hauled again, the load flattening further under his anger. Refusing to look at her, he quickly worked a knot, pulled a loop through a loop, made another and pulled it back on itself, his muscles expanding tighter as he forced up the slack. That done, he shoved the excess rope under the load and went forward to retrieve the shirt he'd hung on the truck's side mirror. It was time to attend to things elsewhere.

But Marilyn claimed his shirt as he reached it; dangled it in front of him as she slipped down to the ground. Her captivating, almondy jade-green eyes swept over him, her perusal tightening his stomach.

He sighed, showing his annoyance as she hung the shirt out in front of him, waved it about, daring him to reach for it. He didn't … wouldn't … and she manufactured that spoilt brat look she'd give when he refused to play the game, a game that required touching, grappling, embracing – a game that always ended with him having no need of the shirt.

He shook his head. Not this time. That game was permanently over, and the further he kept his distance from her the better.

But she moved closer to him, and he stiffened, a mental drawing away from her as those jade eyes wandered over him again before returning to his face.

"'You're looking real good, Nick," she purred.

He stared down at her, ignoring the tailored softness of her voice, almost flinched as her finger found a trail of water running down his neck. His heart flipped over as she traced its path down over his shoulder, down the deeper contours of his chest, followed it down the ridges of his ribcage. Down further. Near his belt buckle ...

He stopped her hand there, removed it from his flesh; let her go, but instantly the finger returned to trace the water line back up, the motion stirring him, taunting his mind with long ago images of their intimacy. He didn't stop her this time, her eyes holding his attention, the pleasant movement of her hand sparking memories he cherished. *Once cherished!*

"So are you," he said drily, immediately cursing himself for saying it. *Now she knows you've been watching her.* Her hand had lowered his defenses so he moved it again from his chest, the strength of his hold pushing the point. She handed him the shirt.

Her eyes didn't leave him as he thrust his arms into the sleeves, but he tried not to look at her. Above everything, he wanted to avoid her seeing the thoughts behind his eyes and he didn't want her to see in his how desperately he wanted her.

The tip of her tongue licked slowly over the delicate curve of her lips, moistening them with the sweet taste of her, a taste he'd so long enjoyed, the motion causing him to survey her a little deeper. *Could it ever be possible ...? Just what chance is there she will change?*

"You're a beautiful sight, Nick. It's a shame to cover it up," she appraised, green eyes drinking in the breadth of him. She lifted her face to his, her dark lashes blinking slowly, the pain he'd felt so long almost mirrored in her eyes. Yet, when he stared down into those incredible jade pools, every second of their intimacy rekindled – the softness of her cheek against his – the velvet softness of her nakedness pressed against his … Then, as always, he shuddered inwardly for his face became someone else's, and someone else's, then became Gary Peters, and the memories burned his throat. "You haven't changed a bit, have you?" he said darkly.

She ignored his tone. "Would it make a difference?"

Maybe it would. He started to button the shirt.

"Can I tuck it in for you?"

"No thanks. I can to do it myself."

She shrugged. "Okay, but it's your loss."

He drew a long breath at that and stared back at her, his eyes darker. How true that was! He'd lost it all: all his plans for the future – any hope of ever feeling safe giving affection to anyone else. She'd done a pretty good job on him. She'd taught him pretty much that he was better off alone. And right now he was better off not letting his need of her rise again. *So why are your hands itching to touch her?*

The thought jolted him like an electric shock, and he tucked in his shirt, turned and walked back towards the street.

Marilyn fell into step beside him like a faithful puppy. "And how are things going with you?" she asked, trying to prolong their time together, trying to get him talking. But Nick was on to it.

"Couldn't be better," he said tightly as he clanged the gate shut behind them and snapped the padlock on. A few more steps and they would be on the path to the hotel.

He avoided looking down at her, the view swamped by the swell of her perfectly tanned breasts.

"I don't see you around much anymore, Nick."

That's right. I make a point of avoiding you wherever possible. I get my fuel down at Barney's at the other end of town rather than stop at the roadhouse. "I've been busy," he said. "You know how it is."

He glanced down at her this time to gauge her reaction, caught an eyeful of curvaceous flesh and noted she'd nodded slightly. Her expression had gone dark though, more thoughtful, and he looked forward again. The hotel was a few steps away. If he could just reach it before she aired her thoughts ...

He reached the first step to the verandah, started to step up when her hand caught his arm, stopping him.

"Nick, do you think we could ever ...?"

He took that first step, his height forcing her hand from his arm. Glancing round, he checked the street, the tightness in his chest and throat choking him as her words hit home. The extra height he'd gained also meant he didn't have to look at her face, at the sombre facade she'd applied. His gaze strengthened on the roadhouse opposite. "Aren't you going to be late back to work?"

She stared up at him, her long silence forcing him to look down, to meet her eyes full on, to see the tears glistening there. Disappointment washed over her face and she swallowed thickly. "I need to know, Nick ..."

His eyes darkened further and he stepped back down in front of her. Close in front of her. This was a private matter and he wanted to keep it that way. Two road trains and a green sedan towing a horse trailer were the only things nearby, and far enough away to be of no consequence. "What do you think?" he said, his words barely escaping tightly clenched teeth.

"I ... I don't know. You won't even talk to me. You avoid me like the plague."

True. He simply couldn't stand being near her when she'd taken so many others as closely as she'd taken him. And she was still taking them. In short, she'd become the town's resident whore.

He leant closer. "Or maybe it's just that you're always so

damn busy with other guys."

Her eyes stabbed daggers into his face. "Damn you, Nick!" she hissed. "Damn you in hell!"

He leant further over her. "You already did that, Marilyn," he said, his jaw and glare hardening. He glanced down the street again; forced himself to breath more easily – it seemed to be working. He had control of it.

'Well whose fault was that, Nick?"

His eyes swung back to her.

"What did you expect me to do for three years? Become a Nun?"

His chest set like concrete as her words poured out, his tension tightening his breathing again. He fought it, leant in close again, struggling to loosen his jaw enough to speak. "I expected you to wait! Or wasn't what we had worth waiting for?"

Hell, he didn't want this discussion, but she was finally pushing it! It had taken a long time, but she was finally pushing it. "Or was I only one of your many good customers at the time?"

A tear rolled, and forged a path down her cheek. She swallowed, her eyes trying to harden with anger, but he knew the ploy for what it was – he knew her that well.

"Maybe I'm not as righteous as you," she said, her chin starting to dimple. She thrust it higher. "Maybe I haven't got the will-power you've got."

Her hand went to his chest, to feel his heartbeat as she used to. He made sure it didn't alter as he stood his ground. She had to see once and for all he was unaffected by her touch, yet even so her next words scored him deeply.

"Let's face it, Nick, I needed your strength and you went off and left me. What else was I to do?"

His breath locked inside him, exploded in his throat, and he scowled. *What's this? A new tactic? Many men went to war, and their lovers waited.*

"I needed someone to love me, and you went off and left

me!" Her voice had softened, her tears now falling freely. Her fingers smoothed the flesh above his heart, made his insides turn to butter. Nevertheless, he removed her hand and stepped back onto the verandah. Looking down at her, he shook his head determinedly. "Forget it, Marilyn."

"I want you back, Nick. I'll do anything I have to do to get you back." The tears had stopped completely, that emotion now turned off.

Nick shook his head and backed away. When he reached the hotel door he shouldered his way through it and disappeared inside. Not once had she ever said she was sorry.

CHAPTER NINE

Same time.

I drove into Cullan from the south, and sighed: only twenty miles to go and this boring nine hour drive would be over. Twenty miles on the other side of town I could get out of the car and sleep, the main thing keeping me awake for the last half hour was the temperature gauge hovering just below the red; that, and the convoy of road trains pushing me hard all the way from Dayton. They would not let up their speed and there had been nowhere to pull over to let them pass so I'd just kept going. Now all I had to do was keep going and hope the air pushing into the radiator would keep the needle from climbing any higher. I had to make Worsley Road without stopping for if I stopped I'd be physically incapable of pushing on again. The last thing I needed in this heat was to be stuck on the side of the road with the boys sweltering in the float. *So just keep going.*

The wide gravel verge ahead however enabled me to pull over a little, and let the road trains pass. I simply couldn't tolerate them pushing me another twenty miles.

I checked the boys again through the wide Perspex window – they were still travelling steady. After this long dry trip they'd be glad to be back on solid ground and have fresh running water.

I groped along the dashboard for the note I'd written when I'd phoned Mum early that morning.

"Take the right-hand turn at the far edge of town," she'd said. The right hand fork would take me home. Well, to Crestwood. It was not my home, just a place they'd moved to in my absence.

I glanced at the dumpy little town in passing. Nothing seemed to have changed since we'd come up to look at Crestwood nearly a year ago. It was still slapped in the middle of nowhere, four hours too far from the show-jumping circuit where I needed to be. *As if Pops didn't know that when he bought the place! And don't call him Pops to his face.* The signpost on the outskirts of town still needed painting, as did Barney's service station which bragged it was still the first in town, but that would depend on which direction you entered, I guessed. The whole town seemed to be two houses, a Post Office, an Ag. store accessed by a narrow lane (no sign that it sold saddlery) and the obligatory hotel on the corner, all contained to the one main street. The hotel was cream and brown, the same as most other country towns I'd passed through. Only one car graced its car park. Everything was built on the right hand side of the road, leaving the left side for the railway line and the barren red earth that stretched from the steel tracks all the way to the roadside, where I now sat idling.

A funnel of dust spiraled up, whirled across the road in front of me as the road trains roared past, an orange film settling over the windshield. When it cleared I noticed a narrow road running between the hotel and the roadhouse, a road I'd not noticed on our last visit. Devlin Street, the sign said, and I shuddered as its name touched a raw nerve. Another shiver surged up my spine. Why I didn't know. Sometimes feelings like this just swept over me, like feeling I was going to meet someone I knew, or responding to a question before the question was asked. Sometimes these feelings were ominous, like something dreadful was going to happen, rarely of anything good.

Shuddering again, I double checked the road and indicated, noticing as I did a man step down from the hotel verandah to talk to a woman. In a second glance I rechecked his size. Impressive. Or she was tiny-tiny. I pulled back onto the road, no time for another look.

With this growing feeling of doom I focused fully on the

intersection and, yawning, made the turn. I drove passed the roadhouse, passed the long white wall of a motel ...

"At the twenty mile peg turn left into Wolsley Road. One mile up is the driveway on the right," my Mum had directed.

I wondered again if going home was the answer – this was not at all what I wanted. *This* kind of homecoming proved nothing to anyone. But the long black road shimmered and blurred in the heat of day, drawing me onward. All around, the land changed from flat brown paddocks I'd been passing for hours to gentle undulations, hills that rolled away from the road. New plains, once formed, stretched away in the distance, some bare or stubbled, others shaded by tracts of scrub. On my right, thickly wooded ridges rose sharply upward; cuttings gouged out through rock-faces so roads could pass to the highway; deep gullies cut the land to channel the winter run-off. *Good riding country,* I thought immediately, *good for fitness training. Stay positive.*

A sign ahead read 'Reservoir', its accompanying arrow pointing to a narrow track on the right. The road sign to Wolsley Road pointed left. I turned the wheel, and a mile further up found the gate to Crestwood. I steered the Fairlane's green nose onto the long gravel drive and headed for the house in the distance, promising myself it would be a limited stay. *So be nice.*

CHAPTER TEN

Same day, late afternoon. Queensland.

Rosie looked up from the kitchen table as footsteps thumped along the back verandah, the potato peel dangling from the knife slipping unnoticed to the floor as the fly-wire door creaked open. Her back stiffened as it banged shut, the black silhouette of medium height and shameless spread blocking the sun in total. The familiar body odour now in the room wrinkled her nose, and her mind completed the picture of a liberally balding dome – sunburnt from his refusal to wear a hat – fatty bulldog jowls drooping below ruddy cheeks, and a red bulbous nose that forced apart two squinting pig-blue eyes over which sat a forest of bristly grey eyebrows that couldn't decide on any one direction.

Pugnacious. That's what she'd heard him called once. She didn't know what it meant, but it sounded about right. Pig by name, pig by nature.

Clearing the doorway, Bill wiped flecks of spittle from his mouth onto the back of his hand, his gaze sweeping the room. His hard reddened eyes settled on Rosie but she focused back on her peeling, and shuddered as the smell of beer reached her. That look and that smell meant only one thing: no matter what she said or did before the night was out she would get a beating.

She drew a steadying breath to calm her nerves and focused harder on the knife. If she remained silent she just might delay the inevitable.

"What's wrong with you?" McCaig huffed aloud as he crossed the room and dumped his kit on the table.

Rosie kept her eyes down. "Nothing's wrong with me," she

said trying to sound cheerful, but realising too late her words were too cheery.

"You're shitty with me, aren't you?"

She flicked a glance at him; saw the hope dancing in his eyes that she'd admit it.

"Aren't you?" he pushed.

She shook her head. She'd lived with Bill long enough to know his little game, how he would push her to the defensive; expect her to try and hide her fear. She did after all have some pride left. But he'd whittle away at her until she could no longer hide it.

"No, of course not,"; the sing-song tone carefully controlled this time.

He drew closer, his podgy hand sweeping the peelings off the table and scattering them over the floor. "Aren't you!" he hissed through discoloured teeth.

His face jutted invasively close to hers, its bitterness sending a shudder to her core. *Why do you stay with him? Why don't you just get out? You don't have to put up with this!* screamed through her head. She shook her head, her chin starting to dimple. *He'll hit you for sure this time,* and she winced with the expectation. *And you can't get out. He broke both your arms last time. What will he do to you next time?*

McCaig straightened over her, his victory smile stalling as footsteps on the verandah drew his attention. Ron was coming in, and Ron didn't like him needling Rosie. He half sneered when she sighed, but leant over her and hissed in her ear, "Well you wouldn't bloody wanna be!"

Ron appeared in the doorway and Rosie breathed with deep relief. Bill wouldn't dare touch her in front of Ron ... but Ron wouldn't stay forever.

She turned her head from the stench of him, knowing the drill too well. Ron's visit would last an hour or so and for that time she'd be safe. The moment Ron's car headed down the drive, Bill would want to play, and Bill played rough. Sometimes he'd want sex, and he liked rough sex. Either way, her evening prospects weren't good.

Pulling open the fly-wire door, Ron entered the kitchen and swung the half carton of cans tucked under his arm onto the table. "G'day, Rosie," he said with a grin. But the smile fell from his face at the room's icy air. He flicked a glance at his father.

Bill McCaig forced a smile and moved around the table; pulled out a chair which creaked under the strain of his weight.

Ron's gaze returned to study Rosie and, by the way she refused to look at him, he knew his father had been threatening her. There was little he could do about it though. So many times he'd told Rosie to leave and make a new life for herself, but she wouldn't, and Bill McCaig continued to torment her. As a very young boy he'd realised why his real mother had left — why she'd deserted him in the middle of the night: she had run for her life and was too damn scared to ever come back for him. He'd often wanted to meet her to tell her he didn't blame her. One day he might just go and do that.

His next glance swept over the light green kitchen, over the walls, the torn dark-green lino, along the white Formica bench-tops that adorned the pale green cupboards. The handle had been torn from the third cupboard door since his last visit, and a pane of glass was missing from the kitchenette. But that was all. Minor things this time.

He'd grown up like this — always something broken; and not always in the kitchen. Holes had appeared in bedroom doors overnight. Treasured ornaments swept from the mantelpiece to obliterate on the hearth below, those that remained intact deliberately crushed underfoot before they could be saved. But to say anything never helped.

He popped the lid of a can and let the liquid pour down his throat, eradicating the dust from the long drive from town. He watched Bill over its rim and wondered if he really wanted to go off shearing after all. His father, for all his fifty-nine years and obesity, was a mean man, one who liked a fight, one who didn't mind starting one if he had to.

His gaze shifted back to Rosie. In the strained silence, she now scraped carrots. She could do with the break, he thought, and he did after all need the money. It would be a pretty good start for him, Kerry and the baby. Hopefully they might get a little place of their own, well away from his father.

"I've made a few calls," he said, turning to his Dad. "There's a wool classer down in Wilcannia who's willing to come in with us. He'll join up with us when we get down there."

Rosie's gaze flicked up but she quickly recovered and dropped it again. Bill was leaving? She'd be free of him for a while? *My, there is a God!*

Nodding, the fat man flipped the lid of a can and cured his own dry patch, a cascade of ale spilling from his mouth and trickling down his jaw, neck and chest till a large wet patch formed on the front of his crumpled shirt. He crashed the can back onto the table and attempted to flick the dampness away. "That old crate of Sweeney's will cart most of the stuff and can take the Classer and Cook," he said, his words slurring slightly after the day's long imbibing. "My ute will take the two of us. You can leave yours here for Kerry. We'll need at least one other, maybe two."

'Lacey's bus will be coming," Ron offered, "which will save us a heap on fuel getting back and forward to the sheds. We won't need anything else with that in the crew."

"Yeah, maybe. But the Taylor boys can bring their own."

Ron's lips pursed at the mention of their name. He'd never liked the Taylor boys. Like his father, they were also too keen for trouble. "I might as well air this now, Dad," he mustered the guts to raise it, "because if you've got something against them I'd rather they didn't come. You and Taylor are always at each other's throat, and I really can't see what they can do to help us — unless you want to shoot the sheep to keep them still when we shear."

'Dobbin, you old worry-wart!" McCaig quipped back, deliberately shoving in the nickname he given Ron as a boy when he'd given him the job of carting cold water up to the sheds, the kid hauling water like a packhorse. "Taylor and I get along just fine."

He leant over and slapped Ron's cheeks three times with both hands, the cruelest of all endearments. "And I have plenty for them to do. I just want them travellin' separate, that's all." He crushed the empty can in his fist and tossed it across the kitchen where it hit the wall near the window and clattered to the bench. "Come on, boy. Get into the spirit. We're gonna be rich!"

Smiling as sincerely as he could, his gaze shifted to Rosie. "We'll get the boys together tomorrow and organise everything. I want to pull out of here by the end of the week at the latest."

Ron's eyebrows dipped. "That soon? Shouldn't we get some contracts first?"

'Nah! We can't afford to wait. We'll rake up business as we go." He ignored Ron's frown. "Don't you worry yourself about it, boy. Your old man knows what he's doing, and if there's anythin' I do know about, it's shearin'. Now you get yourself off home and tell Kerry to pack her stuff."

Rosie's head shot up and her brow creased with worry – Kerry shouldn't be travelling in her condition.

'Is that alright with you, Rosie? ... that Kerry moves in here while I'm away?" Ron asked, catching her concern.

'It's got nothin' to do with her!" McCaig snarled, dragging another can from the box. "This is my house, and I say what goes on here!"

Ron shrugged Rosie a silent apology. It was safer to say no more.

Gathering his empties from the table, he dropped them into the swing-top bin beneath the bench, McCaig following close behind him as he headed to the door.

'And we'll knock that fairy bullshit out of you once we hit the road," his father promised.

Standing on the driveway, McCaig watched the car reverse out and head back towards town, a crimson dust cloud rising high behind it. Satisfied it wasn't coming back, he puffed out his chest and waddled back to the house. It was time to play with Rosie.

CHAPTER ELEVEN

Swinging a leg over a stool at the end of the bar where the archway led into the Lounge, Nick leant back against the wall and sighed as Sheila placed a glass of squash in front of him. She moved away again, wordlessly, which meant she'd seen the confrontation outside. Nick's jaw crossed. She hadn't stopped to talk because she hated Marilyn with a passion and it was her way of keeping it to herself.

He scanned the room, glanced into the Lounge Bar behind him, which was almost empty, like the Public Bar where he sat. Apart from himself, Andy Gilmore perched on a stool midway along the counter and old Jack Pollitt read the morning paper at his usual far corner table. And that was it. Which made it almost perfect. Almost quiet.

He tipped his head back to gain the full effect of the slow turning fans overhead, fans that created a light draught in the heat of the day. His attention settled momentarily on the cobwebs in the corner of the high white ceiling, on the few cracks that marred the pale cream walls. The cracks had appeared at the height of the Meckering earthquake eight years earlier and were now a conversation piece – a conversation though he never entered into.

His gaze lowered to the dark brown carpet, to the twenty black circular tables dotting the room, each table with four black padded chairs pushed in around it. At the centre of each table sat a stack of cardboard coasters, and an opaque yellow ashtray that reminded him that he'd once smoked, a long time ago. Days like this he was tempted to smoke again.

The rumbling of a road-train drew his attention further from

Marilyn, drew it out through the multi-paned windows. The truck rumbled by and negotiated the turn, and he breathed in and out – measured breaths. As the truck disappeared behind the roadhouse, a white sedan with POLICE embellished on its bonnet pulled up outside the window, its duco covered with thick red dust. The driver climbed out and scaled the three front steps to the solid brown door, its opening letting in more heat.

Nick nodded as Senior Constable Rod Willcox entered the bar and acknowledged his presence, a practiced sweep of the officer's eyes determining the other occupants before he removed his cap. No Superiors present. He moved across to Nick and swung a leg over the stool two down from him as Sheila placed a lemon squash on the counter in front of him and moved away again.

"She's a hot one out there today," Rod said, directing his remark to no-one in particular.

Nick nodded. "Looks like you've been doing some travelling."

Willcox nodded in reply. "Some trouble up at Mount Collins." He lifted the cold glass of juice, screened its contents. Lemon, he acknowledged with a sigh. Sheila remembered, and he smiled that she probably remembered every drinker's sin in a fifty mile radius. He expected she knew most things about most people in a fifty mile radius – which covered about the whole of the Dayton's Police jurisdiction. He breathed in and blew out another hard breath.

'You look a bit down, Love," Sheila said as she came back along the bar. "That new Sergeant working you too hard?" She grinned as she wiped the counter in front of him, her excuse for 'stop-n-chat'.

Rod's smile flickered. "News travels fast! And, my oath, he sure is. All six of us are on the hop down there." Of course Sheila would know all about Owen Cussack by now, he realised. It had been two weeks.

He emptied the glass and swung back off the seat. "Well, I've gotta go. I'm due back at the Station in a few minutes."

A smile tickled Nick's lips. The trip to Dayton was a good half hour – fifteen minutes if he put the pedal to the floor all the way, and that was a fact – no-one had ever broken his record. He leant against the wall again.

"Any idea when my fencing supplies will arrive?" Rod asked, his words directed to Nick or Sheila.

"Truck's loaded," Nick said. "I'll be there in the morning."

Happy, Rod nodded and headed out. He glanced at the turn off as he reached the car – no trucks approaching – and smiled. If he hurried, he would only be a few minutes late. The rapid acceleration and short squeal of tyres as the Police car hit the bitumen raised Nick's smile.

The rest of the day drifted by.

Finally, his third squash drained, Nick yawned and looked out the window. The sun had lowered and the horizon blazed with crimson, golds and purple. *Red sky at night, shepherd's delight*: it would be another hot day in the morning; he hoped one not as hot. What he looked forward to now though was a bite to eat and a nice soft bed so he said goodnight to Sheila and headed out.

Just past the turn-off he overtook a road-train, the second trailer's load concealed by enormous blue tarpaulins, the first trailer hauling large crates secured with heavy chains. A Mack, he noted, the little silver bulldog snuffing the breeze above a chrome grill as he surged ahead and resumed the left lane. The red truck shimmered with chrome, its shiny surface reflecting the sunset. *Too much*, he thought. *Absolutely superfluous. Like some of the girls in town ... and Marilyn ... so pretty, then they go and ruin it all with piles and piles of make-up; hiding who they are. A real shame.*

Why do people have to try and change things? he wondered. *All they ever do is change the cover, the book inside reads the same.* His annoyance rose at the thought, but he didn't know why it would. *Face it,*

Nick, he sighed, *you just like the basics – the straight, plain basics.*

He turned left onto Weldon Road and a short way up, left into Northgate. The rumbling road-train roared past heading for the north-west mining towns.

Ahead, the house was in darkness, both vehicles still parked as they had been when he'd left. He cooked a quick meal, accompanied by Pete's heavy snoring which vied for supremacy above chirruping crickets outside, showered and climbed into bed, the competition still reigning.

Outside, the full, yellow moon cast a dull grey hue through the room. He lay letting his muscles loosen one by weary one, his not yet sleepy mind determining the furniture. The dresser, old, polished and mirrored, was his mother's. He could still see her seated in front of it fixing her long auburn hair into the tight knobbly bun she always wore, and his mind smiled. They'd been close, he and she, and he didn't know when he'd stop missing her. He'd thought with the passing of the years that he would forget her, but he hadn't, even after ... seven? eight years?

Not quite eight, he recalled.

He breathed out deeply, releasing the emptiness that had now settled within him, and cast his thoughts elsewhere.

Beside him the wardrobe stood boldly. It was his father's, and was as much a reflection of that man as the dresser was of his mother. The wardrobe was tall and dark. Franco Manetti. Solid and always closed up. Franco Manetti. Unfeeling, and it warranted the same response. You didn't really appreciate it because it was foreboding, dominating everything around it. It didn't listen to your needs – you just got by with what it provided. The dresser on the other hand was flexible. You could move things around.

The bed was them both. Large; soft at times when his body needed soothing – it was his mother – hard at others – when he had problems and sleeping on them wasn't the answer – he would lie awake all night, tossing and turning until he reached a solution, for his father demanded it.

He ran a hand firmly across his rib-cage, his whole body shutting down for the night. His thoughts turned back to Marilyn. God, he wished he'd taken her there and then that day... wished he'd stripped her naked where she stood and taken what she so blatantly offered him. Damn she'd got him going!

The thought pushed another – it was a long time since he'd had a woman in his bed, so long he'd forgotten when. Sometimes he thought it would be nice to have someone to hold; someone warm to lie with ... His blood started pumping and his heart beat hurried. He pressed his eyes closed.

Hold it! You don't need that sort of trouble, and that's all they are. You're twenty-eight, have a farm to run and don't need that complication.

He teased the thoughts from his mind. *They're trouble.*

The noise from Pete's room now dominated: he had won, and snoring drifted rhythmically over the house. *Big, big trouble.*

He fell asleep. For Nick, Sunday was over.

CHAPTER TWELVE

Saturday night, three months later.

The car park outside the Cullan Hotel filled early, cars spilling onto the road verge both sides of the highway. Luckily I'd been able to squeeze the Fairlane in between a dented white Toyota and a navy blue Torana when somebody left early.

Inside, families grouped together dining in the Lounge bar as wives exchanged gossip and men discussed the latest market prices. Quite normal for a Saturday night it seemed. Every so often a cackle of laughter cut through the murmurs, the infectious sound turning heads and overriding the general hum of voices, or someone yelled a greeting and encouraged new arrivers to their table. Through the tall, wide archway in the Public bar where smoke hung like a winter fog, music pounded the walls and balls chinked an irregular Morse code on the pool table across the room.

I'd been watching for my moment to snatch up the pool cue, and did seconds before Ken Wallis claimed it. "Uh-uh, I'm next," I laughed, knowing the boys seldom let the girls have a turn. I moved around the table to set the rack of balls as Roger dragged a cue from the wall rack.

"You're against me, so let's make it interesting," he quipped.

My lips twisted with caution and an eyebrow rose at what he might propose.

"If I win you have to go out with me!"

I scoffed openly – we'd been here before. I pointed the pool cue at him across the table. "Now you're getting bolder. How about ... if you win I'll let you drive my car, once? And that's about it!"

"Oooh, she's raised the stakes!" His gaze swept round, gathering witnesses. "Okay, but I get to say where we go."

Grinning, I laid the keys on the rail. "Who said I was going with you? And what makes you think you're going to win – you've never beaten me yet!" Turning to reach for my glass on the bar I rammed into a solid wall of white, and instantly fought the shudder that coursed through me. That scent of Old Spice, that immense size could only mean one thing. I glanced up; fought back another tremor, and scolded myself for not sensing his presence sooner.

Nick Manetti stood looking down at me, a wry glimmer in his eye contradicting an otherwise blank expression.

I muttered a brief "Sorry," and fought back another wave of tingles as I picked up my glass. As I moved around the table my hands started to quiver, like they always did when he stood close by, and I silently cursed the risk I'd now put my car in by not realising Nick was here.

I avoided watching as he settled on a stool at the bar beside Pete and Sam, the recurring tremor crawling into my shoulder blades that he would be watching the game. I had to ignore him if my hands were to remain steady; if they didn't and Roger beat me I'd look like an over-confident big head. *Stupid, stupid!*

I pulled an elastic band from my pocket and tied my hair back out of the way.

"Oooh, now she's getting serious," Roger jibed, causing Nick to look our way.

'Damn him coming in late,' reeled through my brain. If he'd come in earlier I'd have been sitting at my favourite table in the far corner where I could watch him without being seen. Or I'd have gone home an hour earlier, deciding in my dismay I'd be better off wasting time driving slowly around the back-roads or grooming Jerry and Millstream to gleam in the dark. Either event would have been preferable to hanging out in Cullan on the off-chance Nick Manetti would arrive, while dwelling on the fact that twelve weeks had passed and I was still stuck in Cullan. I sighed as the point pushed forward; slammed the white ball and sent the triangle of bold and striped colours scooting across the green surface. A legal break. The orange ball dropped in the far corner pocket, the red ball into the centre.

"Solids," I said then promptly sank the blue. My next shot missed sinking the green, and Roger sank the purple striped, missed the next while I sipped unpalatably warm orange juice. All the while Nick watched with mild interest, his head only slightly turned as balls disappeared off the table.

I scrutinised the table selecting my next shot; moved around so Nick wasn't in view. I sank the purple ball and the yellow, but was slightly off angle to get around Roger's red ball, which gave him a further chance. He sank two more before he faltered.

"Come on, birthday girl. Finish him off," Sam called from the bar.

I glanced up, noticing Nick had turned to take more interest in the game, and shuddered as his dark eyes flicked over me. *Don't look stupid. Please don't make me look stupid.* I drew a steadying breath, took back control of my heartbeat, and prowled the table for the best angle to take my next shot from. Leaning out across the table I struck the cue ball, which slammed into the green, banking the shot. The ball hit the rail cushion and rebounded out towards the corner pocket. Slowing down on its long roll to the corner, it hovered, teetering at the pocket edge then, almost in slow motion, fell into the hole with a clatter.

"Eight in the side pocket," I said, indicating my intention with the cue. I had to be careful though for the cue ball sat directly in line with the black ball and the pocket, meaning I could easily sink both balls and lose. Trying to shut out the alluring smell of Old Spice, I forced my attention to the table and the cue; moved around the table, lined the cue tip with the base of the cue ball, gave it a sudden short rap and sent the white spinning down towards the black. The balls kissed and the black fled on to the pocket, the cue ball following for long moments before the spin reversed its run and sent it back towards me. It rolled to a halt, kissing Roger's blue ball as the black clunked into the hole.

Heaving a silent sigh, I picked up my car keys and dropped them back into my denim jacket pocket, Roger tearing his hair out as I laid down the cue and walked back across the room. He bought me another juice, and delivered it to my table in the corner.

Smiling, I accepted my liquid winnings, but that was all he got. Anything more might have been misconstrued and I'd made a determined effort not to develop bonds — friends or otherwise. While I was still here in Cullan, still living at home, I wasn't staying, and if there was one thing I hated it was long, drawn out goodbyes.

In my self-inflicted solitude I scanned the room. Ros, Sam and Pete stood at the bar waiting for a turn at the pool table; Carla chatted with Sheila while John Casson, Brad, Roger and Ken stood in discussion with Brian Egan, the local shearing contractor. My boss. He was a good boss, and the job was okay — hectic at times, but fun. Rousing in the shearing sheds was an easy enough way to raise the cash I'd need to get back to the city. And really, it was about all that was available in this sleepy little town. Right now, Jerry was fit and ready for some serious competition, and Millstream was primed for a good and steady showing in the lower levels. I just had to raise the entry fees and get back there to compete.

I sighed with the knowing that I'd already stayed longer than I wanted, and if I didn't go soon it would be too damn hard to leave.

I glanced at Nick and my heartbeat doubled, that familiar tingling rising in my stomach and setting a thousand annoying butterflies to the wing, the chaotic flutter filling my heart and stomach. I lifted my glass and fought the feeling back, turned my gaze to the window as Nick looked my way. His reflection in the dark glass would reveal when his casual surveillance passed and I was free to look back again. This night he wore the trademark white shirt and dark denim jeans he looked so good in, the open shirt front revealing a V of superbly tanned neck and impressively sculptured chest. *Double yummy.* His shirt sleeves were rolled to mid forearm, also showing smooth golden skin and well defined muscles. Just that alone made the butterflies frenetic, much as they'd done since my second week in Cullan when I'd first come to the Hotel.

It had been a Saturday night when Ros needed a lift to town to meet up with Sam who'd been delayed in Dayton; I'd stayed at the Hotel on the off-chance Sam didn't show to avoid having to drive back in to drive her home again. Part way through the night I'd approached the bar to replenish our drinks when the air felt suddenly charged around me. The pleasant smell of Old Spice wafted into my space. I'd shuddered, and turned, only to be blocked by a broad expanse of bright white shirt. I looked up, and locked eyes with two of the darkest brown eyes I'd ever seen. He was six foot four if an inch. My insides reeling, I had gathered my senses, sidled past him and returned to the table, all the while fighting off the tingles invading my skin.

"Oo-oo," I'd whispered to Ros animatedly, "now that's got to be a fifteen." Perfect score was ten.

Ros hiked an eyebrow and scanned the bar. "Who?"

"Mister Adorable over there. Woo-hoo! What a top line! I bet they broke the mould when they built that one."

Rosalind laughed aloud and searched further. "Who? Where?"

"At the bar. Ten o'clock," I whispered, realising we hadn't played this game in a very long time. I continued to study the high, broad brow, the errant black curls that fell across it from the mass of black wavy hair, the tighter curls dabbling the base of a strong thick neck. His rugged face, neither rough nor coarse, was beautifully sculpted and enhanced by high flat cheekbones and full well defined lips. His eyes and lashes were as dark as black peat. I noted his lips curved slightly upward at the corners.

Ros followed my gaze. "Mmmm. Well I'm glad you've taken my advice to forget Tony and find someone else," she scowled, "... but Jesus, Becky, not Nick."

My interest lingered as the man turned and surveyed the room, and I noted the way the white shirt pulled taut across his chest when he moved, across the enormous fabric-encased biceps and the way the whole structure fitted superbly above a narrow waist and strong muscled legs. *Adonis amongst the pygmies.*

"The looks score a hundred but the personality scores subzero. Don't waste your time, Kid. And don't break your heart on him."

I feigned disappointment then whispered back. "I only said: *Oo-oo.* That doesn't mean I want to marry the guy – I mean ... I wouldn't ruin my life like that for quids."

"Oh yeah? Like I believe you," Ros scoffed. "Right now you need to get a bucket because you're positively drooling.'

"Am not."

"Are so."

We'd grinned simultaneously, the old times coming back. It was times like these that made me like being home. Then Rosalind's hand closed over my arm and she leant across the table. "I mean it, Becca. Don't even think it." Her voice lowered further. "You're looking at Nick Manetti, Man of Steel. The man has no emotions; holds no conversations; and hates women ... so much so some of us reckon he's practising to be a monk."

I pulled back my smile. "Oh, what a shame! He has such nice eyes."

"And they'll look right through you. Believe me, I know."

By her sigh I knew she'd been interested herself.

"And while we're on this subject I'd better warn you – no practical jokes. You get on the wrong side of Nick and you'll be playing with Hell."

My 'Hell-sounds-good' eyebrow lifted, invoking Ros's smile. She raised her glass. "Don't say I didn't warn you."

Since then Saturday nights were dream nights, as long as the entertainment arrived. Sometimes he came to town. Sometimes he didn't. Sometimes there'd be action, like the night the blonde from the roadhouse came in with some creeps from Dayton and started a brawl in the bar. If Nick hadn't reefed me up by my jacket and swung me out of the way I'd have been caught up in it. He'd dropped me on my feet behind him as someone crashed through my table, not a word spoken during the rescue. God he was strong! Other nights, it was like an old gunslinger movie when somebody just had to take on the biggest guy in the bar, or in this case the Vietnam Vet. to prove themselves the better fighter. That was Comedy night. Always they weren't and I could sense Nick's frustration; considered maybe that was why he didn't always come to town.

Now, at my quiet table in the dark corner, I pouted for he'd not spoken to me in the whole twelve weeks I'd been here. Ros had been right, and I'd realised that I only bothered coming to town on the off-chance of seeing him. When he did arrive I could sense him before I even saw him, the air seeming charged by his presence. Other than that, a few times he'd nodded a hello as we'd passed going in or out of the Co-op, or when sharing a bowser at Barney's petrol station, and once our hands touched on the door handle as we went in to pay for our fuel. My hand tingled now just thinking of it. But that was the extent of it.

His casual surveillance passed and I turned my head back to the room, watched as he talked to Sam and Pete; as he smiled and spoke to Sheila. A warm genuine smile. Sheila filled his glass, and his hand closed over her arm to detain her as she placed the glass in front of him. Beautiful hands. Big hands I'd noticed at the bowser at Barney's.

Sheila chuckled and smiled back, her fondness for Nick

obvious. And Sheila wasn't the only one, I shrugged with a huff: Furthermore, Rosalind was right – he never showed an interest in women even when they showed an interest in him. Not that I had, nor would. In fact, I deliberately avoided showing the slightest interest – I wasn't staying here! Yet it rankled me that other girls did.

"Shoot," I'd admitted to Ros one night when she'd sensed my deep frustration, "you just don't face a horse at a fence you can't possibly jump." And we'd both laughed at the unintended connotation.

I wondered tonight though if things would be different. Would he at least say "Happy Birthday, Becky", those three words making up for the last twelve weeks of silence.

I returned to the bar for a drink, something with a bit more zing than juice this time. My skin tingled all over when I returned to the table for Nick had looked straight at me, and I'd surprised myself for I'd matched his blank stare by looking straight back at him, just enough to let him know I knew he was there. That was the most attention he'd ever paid me and I reveled in that thought till John Casson arrived at my table and wished me Happy Birthday. I wondered if Ros had sent him for he sat down without asking and started talking, about work, about our soon to be busy schedule, about the weather changing and how everyone would want their sheep done before it broke.

I flicked a glance at the bar. Nick was looking our way – at John in particular. His fingers drummed on the glossy bar-top, his thoughts seemingly elsewhere. I wondered what he was thinking.

Outside the multi-paned window a light suddenly flashed. The night sky lit with such brilliance it exploded through the room, an intense crackling coursing by me so close the hairs on my arms stood up and a hazy blue light trickled over my skin. "Shit!" I squealed, leaping from my chair to shake it off.

An almighty crack snapped like a bushman's whip right beside my ear, and a boom rocked the walls. I flinched again, and leapt further back, almost toppling the chair over. My skin still shone blue as electricity gathered around me, my hand on my throat stifling my next squeal of panic. The room lights flickered then dimmed momentarily as another brilliant flash streaked earthward.

Everyone turned my way, and, though shaken, I was okay, and started to laugh, heat touching my face as I realised the attention I'd drawn. The blue haze slowly faded.

'Storm's coming," John said, glancing round, his voice breaking the silence in the room. "That could be the break I was talking about," he told me.

When Brian Egan walked to the door and stepped out onto the verandah, followed by several others, John reached out and pulled me to my feet. "Come on, Madam Tipsy. We might as well see the other light show," he said.

Outside, to the west, the indigo sky pulsed with blue light, its potency throbbing like a heartbeat through bulging black clouds. I stood against the wall watching nature's power ripple across the heavens; watched Nick at the railing near the step to the car park, as much in my view as the dark threatening sky. Then someone said: "Electric storm," drawing my thoughts back to its beauty and power as it rolled back and forth across the far horizon. How even more beautiful it was with Nick standing in the foreground.

I pulled my coat a little closer as John and the others grew bored and returned to the bar, John's departure freeing a chilly breeze to dance around me in the shadows. I ignored it; continued to watch the sky's rampant shift from black to blue to purple to blue and back down through the colours again, Nick silhouetted beautifully against it. His shoulder rested lightly against the tall brown verandah post, his manner relaxed beneath the angry sky. The cold didn't appear to bother him, nor did the potency of the crisp air around him.

Breathing deeply of the fresh breeze playing more seriously along the verandah, and savouring the slight tinge of Old Spice drifting on the air, I almost choked when he turned his head. "There's no rain in it," he said, surprising me that he even knew I was standing in the shadows.

"Mmm, I know," I sighed, feeling stupid that I hadn't said more seeing he had made the effort. I moved to the railing further down from him, propped my arms on the balustrade and remedied that. "It's so beautiful though, isn't it?"

He nodded, but said nothing else.

We watched the sky together, diverting our gaze as three vehicles pulled in at the roadhouse further over. By the jeering and jostling bandying back and forth between the occupants they were travelling together.

We returned our gaze to the sky until the silence became awkward, and I was glad when Nick nodded that 'that was that', and turned and went back inside.

I remained longer at the railing, more than a little annoyed and somewhat embarrassed. To follow too soon would have been obvious, and I needed time to quell my disappointment that he'd not said anything more. *So what is so damn wrong with me that he won't even talk to me?* funnelled through my mind. *He talks to Ros and Carla; he talks to other girls on the street in town. But never to me. Maybe it's because I'm not pretty.*

I'd certainly not been slapped with the same glamour stick as Ros – she was gorgeous with soft blonde hair and perfect porcelain skin while I was a mousy brunette with a deep olive tan. I'd accepted a long time ago I was totally opposite to the rest of the family. Mum had said I'd thrown to the gypsy side. I had the gypsy looks and the uncanny, unnerving perceptions.

Right now I wished I'd had the guts of a gypsy to have said more. Wished I'd had the willpower to drive Nick Manetti from my dreams. He was a cold, cold fish, *Adonis in scales,* and he had no idea how he affected me. But why would that bother him anyway. I was plain ordinary little Rebecca Cooper, a trait I'd hoped I would one day grow out of. Obviously I hadn't, and I sighed with disappointment. At least I had the brains to realise the uselessness of spurring a dead horse.

Pushing away from the railing, I turned and stormed back inside, the night now dead in the water.

Nick stood directly in line with the door, his back against the bar as he watched Sam across the room. He glanced my way when I entered, but I ignored him and went straight to my table, scooped up my purse and swung past Ros on the way out. "I'm going home," I said without stopping.

Her jaw dropped. "Why?"

"'Cose it's time."

"No it's not! It's still early."

Then Sam intervened as he returned to the bar. "What's the matter?"

Ros scowled her annoyance. "Becky's going home,"

"No you're not," Sam grinned. "You're the birthday girl, and the night's still young."

I shook my head. I'd been here long enough; had two drinks I shouldn't have had, and Nick stood so near my skin rippled annoyingly beneath the surface. Worse, he now stared openly down at me from his superior height.

"Here, have another drink," Sam offered, swinging a glass of whatever it was my way. "See how you feel after this."

"I don't want another drink!"

"Oh, go on," he pushed. "See what you can do, Nick ... tell her it's too early to go." But Nick's jaw tightened and he flicked Sam a dark glare.

"Come on. Just one more glass won't hurt, Ice." Sam insisted, thrusting the glass of an opaque concoction closer.

"No, thank you! And don't ever call me that!"

He winced openly. "Oops. Slip of the tongue."; and I picked his worried expression.

"Yeah ... right ... a big slip!" I could feel the sparks of heat rising in my eyes but not so much that I missed Ros's silent query.

'What's all this about?'

Straightening, I fought the tightness encroaching on my jaw. "Oh, haven't you heard? We are commonly known around here, Sis, as Fire and Ice. You're Fire because you're so-ooo damn hot … so you can guess why I'm called Ice!"

Ros's jaw dropped further. "*Sam!*"

Nick's deep rumble of laughter tumbled out, but he instantly contained it to a grin. I turned on him. "Oh I wouldn't laugh, Nick Manetti, Your reputation's far worse than mine!"

"Oh, come on, Becky! It's only a little fun," Sam countered. "Here, just one more for the road. You'll feel better …"

That damn drink thrust in front of me one more time … I shoved it back with more force than intended. The contents splashed out of the glass as Sam lost his grip on it, and the whole contents tipped up and over Nick's shirt front and arm. Sam juggled and managed to contain the glass before it hit the floor.

Heat flayed my face as Nick's smile diminished. His lips pursed then twisted with discontent.

"I'm sorry," I faltered. "I really am sorry." I glared at Sam as heat glowed on my face. "Oh … damn you, Sam Chapman!"

Feeling red hot, I stormed out, unlocked the car and slid into the driver's seat as the travellers from the roadhouse arrived at the hotel steps.

Part Two

Town Under Siege

CHAPTER THIRTEEN

The dusty white utility pulled off the highway onto the red gravel track; passed the green metal plaque in the grey stone wall at the gateway that announced this was *Ellesbrook*. The chain-hung sign on the green domed letterbox announced the owners were *G & K HOSKINS*.

Picking up speed, the utility bounced and danced along the track, the driver swinging the wheel erratically to avoid sharp stones and deep pot-holes; he didn't however slow down for slower meant rougher.

"We're not going to fool around this time," he shouted across the vehicle. "If this guy doesn't give us a contract today, Taylors can visit him tomorrow."

Ron tightened his grip on the dashboard, bracing himself against the exuberant rocking motion. "Yeah? Well something had better happen soon," he yelled back, his teeth gritting as he tried to maintain balance. "I've just about had enough of this run, Dad." He stiffened momentarily at the expected backlash and flicked a glance at his father. "One way or the other, I'm heading home after this town ... money or no bloody money."

"Don't worry, boy, I'll be with you," McCaig assured him.

Ron breathed easier. He was sick to death of rough country roads, lukewarm motel meals, and of not being with Kerry when she needed him most. She'd be getting pretty big by now.

"... and we'll make money this time all right – and I don't care what we have to do to get it!"

Ron's stomach tightened as he cast a more worried glance across the vehicle.

From the wide front verandah at the farmhouse Geoff Hoskins watched the dust cloud moving closer. He noted even from that distance the car was white and coming fast, and he didn't have the slightest notion who'd be coming out to Ellesbrook unannounced. He certainly wasn't expecting anyone.

He stepped down to the soft green lawn as the utility braked outside the white front gate, and sized up the two men alighting from the vehicle. He knew neither, and therefore strode forward to stop them approaching the house.

"Good morning," the large man greeted as he approached the gate, his baggy brown trousers flapping loosely from his paunch as he walked.

"Morning," Hoskins replied, immediately detecting the man's paltry attempt at a smile. If he'd been a stray dog a man might have got his hand bit. He therefore stayed on edge, treating all uninvited strangers with suspicion ever since his farm bikes had been stolen from the shed six months earlier.

"The name's McCaig," the visitor said, jutting out a broad fat hand. "Bill McCaig. This is my son, Ron.'

Hoskins nodded but shook the hand with reluctance.

"Got a shearing team staying in town," the man stated pointedly. "We're offering our services around the district ..."

The tightness left Hoskins' shoulders and he breathed with relief. "Sorry mate, my contract's already gone to the local crew. The lads have done my place for years, and young Egan's Dad had the contract with my Dad long before that." He maintained an air of pleasantness even though these out-of-towners were trying to cut in on Brian's business. "I have no reason to change teams." He noted the man's blue eyes narrowed. "You'll find Egan's got the whole area on his books by now so I doubt you'll get any takers."

"We can but try," the fat man responded, his tone somewhat taut. "There's a cold front coming in – we could get you done before it hits, save you getting put back when it does."

"Maybe, maybe not," Hoskins retorted, "but I'll hold with Egan anyway."

He caught the disapproving look the fat man shot his son but resisted the urge to glance in the other man's direction.

"Fair enough, but we'll drop back in a day or so to see if you've changed your mind," McCaig obliged. "The weather round here might have changed by then."

"I wouldn't bo ..."

Behind him, the fly-wire door on the house creaked open and Bruce, Geoff's only just teenaged son, stepped onto the verandah. The boy walked along it until he stood directly behind his Dad.

"Nice looking lad," McCaig noted, taking in the boy's likeness to his father. "Bet he's a big help to you around here."

Hoskins pursed his lips and nodded. "He is."

McCaig also nodded and turned on his heel; walked back towards the car.

"... and I won't be changing my mind," Hoskins called after him.

Opening the car door, McCaig squeezed his bulk inside and fired up the engine, Ron taking his lead and slamming his door shut. "You look after that kid," McCaig called back then put his foot on the accelerator.

Turning to Ron, he said: "Next stop, Richardson's.

Hoskins stood watching the dust cloud rise again; watched it drift and settle down across his paddocks. What did the bastard mean by that? he frowned. He shook his head. Surely he'd misinterpreted it.

But his frown deepened.

Tall, grey-haired Paul Richardson looked up from his daughter's car engine where he adjusted the distributor and greeted the men who'd wandered down his drive. He reneged on shaking hands, his fingers smeared with thick grease and oil. What he really wanted to do was scratch the itch in his left eye, but he couldn't do that either, so he listened, slightly distracted by the increasing irritation while McCaig outlined his business.

"No. I'm stuck with Egan whether I like it or not," Paul explained when McCaig had finished his spiel. "My daughter's one of his shed-hands. If I contract you I'd be taking money out of her hands and I can't do that, mate, weather or no bloody weather."

McCaig shrugged and promptly returned to the ute.

"Cooper at Crestwood," he huffed, reading the scrawled print on the crumpled piece of paper Taylor had given him. At least Taylors had done plenty of groundwork for them. They had a good mud map of the area with names and addresses, which alone made him more confident.

"Maybe we should start at the next town after all," Ron aired his thoughts. "This place is all set up to go, and Egan starts here tomorrow." He sighed with deep frustration. "With him so close nobody'll give us the time of day."

But the older McCaig sneered. "No way! We're here, and here we'll stay. And we will make money, you watch! These bastards will change their mind soon enough."

A chilly wind blew over Ron's skin. "Hey, you're not going to start anything here, are you?"

"What do you mean?" McCaig diverted his grin out the window, "... start what?"

"Look, Dad, it was much too close in Wilcannia. Far too much trouble. All of us could've ended up in jail from what I heard."

McCaig grunted. "That's crap! The pigs had no evidence of nothin' ... and just 'cose we was there when the town had a bit of trouble doesn't mean we had anything to do with it!"

"Well that young girl had plenty to say," Ron pushed the point, the details supplied to him during his bout of the flu not quite adding up. "What happened to her anyway?"

"Who knows? And why ask me? Maybe she just got scared and ran off."

"Got scared of what?"

Ron flicked another glance at his father. "It just seems strange ... she disappears and we all get hauled in for questioning. Had to give ourselves alibis, didn't we? And just when they were going to lay charges, they couldn't because the witness was gone. They had one, they said; they just couldn't find her. Sounds real dodgy to me. And what was she witness to anyway?"

Silence filled the cab as McCaig put his attention back to the scrap of paper.

"I have this awful feeling it isn't the coincidence you say it is," Ron persisted. "And where are the Taylor brothers anyhow?" Any thought of trouble immediately conjured visions of those two block-jawed goons.

"God only knows," McCaig shot back. "Probably out huntin' somewhere. They'll be in touch when they're ready ... and damn! ... we just passed Crestwood!"

Stamping on the brake, he clutched the wheel and held the vehicle straight as it slewed onto the gravel shoulder.

A little friendlier than the previous owners, Ted Cooper shook McCaig's hand firmly. Relatively new to farming, he liked to pick people's brains but soon realised McCaig wasn't a local. His answer then was the same as Richardson's, only he had a son and a daughter on Egan's team.

McCaig's nostrils flared and heat rose in his eyes. He glanced over his shoulder as two young blondes cycled up the track towards them, one tall and curvaceous, the other a child in her teens. They'd come from a low-slung shed at the end of the track where two horses munched hay. "Your kids?" he asked Cooper affably.

Cooper nodded. "My eldest and youngest," he said proudly,

watching them approach.

'Bet you need to keep a close eye on them ... to keep them safe I mean," McCaig added.

"Oh I do that all right."

McCaig nodded subtly. "Yeah, well I would too if I was you. Anyway, we'll be at the roadhouse motel if you choose to rethink our offer."

Ted Cooper's back stiffened at the man's sudden gruffness, at the taut drawn expression on his face. He stared after the departing ute wondering, concern growing; he replayed the scene in his head. Yes, he was sure of it. He'd been threatened alright — well the girls had been ... hadn't they? He rehashed it again, right down to the minute detail, the stance, the eyes, the tone. No doubt about it, he nodded. The fat man had warned him to look after his kids.

A chill ripped up his spine and his fists clenched at his sides. He certainly wouldn't stand for that! Nobody threatened him on his own place! And nobody threatened his girls!

So what could he do?

– Phone the Police? Lodge a complaint?

– On what grounds?

He rehearsed the conversation as it had happened, but the words alone did nothing to warrant concern. The tone, the body language was what made it ominous. He shook his head. The Police would call him paranoid, and they certainly wouldn't do anything on hearsay. His only recourse was to be watchful and he'd warn the girls to be careful.

Suddenly he felt afraid.

Farm by farm, McCaig drove on, and by six o'clock when Dave Taylor's voice crackled over the two-way he had a long list of names to pass on. "Persuade them," he ordered. "I want Hoskins, Tatem, Berinson and Tyler, then for good measure push Richardson and Cooper. Tomorrow, I'll try the others on the list." That meant *Minderlay, Northgate, Jerrikulen* and *Castlehill.* "I've had a guts full of this. I want this town and it's going to be ours!"

Later, in the small motel room, he lay on the bed idly watching the team play poker, cards shuffled and dealt but no-one giving two hoots about the hand. They looked shattered, totally fed up with doubling up in cramped motel rooms waiting for the break to come. Their last chance was here for there was little else further north, and they didn't dare go south. Nobody would expect them to head straight to the north, particularly to a dead little town like Cullan.

After this, they'd split up and head for home – nobody would trace them then. Eventually the trouble across the country would be forgotten.

So Cullan was the end of the line – make it or break it time. The locals had so far been loyal to their own but by tomorrow things would change; he could feel it in his bones. His lips twisted in a coarse smile. They'd be shearing by Wednesday.

CHAPTER FOURTEEN

Nick's breaths came in deep laboured gasps, the thick stifling vegetation surrounding him robbing him of air. He was unarmed. On the run. Charlie everywhere. How long he'd been running he couldn't remember, but his exhaustion was complete. His legs felt heavy and refused to function; his arms hung limp, unable to lift. His throat felt painfully dry. He rasped another breath, his mind pushing him. *Go on! Must go on!* He swallowed the order down.

The light! Indeed, a light suddenly flickered through the trees ahead of him, guiding him through the darkness. He had to reach the daylight ... *you'll be safe in daylight.*

He took a step ... *thunk* ... flinched as a chunk of wood cracked and splintered off the tree near his shoulder. It went spinning into oblivion. He chilled and shuddered inwardly – another inch and it would have been his flesh tearing away. He heard laughter, distant and low, but laughter just the same, and knew they had him. Now they'd have some fun.

Thunk!

Another bullet. This one embedded in the tree trunk right beside his head. The next shot would be the one, for he'd stayed too long; he'd given Charlie too much time to get him in his sights.

Move then!

The order overwhelmed him. *Move! Move!*

But he couldn't, fatigue overtaking him.

He could see the enemy now. Red neck-collar points, green tunic; slitted, slanty eyes peering out beneath the green pith helmet ... the long barreled rifle being brought to shoulder. A finger squeezing the trigger.

He saw the flash of gunfire. The bullet moving between them. Spinning ... coming straight at him ... filling his vision. *You're gone,* he groaned, the voice rolling deep in his mind.

His breath left him, and he snatched another, his last, and prepared for impact; stiffened as the bullet reached him; jolted upright as it ripped into his chest. *Thunk!*

His skin freezing, he clenched his teeth and clutched a hand to the hole ...

— shook his head ...

He felt ... nothing.

Why nothing?

His eyes flicked open, and he sucked in a deep breath; let it out again. He turned his head; could see the light better, only now it filtered through a doorway. The laughter was still low and muffled; in the next room. He heaved another breath and exhaled, relief sweeping over him. He was home, safe, another night of tormented sleep over.

Drenched in cold sweat, he lay back down, heaved more air to slow his rapid heartbeat, a heartbeat raised each time by some crazy cocked up premonition that that was how he would die, and each dream brought him closer and closer to that time. He didn't know why he knew, or how he knew, he just knew.

He pulled the blankets closer to eradicate the chill, thought it strange he was more afraid now than he'd ever been back then. Now it was over the memories of those day to day occurrences haunted him deeply, the dreams bringing it back with frightening regularity. God how he hated the dreams. In the real world where it had happened he'd been in control; he could initiate the moves he needed to keep control. But the dreams wouldn't let him have control, and that was the most frightening thing of all: To lose the edge.

He lay staring at the darkness outside the window, his head buried deep in pillows, the cold air making him shiver. He wanted to wriggle down under the blankets again but knew he wouldn't sleep now – and if he stayed in bed he would only think of Nam and lost mates – so he threw back the covers and slipped out of bed. Pulling on a pair of jeans and wind-cheater, he padded down the passage.

Thunk!

In the lounge-room at the end of the hall, another log hit the fire, Pete stoking it high and warming his hands on the flames. He looked up as the high-pitched whistle of the kettle shrieked out "Breakfast!"

A few minutes later Sam handed steaming cups of coffee across the kitchen table, a handful of toast hitting the plate soon after. "You know we start in Cullan today?" he said to Nick. "Clarke's first, then Tovey's?"

Nick nodded and let the coffee warm his throat, let it slowly repel the lingering cold on his skin.

"We'll be in each night for at least a month," Pete added, sounding more than pleased. "I don't think I could put up with another stint of shearers' quarters yet." He flipped a piece of toast over and buttered the browner side.

Sam pulled a chair out and sat down, tight lips masking the glimmer in his eye. "Yeah, and it's perfect timing. After Bec dropped her bundle the other night it's lucky I'm going to be around or Ros just might cool off me."

"You'd better hope she hasn't kept the pot boiling," Pete laughed. "She looked pretty mad from where I stood, and you know she's the type to get her own back."

Sam's lips twisted and his head tipped back in mild thought. "Nah!" he finally said. "She wouldn't do that – she knows we're only funning her."

"Does she?" Pete raised an eyebrow. "You've been pushing her pretty hard lately about going out with Ken or Roger. What part of 'she's not interested' don't you understand?"

Sam shrugged. "Well she can't keep spending her nights driving back roads all alone – Ros worries that she's going to hit a 'roo or something and no-one will know. And The Kid spends so much time alone it's just not normal."

Nick's gaze lifted from his cup. There it was again! *Kid* ... He'd heard them refer to her as that before and wondered just how young she was. She was Ros's kid sister, but how much younger did she have to be to be a kid sister? He forced his eyes down again and studied his coffee. She had to be at least eighteen – she drove and Sheila let her drink at the pub ...

Pete drained his cup and pushed it across the table. "It's her life – if she wants to be a hermit that's her business," he said, rising to his feet.

"I guess," Sam shrugged again. His cup was also empty, and he didn't have time for another so he too rose, leaving Nick sitting in silence pondering the bubbles on his coffee and occasionally looking up at the black sky that slowly faded to the first grey of morning.

Shortly after, Sam and Pete headed out, their headlights breaking the pre-dawn darkness as the car crawled away down the drive. The house fell silent again barring the crackle of the lounge-room fire, its flickering flames infusing a pleasant warmth throughout the house. Nick poured another coffee and planned his day.

By mid-morning he had checked the stock and fence lines, and returned to the house. Black clouds had moved slowly eastward in that time and more clouds lay heavy over the horizon. If they burst, the shearing would be postponed, so he willed them away. In another month it could piss down all it wanted – just blow over this time, he mused.

That was when he noticed the white utility turning in at the northern gate. The car disappeared behind the tree belt for a moment then reappeared around the curve in the track and started its uphill climb. From that distance he noticed two men in the cab. One large, one thin. The engine rattled and clanged, badly in need of a service.

The car drew closer.

The number plate was askew. Green lettering on white base. Queensland plates. His eyebrow hiked.

Stepping out to the middle of the driveway he waited as the men climbed out of the car, immediately recognising them as part of the group at the hotel on Saturday night. He was surprised they were still in town, assuming they were passing through to the mines. *So what can they possibly want here?*

He met them between the house and machine shed, not missing that their eyes surveyed the farm as they came.

"G'day," the fat one called as he approached.

Nick nodded in reply. No hello.

"Name's Bill McCaig. This is my son, Ron."

Nick nodded again, and summed them up quickly. Fat man, stick man. He waited, his thumbs poked into his jeans' back pockets.

McCaig got straight to business. "Nice place," he complimented as he cast a look for other inhabitants. "The Boss around?"

Nick smothered a smile. "You're looking at him."

McCaig's attention swung straight back, confidence sweeping over his face with a broad brush. "You don't look old enough to be runnin' a place this size," he flattered openly.

"I manage," Nick said, his dislike for the man growing. He didn't like the false friendliness nor the squinting piggish eyes; didn't like the patronising compliment nor the way the man had scrutinised the bar on Saturday night. There was something about him that set Nick's back crawling. "What can I do for you?" he asked.

"We're here to offer you the chance to get your wool trucked out of here before anyone else in town, and I might add, before the weather breaks."

"The weather will hold a while yet," Nick said, wondering if

Brian knew he had competition.

"Who can say?" the fat man shrugged, smiling to keep things pleasant. "Now, I have a crack team of shearers in town that can start tomorrow," he impressed. "I can have you finished before the week is out then you're certain to clear the rain." He rocked back on his heels as Ron estimated the size of the flock in the lower pastures.

Nick shook his head. "Sorry, we very much support local labour here, and I'm booked with Egan. You're going to find it hard to get any work in this region."

McCaig stiffened, the piggy eyes closing further. Nick met the look with a bold stare of his own and held it.

McCaig stared back, somewhat unsettled that the young man had sensed his displeasure. He glanced round, ensuring they were alone. "Look," he said, "Egan has plenty of work. He won't miss one mob, and I bet he wouldn't even mind if you said you wanted to beat the rain."

Nick shook his head. "Like I said, the rain doesn't bother me. And I like the arrangements as they are."

McCaig's face flushed with heat. "Listen, I'm gonna be fair, young'un," he said, raising his thumb in assurance. "I'll give you a day or so to reconsider. You never know ... somethin' just might change your mind in that time."

Nick's shoulders tightened. Unconsciously he drew himself taller, his eyes hardening and darkening involuntarily. "That wouldn't be a threat, would it?" he said, a sudden compulsion urging him to grab the man and hurl him off his place. It was an urge he had trouble quelling. He stepped forward, his knuckles knotting as he tried not to make a fist.

"I don't know what you're talkin' about!" the fat man reeled. He backed-stepped down the drive. "Just think about it, that's all I'm sayin'. We'll be back in a few days."

"Don't bother," Nick retorted.

He watched them leave, stewing that he hadn't pushed it

further; rebuked himself for not pushing it hard. And now he worried. He'd dealt with bullies before, and knew a threat when he heard one. Now he would have to be careful. Annoyed, he wondered what they had in mind.

Night had fallen by the time Sam and Pete returned home.

"Six hundred and twelve off the floor today," Pete bragged as Nick flicked on the kettle. "Sam did two hundred and five, top score."

Nick nodded as he ladled the stew he'd thrown together onto plates. He wasn't at all surprised at the number for Egan's crew boasted three 'guns'. He waited till they'd sat down to eat before telling them about the day's visit.

"... same group that was at the hotel the other night," he said.

"So what did they say?" Sam asked with a frown.

"Just that they can have us done before the rain hits." They didn't need to know much more than that. "I don't know if Brian knows of this, does he?"

Sam rose and picked up the phone. At call's end, he hung the receiver back on its cradle and leant against the wall, his face drawn. "Berinson's cancelled his contract and taken up with the new crowd."

Pete's lip curled in a sneer of betrayal. "Well that'd be on the cards. He's fairly new to the area ... and he's got a cash flow problem. Maybe he got nervous with this weather change that's coming." He shoved another forkful of meat into his mouth.

"Mmmm, maybe," Sam answered. His stare fixed on Nick, noting the man's silence, noting the deep thoughts behind his eyes, like when he told stories of Nam, sifting through details, not telling all. "Hoskins cancelled too. How do you explain that?"

His suspicions were founded for Nick's dark eyes flicked up and his jaw set firmly. He wouldn't ask what stirred him though for Nick only ever told what Nick wanted to tell, and never anything more.

Pete almost choked. "Hoskins? You're kidding!" He coughed a few times then swallowed the lump in his throat. "But he's been a regular from way back, even when Brian's dad had the team. Why would he want to change now?"

Nick stared at his untouched plate and remained silent, suspicious as to why the contracts had been cancelled. He said nothing – wouldn't yet. He folded his arms on the table and ignored Sam's constant stare. Tomorrow, he'd look into it.

CHAPTER FIFTEEN

Next morning, Nick stood in front of his yellow Ford outside Hoskins' gate, Hoskins looking across the left fender at him.

"Look, Nick, I'm not going to change my mind if that's what you're here for. And since when have you been working for Egan?"

"I'm not," Nick replied. "I'm here because something's not right. And I'm not asking you to change your mind. I'd just like to know why you did." He focused on the paddock, waiting for an answer, listening for inflections in the older man's voice.

A door on the house creaked open before Hoskins could reply and Nick's gaze swung that way. Immediately he picked up Bruce standing on the verandah, the boy's right arm supported by a white fabric sling. Hoskins' attention also shifted, his expression changing from anger to resignation.

"Were you threatened?" Nick asked, detecting that his question made Hoskins' back straighten. "I sure as hell know I was."

Hoskins studied Nick's face but he didn't answer that. "Are you changing teams?" he asked instead, his voice dull with defeat. And there was something else in the tone Nick couldn't quite pick – maybe grief; maybe concern. Possibly both.

He glanced back at Bruce, expecting his response would bring a whole heap of trouble. "Nope."

Hoskins lowered his gaze. "Yeah ... well I have a family to protect." And Nick had his answer. "If they threatened you, mate," Hoskins looked up again, "guard you're back. Guard it close."

"What happened?"

"Car ran him off the road yesterday. Broke his arm, grazed his face, wrecked his bike. The kid's bloody lucky to be alive. And the bastards just left him there, Nick. Can you believe that? They just drove off and left him there."

Picturing the kid writhing on the roadside, Nick shook his head. "I'm real sorry to hear that, Geoff, but I'm wondering how many others are in the same boat?"

"I don't know," the man shook his head, "but I'm playing it safe from here on in. They can have my bloody sheep if that's what this is over. I only have one kid."

Nick nodded. He knew now what he had sensed: guilt. The man felt guilty for not agreeing to change sooner. If he'd agreed a day sooner his son wouldn't have suffered.

Straightening, he returned to the driver's door. "By the way, did Bruce see who hit him?"

"No ... but he says it was a white car."

"Do you think it was McCaig?"

"I was sure it was!" Hoskins growled as he moved away from the truck. "I was going out to kill the bastard but the Police got to him first. They say McCaig was at the roadhouse at the time – and Jack Pollitt's grand-daughter verified that."

Nick tensed at the mention of Marilyn – Cullan just seemed too small at times. He pushed the image of her face from his mind and frowned. "Got anyone else in mind?"

Hoskins shook his head. "I can't imagine anyone hitting a kid and not stopping, and certainly no-one in Cullan would do it. And what's more, without some sort of clue, the coppers can't do anything more than what they've done – which is sweet bugger all!"

Nick heaved a sigh; nodded again. "Well, I gotta go. I'll see if others have had any problems. Maybe, if we rake up enough evidence they might get further involved." He climbed into the cab and turned the key.

Hoskins leant down to the window. "Watch your back, you hear," he warned again. "Just watch your back."

Nodding, Nick put his foot on the accelerator, and Hoskins stepped back; turned and walked back to the house. With a protective arm around his son, he watched Nick drive away.

"Trouble's brewing all right," he said to Bruce. "For that man to take the time to mingle something's got to be wrong, and he's the type who doesn't back down to anyone." He felt more guilty then for giving in so quickly.

Directing most of his anger at himself for submitting to pressure, Doug Berinson stood a short way from Joanna, who stood inside the open shed, heavily pregnant and looking exhausted. Her eyes were red from crying.

"Of course we changed teams," the man growled. "They shot her dog on Monday night. The poor old thing didn't stand a chance. Now look at Jo ... she hasn't slept a wink since fretting over it. You've got to see my reasons – I couldn't take the chance of losing my top rams the same way. That's why I changed."

A smallish man, Berinson looked even smaller alongside Nick, his high receding hair-line and heavy framed spectacles making him look older than his years, and he seemed to have aged more overnight.

"... you report this to the Police?" Nick asked, still watching Joanna and feeling her pain. He'd had a dog himself once when he was much younger. He'd never have another for anything that gets that close hurts too much when it dies. And everything dies sooner or later, no matter how hard you try to stop it.

"... problem is," he heard Berinson say, "McCaig and his bunch were at the roadhouse. All three cars were parked outside the motel all night." He shook his head. "What frightens me," he continued, leading Nick away from the shed, away from Joanna, and speaking more softly, "...is they crept right up to the house and blew Robbie's head off right on the back step." The man's chin started to dimple revealing his own stress and pain at finding the slaughtered dog, but he contained his grief. "By the time we got outside they were gone. We didn't see a thing. No tracks. No shells. Nothing. Now that's too close for comfort."

Looking back at the house, Nick scanned the area for a suitable blind, but Berinson was right. There was nowhere, the yard completely open. Maybe the side of the house had been their shield, or the large dead tree at the very end of the yard, both places uncomfortably close to where the Berinsons had openly reacted to the dog's death.

"As bad as it is, you're lucky it's only the dog," Nick said. "With Geoff Hoskins, it was his son."

Berinson removed his glasses and pinched the bridge of his nose. "Oh God, no! How bad?"

"Just a broken arm and grazed face, but it could have been worse."

Berinson slipped his glasses into his top pocket and turned to Nick. "So you can see why I gave in then, can't you?"

Nick nodded.

"Look, I know I've not been living here long enough to be considered part of this community, and I know my decision will upset a number of people," Berinson expounded, "but all I have in this world is Joanna and this farm, and I'm not about to risk either."

Nick looked back to Jo. "Yeah, that seems to be what they rely on. I just can't figure how they're doing it."

He looked again at the step where the dog had met its end. Another cowardly attack. In both cases, sneak scare tactics had changed people's minds, and it wasn't fair, for how could you fight what you couldn't see? *Gives about as much chance as a sniper attack in a defol. zone,* he sighed. He wondered then what was in store for him. A sneak attack in the middle of the night? On what? He didn't have much he couldn't live without.

– No ... but other people do.

He stood a moment thinking, Joanna Berinson's pain stabbing home a hollowness in his gut. He thought of young Bruce, and the useless loss of the dog, both innocent victims. Whoever did this had to be stopped. He drew another deep breath in and let it out – as much as he didn't want to get involved in whatever was going on there seemed little else he could do. And he certainly wasn't about to sit back and let it continue until he became a victim.

His gaze drifted from Joanna's tear-stained face to her husband. "If I arrange a meeting with others in the same situation will you come along?" he asked. "Maybe the only way to fight this thing is together."

"Aah ... I dunno," Berinson hedged. "That just might rile them further."

Nick's lips thinned. He understood Berinson's fears, and he understood the sort of men they were dealing with. "Okay, what if we hold it somewhere out of the way, somewhere they won't know. If there's enough instances to show the level of trouble we're having here Dayton cops will have to get involved."

Berinson lit a cigarette with shaky hands and inhaled. "Well ..." He studied the red glow of its tip for several long moments, watched Nick for a short second longer. "Okay ... I guess I'll come," he agreed, "if you think it will help."

Nick nodded. He'd need full support from everyone, and he needed to know what they wanted to do. He already knew what he wanted to do but he wasn't about to make it worse without them being prepared. And it would get worse, he nodded inwardly, before it got any better. Silent wars were like that.

For the rest of the day he drove from farm to farm gathering support. Apart from Hoskins and Berinson, there'd been no other trouble, and he was thankful of that. He realised though his uncharacteristic visits had put some people on edge, a fact he regretted but couldn't avoid. He knew most of them feared him, a legacy of his mistake those years ago. Or were they simply scared of his size? Maybe they all thought the same as old Jack Pollitt once remarked: "You can't trust those strong, silent types ... the silence is their dark side trying to get out."

Well I don't have a dark side, Jack, he thought as he drove, and he didn't consider himself a 'silent type' either. Most times he just had nothing to say – and he wasn't comfortable making idle chatter because it was more socially acceptable than saying nothing at all.

Anyway, it didn't alter the fact that trouble was brewing and they would need to be ready – trouble he felt was now too late to avoid.

Gwen Sampson offered their machine shed for the meeting, which was far enough from town to be secluded. Most of the townsfolk would be there on Thursday night anyway for Sue's twenty-first party. The event would be a good camouflage for the meeting, and those not already invited would be. She offered to make the phone calls knowing Nick hated telephones, remembering him saying once when she'd visited his mother that he was a face-to-face person. She'd been close to Eliza Manetti, and she had a soft spot for Nick. From the hard-working lad she'd known when Eliza was alive, he had grown into a powerful young man, both physically and mentally. He would be the steadying influence in a relationship if he ever married – and how often had she told her Susan to go after him? "Catch yourself an unspoilt, fully established young man," she'd said time and time again. Unfortunately, Nick had been hard to pin down.

As Nick climbed back into the cab and closed the door, Gwen stepped closer to the vehicle, that sympathetic expression she always viewed him with sliding down her face like an avalanche.

"We don't see enough of you, Nick," she said pointedly.

Inwardly he drew back, expecting what came next.

"Why don't you come over for tea one night? Open invitation," she said with a fleeting smile, her hand resting encouragingly on his arm which draped along the door ledge. Her warm insistence.

He nodded and smiled. "I'll take you up on that ... when this thing is over," he said, though he doubted he would. Family dinners and socialising wasn't his idea of a comfortable evening. If she'd set a date, he'd probably have felt guilty and accepted – it would have made his mother happy – but while the invitation was open he'd leave it well open, at least until Susan was married. Right now though, he had other things on his mind.

McCaig was in for a fight!

CHAPTER SIXTEEN

On Wednesday night, McCaig's men returned to the roadhouse aching, dirty, but thoroughly satisfied. McCaig had pulled off a beauty! They were shearing again, and the flock was immense.

They sat around the cafe for an hour after eating then showered and trailed across the road to the hotel. McCaig, however, remained behind in the motel car park waiting for the Taylors' routine call. McCaig needed to talk, and he needed to talk in private. All day long he'd been scheming how to do better and had come to a decision: they would push this stubborn little town while it was moving his way and they would push it hard.

The two-way radio they'd fitted to the vehicle before leaving Queensland crackled. "Big Brother to Poppa, do you read me? Over."

McCaig cringed at the idiotic callsign Ben Taylor had drummed up, making everything sound like some farcical army mission; he considered that, while the Taylor brothers had left the Army, they had never really left the Army. He did however note how at ease Dave Taylor sounded over the airway.

He lifted the mike from its hook. "Yeah, I read you. You got a pen there?" He avoided using a name that might be traced – if anyone had the equipment to listen in they could end up in real trouble.

"Uh, somewhere, I think ... hold on." A lengthy pause. "Yeah, got one."

"Okay. Ring me on this number." McCaig reeled off the number of the public phone at the corner of the roadhouse. "Got that?"

"Got it!"

"You in a position to ring now?" He lowered the microphone from view as Jack Pollitt hobbled on crooked legs towards the hotel. No point advertising there were more of them than were visible. He was thankful of the time it took for Taylor to reply.

"Not yet," the voice came back. "Give us half an hour and we will be."

Glancing around to make sure of his solitude McCaig raised the mike again. "Okay, half an hour."

It would be eight o'clock before they'd call so he waddled across to the hotel, bought two bottles over the bar and ambled back to the car. Winding down the window, he waited for the phone to ring, his head resting back against the seat, his eyes closed and his mind chanting. *Push ... Push ...*

Push. Push. Push.

Tring ...

Tring ...

Tring. Tring. Tring.

McCaig bolted upright; blinked quickly to focus on his surroundings. He felt slightly annoyed he was no longer the Lord High Commissioner sprawled across thick, embroidered cushions, with naked dancing girls flashing their long legs and voluptuous bosoms in his direction, that their golden finger castanets now rang in single rings instead of intrinsic rhythmic jingles in time to their thrusting, advancing hips. *The phone! The phone!* he cursed, groping for the elusive door handle. He flung the door wide, bolted to the phone box, the open bottle he'd tucked between his thighs spilling onto the bitumen. His massive frame almost jammed in the doorway as he snatched the receiver off the hook and stopped its incessant ringing. "Hello!"

"McCaig?" Dave Taylor's voice.

"Here."

"What's up?" the man asked gruffly.

"I got an idea," McCaig said with subdued excitement, "and it can't go over the air. By the way, you two are doing okay. We got two jobs so far."

"Ah-huh." The voice sounded muffled as if Taylor's mouth was clogged with rag. "Came close to getting caught though." A long pause then he sounded clearer, more jovial. "We ..."

"I don't want to know! The less we know the less chance of slipping up if the cops come snooping."

"You're the boss," Taylor declared, a little miffed at being cut short. He leant back against the cabinet wall and prepared to take another mouthful of the 'burger he'd bought at The All Night Diner. "It's not going to be easy to get another though. We pushed the easy ones already." He surveyed the area around where he stood, where Ben sat stuffing his face outside the dimly lit eatery. The place was otherwise deserted.

"Yeah ... well I've been thinking ..." McCaig swatted at a moth that hovered around the light, its activity throwing shadows round the phone box. "... why not push Egan's crew a little? One or two of them not turning up to work will slow 'em down."

He swiped again as the moth fluttered past his ear. "That'll force a few more our way."

Taylor's smile widened and twisted. "Probably would."

"By the way, where are you boys staying?"

The moth had settled on the window pane, its wings fluttering to keep it there. McCaig watched it a moment longer, distracted.

"Not far away," Taylor responded. "There's an old abandoned mine-shack about twenty miles north. We're holed up there. We're staying in tonight, but be ready, we'll shake a few nerves tomorrow night."

McCaig's hand cupped over the moth on the glass, slowly closing to contain it within his grasp. "Okay. Good hunting. And listen ... stay off the air as much as you can. Ring this number Friday – same time. You got that?"

"Got it."

McCaig hung up. Slowly he opened his hand and inspected the beautiful patterned wings that vibrated on his skin, admired the shimmering teal peacock feather design. Then he lifted his hand, holding the fluttering insect to the wind, and slapped his hand hard against the glass. Sticky ooze smeared across his palm, which he wiped off onto his trousers. Without another thought he wandered back to the others.

Through the tall multi-paned windows, his men played darts and he thought: 'Good. With the Taylor boys inactive, they could all get an early night.' And by God he damn well needed it.

CHAPTER SEVENTEEN

As McCaig's call disconnected Northgate's phone started ringing. Sam answered it and passed the hand-piece to Nick as he entered the room.

"Nick here," he said, still toweling his hair dry from his shower.

"It's Brian. I just got your message about this new crowd," the man said tautly. "Are you serious?"

Nick pictured the stocky-built man on the other end of the wire. "Yeah," he said. "Why else would anyone drop your team?"

"Mmm. Well I'm glad it's not from anything I've done, and I can say I'm relieved that it's a very valid reason." Brian cleared his throat. "I hear they threatened you. Is that true?"

"I guess," he shrugged, "but they've threatened everyone." He noticed Sam look up with interest and turned to the wall to avoid the questions in his eyes; he hoped Sam would be his usual wise self and not broach the subject. It was, after all, not Sam's problem.

"I spoke to the Police today," Brian said next. "They can't give us much help until they've something more tangible to go on. And that Queensland mob did have concrete alibis ... both times. The problem couldn't just be coincidental, could it?"

Nick blotted droplets running down his chest. The warmth the shower had given him was slowly dissipating, the water dripping from his hair now cold. "Unlikely," he said, draping the towel around his neck to stop the drips; he leant his shoulder against the wall but its iciness forced him off again. "Maybe tomorrow night will shine better light on this. We just have to hope nothing happens till then."

The verbal thought was as much for himself as for anyone else, and he wondered again what they had in mind for him; felt uneasy for they had the controlling factor: surprise.

"Yeah, right," Brian agreed. "I guess I'll see you tomorrow then ... and listen mate ... look after yourself ... okay?"

Nick nodded inwardly. "Yeah. I'll see you later."

When the line buzzed he dropped the receiver on its hook and turned back to the table. Sam stared straight at him so he stared straight back, his gaze hardening as if daring the man to mention what bothered him. They'd been through the 'we're mates, and mates should help each other' thing before and knew where they both stood on the issue. He ignored the heat in Sam's eyes as his friend rose, picked up the phone and dialed a number.

"I'm calling Ros," Sam said darkly, "... to see if they're going to Sampson's tomorrow night." His jaw muscle flexed that Nick simply shrugged and ignored his tone as if it didn't matter, Nick dallying at the table, wondering if all the Coopers would be there.

The cat weaved itself back and forth about his legs and he picked it up, stroked it gently as it purred and nestled against him. Then visions of Berinson's dog flicked to his mind and he put it down again. *Don't get too close to anything*, he reminded himself sharply. *And don't get attached.*

He filled the animal's bowls with left-overs and called it a night.

CHAPTER EIGHTEEN

On Thursday night a cold brisk wind swirled orange eddies up and down the highway spiraling them around the streetlights then dancing them away into Cullan's darkness. Nick drove through the dust clouds, passed the empty roadhouse and pulled up outside the hotel. Inside, Jack Pollitt sat at his usual corner table reading the morning paper while Sheila perched on a bar stool flicking through a tattered Woman's Weekly she'd bought weeks ago. Jack nodded as Nick strolled in and went straight back to reading. Sheila flipped closed the book and climbed down from the stool.

"Hello, darlin'," she said, her face brightening. "I've been wondering where you'd got to."

Nick's lips hinted at a smile. "I've been around," he told her, having no intention of telling her what he'd been up to. "I just dropped in to see if everything's okay." He glanced around appreciating the quiet.

"Of course everything's okay. And it'll stay that way," she said, "... seeing everyone's out at Sampson's party." She glanced at the time. "Isn't that where you're supposed to be?"

Nick nodded. "And I'm going." He walked behind the counter and went into the cool-room, shouldered a carton of cans and came out again. "It just worries me," he said, laying his money on the bar, "... that you're here alone with them."

Sheila chuckled. "Don't you worry 'bout that, ducky. They're no trouble. Besides, I have Jack here."

She gave the old man a wink, and Nick shot Jack a cursory glance. The old man's days were well past being of use to anyone, which was why he worried.

"Well if you do have any trouble you know where I am."

Sheila smiled and nodded, and Nick left. If he'd had a choice he'd have stayed at the hotel in the quiet rather than suffer the interruption to Susie's birthday bash.

Driving back passed the motel again he noticed McCaig's utility sandwiched between the bottle-green rattle-trap truck and the apple-green mini-bus, and nodded his approval. They were all in early, and he hoped they would stay in.

He drove back past Crestwood, Northgate, and continued on to Sampson's farm five mile farther down the highway.

Parking in a veil of darkness behind a long line of cars he shouldered the carton and headed for the shed, passing Sam's blue station-wagon, Richardson's cream Fairmont, a few other cars with city plates, probably belonging to Sue's extended family, and Tatem's gold Mercedes. He reached the familiar sage-green Fairlane, noted it was a mighty big car for a 'kid', and became aware again how that word grated on his nerves. He peered through the car window as he passed for he'd seen the car on the road many times, or parked in town, but never been near enough to take a real look.

Even through the dim interior he could pick its stylish simplicity – nothing elaborate – nothing more than needed, yet beneath the unobtrusive exterior lay a gutsy V8 motor – he'd heard it gurgling when she cruised through town, almost making a statement of power without needing to show it. A rubber spider dangled from the rear-view mirror and he smiled and moved on.

At the shed doorway John Sampson stood watching for unwanted guests, his taut stance easing when Nick appeared from the darkness. "I was wondering where you'd got to," he greeted. "We were just starting to worry seeing rumour has it you might be next."

A cold chill crawled across Nick's skin that that wasn't an impossibility. "I had an errand to run," he excused. "Is everyone here?"

The man nodded and remained on watch as Nick entered the shed through the wide sliding doors. Nick's dark eyes swept the room, and he noted Gwen Sampson had been a busy lady: gay-coloured lights swung back and forth in the night's light breeze; twisted streamers looped from all points of the shed to the ceiling centre; chromatic clusters of balloons hung about the walls while decorative plates of cold meats, salads, sandwiches and cakes for the evening's buffet covered long trestle tables. Planks lay on drums and folding chairs bordered the lower walls while bales of hay and anything else considered sit-able filled the spaces between. Slim Dusty tunes drifted on the wind, low in volume and tolerable to all, but that would probably change when the oldies wandered off and Susie's party began in earnest.

Nick moved on through the shed, noting Ross Tatem and Paul Richardson engaged in solemn conversation on the far side, that Gwen Sampson tended an elderly woman in a lounge chair – probably her mother. He lowered the carton by the drums of ice and took a cold can from the top, preferring not to be lumbered with a glass from the keg further over. While he absently screened his surroundings, he hadn't missed noting how many people moved aside as he passed – like parting the Sea of Galilee. It further confirmed his theory that, despite their tight G'days, they were wary of him. He found an empty place against one wall from where he could watch the room, that mute point hitting a sore spot deep inside him for he'd done nothing to them. Not a damn thing. The thought provoked his anger for what had happened those years ago had no effect on anyone but the few involved yet they'd made him feel like an outcast ever since, like some over-sized freak who would break them limb from limb without any provocation.

His throat tightened, and he wondered if Sheila was the only one who really knew him. Subtly softening his stance to try and look less built so they'd feel safer, he tried to shrug off the dark mood covering him. That's why he hated gatherings like this, and he just couldn't see things ever changing.

Huffing a deep breath, he took a swig from the can and listened to the chatter going on around him, anger fuelling many words while fear prompted others. He stared at his can, images of what he soon expected drifting to his mind. He took another long drink hoping they would not make this a total waste of time; he needed all to agree to fight back because he sure as hell wasn't giving in to anyone.

Above the noisy chatter, Pete's loud laugh drew his attention. He scanned the far side of the shed until he found where Pete, Sam and Carla stood. Fire and Ice, and he smiled at the apt comparison, sat on the grandstand of hay bales, the kid laughing heartily, her blue eyes twinkling at whatever had touched her fancy. He smiled inwardly, recalling how quick she was to smile or let loose with a laugh, how instantly she saw the funny side of things – even if it was only how crazy her hair had blown while driving with the window down. Tonight her dark hair hung loose against the shimmering white top she wore; it would be crazy-crazy hair by the time she drove home tonight, he smirked. He watched as she rose, dusted hay off the seat of her dark-blue jeans, and turned. Her gaze swept from the doorway to the far corner to the keg. He waited till her gaze reached him at the far wall, almost smiled when her eyes reached his. When they did she turned and plopped down again.

His eyebrow hiked for this wasn't the first time she'd done that, and he half grinned. She was probably still embarrassed from bathing him in alcohol and flinging his 'reputation' at him. He almost considered wandering over and proving the rumour wrong, but fought the inclination; forced his attention elsewhere.

Listening more intently to the conversations around him, his impatience grew at the need to get things moving.

CHAPTER NINETEEN

My nerves rankled that Nick had arrived and I hadn't sensed his presence. He now stood across the room watching us. More annoying, he'd caught me searching the room, as if he knew I would, and that he blatantly stared my way then stared beyond me as if I wasn't there. This had happened before. I forced myself not to watch him, avoided looking in his direction – unless he was thoroughly preoccupied. But even then he'd glance my way. He seemed to be aware of everything around him, including my brief perusals. Which meant I could only watch him when his back was turned, which I did when he talked to farm owners, some of whom I knew through being on the team, others I knew only by name.

Always Nick looked serious, his eyes dark and determined, his size unintentionally dwarfing them. At one time during the night Ros nudged me and flicked a glance across the room. I'd almost drawn blood on my lip for Susie Sampson stood beside him, hanging on his every word; both her hands had locked around his massive arm. I'd not seen Nick with a girl the whole time I'd been in Cullan, and this threw chills up and down my spine. But Susie looked so small standing beside him the match was ridiculous, so I slackened my jaw and forced my back to loosen. Nevertheless, when he leant over and kissed her softly on the lips I wanted to snatch up my jacket and drive away so fast ...

"It's only a birthday kiss," Ros chided, nudging my ribs. Then Brian Egan blocked my view as he stepped onto a crate at the centre of the shed, placing his head above all those he'd been talking to. He raised his hands to quieten the worried voices.

"Everybody! ... Everybody!! ... Look ..." he shouted over the noise, "I won't hold any of you to your contracts if you choose to change over, but I will say this ... if you back down to these outsiders now you'll open the way for others to come and pull the same tactics." He paused, scanning the faces around him. "And I put this to you ... just how far are you prepared to lie down before you stand up again?"

A number of heads nodded. Murmurs hummed. A few shot a glance in Nick's direction. He stood, his shoulder resting against the wall, his eyes fixed on Brian, the hard set of his jaw and dark eyes denoting his resolve.

Finally a voice from the back overrode the mutterings. "How are we supposed to protect ourselves? Tell us that, Egan, and we'll stay with you!" It was Doug Berinson.

"I don't know what to tell you," Brian said with a shrug. "I've spoken with the Police but until something incriminates this new crowd there's nothing they can do. So all I can say is ... protect each other – watch each other's places. Don't let your kids go out alone. This thing will blow over soon enough."

More mutterings rose, and the hum of discontent increased.

"Wait! ... Wait!" Brian raised his hands again. "Look, nobody had any trouble yesterday, did they?" He looked around as heads shook, as people turned to see if anyone nodded. "No! So maybe nothing else will happen. Maybe they've done enough to get you scared."

Positive sounds rose this time and heads began to nod.

"Okay," Paul Richardson said firmly. "I'll stick with you, Egan. They'll be in for a fight if they start anything with me."

I sighed on hearing that – we would at least have work for a while yet, and I wondered if they realised the fallout of them cancelling their contracts: people would lose income and I'd have to postpone getting back to the city.

"Here, here," someone else added. Then another. And another. And the tension in the shed slowly waned.

"Good," Brian sighed openly. "If you want to talk some

more I'll be here for a while but for now let's get back to celebrating Susie's birthday."

I caught a glimpse of Nick as he took a drink from his can, but he stayed where he was as the crowd broke into smaller groups.

Shortly after, people started leaving, families with younger children going first – Tatem's, Hoskins and Hiltons. My folks gathered their jackets and dragged Jason and Susan away, hinting for Ros and I to follow, but, as Nick had offered to drive Sam and Pete home so Carla could drive Sam's wagon home, we opted to stay longer.

By eleven o'clock a bitter chill had infiltrated the shed even though Nick and Susan's Dad had closed the large doors to the wind hours earlier. Nick had remained outside with Susie's Dad and I'd only caught a glimpse of him once or twice when he'd glanced inside in his eagerness to leave. I buttoned my jacket, tossed Ros her heavy coat and headed for the small access door that led out into the night. It was indeed time to leave.

As I reached the door Nick stepped into the opening from outside, his size blocking my way. He stared down at me, his dark eyes tumbling my heartbeat. My teeth clenched. *Damn it! You go on a diet and your favourite food keeps getting shoved in your face.* I pushed Ros ahead of me, giving Nick a chance to clear the way but he simply pressed back against the frame to let her by.

"Goodnight, Nick," she said as she sidled passed him.

"Night," he replied.

I glanced up, but dropped my gaze again. His dark eyes hadn't left me. My heart thumped like a tom-tom in a mad drummer's hands and I worried he would hear it. I needed to retreat to get it under control but Ros had already left the doorway and had headed down the drive. I would look pretty stupid if I didn't follow her.

Glancing up, I caught Nick's tight smile, noticed he'd

pressed further back to give me more room. I sidled past him, my breasts brushing against him as I stepped through the gap. I said a meek "Excuse me", to which he made no response, and hurried after Rosalind.

She looked back as I caught her up. "For God's sake, will you stop drooling!" she laughed.

"I am not," I hissed in the darkness.

"You are so. You need a bucket."

"Oh shut up!" I snapped as we reached the car.

CHAPTER TWENTY

Nick smiled as the kid hurried away in the darkness, her sharp tone but not the words carrying to him on the wind. He watched, and though slightly annoyed she'd not said a simple goodnight, he smiled that Sam was right – her feisty temper was as quick as her laugh – and right now something had obviously spiked it. He strained to pick up words but the voices faded into the distance. Then he heard the click and clunk of car doors and the thunderous roar of the V8 pumped by an angry foot. Headlights flared, one minute large white moons glowing in the blackness, the next red slits slowly fading towards the road.

Further down, the light beams shone up the roadway as they turned and headed down to the highway.

Enough fun for one night, he sighed, killing the smile.

Bidding John Sampson goodnight, he strolled towards the truck passing where Pete and Sam were showing Carla the dashboard switches in the wagon; he climbed into the cab and turned the truck around then waited, engine running, door open, while they sorted themselves out. Finally Sam and Pete slid onto the seat beside him.

As the F100 pulled away Pete watched Carla out the back window, the blue car leaping and lurching like a drunken kangaroo as Nick led the way down the drive. The car however smoothed its line by the time they reached the highway. The sedan's horn tooted several times a short while later as the F100 swung right towards Northgate leaving Carla to go the last six miles alone. Nick tooted goodbye in return.

CHAPTER TWENTY-ONE

The Taylor brothers had sat in their car for hours on a side road overlooking Sampson's shed as the night slowly drifted away around them. Several times, when the boredom became too great, they'd driven passed Sampson's farm, and once even turned around in the driveway.

"The whole bloody town must be there!" Ben had muttered as the long line of cars shone up in their headlights.

Dave simply nodded.

They drove back to their point on the hill, and sat in silence, looking like concrete statues in the darkness, their square, chiseled and seriously overloaded jaws further compounding the image. Short cropped hair, deep green eyes and bulky statures revealed the close family tie. At thirty-six, Dave out-aged his brother by three years, and had looked after Ben for more than half his life after their mother had abandoned them for a life on King's Cross. She'd simply gone out to work one day and never came home. They'd survived by sticking together and eventually joined the Army, separating only when Dave gained a place in Special Forces.

In the comfortable silence Dave glanced across at Ben, who now stared out the window. He wondered what their future held; wondered what they would do after this job, and wished he'd learnt some skills in the Army other than killing. But fighting was in his blood his Uncle had told him. His Dad had been a scrapper and that's why he was good at it. He huffed inwardly at the thought then at the thought of the father he'd never known. He'd always thought he was good at fighting because he liked to win, at whatever he did. The skills he'd learnt in the Army – his special skills – had helped him meet that goal, but it hadn't helped him hold down other jobs. And no job held the excitement he'd found in the SAS. The closest he'd come to employment bliss was his last job: a culler on the stations. A shooter. A hunter. 'roos, donkeys, injured stock, he'd tracked down whatever they wanted obliterated and snuffed it out. That included the massive Pit slaughter they'd recently completed. But that had become boring after a while, so many sheep just standing for the bullet. He'd eventually made a test of it to see where he could hit and cause the least amount of blood to spray.

He shook his head. That damn drought had cost him his job, the bare earth and dry water-holes leaving nothing but rotting carcasses bloated by intolerable heat, gut-wrenching stench and layers of bloody flies. No skins, no meat, no money. Nature had completed its own cull. He huffed silently in the darkness, feeling lucky that McCaig had come along and promised good money for their time.

His jaw crossed as he glanced at Ben again. Whatever they'd do next it would be together, as usual.

He noticed Ben flicked a glance his way but turned his attention back out the window – if he acknowledge the look it would only set Ben talking again and he was enjoying the quietness of the moment.

Long minutes passed, and the lights strung on the distant shed began flickering in the rising wind. Trees around them on the ridge began to sway. He glanced up at the branches under which they had parked, looking for weak or damaged limbs that might come crashing down. That was when Ben piped up.

"Can we make a start now?" he asked for the third time.

Dave groaned and shook his head. He was more used to long stretches of watching than Ben, a legacy of his rigorous surveillance training. He simply responded with "Soon," wishing Ben would stop his fidgeting.

"You said that last time."

"Well, so I did! And it will be, but not yet! There's still too much movement going on." His hand stopped absently stroking the rifle barrel between his thighs and he lifted his beer. "If we go now, we could be in the middle of doing something and get sprung by them coming home. Now that would be a little bit hard to explain, don't you think?"

Ben slumped back in his seat, accepting Dave's reasoning.

Another hour ticked by, Dave sitting rock still, staring out the windscreen, Ben agonising at the silence. His left buttock had gone numb where a broken seat spring had poked up, and his legs had lost circulation. He stepped out onto the road and ran up and down on the spot, the heavy thump of boots further annoying Dave.

In the valley below, a procession of early party leavers single-filed back towards Cullan. Some cars branched off left, some right, gaps in the convoy closing up as soon as they appeared. Ben jumped back into the car as Dave prepared to move lest a car ventured up Brixton Hill. But none did.

Just after eleven, a big V8 bellowed by under full throttle.

"Sounds like that truck from Northgate," Ben commented mildly.

"Ain't!" Dave shook his head. "Headlights are too low and the high-beams are side by side. It's that Fairlane from Crestwood."

Ben looked up keenly and raised an eyebrow. "The Cooper girl ..."

Dave looked across at him. "How'd you know who it is?"

"Lacey found out. She drove out of town the night they arrived. Not too bad on the eyes apparently." His eyes sparkled with a thought. "Why don't we follow her? We could get ourselves some amusement for the night ... and cure a nagging urge."

Dave shook his head. "Too risky."

A short while later though he was ready. "We'll cruise around a bit," he said, his eyes squinting with anticipation. "We'll find a place with the lights still on, wait for them to go out and hey presto! – when all is dark, we'll check the place out and scare the living hell out of 'em."

"Cooper's ..." Ben hoped.

"I'm laying my odds on Richardson's or Tatem's," Dave dampened his interest. "Tatem's will be a problem though – they've got those three mongrel dogs. We won't be able to get close to the house without rousing one of them, and they're not half deaf like Berinson's mutt."

Ben laughed. "We actually did that old bugger a favour, didn't we?"

Starting the car, Dave let it roll down the hill and turned left onto the highway then he put his foot to the pedal. It was time to check out the options. Time for an adrenalin rush.

They hadn't driven far when Ben said, "Pull over. Nature's calling."

Grunting, Dave turned into Wolsley Road and pulled to the side of the road. He turned off the engine but left the headlights on to avoid looking suspicious. Ben alighted and scuttled into the bushes. A few moments later headlights appeared at the turn-off and a car turned onto the side road and came slowly up behind them.

Zipping his trousers, Ben stepped to the front of the vehicle. He knew the drill. They'd be polite and ask for directions; say they were just passing through. If it was cops, they'd plead ignorant to the missing number plate and promise to send for another. Other than that, they'd play it by ear.

Two miles from home, the red tail lights of a parked car reflected back at Carla as she turned onto the home stretch of road. Maybe somebody broken down on their way home from the party, she thought, and pulled onto the gravel. Parking behind the vehicle, she wound the window down and poked her head out the opening. Even like that she didn't recognise the car in front of her.

Ben Taylor strolled along the road towards her, squinting in the glare of the headlights, desperately needing to read the situation. He knew immediately it wasn't the Law. He could pick a cop car ten miles away.

When a young girl's head appeared through the driver's window, he stooped near Dave on passing. "Lordy, Lordy, sweet Jesus," he whispered in his best Gomer Pyle voice. "Our luck is in tooo-night."

"Are you all right? Is everything okay?" Carla called as the man strolled towards her. A shudder ran down her spine at his manner of approach. He seemed far too casual. She dropped her arm down on the door lock, securing it, her hand falling to the window-winder, ready. The man topped six foot and was broad in stature, his hair closely cropped like a soldier's, yet there was something about this soldier-type she didn't like.

"Not really, love," he responded, his pleasure that she'd stopped obvious. "We have a flat, and would you believe it, my wife has the jack in her car."

Inside the utility, Dave stifled a laugh.

Ben sensed the girl's scrutiny of him and the car. If he played his cards real careful they would have something to occupy their time for a while. And good things always come to those who take! he fought back a smirk. "You wouldn't have a jack we could borrow, would you, love?"

Shielding his eyes from the glare of her headlights, he concealed as much of his face as he could and walked closer.

And closer.

"Well I don't know," Carla said warily. "It ... it's not my car." She knew should have kept driving; knew she should have gone straight home and sent her father back.

"Can you have a look, love? My wife's due to have a baby any time now, and I don't like leaving her alone too long. If we don't get this tyre done we'll be sitting here all night."

Carla sighed and tried to shrug off her caution. 'It can't be too bad,' she thought. 'He has a wife, and a child on the way'. She unlocked the door, removed the keys from the ignition and climbed from the station wagon. Without another thought, she walked to the back of the car to hunt for the jack.

The man caught up with her; followed a few close steps behind her.

CHAPTER TWENTY-TWO

Nick didn't know what time it was, but something had woken him, and it hadn't been a dream. The sound was too far away and repeating. He rubbed his eyes and noted through the blur of his eyes darkness filled the window.

The jangling came again, rankling his nerves, its gringing in the darkness insisting on a response. He threw back the covers, swung his legs out of bed and padded across the passage, naked except for black jocks. His skin immediately goose-bumped from the cold. Snatching up the hand-piece, he reached over and flicked on the light switch. *Damn! Three o'clock! Who the hell's ringing at this hour?*

Shivering, his shoulder muscles knotting as the cold penetrated his bones, he said a simple "Yeah?"

"Pete?"

"No, it's Nick." His voice sounded thick and hoarse and he cleared his throat. "Who's this?"

"Paul ... Paul Richardson, Nick. Listen ... is Carla there by any chance?"

"Carla? No. Why?" He scratched his head, and yawned; thought he heard muttering in the background on the other end of the line.

"Listen, Nick ... I won't be angry if she is," the man assured him. "Maybe she snuck out with Pete or something. Can you check? ... Please!"

Nick instantly picked up the tone, the desperation making the hour irrelevant. "Okay. Just hold on ..."

He rested the receiver on the bench, snatched his jeans from his room and stepped into them as he headed for Pete's room. By now, the cold was painful.

Pete's door stood ajar, the interior dark, silent. No snoring. *Promising?* He knocked loudly, the sound echoing hollowly through the house.

"Mmm," Pete's voice droned from the darkness. "... what?"

"Are you alone?" Nick stayed in the passage in case he wasn't.

"What are you on about?" the words drawled out, "... of course I'm alone."

Nick ran his hand along the inner door frame and flicked on the light as Pete turned over and faced the door. He blinked at the sudden brilliance. "You'd better get up then. Something's wrong."

Nick returned to the phone, bad vibes flowing. "Paul?"

"Yes?" the reply snapped. "Is she there?"

"No. She left us around eleven-thirty, driving Sam's car as arranged. She hung behind us all the way until we turned off."

"Well she didn't get here, Nick ... and we're going crazy. Where else can she be? Where else would she go?"

"I don't know, Paul. Have you rung the Police? ... in case there's been an accident."

"No. We just woke up. When we realised she wasn't here we phoned to see if she was with you boys."

Nick shivered inwardly. "Okay, you ring them now, and stay by the phone. We'll head out and see if she's broken down anywhere."

"Jesus! she could have walked home by now if she had," Paul moaned. "Where the hell is she? Something must have happened!"

Nick nodded, bad vibes seeping deeper into his bones. "Just ring the Police, Paul, see if they've heard anything. We're heading out and will be round your way in a minute." His adrenalin, now pumping like a piston, tightened his nerves.

Pete appeared in the doorway, his dressing gown hanging

loose, his furrowed brow besieged by tousled hair. "What's going on?" he yawned widely, rubbing his head to stir his sleeping brain.

"Carla didn't get home tonight."

"What? What are you talking about!" He glanced at the clock. "It's three in the goddamned morning."

"I'm saying, she didn't get home! Get Sam up, and get dressed. We're going out to look for her." Nick picked up the phone again.

"What are you doing?"

"Ringing Coopers. They're the closest neighbours. Maybe she's there, or maybe they've heard something. It's worth checking."

The phone rang long and full at the other end, and Nick's goose-bumps rose higher. He wished the cord stretched far enough so he could reach into his room for a sweater, but it wasn't so he warmed his skin with friction.

Come on, come on! he prompted. *Come on!*

Click.

"Hello?" A young girl's voice, wary and soft with disturbed sleep. Possibly the youngest Cooper he'd seen several times.

"Hello." He spoke just as softly, not wanting to alarm her. "Who's this?"

"Who's this?" the reply came back.

"It's Nick next door. Is there someone there a bit older?"

Silence on the other end, but only for a second. He heard the girl mumbling in the background and imagined the whole house had been woken by his call.

"Hello!" A man's gruff voice this time, taken over from the sleepy-headed child. Nick pictured the stern-faced, grey-haired Ted Cooper, a man he'd had little to do with – a man who didn't think much of Vietnam vets and openly said so. "Who's this?" the man demanded.

"It's Nick from next door ..." Now he regretted calling.

"What are doing ringing at this ungodly hour?"

Mean Poppa, Nick huffed, but he understood. He hadn't been impressed either at being woken so early. "Mr Cooper," he said, keeping an air of formality seeing he didn't know the man that well – and preferred to keep it that way – "Carla Richardson didn't arrive home from the party tonight. We need to know if you've seen her since then, or if you've heard anything unusual tonight ... and ..." He heaved a deep breath. "... did your girls get home all right?" *There! It's out!*

"Yes ... yes, my girls got home okay. And no, we haven't seen the Richardson girl. And I haven't heard anything unusual either. Have you heard anything unusual tonight?" The voice muffled, like he was asking those beside him. "No," he came back. "No-one has heard anything."

"Okay. Sorry to disturb you." He began to hang up.

"Hey, young'un – wait! ... Do you need any help?"

"No sir, not yet," Nick replied. "We'll be going out looking shortly. I was just eliminating possibilities. Thanks anyway."

Ted Cooper cradled his receiver. "Nice respectful lad, that young Manetti," he said. "He wanted to know if you two got home all right. The Richardson girl apparently didn't."

CHAPTER TWENTY-THREE

Sliding his arms into fleecy sleeves, Nick dragged a windcheater on over his head and topped it with a heavy woollen jacket. He pulled on his dark leather boots and grabbed the bunch of keys from the dresser then returned to the kitchen where Pete and Sam waited, Pete pacing the kitchen muttering to himself. Nick didn't make him wait any longer.

"Sam, you take Pete's car. Pete will come with me. We'll follow the highway first to see if she's broken down anywhere. You got a torch?" Sam nodded. "Let's go then."

Two vehicles pulled onto the highway one behind the other, travelling slowly south. Lights on at Crestwood flickered through the trees, twinkling at them from the side of the hill as they passed. Coopers hadn't returned to bed yet, Nick noted.

The road sign reflected in the headlights and Nick swung the truck onto Wolsley Road, the fluorescent registration plates of Sam's car immediately lighting up like a beacon.

"Jesus! Look!" Pete shouted, pointing ahead, but Nick had already seen it. He pulled over well back from the wagon, two sets of tyres scrunching on the gravel as Sam parked close behind him. They alighted to the road, flicking concerned glances at each other, the gusting icy wind penetrating every layer of clothing and making Nick's goosebumps pop even higher. The tip of his nose burned with its cruelness. He wondered though if the shudder coursing through him was from that or from his growing fear for Carla.

The wind howled in circles around them, blew up clouds of gravel dust and whipped it in their faces till they tilted their heads to keep it from their eyes.

"Don't get too close," Nick shouted above the wind's rising moan. His fears for Carla doubled when he noticed the set of car keys swaying in the tailgate lock. *Something definitely wrong here.* "And don't disturb anything," he added, noting after he'd said it that the wind had probably obliterated any tracks before they'd arrived.

Raising his torch, he directed its wide yellow beam into the vehicle, penetrating its darkness while seriously praying Carla was asleep on the seat; he kept telling himself she had broken down and didn't want to brave the cold by walking home – she hadn't been greatly rugged up at the party, he recalled.

The torchlight played over the seats. Front. Back. Rear compartment.

Nothing. The car was empty. The window down. The door unlocked.

"Carla knows better than that!" he scowled.

Turning frantic circles, Pete shouted her name to the wind, his hands cupped to project his words through its force. He ignored its merciless sting as it whipped across his face and blew her name straight back at him.

Nick shivered constantly as he listened for the faintest response, his eyes closed at times as he honed in on sounds farther afield. There was nothing significant, just howling wind and trees creaking under its pressure. At one point he thought he heard a scream, a long, high pitched scream, but the second one dashed his hopes – one of the kid's horses was answering Pete's call. It was pointless standing around any longer.

He drove on to Richardson's while Sam waited in Pete's red coupe for whoever arrived first – Carla or the Police. Paul had no better news, except that Dayton Police would send someone over. He pulled back onto Wolsley Road again, hoping a general drive up and down would find her, fully aware Pete was better doing something other than out-pacing Paul Richardson on the wide lounge-room rug.

Maybe she tried to walk home. Maybe she's fallen; hit her head; hurt her leg. Something! he reasoned in silence. *Maybe there's some other reason, other than the one I so strongly suspect.* For his mate's sake he kept his thoughts silent, spoke only of the brighter side of finding her. Most of all, he wanted to go back and start Sam's wagon, doubting it had broken down. Sam had never had trouble with it for as long he could remember. And the keys swinging in the back lock gave him the screaming heebie-jeebies. Carla had stopped voluntarily. There were no skid marks on the road or gravel, and the car was heading uphill so she definitely hadn't pushed it. But the only way of knowing for sure was to start the engine, which meant touching. And touching would destroy any clues that might be needed later.

Deep down, he knew the Police would get involved this time.

From the passenger seat Pete cast the torch beam outward, lighting up the paddocks, searching, seeking out the slightest movement, any sign of anything abnormal. *Futile, absolutely futile,* Nick sighed, but he kept driving – it was better than sitting around doing nothing. He continued along the highway towards Cullan at snail's pace, feeling not much better than useless.

When they reached the junction of Adanti Road, he stopped the truck and stared into the darkness. *Surely, if she's out here walking she won't be any farther south than this.* Fear churned his gut.

With his intuition nagging, he swung the truck right and started up the slope of Adanti Road, barely crawling along as he peered through the billowing dust that buffeted their progress. Topping the crest, the wind blew stronger, rocking the truck, and red gravel dust swirled more wildly into the headlights. Through the thickness of its haze Nick sensed first then noticed a shape, its faint density moving in the cloud. The darkened shape became darker and clearer in the whiteness of the headlights. He drove closer.

"There! There she is!" he said, punching the words out with

relief. Exhilaration flooded through him that his previous thoughts were wrong, for there she was – Carla – walking with the wind, coming straight towards them, the gusts almost blowing her along.

He braked in the middle of the road, realising as he did that something wasn't right – something in the way she walked. She was stooped over … *but she would be in this weather*, but she wasn't huddled as she should have been in this wind. And her steps seemed aimless, plodding one foot after the other. She should also have responded to the approaching truck and moved off the road … *she should have done something.*

Pete flung his door open. "Thank God!" he huffed, leaping from the truck. "Now I'll kick her silly arse for scaring the hell out of us like that!"

He jogged towards her before Nick could stop him; called out to attract her attention, not yet realising the headlights would have done that. Nick swung down from the cab and strode after him, more wary now at what they would find. He knew it wouldn't be pleasant.

Pete had almost reached her when she lifted her head, inch by inch exposing her bloodied features to the light; fresh blood trickled from a split in her swollen lips. She saw them, as hazily as that must have been through the puffy slits of her eyes; she stopped; straightened at their closeness, and let out a long piercing scream that brought Pete to a standstill. Another shriek ripped from her throat, and another, as she stood in the windstorm, her fists clenched and her arms locked to her sides as the red earth whipped up a fury and swallowed her again.

Nick's shoulders slumped. *Shit …*

Then Carla started crying, gut-wrenching sobs that mingled with the screams. Pete moved closer, reached out to lock his arms around her, to hold her, but she lashed out, her arms flailing wildly to keep him away. Like lethal talons her maroon painted nails swiped at his face as she resisted his touch. She was a beast trapped and enraged by her fear. Her eyes, barely visible now through the pulpy mass of her once pretty face, shone with wetness yet Nick doubted she could see very much; she more sensed where they were, a primordial instinct, and Pete couldn't get close without being slashed.

"Fuck!" he yelled back at her. "Is that you, Carla? Is that you? What the hell's happened to you? What have you done?"

He spun a circle, clutching his head, his eyes begging Nick to tell him what had happened, that everything would be okay. He turned back to her in disbelief. "Oh Jesus!" And turned away again.

Nick drew level with him then passed by him.

"Jesus, Nick ... what's happened to her?"

Striding closer, his attention on the sharp striking nails, Nick knew to be careful or he'd be on the receiving end of her claws. As he expected, she slashed at his face but he clamped a grip on her wrist as he reached her, stopping its flight. Her other hand struck automatically, and he grabbed that too. Continuing the flow of her strike, he drew her hands high and twisted her away from him, crossing her arms over her body and pulling her back into him until she was locked against his chest. Like that she was helpless, her talons secured.

Carla screamed again, the shrieks now more terrifying. Nick felt her body tighten like a board against him, her back pressing hard into his stomach, every fibre of her committed to escaping from his hold. He shut his mind to the noise; held her tighter, saving them both from damage. She felt icy, the sheer blue lace of her torn blouse affording little protection against the night's bitter wind. He turned around; used his body to shield her from it.

Images flew to his head. Memories. He'd done this before — young Vietnamese girls after the soldiers had finished with them, their actions the same. So he held her closer, tried to console her, chanted over and over: "It's okay. We've got you. You're safe now." Yet the words were incomprehensible to her, and he knew they were useless.

Above her screams Pete shouted, incoherent babblings that avoided him finding ... accepting ... the facts. Nick yelled at him: "Get the truck!" But Pete kept shouting. "I said ... get the goddamned truck!"

Instantly Pete went quiet. He watched as Nick covered Carla's body with his own, shielding her from the wind; watched as Nick's head nestled close to her pale cheek, his massive arms folding further around her. He heard Nick's voice softly chanting: "It's okay. It's okay ..." But still Carla writhed to be free. She would never get free of Nick, not in a million years.

"Move!" Nick barked at him.

The command snapped Pete into motion. He sprinted forward, swung into the truck and released the brake to roll it forward; he braked beside them, leant across the seat and flung the door wide open.

Nick backed up to the passenger side, eased himself up into the cab then dragged Carla with him. Only when he had her contained inside the cab did she stop screaming. She sat taut, a marble statue in his arms, her stiffness warning Nick she was summonsing her strength for an all-out bid for freedom. He pulled her in tighter, kept her warm with his body, his strength measured to match her resistance. And he rocked her, closely watching the grotesque hands, those sharp nails curled and trying to find their target.

Hunched over the steering wheel, Pete stared at them.

"The hospital," Nick ordered, his head pressing harder against Carla's cheek. He flicked a glance at Pete, noting his distress but right now he could do nothing to help him. Not yet. If ever. He started chanting again, almost singing in Carla's ear.

Dayton was the closest medical centre and Nick urged Pete to push the truck to its limit, thirty minutes ticking by before the pickup slewed to a halt in the emergency parking bay outside the wide glass doors.

Pete leapt out, scurried around and reefed open the passenger door; stood back as Nick eased Carla down to solid ground. She hadn't said a word since they'd found her, not even in her violent struggle during the trip to town, the dark mark now on Nick's jaw a souvenir of where she'd slammed his face with her head.

The moment her feet hit the asphalt Carla braced her heels and pushed back. Nick took her weight against him and physically manoeuvred her forward, moving her closer and closer with his body towards the glassy entrance. More than anything he wanted to hoist her into his arms and carry her but her primed claws negated any chance of that.

They entered the hospital, Pete holding open the doors, Carla's resistance doubling as Nick nudged her down a long narrow hall. She kicked out to gain a foothold on anything that would block her forward movement, anything to stop moving in the direction he forced upon her. She screamed over and over, words now: "No!! No-o-o! No-o-o-o!"

"It's us, Carla. It's us." But she didn't hear him, and she didn't understand, and when she started whimpering, Nick realised her defeat, and moisture rose in his eyes.

When they reached the brighter lights at a junction of corridors Carla lurched forward then flung herself bodily against him, smashing into his chest and almost winding him. Two men sprinted towards them and she twisted and growled like a snared animal. As they drew closer she cowered, the guttural sounds erupting again into shrieking that seared Nick's eardrums. Her torment echoed up and down the hallways. Nick kept her wrists locked in front of her but she started slipping down, her weight putting strain on his grip. Suspecting her ploy he followed her down, his muscles tight and aching from the long effort it had taken to hold her, her strength awing him. His face felt sore and swollen where she'd slammed her head against him, his chest bruised from the repeated backward head butts.

At the sight of her frenzy, the approaching runners stopped. From the name tag on one white coat, Dr James had arrived. Nick hadn't seen him before. The other guy was a blond-haired, broad shouldered orderly who lived in Dayton.

Both men stepped back as Carla kicked out in their direction, the whiteness of their uniforms dazzling against the drab grey corridor walls. She smashed her head back against Nick's chest again and he pinned the offending weapon by pushing her head into the inward curve of his shoulder, his jaw holding her there. Her heart pounded so hard and fast beneath his arm he could barely determine the beats.

Above the ear-splitting screams, Dr James shouted at him. "What is it? Car accident? Drugs? What?"

Nick's jaw tightened; he shook his head. No way did he want to say the words that had filled his mind since they'd found her, let alone say them in front of Pete. Hell, he didn't want to say them at all.

He shot a glance at Pete, his friend now standing off to one side, ashen-faced, and helpless.

He shook his head, resisting speech, but the man opened his arms and palms in askance. Swallowing thickly he looked at Pete and said hoarsely, "I think she's been raped." And hated himself for saying it.

Immediately Pete slumped to the bench near the wall and buried his face in his hands.

Raking a hand through his crop of dark red hair, Dr James studied Carla's battered face then turned to the man beside him. "Get Dr Peters down here, stat. She should be in quarters," he said.

The blond orderly retreated down the corridor, passed a short dumpy nurse who hurried towards them. The intern signaled her and issued brisk instructions then she too retreated. Nick couldn't hear the instructions above the screaming but saw the woman's acknowledging nod before she hurried off. He imagined her white shoes squeaking on the highly polished floor: nurses' shoes always squeaked – it was something he'd discovered in the Army Hospital. He'd even made a point of counting all those that didn't, and found there were none. He tightened his grip further as Carla made another attempt to wrench free of his grip.

"Do you know who she is? And where did you find her?" Dr James asked loudly.

Who cares! Do something for her, Nick thought sharply, but instead he simply said, "Outside Cullan," as Carla started slinking down again. This time she almost slipped below his grasp. He bent and followed her down again, restructuring his hold to force her back up and narrowly avoiding her bared teeth biting him. He pinned her head back against his shoulder and eyed the resident critically. The guy looked nervous, inexperienced; didn't seem much older than himself. Above everything though he wished they would hurry and do something for his back now ached, his jaw throbbed, and very soon he was going to lose his grip on her.

In the middle of the next long high pitched scream, Carla fell silent, like when a snake takes a frog, Nick considered, the sound ceasing the instant the jaws clamp shut. He steeled for the next reaction.

Then Carla started to cry, loud heart-rending sobs as if something inside her had snapped and she'd realised the futility of fighting, as if she'd accepted her cruel and terrible fate and it was beyond what she could cope with. Nick wanted to turn her round and hold her; wanted to tell her he didn't mean to hurt her, that he was holding her so for her own good. But he knew better than that. He couldn't do anything more than he was doing. All those days of seeing her in town, seeing her growing up with her friends, watching her herding sheep up to the shearing shed with her Dad, her pigtails swinging like a windmill as she ran, and later, when he'd come home from the war, her sitting on the hotel steps talking to boys ... all those things came back to him. Such a great kid, he thought, turning hollow inside. So good for Pete. Swallowing thickly, he maintained his crushing restraint.

Seconds later the female nurse reappeared carrying a silver tray, at its centre a syringe.

"Phenobarbital," the intern said as he took up the phial and ejected air from its contents. "It'll calm her down.'

Nick locked her body tighter to his own, securing her arm to avoid damage to her skin if she moved. Within ten seconds her strength diminished, her body sinking lower, growing heavier in his arms. She slumped, and her heartbeat slowed and became more defined.

Another white coat scuttled round the corner at the far end of the corridor as Nick straightened and took Carla's full weight in his arms. He looked up as Dr Peters hurried into the light, her open coat swishing out behind her in her rush. Behind her came the same blond orderly, the man grabbing a gurney from against the wall and dragging it with such finesse it seemed a part of him.

As the woman drew near she ceased running, the additional moments gained used for assessment. Her blue-grey eyes locked onto Nick, at first in mild perusal then in recognition. The eyes hardened, became accusing as she assessed Carla's battered form and the strong-arm hold Nick had on her.

His jaw set in disgust. *No way, lady.* But he knew she would not have forgotten what his fists could do, and realised Carla's disfigurement probably resembled what his fists had done in the past.

He dropped his gaze, his guilt stirring but for a long time ago – she had no right to accuse him of this.

Lifting Carla's chin, Dr James shone a light into the slits that hid her eyes; he checked her pulse. She was still conscious but remained quiet, and the hospital halls resumed their silent ghostly feel again. Only the squeaking white soles heralded movement.

The intern nodded for Nick to release the straight-jacket

hold he had on Carla and helped him lift her to the gurney. They draped a white blanket over her, Carla now seeming oblivious to everything, her eyes overtaken by the swollen mass of her face. Pale, submissive, uncaring … Nick remembered the wounded soldiers he'd found in the jungle – soldiers lost, critically injured, weaponless. They waited to die; they wanted to die; and he chilled at how similar they looked.

The gurney started moving, Nick following a few steps behind as it was wheeled away and around a corner; he watched as it disappeared through a doorway, Dr Peters close behind it. She stopped in the doorway, cast another glare his way before stepping into the room and closing the door behind her.

Nick stared at the solid barrier for long minutes before realising there was simply no point. There was not much point to anything. Turning, he felt a trickle of blood seep from his lip, and dabbed it away with the back of his hand. Carla had got him a beauty. He blotted again but the flow persisted, and he smoothed the cut on the inside of his lip with his tongue, gingerly prodded the tenderness of his jaw.

Picking up a clipboard from the glass-paneled office, Dr James watched as Nick sucked in long, deep, calming breaths. "Are you okay?" he asked, reaching up to turn Nick's jaw to the light.

Nick pulled his head back and nodded, but more blood oozed at the movement, and the intern reached back into the office and handed him a wad of tissues. He glanced across at Pete on the bench, Nick's gaze following as he dabbed the warm red trail on his face.

"You'd better give us some information," the resident said, drawing Nick away.

Nick nodded though he knew he should be making a phone call. But the time never seemed long enough and he forced himself to pick up the phone at the emergency entrance rather than use the office phone offered him.

Richardson's phone barely rang when Paul's voice answered sharply. "Yes!"

"It's Nick ... We found her."

"Oh thank God!" The man's voice broke. He was crying.

Nick took a deep breath, hating to finish the news. "She's at the hospital, Paul. You'd better get down here."

A groan of dismay followed. "No ... oh no ... What? What's happened, Nick?"

"I don't know what's happened," Nick lied. Nothing was conclusive – he was only surmising – it wasn't his job to be the bearer of bad news. "We found her, we brought her here. They don't know what's wrong yet either. Can you just get down here?"

"Yes ... yes. I'm coming. We're leaving right now."

"Just drive ..." Click. The line buzzed. "... carefully."

He dropped to the bench beside Pete and waited.

In the silence of the corridor, his head and back propped against the wall, the cold of the night seeped through his skin, groped its way into his stomach. He didn't fight it this time. It just didn't seem to matter.

CHAPTER TWENTY-FOUR

Things happened pretty fast after that. Within minutes, a Police car skidded to a halt on the apron outside the Emergency entrance. Rod Willcox strode in through the swinging glass doors, cap in hand, a folder tucked under his arm. Young Brett Waddell strutted behind him, like a chicken in a hen-house not wanting to miss out on the food. Rod stopped for a moment in front of Nick; stood looking down at him. Nick's eyes were closed but he knew he was there. He'd heard the doors thump open; heard the brisk heel-clunking footsteps of authority. He opened his eyes. And that was all.

"Did you find her, Nick?"

Nick nodded.

"Did you see anyone? ... anything?"

Nick shook his head, his face feeling sore and swollen with the movement.

"Okay. Just hang for a bit and I'll get your statement then you can go home."

Nick nodded. He knew the worst was yet to come. Paul Richardson was due at any moment and still no word had come from the room. Pete still sat with his face buried in his hands as if the darkness buried reality; as if not seeing anything would blot out the vision of Carla's battered face and what had happened. He could hear Pete's short, sharp breaths, and knew he would have to be ready. Something was going to break pretty soon.

Suddenly the emergency doors burst open. Running steps this time, clunking and squeaking from the street. Nick looked up to see Paul and Marjorie hurrying towards him. The man drew closer, stopped, his eyes and arms asking.

Nick rose to meet him but both doctors appeared round the corner of the corridor and Paul diverted his attention in that direction.

"Mr Richardson? Mrs Richardson?" Dr Peters took control and introduced herself and the red headed intern.

"What's happened? Where's my daughter? I want to see my daughter," Paul blurted out, his demands all running together in a splutter.

"Mr Richardson," the woman interjected, "Carla is under heavy sedation ..." She maintained that professional aloofness that indicated she'd severed herself completely from the world of bad things and bad emotions. Bad things just happened. She lowered her voice and drew them further down the corridor. "Your daughter has been assaulted, quite brutally I'm afraid, and we believe she has been raped. We have made her ..."

The words became too faint for Nick to hear.

But he didn't need to hear the words as Marjorie turned ashen and burst into tears and turned into the strength of Paul's arms. Paul stood holding her, the colour draining from his face as he shot a glare over her head at Nick. The cold black look he returned Paul was enough to confirm the truth, and Nick's jaw flexed involuntarily as he dropped his gaze to the floor.

Paul swung back to the strangers. "I want to see my daughter! I want to see her now!"

Nick lowered his head. They were in for one hell of a shock and there was nothing he could do about it. He shook his head and sighed. The pain people suffered because they got too close. They all got too damn close.

Then noise filled his ears, shifting his thoughts completely.

"No! *No-o-o-!* Those bastards!" Pete bellowed as he exploded from the seat. "I'll kill them for this!"

As Pete charged down the corridor Nick thrust an arm out to restrain him, but Pete lunged forward and double-handed shoved him so hard his feet almost slid out from under him. Only the wall at his back stopped him hitting the floor. The noise brought Rod and Brett out of the glass-paned office.

Rod signaled Brett to move and together they bolted after him. But Nick was closer, and quicker. He shot out the glass doors before they fully closed, flinging them back on their hinges as he shouldered his way through. Striding across the car-park, he grabbed Pete's arm and hurled him around, deftly ducking beneath the fist that arced his way.

"Don't try and stop me, Nick! I'm going to get 'em – I'll get 'em once and for all!"

"Yeah? ... Get who?" Nick shouted.

"Don't play me stupid, Nick!" Pete jabbed a warning finger as he back-stepped towards the F100. "You know damn well who!"

Nick realised then Pete still had the truck keys. "Look, mate ... I don't want to see you do something you might regret."

"Then back off ... just stay away from me. I don't want to have to hurt you, Nick." His clenched fist was partly armed.

Nick glanced behind him as brisk footsteps reached the car-park. Things were getting sticky. He stepped forward, fully arming Pete's blow.

"I'm warning you, Nick, stay back!"

Nick didn't and, as Pete's fist smacked a mighty blow straight at his face, his big hand shot out and closed over it, stopping its flight. Without stopping, he slipped his grip to Pete's wrist, swung his arm down and spun Pete around with force then wrenched Pete's arm up behind his back. Pinning it against his shoulder-blade, Nick's left arm locked across Pete's chest, and like that he shoved Pete into the side of the truck.

"You bastard! Fuck you, Nick!! I'll get you for this," Pete raged as he struggled against the hold, but any attempt to fight only increased his pain.

"Calm down," Nick hissed, his jaw set firmly. He'd just about had enough of this shit for one night. "Do you want to get yourself locked up again?"

Rod Willcox reached them, his white peaked cap back on his head to keep off the crispness of morning. He looked up briefly, noting the grey sky hinting at dawn. It had been a long night, and the way things were going it was going to be an extremely long day.

Eyeing the figure under Nick's restraint, he smirked – he'd seen Nick's work before and Pete Kennedy wasn't going anywhere.

"Everything okay here, Nick?" he asked, casting a glance down the street to see who else was around at this ungodly hour. So far nothing had happened to warrant their involvement, and if Nick had opted to take control of the matter Nick was welcome to it. Without the problem of Pete Kennedy he could get back inside and wait for news.

"Everything's fine," Nick said deeply.

"I can leave him to you then?" He accepted Nick's nod but caught the willful glare on the other man's face. "But you, Mr Kennedy ..." he said, pointing a stern finger, "I'm putting you on a caution. This is strictly a Police matter and any interference from you in any way whatsoever will not be treated lightly. You got that?"

Pete stared vacantly at the landscape; said nothing.

Rod sighed and let it go. "He's in your hands, Nick," he said, to which Brett Waddell grinned, then realised the pun wasn't intended and quickly pulled it back. He hoped Rod hadn't seen – it didn't do for rookies not to take their job seriously.

"I'd take him home if I was you," Rod suggested strongly. "There's nothing that can be done here tonight."

The officers strode back towards the hospital, Brett glancing back to watch the ex-Nam Vet. manoeuvre his captive, realising the stories he'd heard about Manetti weren't exaggerations. The man was fast, silent and deadly. He still couldn't believe the speed of the apprehension.

As an afterthought Rod also turned back. "Come and see me later, Nick. I'll get your statement then."

Nick nodded that he'd heard but kept Pete restrained. When they were gone he said, "Are you okay now?"; gruffly enough that Pete knew his mood.

Pete didn't answer and Nick increased the pressure on his arm, his muscles bunching under his annoyance. "I said ... are you going to be more reasonable?" His right bicep cut off Pete's air.

Pete started coughing. "Yeah ... yeah, okay ... just let go," he rasped.

Nick released the pressure, and when there was no further resistance he released the hold completely but held his position in case it was a trick to catch him off guard. It wouldn't take much to put the hold back on.

Lowering his arms, Pete shrugged the tightness off his strained muscles; massaged his throat where Nick's arm had crushed it. "You're still a bastard," he muttered, shrugging his clothes back in place.

"Yeah? Well tell me something I don't know. Now get in the truck – we're going home."

Pete shook his head and turned towards the Hospital, his focus on the double glass doors. When Nick's grip clamped on his shoulder and turned him back to the cab, his other hand demanding the keys, Pete knew he didn't have a choice.

"Tomorrow, mate," Nick said softly. "Tomorrow."

CHAPTER TWENTY-FIVE

Heavy clouds filled the grey sky, their thick lumpy layers blocking any chance of anything but rain breaking through. The first drops landed on the truck roof as Nick slammed the Ford's door shut. He was home … home in the pleasant silence. He watched as Pete climbed from the cab and trudged up to the house, the man's shoulders hunched, his head low. Pete hadn't spoken a word to him since they'd left the hospital.

Stepping out to the verandah, Sam frowned as Pete approached then looked beyond him to Nick. When Nick shook his head he stepped aside and let Pete pass.

Nick reached the verandah, watched a moment longer to make sure Pete turned right down the passage to his room and not left to the front door then turned and looked at the sky. "Bad day all round," he said darkly, still perusing the clouds. "Where are the keys to his car?"

Sam patted his back pocket.

"Don't let him have them." He poked his own keys deeper into his jeans.

"What's going on?" Sam asked bluntly.

Nick shook his head again and drew a deep and tired breath. It didn't fill the hollow in the pit of his stomach. "They raped her. It's not good." He stood in silence watching the dawn battle the gloom, long minutes passing without either man speaking, each contemplating the trouble, and Carla, till the chortling of a magpie drifted from the trees.

"You'd better ring Brian," Nick said. "He's going to be short staffed today." Then he turned and went inside.

Sam followed, flicking on the kettle before picking up the

phone; he watched as Nick sank to a chair at the table and wiped the fatigue from his face. The call connected.

"Brian? ... Sam. We thought you'd better know there was more trouble last night." He pulled two cups from the dish-rack. "... Yeah, pretty bad."

Nick could hear the voice on the other end of the line, but not the words spoken. He didn't bother listening any harder.

"You won't have a team today," Sam went on. "They grabbed Carla last night. ... Yeah, mate. ... Yeah. She's in the hospital in a right mess. Nick and Pete just got home."

He heard the groan, the tone of despondence, and noticed Sam's expression tighten. He knew what was coming before it was even out.

"I say we go sort them out," Sam asserted, his voice unusually gruff.

A long period of silence reigned while Brian stressed a point, for good or bad Nick didn't know, but things were getting out of hand.

"Look, they aren't getting anywhere!" Sam dumped coffee and sugar into the cups with an aggressive spoon, and Nick eased a relieved breath that at least Brian seemed to be holding sense.

"... but the trouble's getting worse. If we'd acted before this Carla might not be so bad off!"

Another pause.

Sam huffed a breath and rolled his eyes to the ceiling, oblivious to Nick's dark stare. "How much proof do you want, Brian?" Then he did notice. "Yeah? ... Well I don't agree ... but ...."; his voice dropped slightly, "... okay." He held Nick's gaze a little longer then flicked the kettle off, curtailing its insistent scream. "I don't know," he said next. He turned to Nick, offering him the receiver. "He wants to talk to you."

Nick winced openly. The last thing he wanted to do was talk, for his body was starting to pleasantly sag. He yawned, and looked annoyed as he reached for the hand-piece, mildly thankful the cord extended that far across the room. Sam poured water into the cups, the pungent aroma promising a strong and bitter flavour.

He raised the hand-piece to his ear. "Yeah?" he sighed openly.

Brian wanted to know how Carla was, if she was up to seeing anyone, but Nick didn't think so. She was bashed so badly he doubted she'd want to see anyone for a long, long time. But he didn't say that. It was really none of his business.

"Probably just send chocolates or something at this point," he offered.

"How's Pete coping?"

Nick sipped his coffee. It warmed him internally and slowly worked its way outward. He almost yawned again. "Not too well. He went a bit crazy this morning, but will hopefully be more reasonable after some sleep."

"Yeah, well keep an eye on Sam too. He's a bit hot under the collar."

Nick looked up at Sam. "Yeah, I guess we all are."

"Well let's all keep our heads then." When no answer came to that, Brian came back with: "Well I'll let you go. I'll check back with you later, okay?"

"Yeah." Nick stifled yet another yawn, not looking forward to the prospect of another phone call.

When Brian's phone clicked off, Sam returned the receiver to its cradle and stood studying Nick. The big man's hands supported his brow, his elbows propped on the table to keep his head up. His dark eyes looked heavy and dull.

"You look like shit," he apprised. "Why don't you go get some sleep."

"Can't. I have to make sure Pete stays put," came the taut reply.

"I'll do that." Sam leant back against the bench and waited for a response. Through the window behind him, dark clouds rolled heavily in from the coast.

"And who's going to watch you?" Nick asked, looking up. "You sound a little too ready for action yourself."

"Hey, I'm fine, don't you worry. Steady old Sam, remember, and I'm not about to do anything stupid. So go on, go and get some sleep."

Nick didn't argue. Rising, he crossed the passage to his room, flipped off his boots, shucked the jacket from his shoulders and pulled the covers over him. Sleep rolled over him like a soft, dark cloud, his last conscious thought hoping Sam would keep a steady vigil.

Some time further on, occasional clinking drifted on the air, penetrating his sleep. It was very faint, but there just the same. A scream cut short in full pitch and Nick's eyes flicked open, his sharp mind gauging his surroundings in a second. The room was brighter now, though the heavy clouds outside the window hung lower than before and still rolled in from the coast. The land was dark with shadow and cringed from their threat. Voices drifted next, muted by the length of the passage and sounding a long way off.

He recognised Pete's voice, and his tension abated. He was still there.

Blinking heavily, he pushed the covers aside and sat on the edge of the bed. The clock on the dresser ticked over noon, and he thought: 'Shit'.

Reluctantly he rose and followed the sounds to the dimly lit lounge-room where Pete bent over the grate laying wood in the fire-place. His fanatical habit: always the grate had to be ready. Even in summer, logs crisscrossed in the fireplace, enhanced by silver threads from a few resident spiders, but it was ready just the same. If there was one thing Pete hated it was being cold. He quietly poked another log on the pile, stacking it higher for maximum warmth.

Nick remained in the doorway, weary, but satisfied things looked calm. Pete was busy; Sam leant nonchalantly against the mantelpiece. The sight of them made it hard to believe the night before had happened.

As Pete reached into the wood-box he turned slightly and noticed Nick in the doorway. His face immediately hardened. They'd almost come to blows only hours before. Rising, Pete dusted his hands and approached him, Nick drawing taut as he drew closer. He moved aside to let Pete pass but said nothing.

But Pete stopped in front of him, his face pale, his eyes red from crying. The man rubbed his head with embarrassment. "Listen ... I'm sorry for this morning," he rasped. "I didn't mean to take a swing at you."

A snort of laughter came from across the room but Sam killed it in an instant as Nick glared his way.

"I was just so bloody angry. I ..."

Nick nodded. "I know," he said, flicking another glance at Sam, another warning to remain silent. The man's face was dead-pan straight. Falsely straight.

Pete walked passed him and turned in at the kitchen while Nick returned to his room to pull on his boots and make the bed. Funny that, he pondered as he pulled up the covers and tucked in the edges, he was almost as fanatical about a well-made bed as Pete was about his fire. His habit had form in the Army; he wondered where Pete's had formed.

Muttered exchanges bandied across the kitchen and, although he was just across the hall, he thought them unusually muted.

Across in the kitchen Sam had deliberately lowered his voice. "Christ, you must have been off your rocker ... you actually took a swing at Nick?"

Pete nodded, his lips tightening, eyes lowering.

"You're lucky he didn't break you in two."

Pete rubbed his arm. "He nearly did."

Coffee cups clinked as Sam lowered them steaming to the table. "You okay now?"

"Yeah, I gotta be," Pete said. "I'll be going in to see Carla soon and I'll only make things worse for her if I can't keep control."

Nick entered the kitchen and breathed easier at the comment. He wasn't ready to cope with any more trouble just yet. He dropped a hand to Pete's shoulder on passing. "Do you want a lift in? I'm going in myself this afternoon."

Pete shook his head. Taking his own car meant he could stay with Carla as long as he could, and he didn't want Nick waiting around for him. Nick nodded that he understood, and rubbed the tiredness from his eyes. Then he slowly flexed his muscles and stretched, the bones in the back of his neck cracking softly; he felt the bruise on his jaw and fingered the slight swelling on his bottom lip. "You can tell Carla she's got a hard head," he said, making light of it.

Pete merely nodded. His guilt had already risen at not being with her, for not staying at the hospital to hold her hand, and he wondered what she must think of him for up and leaving her there. He wondered if anyone had explained that they'd made him go, or would she think he'd abandoned her because of what had happened? He wouldn't do that. Never! And he hadn't realised until this day just how much she factored in his life. When he got back to her he would assure her what had happened wasn't her fault, that it didn't matter to him … that the bastards that hurt her would suffer soon enough, one way or another.

He looked up, realising Nick's eyes had narrowed as he watched him across the table. "Are you sure you're okay?" he asked.

"Yeah … Yeah, 'course I am," came Pete's rapid reply. He forced back the brutal images floating on his cup.

CHAPTER TWENTY-SIX

Sometime later at the fork at the north end of Dayton, Pete's red coupe sped right towards the hospital while the solid F100 turned left into the Police Station driveway. Inside the Stationhouse Ken Carter had desk duty, a role he always hated and one he deplored when action plagued the streets, which wasn't very often. He'd noticed the yellow Ford pull up outside and waited, his elbows propped on the wide front counter as the man from Cullan approached the station-house. He knew of Nick Manetti; had seen him in action when they'd been called to skirmishes at the Cullan Hotel. One time when he'd broken up a fight between towners and miners, he remembered asking why they'd bothered calling the Police.

He mused as Nick appeared at the glass-paneled door that he'd never be missed in a crowd – the guy stood two axe handles wide at the shoulders, but more worrying than that, he held an air of quiet self-confidence that made one immediately cautious. He hoped if he ever had to tangle with the guy that he carried a bloody big stick.

The man opened the glass door and entered.

"Can I do something for you?" Carter asked as Nick's eyes swept beyond him to the desks throughout the station-house.

"Is Rod in?" Nick replied, preferring to speak to someone he knew rather than with someone he didn't.

Carter shook his head. "Nope. He went off shift at nine. Is there something I can help you with?"

Nick scowled inwardly. "Rod wanted to get a statement regarding the trouble last night."

"The rape case?"

So it was rape. Nick nodded, his back tightening at the news.

"Sergeant Cussack has the file on that one, and he's out at the moment. I think he was going to call at your place from what I heard. But they really can't do a great deal until they speak to the girl ... unless of course you saw something."

Nick shook his head. "Afraid not," he said quietly, his gaze drifting out the window to the Dayton District Hospital, its upper wing visible above the town's red roofs. "They haven't spoken to her yet?" He turned back and glanced at the clock on the wall. It was now three o'clock.

"No, not by last account." Carter put his pencil to rest behind his ear and leant his forearms on the counter. "She's still heavily sedated apparently."

Nick didn't like the sound of that either. *Sedated over ten hours.*

"Best thing you can do is go home and wait," the officer suggested. "The Sergeant will be around to see you sometime this afternoon."

Nick nodded. "Yeah, I'll do that, but will you tell Rod I was in."

He headed straight home, seeing no point in going to the hospital. He could do nothing there, which annoyed him. It annoyed him even more that he'd come in so late and missed Rod for Rod would hopefully divulge the information they had, and he wondered what inquiries this Cussack was making, and where.

CHAPTER TWENTY-SEVEN

At the end of the upper floor corridor Pete found the Waiting Room, where Carla's father paced back and forth across the flat brown carpet and her mother stood at the high window looking down on the street. He opened the door and entered, ready for their accusations, their glares, for he'd had no right to leave the way he had. He'd stupidly abandoned Carla when she needed him the most. But the accusing looks didn't come. Carla's mother simply turned and smiled thinly. Her father stopped pacing and huffed with open annoyance.

"Thank goodness you're back," Marjorie said mildly. She'd seen Pete arrive and park the sleek red sports car, and felt enormous relief. For a while she had worried he might not return at all and that would be too traumatic for Carla who would need the full support of all of them to recover from this. "And thank you," she said sincerely.

Pete moved across to her. "I hope you don't think I left here ..."

"We know what happened," she said, touching his arm reassuringly, "and we understand."

Paul turned back from where he'd stopped at the window. "Pity you and Nick didn't go and blow them all away," he grunted. "It's what you're trained to do isn't it? It's what you do?"

Guilt crossed Pete's face. "I was going ..." But Paul turned his back on him and directed his gaze out the window.

"Don't listen to him, love. That's not what's important at the moment. We have to be strong and hold together for Carla," Marjorie consoled.

"How is she? When can I see her?" Pete almost begged.

"Humph! You're guess is as good as ours!" Paul grumbled, his back still prominent. "We got in to see her over four hours ago, for five lousy minutes. Not that she knew we were there! They've got her so drugged up she doesn't even know who she is."

"Take it easy, Paul. They know what they're doing," Marjorie appeased.

"I can't help it!" he retorted. "I can't help feeling like this! My daughter is lying in that room beaten to a pulp by some sex-crazed butcher, she's probably scared half out of her wits ..." His chin quivered and his eyes moistened, "... and we can't go in there and sit with her? What sort of hospital is this!" He plonked down into a chair and buried his face in his hands.

Voices at the door raised his head again as the dark-haired Dr Peters appeared behind the glass. The door opened, pushed for her by another doctor – not the resident Dr James. The man ushered her in and closed the door behind them.

"Mr and Mrs Richardson, this is Dr Edmunds," she announced.

The short, balding, fat man in the drab grey suit had the most crystal blue eyes Marjorie had ever seen, albeit distorted and magnified by a pair of thick, horn-rimmed glasses. He appraised them quickly then glanced back at the folder in his hand.

Paul ignored him. He was just another medical attachment that delayed him seeing Carla. He turned to the woman. "When can we see Carla? And what's taking so damn long?"

Her colleague signaled him to stop, directed them to the seating at the far corner of the room which was more conducive to group discussion. "Please, sit down," he said. When they had he pulled a seat around for himself. Fingering the new looking file in his hand, he cast his eyes over their faces.

"When can we see Carla?" Marjorie repeated Paul's question.

"Soon," came the promise, "but first you need to know a few things." Paul started to interrupt again but the man stopped him with a hand.

"Dr Peters called me in about noon today when certain elements of Carla's case weren't running to norm, and rightly so," he said. "It appeared then a problem was developing and we have been monitoring your daughter ever since … to be absolutely sure our diagnosis is correct. As you can appreciate, we didn't want to alarm you unnecessarily."

Paul and Marjorie scowled and glanced at each other. The man pressed on before either could speak. "The rape itself was rather brutal I'm afraid, and some internal damage has occurred. Whether this will prevent her from conceiving in later years is, at this point, unknown. But that is not our greatest concern." He flipped open the file and scanned the uppermost page.

"What we are worried about is a blow Carla sustained to the temporal region, here." He pointed to an area in advance of and slightly above his ear. "We have reason to believe the blow has started some cranial bleeding which is causing pressure on her brain." His expression tightened with such concern Paul's face turned white.

"So what does that mean?" he asked as Marjorie clutched his arm. "What's going to happen to her?"

"What it means, Mr Richardson, is that we have to reduce that pressure quickly before too much of the brain is damaged. Now, this hospital doesn't have the facilities to do that here so we've arranged for Carla to be flown to the city. The ambulance is already waiting to take her to the airstrip."

Marjorie's fingers covered her mouth, forcing back her grief; she nodded keenly. "Thank God," she murmured, tears filling her eyes. "Thank God something's being done."

Paul remained rigid, expressionless, his gaze following Edmunds as the man rose from the seat. "You said … before too much damage is done. What exactly do you mean by that?"

Dr Edmunds closed the file and tucked it under his arm. "It means, Mr Richardson, we suspect some damage has already occurred. Now I do say, suspect. The city specialists have all the equipment to ascertain whether that is the case, and if so, how much. It is certainly early days yet."

Forgotten throughout the discussion, and visualising more than Paul or Marjorie could ever expect to know, Pete rose from his chair and walked to the window. The sky outside was darkening again, the approaching blackness reflecting the rest of his life. In a while it would be a shadow of blackness – non-existent – for without Carla there would be nothing. Without children of their own, there would be no future. Carla wanted children. Lots of children. She wouldn't feel whole without them. So what was life going to be like from here on in? He shook his head, and turned back to the room, moisture filling his eyes. The doctor was speaking to him.

"... you can see her briefly before we take her, and we are sorry but there is only room for one parent in the ambulance, and it will be strictly family visiting for a while."

Pete nodded. If he spoke, he would lose control.

Minutes later, he stood beside Carla, staring at her swollen, battered face, a face he could only presume was hers. The men who had done this were worse than animals and obviously enjoyed what they did.

He lifted her hand, held it to his cheek, just to hold her for a minute, but tremors racked her body even though she slept so soundly. He wished he'd mistakenly stumbled into the wrong room and this wasn't the beautiful girl he planned to marry.

His anger doubled when they came and took her from him, and he slipped back into the long grey corridor and watched as the ambulance sped away, its siren wailing, its red light flashing as it headed south to the airstrip.

He returned to his car and headed back to Cullan, visions of the life ahead of him playing on his mind. The black-grey clouds had moved in the time he'd been inside and now hung lighter over the horizon, blacker and heavier to the east, and a faint tinge of sunset peeped its rays through the lesser grey.

'McCaig's team should be in by now,' he thought as the miles clicked by. 'You don't have to add two and two to know who did this.' His jaw clenched and a smile twisted his lips. They would pay, and revenge would be sweet! Full redemption would take a long time and this was just the beginning.

He knew he'd have to be careful though. Revenge was pointless if you died before seeing its result – he'd learnt that in Nam. Priority number one was to stay alive for the second and third assault.

He nodded at his judgment, at his own common sense. He had no hope of surviving a full on assault on the men, not alone – there were far too many of them – and without weapons he couldn't do much. Whatever he did in Stage One would need to be quick. Get in, do it, and get out again before they could get a hold on him – much like the Army sorties they'd been on. Surprise assaults. He wished Nick was here with him now.

He passed the Cullan road sign on the outskirts of town and slowed the car, cruised quietly down the main street studying the lie of the land. Two road-trains parked opposite the roadhouse on the western side of the turn-off made an impressive shield as he rolled his car smoothly in beside them. Both cabs were empty, the drivers either sleeping or eating at the roadhouse before taking the long haul north.

He stepped from the car and quietly clicked the door shut then slipped around in front of one of the trucks. The darkness was almost complete now, but the lights of the roadhouse shone brightly over the corner and lit up a short stretch of Devlin Street. Across the road, the hotel's windows blazed with yellow glow, giving clear view of its interior. He waited, scanning, thinking.

Three vehicles outside the motel told him McCaig's boys were in ... but where?

– the motel?

– the roadhouse cafe?

– the hotel?

And what could he do? All he wanted at this stage was to make them suffer. Nobody else. Just them. They would suffer repeatedly for their violation of Carla. An eye for an eye. His gaze returned to the vehicles, to the white utility with the missing number plate ...

– to the dilapidated green truck ...

– to the apple-green Mini-bus.

Sure. Sure. Stage One. No vehicle, no work. No work, no money. One battered body for another. He almost laughed at his logic.

Scooting back to his car, he scrounged around and found a few items to help his quest then went back for another look. Be quick, he reminded himself. But where the hell were they?

His gaze shifted from motel to cafe to hotel. He had to know where they were so he could act without detection. Bide your time, he muttered. Just bide your time.

A large figure crossed in front of the hotel window. Too large for Sheila. He smiled and wandered across the road, staying out of reach of the light to avoid being seen as he passed the roadhouse. An adrenalin rush shortened his breathing.

He crossed Devlin Street and stood in the hotel parking lot, a shiver of excitement rippling up his spine as he stole onto the wide hotel verandah and pressed himself against the wall. Edging carefully forward, he peeked in through the multi-paned window.

Lining the bar, McCaig's crew drank and laughed as if nothing had happened.

Another quick look. Pete counted six. There should have been eight. He had to find the others.

Another look, but still only six.

Crouching below the window sill he diddy-bopped to its other side from where he could see the pool table and the dart board, and there were the other two, playing darts. He almost let rip with a cry of victory. Yes!! The bastards, the silly bastards were all inside!

His chest vibrating with suppressed laughter, he scurried, his feet sprinting the moment they hit the tarmac. Scooting through the darkness he slipped around the corner of the roadhouse to the motel where all was pleasantly quiet. Even the activity at the roadhouse remained internal.

No cars! No lights! No witnesses!

The hissing of air became almost a scream as his knife withdrew from the rubber. One, two ... three, four. The white utility lowered to the ground, listing left before the pressure equalized. Pete smirked, his smile prolonging as he pictured McCaig's reaction to the damage.

You got a flat, McCaig? Don't worry, they're only flat on the bottom. Old joke but incredibly appropriate!

His jaw set at the new squeaking sound, as, from flat on his back on the gravel, he reached up under the old green truck and groped around in the cavities. Thick cord-like wires branched off in all directions and he yanked down on them sharply, sneering as the truck's life lines gave way. He pulled harder till they popped and snapped loose in several places further away from him. Then he slid back out from beneath the truck, thankful he'd not been caught in that position – no chance of running.

Tightness gripped his stomach as fear rose higher. He picked up the jack handle. This was the noisy part.

Tapping it loosely on his hand, he calculated where to start for he wouldn't get much time before he'd have to run – just a few good swings and away.

He raised the metal bar as car lights appeared on the road, coming south. Two sets! Now he'd really have to hurry.

Across the road, McCaig stepped out to the hotel verandah and stretched his arms as he yawned. It was almost time for Taylor's phone call and he needed to be waiting. Looking up, he surveyed the night sky, his thoughts on the morrow's weather, but the sound of something crashing drew his attention down again. The sound came again, a loud cracking followed by lots of tinkling. Glass breaking, he realised with a deepening frown.

The sound came again, and again. Someone was having fun over at the roadhouse!

Grinning, he pushed open the hotel door. "Hey, come on. There's something going down at the roadhouse," he yelled across the room. "Should be fun."

Pete darted towards the roadway in a low crouched run. The headlights however were much closer than he'd thought and were almost on him. He put on the speed but too late – the lights shone him up like a rabbit in the spotlight, his presence stopping the first vehicle in the middle of the road. It was a big car with high headlights, and he breathed with relief. It was Nick.

The second car pulled into the roadhouse, short-cutting the turn-off by veering along the gravel of the motel car park. It braked abruptly, skidding a short distance on the loose stones before reversing back to shine its lights on the three parked cars.

Pete cursed his luck.

Alighting from the sedan, Rod and Brett donned their caps as they unfolded from the front seat, and Pete turned to face them. Smiling, he tucked the jack handle behind his back, endeavoured to poke it into his belt to free his hands. His smile faded however as McCaig's men stepped around the corner of the building, his night's efforts noticed immediately.

Shouldering his way to the front of the group, Steve Beattie swept his hand along the camper's soft-green duco; tapped the shattered back window, which fell inward. His jaw set as he flicked a glance at Lacey.

Lacey's madness erupted on his face, which flushed red as he lunged forward. "I'll kill you, you bastard! I'm going to fucking kill you!" His clenched fists swung at Pete but Merv, the cook with no last name, caught him mid lunge.

McCaig strode round the white utility, examining the slaughter, sadistic intentions dancing in his eyes.

"Drop it, Mr Kennedy," Rod Willcox ordered. "You've some serious explaining to do." He tossed a glance behind him at the vehicles, assessing the possibility that this was not the young man's work, but shook his head and sighed. From the corner of his eye, he caught sight of the fat man – McCaig – advancing, and realised the shearing crew moved with him. He signalled Waddell to step between them to keep them from the offender.

Nick arrived, his truck now parked on the opposite side of the road. He moved in beside Waddell, widening the defense.

"Stay back," the rookie ordered, his voice tremulous. "This is a Police matter. We'll get to you in a minute. You just stay back and stay calm."

But the men kept coming.

Willcox's attention returned to Pete. "I presume this is your handiwork!" he said, annoyed at the prospects of another long night.

Pete nodded, a wide grin forming as he held out his wrists for the handcuffs.

"Well, Mr Kennedy, you've certainly earned it this time. I am placing you under arrest ... this time for willful damage." He looked down at Pete's offered wrists unamused, and scowled deeper. "You can come quietly or we can restrain you," he added dryly. "It's your choice."

Pete shot a glance over his shoulder, assessing the strength of McCaig's crew. "No. I'll come. In fact, you came along just in the nick of time ... for a change!" He slapped Nick on the shoulder and headed for the patrol car. "The breeze-mobile was the best," he laughed, thumbing at the windowless camper. To its owner, he gave The Finger. "Bye fellas," he said as he slid into the back seat of the squad car.

McCaig's skin turned scarlet. "I'll have you, you little ...!" he boomed across the distance. "I'll have you!"

He strode forward but Nick stepped across his path, blocking his access to the Police sedan. "Get outta my fucking way unless you want to be first!" McCaig snarled.

Nick straightened. "I don't mind being first."

McCaig's piggy eyes quickly assessed his opponent, the man young and powerful, the broad muscled shoulders and chest already drawn with aggression. A young bull, he considered swiftly. Well he was an old bull. He carried more weight and experience. He could certainly take him. Yet he hesitated, for there was something else about the man that bothered him. He cast his eyes over Nick again, settled on the intensity in the dark brown eyes. It was the look – that cool unperturbed look that showed he wasn't afraid – the absolute air of confidence, as if he knew something nobody else knew. There was definitely more to this kid than met the eye. And there he faltered. This was what he'd sensed that first day at Northgate.

A blue shirt stepped between them and put a restraining hand on the young man's chest, pushing him lightly back. "Okay, settle down! Back off, Nick," Rod said. "You too, McCaig. In fact," he said, pointing a warning finger at the fat man, "I strongly advise you to take your group back to the hotel and wait until we get there."

McCaig reeled. Part of him felt defiant enough to throw a punch, the other part remained highly cautious. Under normal circumstances he'd have brawled right there and then, but this time, and his eyebrows dipped with careful thoughts, they could use this moment to advantage ... this time things were going in their favour. He didn't dare create further trouble.

Grumping, he ordered his crew back across the road and Rod released an audible sigh that a physical confrontation had been avoided. Furthermore, he felt relieved he'd managed to avoid turning Nick loose on them. As McCaig's men disappeared around the corner, he lowered his hand from Nick's chest and relaxed as Nick's tautness subsided.

Safely hidden behind the corner brickwork, McCaig hung back by the phone box, a sneer lifting his lip as he listened to the conversation going on around the corner ...

Nick leant down to the car's open window, his dark eyes criticising the occupant within. Pete's smile had vanished, his attention now on the truck bay opposite and the two men crossing the roadway. "My car!" he said with sudden worry. "They'll trash my car!"

Leaning back against the sedan's front door, Willcox folded his arms and looked down at him. "Well you should have thought about that before you trashed theirs. What the hell did you do that for?"

Pete's jaw set and his gaze fell. "Payback," he said deeply, "for what they did to Carla. ... And I'll do it again!"

"Then aren't you the mistaken bunny," Willcox gibed, shooting Pete a derogatory glance. "They had nothing to do with it. They were here all night – all of them." He shot a harder look at Nick. "And they had a witness. Young Barbara Bradley had the night's bowser duty."

Nick straightened and shook his head.

"Their cars were here all night too," Rod continued, looking more pointedly at Nick.

"No," Nick drawled in reply, his head still shaking. "Something's not right here. They're tied into this trouble somehow. They have to be for they're the only ones benefiting from it."

"Well, going on the facts," young Waddell interjected, "there's no ..."

"Don't you give me that crap about proof," Nick turned on him, poking him in the chest. "Everything points one way! And it's about time something's done before somebody gets killed."

Shrugging off his anger, he turned back to Rod. "Or is that what it's going to take before something is done here?"

Rod shrugged his shoulders and lifted his hands in futility, his loud exhalation indicating he wouldn't argue the point.

"So what's going to happen now?" Nick asked, glancing at Pete again.

"We'll lock him up for the night, as much for his own protection as anyone else's."

Nick blew out a heavy sigh. "What time shall I pick him up?" he asked dully.

Rod scratched his head and straightened his cap as the road-trains cranked up and pulled out northward, leaving great clouds of dust swirling beneath the streetlights. An eerie ochre haze filled the corner like magician's smoke, revealing the sleek lines of the little red Silvia when it cleared. Few cars like this existed, Rod noted, and he'd often admired the car when Pete went zooming by. He rubbed his jaw, considering there would be one less by the end of the night if he left it a sitting duck. And after tonight's little episode, duck season was definitely open.

"Okay," he said, "and I shouldn't be doing this, and wouldn't be if I didn't think I could trust you ..." He rubbed the tension in his brow, knowing the trouble he'd be in if anything went wrong. "If Pete promises to behave himself on the way in, Brett can drive his car back to Dayton and save you a trip. Then Pete can drive himself home tomorrow."

"Yeah, sure!" Pete this time. "I'll do anything you say ... just don't leave it there ...."

Skulking around the corner of the brick wall, McCaig wished they would leave. A cold sweat had risen on his skin as he stared across at the phone box. Any time now, Taylors would be ringing ...

Nick leant down to Pete again as Rod fired the engine. "Have a good night," he said, one eyebrow rising dubiously.

Then a thought crossed Rod's mind as he looked towards

the hotel. He looked back at Nick. "Listen, I don't want you going to the hotel tonight, you hear? Things might get out of hand while we're gone. So go on home, will you?"

Nick's gaze shot across the road, and the muscle in his jaw flexed.

"If you're worried about Sheila, go home and ring her. We'll be back at the hotel in an hour. And don't you worry ... Sheila can look after herself."

Nick's stare hardened at the yellow lit windows.

"I'd rather not, Nick, but I can make that an order if I have to," Rod insisted, looking stern. "So what's it to be?"

Exhaling with frustration, Nick raised his hands and backed away from the car. "Okay, okay. I'm going." He didn't really have a choice unless he wanted to cross sides of the law, and it wasn't that important. Yet.

As he climbed into the truck and the Police sedan pulled out heading for Dayton, McCaig snatched up the phone on its first ring.

Taylors had a job to do.

CHAPTER TWENTY-EIGHT

Down at the makeshift stables, Dad hurled another bale of hay into the yard and scatter-kicked it around, breaking it into sections. "We're not taking the horses with us!" he bellowed back at me. "There's nowhere to put them!"

I glared at him as Jerry and Millstream crowded into the far corner of the yard, agitated by the shouting and the ferocious scattering of feed. "Stop it! You're frightening them! And I'm not going without them!"

Dad's eyes narrowed as he stormed across the yard, his hand rising to strike me, but he didn't carry it through. Just as before, he knew it would make no difference. "You're not putting those blasted horses ahead of this family again, girl. Never ever again." His voice in night's darkness doubled his convictions.

"Well I'm not leaving then!"

He yanked the electric cord out of the wall socket, plunging the stable area into greater darkness. Only Jerry's white head was discernible in the gloom, Millstream and their dark blue rugs blended in with the night. Dad strode closer, then suddenly lunging, grabbed my arm and dragged me up the driveway, the pressure of his fingers crushing so tightly I couldn't wrench free.

"There's nowhere to keep them in the city at such short notice," he growled, shoving me ahead of him. The force of his anger almost spun me around and I lost my footing on the gravel; almost fell but he dragged me up again and pushed me on up the track. "... you yourself know that!"

Scrambling to stay upright, I wheeled, burned his face with my eyes, but he didn't stop and I had to keep backing up the track to prevent him shoving me over or locking a hold on me again. "You're insane if you think I'll leave here without them! They're all I have!" I screamed.

The look on his face darkened as the meaning of my words hit home.

"You said that yourself," I flung at him. I stopped retreating. This was the time to have it out once and for all, what had been eating away at me all these years. "I've got no looks, I've got no brains ... hell, now you want to take away the only thing I do have!"

"Don't be pathetic. Nobody said that."

"Yes, yes you did ... you said that. 'It's a pity you don't have Rosalind's charm and beauty', you said. 'She makes good money with the way she looks and moves'." My head rocked and tilted in morbid mimicry, exactly as I'd remembered it. "'It's a pity you don't have Jason's brains — you could someday make something of your life.'"

Tears welled in my eyes but I forced them back — I'd cried too long already over never being good enough. Hell, I didn't fit into this family at all and it was oh-so obvious every time we came together. "Hell, you couldn't even appreciate me when I did show some talent at something ... and I bet it killed you that I've made a good living doing what I do. That's why you want to take it away from me!"

"Take what away?" he snarled, his nostrils flaring as heat flooded his face. "The chance to break your goddamned back and end up in a wheelchair every time you ride? And you make a good living be damned. You made a good living as a whore and milked it for all it was worth."

We'd reached the end of the enclosure and he flung the gate wide. "Look, the gate's open. They can get out onto the farm ... there's plenty of feed for them out there."

Tears flooded my cheeks. Is that what he really thought of me? That I was a whore? My hand rose, seeking retribution, and found his cheek as he turned. "How dare you accuse me of that! I had no idea he was married! He never told me!! And I wouldn't have been forced into that situation if you'd ever given me one thing I cared about."

I had no time to say any more as his hand clamped tightly to my throat. He hurled me back, the gravel skidding out from under my boots and toppling me onto my seat; he grabbed my arm again, half dragged me behind him, the stony ground doing little to field a foothold.

"You're coming with us!" he snarled again, "and the horses are staying."

"But they killed Berinson's dog!" Indeed, images of the poor dog with its head blown off turned into horses, a grey horse and a brown horse lying stiff in the paddock. "What if they come here? They'll shoot them! Don't make me leave them, Dad. Please don't make me leave them." I tried to wrench my arm free but his grip tightened further. "I'll keep them on the float. They can stand there till morning ..."

We had almost reached the house, almost reached the driveway where two cars lined up one behind the other ready to pull out for the city.

"Rosalind, you drive Becky's car! Jason, you go with her, and stay behind us all the way. Now, you, get in the back! And that's the end of it!"

He shoved me into the side of the Holden, not daring to release his hold until he'd fully blocked my escape from the opening.

"They don't stand a chance with nobody here!" I cried. Behind him, down the track I could just see Jerry pacing the fence line, his agitation evident. If I left, would this be the last time I'd see him? Would this be my last lifetime memory of him? Tears poured and blurred my vision, blocked my throat.

"You don't stand a chance if you stay here — none of us do!" He shoved me onto the seat and slammed the door behind me. Before I could grasp the door latch and unlock it, he had slid into the driver's seat and was pulling away at speed. "I'm telling you, Becky," he bellowed as the car fished slightly on the gravel, "we're not sticking around to end up like Berinson's dog!"

He waved his hand out the window for Rosalind to take the lead and both cars pulled out and sped east along Worsley Road. Fleeing, he abandoned the farm and his stock and left my horses to the mercy of the night. I would never ever forgive him.

CHAPTER TWENTY-NINE

Late the following afternoon, Cussack strode down the narrow corridor and pushed open a small metal door part way along its length. "Okay, young'un, time's up," he grunted, pushing the door wide open so the jail's solitary occupant could step into the hall. "I hope you've got control of yourself by now."

Nodding, Pete followed him down the hall to the office. Indeed he felt less smart than he had the night before – the boredom had driven him crazy and, while he'd expected to be out by morning, spending his lock-up time sleeping, the Sergeant had played 'smart-arse' and kept him in all day to teach him a lesson. Now he felt like a school kid being let out after detention. On top of that, he'd hated the interminable time he'd had to lay and think. Now all he wanted was to go home. And he wanted to be with Carla. During the restless hours he had thought about driving to the city, an idea he hadn't yet discounted.

In the outer office, Cussack tipped Pete's belongings onto the wide counter, emptying the yellow envelope completely. "Check it and sign for it," he said dryly. "You will be required to appear in a Court of Law in due course. Notification will be by mail. If you want to contest the charges, get yourself a Lawyer." He looked straight at Pete with stark blue eyes, "... but make sure it's a good one. Personally I think you'd do better earning a lot of money shearing between now and then." He grinned smugly – not exactly a felon's best friend – "... I think you're going to need it."

Gathering his bits and pieces together, Pete stowed them back in his pockets; his car keys he tossed lightly in his hand, trying to impress that the stay-over hadn't bothered him much.

He turned and headed for the door.

Outside, a slight wetting drizzle rained down but to Pete the fresh smell of first rain felt as blissful as his release.

"I don't want to see you again!" Cussack warned as he pulled open the door.

"Don't worry, you won't," came the tight reply.

Stepping outside, Pete didn't look back. He found his car safely locked at the rear of the stationhouse and quickly scrambled in. While he loved the rain, getting wet was a totally different story. Wet meant cold! And he loathed being cold.

Beneath the weeping peppermint tree outside Johnson's Hardware Store, Lacey sheltered from the constant spatter dripping from the leaves. He'd been waiting for hours, watching for Kennedy's release. Finally it had come.

As the sporty red Silvia pulled out onto the highway and headed north he sprinted back round the corner, a sinister grin and a slow thumbs up through the nonexistent windshield giving Beattie the okay to grab up the microphone.

Beattie pressed the button. "Big Brother, this is Goose.'

CHAPTER THIRTY

Entering Dayton from the south, I lifted my foot and let the Fairlane gurgle down for the town limits. The windscreen wipers slapped in rhythmic monotony at the rain, as they had for the last few hours. I yawned and sighed – it had been drizzling like this all day, getting heavier the closer I drew to Cullan. Indeed, heavy black clouds pressed earthward, their ominous presence matching the mood created by my heated arguments with Dad which had raged like a storm into the early hours of morning.

Sighing deeply, I recalled the giant can of worms I'd opened that night, having said some pretty nasty things. I'd reminded him that Grandpa had been more like a father to me than he ever had – Grandpa had been my trainer and provided all the things I'd dreamed of, or opportunities to gain them. But Dad said some pretty bad things too. So here I was, leaving again. This time I wouldn't be back. No amount of destitution would ever bring me back to this place. He didn't understand me – he never tried: I wasn't pretty enough; I wasn't smart enough, and no other talent I showed ever mattered. More than that, I'd been totally disrespectful bringing it to his attention. And that was the last straw.

I shrugged inwardly. Maybe I did disrespect him. Yes, I did. For a start I believed in committing totally to whatever I took on; I believed in fighting for what was right no matter what, and obviously he didn't or he would have been committed to me as his child, or at least accepted my right to be me. He would have allowed Mum to make her own choice on where she stood in our argument; listened to her when she tried to stand up for me – but he didn't. I would have respected him if he'd stood up for what was the right thing to do in Cullan – and that was stay and band together. Yes, I would always disrespect him, for leaving his stock that relied on him for their protection and forcing me to leave mine.

Right now my head felt like someone had grabbed it and was squeezing inwards, and rubbing my brow did nothing to ease its tightness. My eyes burned from lack of sleep – we'd been hollering at each other all night ... until Ros had slipped the car keys under the table and I was able to sneak them into my jeans.

Sucking in a deep breath, I sat taller, forced back the tiredness overtaking me. I had to get home before it did; I had to get home, hitch up the float, load up the boys and get the hell out of there. I certainly wasn't about to let Jerry have his head blown off. Nor Millstream. They were my best mates. My only mates. While I was helpless to ward off the cruelty going on in Cullan, I could at least protect my boys. That was my commitment: doing whatever I had to do to keep them safe. *That's what Love is all about, isn't it?*

That thought kept me going, that and wondering why I'd missed out on all the love at home. As I'd headed for the door, I'd apologised to Mum that I was going, wishing she'd have stood up for me for once; just once. With so much on the line she should have said what she wanted to say – even to say she understood why things were they way they were – it would have been enough. I knew she loved me the way I was, but I needed to hear that she didn't want me to go. For once she could have stood up to him – rebelled against his martial law – but she didn't even say I could come back and we would work things out. She hadn't said anything – just stood there teary-eyed – and I realised then she'd never gone against him the whole time I'd been old enough to notice.

So here I was, on the road back to Cullan, waltzing back into its shitty little problem and taking a risk doing so. But, I wasn't staying. This was just a "snatch and grab" raid – toss as much as I could into the boot of the car, get the trailer on and the boys away. Get well away from this town. I shrugged again. When all was said and done, I was doing exactly what Tony had said I'd done – I was running. Running from my problems. Running from Daddy's rules. Running from his domination. And like before, I didn't have the foggiest idea where I was going next. At least this time I was wiser. I would focus solely on getting back to the Showjumping circuit. Get back on my feet. I'd stayed longer in this town than I'd intended anyhow. Maybe I would take a trip south and look up Tony; get some of my money back.

I estimated two hours to pack everything I owned, and load up the boys. *If they're still alive ...*

A shudder ripped up my back.

No! They have to be alive, otherwise all this is pointless!

I huffed a breath, pulling it in, pushing it out with force; pushed away the vision of dead horses, visions I'd had every time I closed my eyes. Sometimes I'd see Carla's face, and shudder. They'd said she'd been so badly beaten only her family could see her. That had to be bad.

It was about four-thirty when I crossed the railway line on the other side of Dayton, which meant I had to hurry if I was to get all my stuff packed and be gone before dark. Cullan after dark was a nightmare town. If I timed it right, I'd be back in the city by midnight and have the horses bedded down in the stables I'd rented on my way back. All I had to do was hurry.

Prompting the accelerator to do a better job, I sighed with relief as the motor grunted and powered up in response. *Not far to go now.*

Beyond the town limits I put my foot down harder, but this time the engine objected to the request and gasped instead of growled. Frowning, I presumed it was just a strong head-wind, and pressed the pedal further. The motor roared loudly and barreled on. *Must have been the wind.* I kept my foot down and the next mile clocked off slightly in excess of the speed limit, the wind whistling mournfully past the side mirror, droning, the sides of the road a blur. Only the road ahead warranted my interest.

A mile or so further on, and without warning, the engine dragged again, an air-sucking sound coming from beneath the bonnet. *Definitely not the wind this time.* The motor faltered and the speed dwindled.

I pumped the pedal, twice — hit it hard a third time — stamped on it and held my foot down. The engine finally surged, backfired, and powered on again. *Yes!*

I checked the fuel gauge yet knew it wasn't a lack of fuel — I'd filled the tank at Bendori — and yes, the gauge still hung at the three-quarters mark. Maybe it was sediment: Ros had really drained the tank on the trip down. *And if it is, what can I do about it?*

Feeling cold, my attenttion stayed on the motor, on its irregular sounds as I tuned in to how the car felt on the road. It ran smoothly for the moment.

But what if she stalls altogether?

Your nightmare will start in earnest if you stay in Cullan after dark.

A tremor erupted and worked its way up my spine. *If I can reach the roadhouse before Tom leaves he can look at it before I continue on to Crestwood.* That became the plan, and I breathed easier for it.

A short while later the engine gasped again. Backfired. Then went frightfully quiet — Cullan seemed a long way off.

Frantic, I pumped the pedal again fearing the motor would die altogether. The worst place to have mechanical problems was on the Northern Highway. If I had to pull over on the very narrow shoulder in this poor light the road-trains would probably drive right over me as they had done to the small flattened Mini in Tom's wrecking yard.

From the distance I'd travelled, Nundajora Siding was just up ahead. If I could reach there I would pull over. At the rate the engine was chugging I sure as hell wasn't going to make it to Cullan.

With that thought, the car surged again, the engine roaring

back to life and my hopes lifted again. Wisely though, I stuck to my new plan – I would pull into the railway siding, a gravel sidetrack that curved in from the highway and back out again. It was well concealed by trees and scrub and barely discernible from the road – unless one knew it was there. There, I would attempt to blow the blockage clear. If I couldn't, I would lock the car and sleep overnight, which was preferable to being crushed by a barreling Semi ... and preferable to staying in Cullan after dark.

The siding soon came into view.

Part Three

Rebellion

CHAPTER THIRTY-ONE

Pete drove towards Cullan, taking care not to slide on the wet, slippery road; he cursed that the journey took longer than usual for he wanted to be home, but one slip of judgment, he feared, and it might take even longer. So he shifted his thoughts to things other than putting his foot down.

He'd fully decided now to pack a few things and head for the city, and just sit around in the hope they'd let him in to see Carla. It had also crossed his mind that he'd been fairly lucky this time, that if it hadn't been Nick and Rod catching him he would probably be lying in a hospital bed beside her. The thought of Carla pushed his foot down and he pushed her away again; grinned slightly at the next thought and shook his head. That silly old fart McCaig had actually threatened Nick. His grin widened: Nick would have slaughtered him. He nodded at the pleasant image that flicked through his mind. But his smile thinned again. It's a pity Rod had stopped it. It would have been ...

His attention snapped back to the road.

Through the grey surrounds and the light sheet of drizzle something moved on the road ahead. Someone, barely visible through the windshield, was waving him down. He frowned, braked and pulled to the gravel shoulder.

A red chequered shirt, similar to those worn by the miners further north, filled the windscreen as a tall man trudged around the front of the car. He was soaked through, rain pouring off his chin and blending with the flow trickling from his clothes. Hunched against the increasing rainfall, he arrived at Pete's window. Pete wound it down, his eyes casting up and up at the sheer size of him.

"I've got a problem, mate," the man explained, raindrops flicking off his lips as he spoke. He wiped them away on his arm. "My car's broke down on the siding over there, and I've flattened the battery trying to get it started. Do you think you could give us a hand?"

Pete looked the man over again. He was drenched and looked cold; nightfall was not far off and the sky promised worse weather to come. As much as he wanted to be home by his fire or on the road to Carla, he wouldn't rest comfortably knowing he'd left someone stranded on a night like this.

"Sure, mate," he nodded. He looked around. The thick belt of trees buffering the siding from the highway prevented a view of the car so he couldn't tell which way it faced. Nevertheless, it was easier to reverse and pull in than to drive forward and make the extremely sharp turn in from the farther end. He dropped the gear lever into reverse.

As he reached the gravel in-road headlights appeared behind him, a vehicle fast approaching. He dropped back into first gear to clear the road, his wheels spinning and sliding on the slush as he moved onto the rain soaked track.

CHAPTER THIRTY-TWO

As I approached the siding I noticed through the heavy rain the reversing lights of a car up ahead; noted through the constant swish of wiper blades the car was red. As it moved off the road, I thought it looked like Pete's car; hoped dearly it was. Pete could help me fix the Fairlane – we could wait until the rain eased, work on the car and he would at least see that I made it through to Cullan. I crossed my fingers that he indeed intended stopping till the rain eased, and would still be in the siding when I reached there.

Indicating, I pulled off the road; followed the coupe onto the slushy side track; crawled up behind it. Steering to pull alongside him, I smiled, knowing how surprised he'd be; smiled wider and prepared to give him a thumb-to-nose wave, and say "Isn't it funny the people you meet in the strangest places?" when I wound down the window.

Braking, I looked across at Pete; his attention however was fixed forward. *Hasn't he seen me?* I followed his line of interest, noting immediately that others stood in the siding – two men stood in front of a white utility, the ute more in front of Pete's car than mine. The men gestured across the distance, their voices lost in the wind.

I glanced at Pete again. His window was still up, and I realised the men weren't talking at all. They were pointing.

Odd. Pointing at what? Peering more intently through the misting glass, I frowned as the wipers slapped back and forth, distorting my vision. No, they weren't just pointing, they pointed something ...

A loud explosion rent the air and I leapt at its sudden retort.

For a moment I thought the Fairlane had backfired again but realised it hadn't; it was just sitting in idle. I shook my head, pressed the accelerator to check, but the engine powered up in an instant. *Not a backfire.*

I looked across at Pete, unwanted calculations churning my stomach, turning my blood cold. My heart shuddered. They had pointed a rifle and the rifle had gone off!

The sound of glass shattering filled my ears as Pete's windscreen crinkled, turned white and fell apart, tinkling as it fell inwards in pieces. Big splotches of red splattered across the driver's window forming in a wide thick band. Red blotches splattered the back passenger's window until Pete was obscured within. Then streaks, like heavy raindrops massing together before sliding down the glass, turned the rain blood red. Pete's car horn blurted, a long, loud protest as he pitched forward.

Involuntarily my hand stifled my scream, as if silence would make it go away; remove the reality. But other things poked my brain ...

– the gun hadn't just *gone* off – it had been *made* to go off.

No, no. It couldn't have. I'm just tired ... must have fallen asleep at the wheel.

I leant forward and swiped the fog from the windscreen.

No, the men are there ...

And they stared straight at me, somewhat stunned. I'd surprised them more than I surprised Pete. The smaller of the two suddenly charged at the car; the other remained stock still, and, through the increasing breath haze on the windscreen I watched him reload the rifle.

Shit!

Halfway to me, the runner veered to one side, and I saw the rifle rise to the shooter's shoulder.

Shit! Shit!

I braced for impact as another loud boom bruised my eardrums and sparks flew from the Fairlane's bonnet. Steaming shards of what I didn't know showered the glass. My foot landed on the accelerator as I braced again for impact, the low rumbling motor bellowing as the Fairlane powered up. The front end lifted at the sudden impetus, the surge forcing me back to the seat as it hurtled towards the shooter.

The next noise I realised was my own shrieks of panic as I lost control of the car on the gravel. I clutched the wheel, and through the foggy windscreen and slapping wiper-blades I saw the shooter again, looming larger. He stood directly in my line of travel. Automatically I spun the wheel to avoid him, but another boom echoed in my ears and shot peppered the fender, making deep crunching sounds and sharp squeaks. My new direction now headed me straight at the utility. *So close!*

I shrieked again. I was going to hit it! Frantically I spun the wheel the other way and more sparks flew up in front of me and a tinny sound rattled in my ears.

Beside me, the runner made a grab at the door, his face looming in at the window as I sped by him. But my brain now worked overtime. I powered on, my foot deliberately down, gravel spewing up in a wave from the tyres. Slush and rocks sprayed outwards from the car, pelting the men as they dived sideways into the bush. They rolled to their feet as the Fairlane's rear swished left then right and tore past them.

A few seconds later the tyres hit bitumen, gained traction, doubling the car's momentum; the sudden speed catapulted me straight towards the ditch on the other side of the road. *No!*

My grip locked on the wheel as the ditch drew closer. *No!*

The Fairlane's long bonnet crossed the white line and I saw myself propelled down the steep embankment, the car smashing into the opposite bank. I saw the men catching me and reeled at the image; spun the wheel left; thrust my foot down on the pedal and sent the car hurtling forward again. The chassis rocked side to side through furious steering as I pulled it back to the road, my wildest prayers answered as all wheels gripped on bitumen.

Miraculously I was on the road heading away from them.

The bitumen ahead panned out grey and clear, and I shuddered as the scene replayed vividly in my head – the incredible boom – the blood – the rifle – the horn ... *Oh my God, it had really happened.*

Images of Pete prised their way deep into my head, even though I tried to reject them. I couldn't think about that now – *you have to get away. Save yourself. Get help. But where?*

Glancing around, I realised I was heading for Cullan. The Police were stationed in Dayton, in the other direction, so somehow I had to turn around; do a U-turn.

In the rear-view mirror headlights appeared from the siding. *Jesus! They're coming after me.* I hadn't thought of that. In such a short space of time I hadn't considered anything, like ... *Who are they? And why?*

Another glance at the mirror: they'd reached the highway.

I put my foot down harder; my only chance was to outrun them. I had to get straight back to Dayton.

But this is the only road to Dayton and you're going the wrong way!

In the many months I'd been living in Cullan, driving quiet back roads getting Tony out of my head, dealing with the anger and humiliation, I'd learnt all roads leaving the highway led back to town. Only the highway itself led to Dayton.

Blood pumped in my veins; pulsed through my ears. If I could just get onto the back roads I could keep them well behind me. If I could link back to the highway on the other side of Cullan I could head south again, as long as they stayed behind me. My only chance of survival was to reach Dayton Police. Only there would I be safe.

Even though my hands now trembled on the wheel I pushed my foot down further. Brenton Road lay on the right up ahead, a gravel bypass road that wound interminably and eventually linked to a road that ran back to the highway miles north of Cullan. I hunched over the wheel, peered through the windscreen, searched for the road through the foggy glass and rain. I set the wipers faster; slowed my reactions. *Breathe. And breathe.*

Yet it felt as though no air had touched my lungs. *Relax. And think. Come on! Think! You're good under pressure.*

But my heart continued to pound in my brain. There was indeed more at stake here than a crisp new blue ribbon and a few thousand bucks. I leant back against the leather quilted seat.

Apart from the one set of lights behind me, no others lit the road. I turned my lights off so I wouldn't be so easily followed, and forced myself not to indicate.

Easing up on the pedal, I turned the wheel smoothly and slid the car subtly sideways on the wet bitumen. The Fairlane's nose lined up beautifully with the gravel side road and I eased out a breath as its nose tipped over the hump at Brenton Road. I now hurtled along it, large wads of mud and rocks flying up in my wake.

About five miles ahead was Foxley Road, a T-junction, and just after that a sharp bend. If I could get far enough ahead and make a quick turn into Foxley Road they might not see me and go straight on, travelling miles of gentle winding S bends, thinking I'd be just around the next curve. They'd go for miles before realising their mistake – and I would be streaking along Foxley Road heading for the highway, a long twelve mile stretch.

Two miles north of where Foxley Road hit the highway was Crestwood.

I can make it home. I can go home and hide out!

— and risk leading them to Jerry? No way! Absolutely no way!

I turned cold at the thought.

Which is the same reason you can't turn down a driveway and ask to use the phone. Wherever you go they just might follow and do the same to others as they'd just done to Pete.

I shuddered again, seeing Pete; imagining what he looked like, the image so gruesome tears flooded my eyes. I fought them away, rejected the images each time they came to my head, like it didn't happen.

Brian Egan's driveway flashed by, the front sign left splattered with slush and mud. Blackboys and heavy scented wattles draping bright yellow blooms whizzed by on my right, but that wasn't what I searched for. Eventually the landmark appeared: a black stump sawn off at waist height. I passed it. A second stump appeared. The third was just before Foxley Road.

And there it was! – barely visible on the left, growing larger by the second. Way back, headlights still hunted through the dimness, reaching through the grey shroud of approaching nightfall. *Coming fast.* I eased my foot on the pedal, needing to be careful on the wet, loose gravel. I touched the brake two ... three times, nudged the wheel left, straight, left, then straight again; pressed my foot to the floor as I straightened the wheels on the red shifting ooze. The rear end swung violently out but righted itself on acceleration. I'd made Foxley Road and breathed easier; prayed they would go straight on.

Easing each breath slowly out to regain my composure, I begged my hands to stop shaking; begged my chin to stop quivering. Nothing worked, not even when the rear-view mirror revealed an empty road.

They must have gone on by. They must have!

The chant penetrated my head. Soon I would reach the highway and be well on my way back to Dayton. Once I reached the highway no-one would catch me.

But what if they turned back? The thought seared my brain.

What if they expect you to try and reach Dayton? They could easily double-back to the Highway and be waiting when I got there. What would I do then?

My lips trembled and I groaned with the realisation that I didn't stand a chance. I couldn't go home. I couldn't stop at a farmhouse, and I probably wouldn't get through to Dayton.

So what are you going to do?

It doesn't matter ... I'm going to end up like Pete.

Those horrific images filled my head again.

No! ... Shut up! Don't think like that! – just keep driving.

With a hard lump blocking my airway, I snatched a look at the rear view mirror. *"Shit!"*

Headlights had appeared on Foxley Road.

"No ... they're still coming!"

I stomped on the pedal again, demanding more speed, the promise of a clear road to Dayton my only consolation. Then I shrieked as a loud explosion resounded around me. *They're shooting!*

The car rocked, and I ducked beneath the height of the seat, kept my head only high enough to see the road.

From the view in the side mirror I noted they were still a fair way back. *Much too far for a rifle shot to be so loud.* I went colder. *Oh no ... not now!*

Right then the car backfired again. *Boom!*

The Fairlane surged for a moment then the motor sucked air, gasped, the speed slowly dying.

"No! Don't you dare!" I cried, pumping the pedal. "Don't you dare stop now!"

Tears blurred my vision, and my life played out in my head. All the good things. All the bad things. Going out like this on top of the arguments with Dad. All unresolved. Not right. I wasn't ready for it.

The motor surged to life again. "Almost at the highway. Come on. Come on!" I sobbed. "We're nearly there. Please! Come on!"

Then another fierce retort rocked the car as the engine banged beneath the bonnet. The motor coughed and whined. Red lights lit up on the dash. With a sudden lurch, the car's front end lifted then dipped, the engine choking. The constant throaty drone of its power diminished, and the heavy chassis brought it to a quick and final halt. Next, the power steering locked and the chassis took control of the wheel and swung the Fairlane left towards the ditch, its nose dropping over the soggy embankment before it came to a halt. I bashed my fists on the steering wheel. "You bitch! You rotten bitch!"

Behind me, headlights loomed larger, the distance closing.

I groped for the door latch, flung the car door wide. As I scrambled out, the threads of my sweater caught on the door latch; I tugged to pull it free but the strong wool trapped me there, my gaze fixed on the approaching car.

As the blinding headlights loomed even closer, I reefed the sweater off over my head, peeled it from my arms and left it hanging. I was free. *But what now?*

Like a frightened rabbit, I scanned the surroundings. Scrubland, thick and dark, grew on the right hand side of the road. To my left spread large open pastures low in crop that provided little cover.

Hide! bellowed through my head. *You have no choice now — head for home.*

Yes, that was my last chance. Get home, toss a bridle on Jerry and get the hell out of there. I could ride up into the hills and across farmland where they couldn't follow. But I had to get home first.

As I dashed across the roadway a road-train on the highway further down sped past the intersection. Though a fair way off, it was reachable. I just had to get there unseen.

I plunged through the bushes, the slam of car doors penetrating the bush sending me crashing deeper through the underbrush. Almost immediately I found a narrow track and hurried north-west, stopping only occasionally to listen. The rain started again, at first just a light drizzle.

CHAPTER THIRTY-THREE

Scrambling from the utility, Dave Taylor reached into the cab and pulled the shotgun from behind the seat. He stood surveying the land as Ben unzipped the leather sheath from his .303, Ben tossing the case back in on top of Dave's. The light drizzle eased as they headed down the road, Ben side-stepping down its centre, rifle breasted, to check that the Ford was empty.

"I don't like this," he said as he eyed the bushes beside them.

"Don't like what?" Taylor snapped as he approached the green sedan from the ditch side. He raised his rifle hip height, ready to pop a shot into the driver's seat.

"Killing this girl. I mean, this thing's gone too far, and I don't like it – not when it comes to killing a girl."

'What are you going on about? Are you going soft on me?" Taylor barked. They reached the Fairlane and he raised the stock higher, his finger twitching. "What about the other one? You had fun with her." He released a frustrated sigh that the front seat was empty.

"Yeah ... but we didn't kill her. She'll get over it." He paused a moment as portions of his life flicked through his mind. "Even in the Army, I never had to kill a girl," he muttered as he too noted their prey had fled and deflated. He followed Dave across the gravel shoulder.

"Yeah, well if you were in the right Unit that might have changed." Taylor cast him a disparaging glance. "Well if you get squeamish, I'll let you look the other way, how's that?"

Ben looked unimpressed.

"Now, come on, we'd better hurry and get this over with — we've still got some unfinished business to do back there."

At a narrow entrance of newly broken bushes, they entered the scrub, Dave stepping lightly as he listened for sounds of a panic-stricken prey, as he looked for newly snapped twigs and branches. Like this, slow and stealthily, they tracked her further in.

CHAPTER THIRTY-FOUR

As the windshield wipers slashed and swiped their way against the glass clearing the drizzle, Nick's jaw tightened – the rain had finally broken and would put a stop to the shearing. It would take several days of no rain for the sheep to be dry enough to start again, and because of that he sighed.

He cruised down Wolsley Road, having just checked on the Richardson's stock – they would be away for a while he'd heard, and he didn't know if arrangements had been made for the farm in their absence. For the moment though everything was fine.

The sky had darkened considerably since he'd left home, he noted looking up, and nightfall was not too far off. It was Saturday. Maybe he would go into town; maybe see if Sheila had any news; see if she needed anything.

The thought tightened his jaw further ... *Even if McCaig is in.* He'd stayed away long enough, and tonight he might even stay over. Sheila must have heard something about the outsiders by now.

Topping the hill, his eyes lingered on the red and white hand-scripted sign on Crestwood's gateway and his lips thinned. Word had spread that Coopers had packed up in the night and pulled out too. They'd run back to the city. The news irritated him though he didn't know why it should – Ted Cooper had every right to protect his lovely daughters. And after what had happened to Carla he didn't blame him in the least. Maybe, if he really thought about it, he was glad.

Reaching the highway, he turned the wheel to the right and headed for town, ignoring the Ford's meandering as he glanced down Foxley Road. On the side of the road well back from the corner he caught a glimpse of a car, and hooked to it like a starving fish to a worm. Something about the car didn't look right. He braked and stared harder. If he wasn't mistaken it looked like Becky's Fairlane. But Brian had said all the Coopers had left. Uneasiness creased his brow.

Stopping the truck, he spun the wheel and headed back to Foxley; pulled up slightly in front of the Fairlane. As he climbed down from the cab, his heart started double-beating. There were two cars: Becky's Fairlane and McCaig's white utility. And it didn't look good. The Fairlane's front door was flung wide open, and Becky's soft white sweater lay part in the car, part on the bitumen, hooked by several threads on the door latch. The car itself was angled over the ditch, the suspended left front wheel rotating slightly in the wind. Across the olive-green bonnet deep gouges marred the paintwork, made by what he could only guess, and deep penetrations through the grill provided an escape route for wheezing, hissing steam.

Nick stalked forward, the empty white utility raising hairs on the back of his neck. Another Carla, he thought, his stomach knotting. He scanned the ground for signs of a struggle, but none showed. As he wiped the rain from his face, he noticed the gap of broken bushes opposite.

Moving away from the utility, his attention caught again and drew him back. *Maybe worse than Carla,* he chilled. Rifle cases spread across the seat. Two. Both were empty. How long had they been after her? How far could they have gone?

Maybe he was already too late.

He laid his hand on the wet white bonnet. *Still warm* ... so they hadn't been there that long. He returned to Becky's car and tested the hood. It was also warm, maybe slightly less so than the ute. That would mean, and he strongly hoped he was right, that she had a lead on them.

Crossing back to the truck, he listened for sounds coming from the catchment; heard only a rustle of leaves, which could have been them, or it could have been the wind. He checked the ground again – the soft earth at the roadside indicated three sets of footprints, and his stomach knotted tighter.

He wiped a nervous hand across his mouth. *Come on, Nick! Make a move. Go in after her.*

Inwardly, he shook his head. They were armed, and there was no easy way to overpower them.

So come on! Think!

He scanned the land for a sign that would give him other choices, but nothing showed, only a minor observation that the clouds rolling low and dark from the north-west promised a harsh, unpleasant night.

He stared at the sky, his eyes dancing with thought. *Of course! From here, she would head for home! There's nowhere else for her to go.* His jaw flexed as he scanned the bush again. *So close, yet so damn far away.* Well, he huffed a breath, at least she had the advantage – she knew the area: she'd been riding her horses in and out of the catchment for months.

To be of any help though he had to get ahead of McCaig ... he had to somehow put himself between her and them.

Studying the scrub again, he shook his head. It was far too risky to overtake them from this end; he would stand a far better chance of helping her if he came in from the other side and met her on her way home.

Satisfied with the plan, he hauled himself back in the truck, fired the engine, and spun it round behind McCaig's utility, noting as he did the absence of a number plate. The dust and grime in its place told him it had been gone a long time. He turned right onto the highway and quickly put distance between him and Foxley Road.

The catchment area ended about a mile further on at an old inspection track running east-west, an undeveloped extension of Wolsley Road. Bounded by the highway on its western edge and Brenton Road to its east, it was that inspection track Becky would be heading for. The track would link her up with the roadway home. Maybe, he pondered further as his eyes tried to penetrate the thick scrub whizzing by, if he pulled up on Wolsley Road, he'd be right on line when she came out onto the road. He'd bundle her into the truck and they'd be out of there.

Maybe too, he countered just as quickly, McCaig would expect that and try to head her off. Therefore he eased the truck past the road blockade that prevented public access to the reservoir, and drove a short distance along the eastbound track. He stopped the truck on the far side of a culvert and climbed from the cab, all the while listening for any sound of movement. With darkness rapidly approaching, he prayed the kid was still ahead of them; that she wasn't hampered by the falling shadows of night. If she was, they played too rough for her to cope for long.

Removing the heavy jacket that had until now kept him warm, he tossed it back in the cab. Its bulk would be a hindrance if he had to stand and fight, and besides, he consoled himself with its loss, he would need it later to get warm again. His crisp white shirt quickly dampened in the rainfall and clung to him like an icy skin, its sudden chill making him flinch and shudder. Noiselessly he pressed the Ford's door shut and stepped into the underbrush.

Away to the south, muffled voices echoed back and forth, men shouting to each other above the rustle of leaves. He detected only male voices, and no screams. They were pretty sure of themselves, he noted, for they weren't even trying to conceal their position. Then his anger grew that their loudness was intentional to keep the kid in panic.

He stood a moment longer pin-pointing their direction, his chest tightening at the thought of the coming fight – at the thought of what the outcome might be – of what he wanted it to be.

He started to move, slipping quietly from the protection of

one tree trunk to another, staying ahead of the voices. If all was still in their favour the kid should be somewhere between them and him, but how far ahead of McCaig he couldn't predict. Maybe she was much closer to home than he expected. Maybe she was even heading on a different tangent to him and he would miss her by a mile. Nevertheless he kept moving. His first priority was to intercept McCaig.

From giant wandoo to stout eucalypt he moved across the catchment, silent and unseen, and eventually stepped from behind a stringy bark onto a narrow muddy track, one barely wide enough to even be a 'roo trail. He stopped to listen. The voices however had gone quiet and had been for some time. The silence of the voices bothered him for it was hard to determine which way to travel. Maybe, he considered darkly, his previous thoughts were right and they had deviated. Maybe they were now on a different path to him altogether. Maybe he was passing them by rather than intercepting. Maybe ...

The rustling of leaves and snapping of twigs slightly to the south stopped his thoughts, and his eyes darkened quickly, the muscles in his chest and shoulders tightening as his glare fixed to the scrub beyond.

The sound had come from just around a bend, somewhere near the steep gully that bisected the catchment area.

Noiselessly, he scarpered along the path and found cover behind another giant tree; pressed his back hard against it. And there he waited.

The rain became heavier, soaking him through, chilling him with its icy sting. He forced his breathing to slow, forced his rapid heartbeat to quieten for its thudding in his ears blocked out all other sounds. He prayed the bubbling whoosh of water tumbling along the gully would amply cover his presence as he summoned the strength he'd need to put his plan into action.

If it was McCaig he would take him by surprise, which would give the kid more time to get away. Maybe he could even snatch a rifle and even up the score. If it was the kid, he would wait until she reached him then make himself known — without her screaming and giving them away.

He rolled his shoulders to loosen the tension in his neck and chest, tension that had grown at the thought of a fight, tension that would only slow his reflexes. He pushed back the fear that had steadily grown since he'd seen the cars on the road, and silently coaxed them on, his eyes dark with intent. *Come on, McCaig. It's Payback time!*

CHAPTER THIRTY-FIVE

Loud voices whipped by me on the wind, distorted and undecipherable, but the tone was not. They were getting closer which almost forced me to run. I fought the urge not to on this dark, rutted track. Above all things I had to stay calm and keep moving steadily. I had to keep my wits about me and make sensible decisions.

Moving along the red mud trail that skirted the gully, avoiding touching brush or bush that might leave a tell-tale sign, I headed in a roundabout way towards home, knowing that the track ahead curved left then travelled straight down to the highway, and that was the track I needed. Any bend that would keep me hidden longer was a good bend, so I pressed on, never daring to look back.

The rain began in earnest then, the drops heavier and roaring with noise. Large splotches dumped down from the salmon gum canopies, seeming to mass there until I arrived, then ... *Bullseye!* I shook the last deluge from my fingers, wiped it from my chin; tried to suck air back into my lungs. The rain was like melted ice-cubes. I started to ache; the cold sapping my strength. I wondered how long I could expect my stiffening muscles to keep moving. And how far did they intend chasing me before giving up, whoever the hell they were?

Gulping more breath, I shuddered, remembering the size of them. Huge. They were freakishly huge. Then I remembered their intent and hurried faster, slipping and sliding along the slimy trail. The muddy ground and low hanging branches hampered my way, rocks and boulders hidden beneath the puddles threatening to roll my ankles. If I fell, that would be the end of it. So I steadied myself, trod more carefully, focused more intently on what I was doing ... till a twisted Grevillea root hooked my foot and tossed me down, that same damn bush that pricked my legs each time I rode this trail. I cursed as I toppled forward, my hands hitting hard on the rocks as I slewed along the mud, my body thudding as I hit the ground. A wave of mud and slop flew up and poured over me; my palms burned and stung where stones sliced through the skin. I cried out, too late to stifle it.

Groaning mentally, I regained my feet, noting my sludge-covered jeans and the orange mud soaking through my shirt. "Damn!" I hissed. That had been a nice shirt.

They must have heard me for the voices came again, closer now, the frantic rustling of bushes more audible than before, more defined above the quietening wind. Cold clutched my stomach as I turned.

Get going, for God's sake! Get going!

My heart leapt as more bushes snapped behind me, and I started moving – started running – sought more stable ground so I could sprint. The time to be careful was over.

One second I had clearly put distance between us – the next I wasn't ...

– I was airborne, my legs pumping in mid-air. Something had ripped me from the ground. Then something hard encircled my waist. Something clamped over my mouth. I was dangling in the air and being hauled backwards.

"*NO!*" I fought to scream, but the hand crushing my face was so incredibly strong not a single word escaped. I thrashed against the force, kicked my legs, twisted, and writhed, did everything I could to loosen the grip that smothered my cries for help. Someone had to hear me!

Further back I was dragged, the huge arm yanking me so hard against a solid body I had no hope of escaping. They had me. It was over.

But I would fight until I had no breath to fight with. As long as I still breathed I had a chance. Thrashing my head from side to side, I attempted to scream again, but the hand over my mouth wrenched my head back, straining my throat. If I continued moving like this, I would break my own neck. So there I was, so hopelessly subdued one moment, the next spinning in mid-air, my feet dangling. I glanced down: I was suspended over the fragile rim of the high gully wall. Rain bucketed down while a torrent of water rushed beneath my feet, more pouring over the edge into the murky tumult below. The next thing I was moving again — either the ground had given way or I'd been tossed like a rag doll down that fragile embankment. Regardless how it happened, I now hurtled towards the tumbling churn of thick brown sludge that swept along the gully.

Everything happened in slow motion after that: I hit the bank, my back jarring with the hard impact; mud, rain and rubble poured down around me, raced me down the steeply rutted ground. I threw my arms out, ready to dive away from the landslide, ready to protect my face and torso from hitting the water, but a massive arm whipped round me again; hauled me back so suddenly the air burst from my lungs. Another solid whack and I was thumped against the gully wall well above the water, my head, back and shoulders hitting so hard the force collapsed the gully wall around me. It felt like a giant bird sitting on my shoulders.

The down-slide created an overhang in the gully wall above us, and I feared the whole embankment would soon give way and bury us alive. A huge body slammed into mine, pressing me deeper into the ooze under the overhang. Any second it was bound to give way.

Mud seeped into my clothing, matted my hair, turning it into a thick orange curtain the full length of my back. My lungs burned from the winding and I was suffocating under the overwhelming weight pressing on me.

Desperate to breathe, I prised my arms into the narrow space between us, screamed into the void: *"GET OFF ME!"*

I hammered the broad wall of chest with my arms, where they could move; shoved against him in almighty panic with all the might I could muster. *"GET OFF!"*

The pressure eased, but only slightly. And I heard his voice in the void between us, his tone deep and brutal. He said four words: "Shut ... the fuck ... up!"

From the gruffness of his tone, I instantly obeyed. At least for the moment I could breathe.

In the resulting silence I focused on surviving, questions ripping through my head. *Why? ... Why has he softened the pressure?* He was suffocating me so successfully with his size, why did he ease off? *Is there some other way he intends to kill me?*

I shook the thought from my head. *He can go to Hell! I am not going to die today!*

Prising my hands higher, I braced against the muddy bank and pushed with every bit of strength I could muster. In these conditions, on this precarious ledge, I had a chance to break his hold.

Behind me, more earthen wall slipped away, sloughing down around me and encasing my feet which slowly began slipping down the soggy slope. If I could only shift them further ... move them off the ledge.

Wriggling my foot in the mud, I tried to make the ledge give way. If it dropped I could maybe slip out from beneath him and let the swift flowing current in the gully carry me away. It was my only hope of escaping ... if I could only just get free ...

Beside my cheek, a thick muscled arm braced hard against the wall, the veins of the forearm standing proud. A huge hand clung to a tree root the falling mud had exposed, and I prayed for his grip to fail as mud oozed through the broad, clenched fingers. His feet shifted then, embedding deeper into the slush beside mine as I started to squirm beneath him.

I slid my foot away again, needing only a little space to twist out from beneath him, using the slipperiness of the wall to ease my body past his. But a hard muscled thigh thrust deep between mine and locked me to the wall again. I was stuck – no chance of going anywhere.

Above the howling wind and roar of pelting rain, above the noise of tiny waterfalls pouring over the gully's edge, voices carried in broken syllables. "Check ... there. ... can't ... far ..." The wind whipped the words away as soon as they were spoken.

My abductor pressed in closer, his massive body covering mine again. He didn't reply to the voices, and I frowned. Why didn't he call back? Why did he not alert his friend to my capture? What was he ...?

In that moment my jaw fell open. I drew back further and took in more details: the superb musculature that I'd been beating on – the heavily contoured chest beneath wet, transparent fabric – the massive body that so callously pressed mine into the oozing slush, that shielded me from the stinging, torrential rain ... it actually shielded me from something far worse. My heart leapt wildly for why else would he stay so silent?

And the voice. *Oh yes, the voice.*

My fists stopped pushing against him, instead clung to the sodden fabric, his heartbeat pounding beneath my hand, giving rise to my own. I forced my head back and looked up, not really needing verification. My heart somersaulted. Cart-wheeled. It was Nick Manetti: Man of Steel.

CHAPTER THIRTY-SIX

I watched him as he scanned the track above us, mud and water dripping from his hair, opaque orange trickles streaming down his neck. He felt taut, the muscles in his neck and shoulders bunched, his jaw rigid. More rain trickled down his face, poured down his smooth tanned cheeks and cascaded off his chin. He shook his head to keep the rain from his eyes; lowered his head to wipe the trickles onto his chest. Our eyes met briefly in that moment then he looked to the track again. I could not mistake the worry on his face and wondered if he was thinking the same as I – what if we'd left tracks that led them to the edge?

Then Nick shot a glance over his shoulder, and I felt him tighten further; his heart skipped as he looked to the other bank. I hadn't thought of that. But did now. What if they'd split up to cover both sides of the gully? They could pick us off one by one. The though made me shudder.

The voices came again, shouting from the same bank – the bank we hung below, and Nick turned his attention back to the track above us. On they came, their voices louder and still distorted. I shuddered again and Nick pressed closer to me, his face close to mine.

'What the hell did you do to get them so riled?" he accused in undertones. I shook my head. What could I tell him? ... how could I tell him? You just don't break news like that about one friend to another? I couldn't. I just couldn't. Not here.

He'd eased back a little but soon pressed hard against me again, and I felt the skip of his heart on my cheek. Then I realised he'd stopped breathing.

I glanced up, and did likewise. The toe of a boot had

appeared over the edge of the embankment, and Nick's gaze had fixed on it. Pete's killers were directly above us. If they looked over the edge, if the edge gave way now, it was over.

Nick moved, but only slightly. I sensed he was preparing to act. His breathing returned, deepened, and his heart beat grew more fierce against my cheek.

He glanced down again, his face close to mine. "Get ready, and don't fight me this time."

I nodded, my own breath locked in my chest for I had no idea what he intended. All I could do was wait and follow his lead. He smiled thinly then looked up again, my gaze following his. The boot had gone, the men moving on.

In the time we'd stood on that flimsy sodden ledge beneath the overhang the storm had intensified, the buffeting wind moulding the land to its will. Through its low moaning the voices began to fade.

After a short time standing in the eerie silence Nick nodded it was time to move. He shooshed me with his finger then, just as suddenly as he'd secured me against the gully wall, he swung his leg aside and sent me sliding down the muddy embankment to the water. I landed with a splash, my feet sinking in mud and toppling me forward towards the raging froth rushing by me. Nick landed seconds behind me, his arm lashing out and reeling me back before I went down in the foam. Fixing a vice-like grip on my wrist, he hauled me after him along the gully floor.

Water churned and roiled around us but I battled on through it, Nick hauling me off my feet every time the bubbling slush threatened to drag me to a standstill. He lifted me clear, kept me moving each time the suction attacked my feet and tried to pull me under. I struggled to keep up with him, fearing he would tear my arm from its socket if the water won the fight.

We scrambled against the current, staying close to the gully wall, the water's turbulence and noise of the rain camouflaging our movement.

Some way ahead, the gully curved then narrowed, the water funnelling fiercely through large concrete pipes that stabilised the narrow bridge ahead. Nick slowed, the force of the water and the strong current attacking his feet making it difficult to maintain a foothold. I clutched his arm as the torrent swirled about my knees and pulled me down, the water becoming deeper the closer we neared the bridge.

Then Nick reached around me; dragged me closer, thwarting the water's efforts to pull us apart. Only a few more yards and we'd be at the bridge. He ploughed on through the orange froth, found a stable footing on the edge and started to climb the embankment. His incredible strength dragged me up from the water with him. Reaching around, he suspended me by one arm over the wash and safely drew me across to stand in front of him. If he dropped me I'd be swirled away and sucked under the thrashing water.

We now stood on the edge of a reinforced wall. Above us, water cascaded from the track, the wind driving the rain sideways. For now though, we were shielded from its wrath.

Nick pulled me closer, locked his hands around my waist. His eyes flicked up directing my attention to the rock-filled embankment beside the gaping pipes. "You're going up," he said, his body blocking the wind from taking his words. "I'll be right behind you."

He turned me to face the rocks, and I had no choice as he hoisted me up, his hands on my waist, seat, legs then feet as he pushed me up to grasp the top of the bridge. With effort, I dragged myself over the top and rolled into a deep muddy pool on the track above.

Then Nick locked his hands onto the protruding pipe and hauled himself up in one smooth lift, his arm muscles bulging as he kicked himself forward to lay beside me. Rolling, he regained his feet and crouched, scanning the area.

Coated in mud and dripping orange rain, I waited; listening

as he listened, but apart from the noise of my rasping inhales, all remained silent.

Nick's truck stood in the darkness across the bridge yet he made no move towards it. Instead he turned slowly, scanning all around us again. I rose slowly, his breadth blocking the icy wind from my skin, but even so its bite was cruel.

"So far, so good," Nick said. Indeed, he looked pleased that no rifle barrel had appeared in our faces as we'd lain on the track defenseless. He cast one more glance around then clasped my hand. "Come on," he said, dragging me forward to the truck.

Opening the door, he bunked me up onto the passenger seat then hurried around to the driver's door and hauled himself inside. Glancing down at me again, he turned the key and the engine grunted to life.

"This will bring them running," he said, "so get your head down and keep it down!"

His big hand pushed me below the height of the seat.

Leaving the lights off, he steered the truck carefully, the fierce wind buffeting the cab, rocking it almost as much as the rock-strewn path. When the track grew rougher, Nick turned the headlights on.

Closer to the highway, Dave Taylor spun on his heels and listened. "Do you hear a motor?" he asked Ben, scowling at the implication.

"Sure do," Ben answered. He turned slowly to let the sound filter to his ear. "Can't make out where though."

"That way." Dave pointed north.

Simultaneously, they sprinted through the scrub, hurdling bushes to reach the eastbound track. Way ahead, red tail-lights glowed in the darkness but only for a second as Nick touched the brake. It was enough that both men noticed, and they listened as the engine slowly faded in the night.

"You reckon?" Ben frowned at his brother.

Dave thought a moment then shook his head, his lips thin with uncertainty. "I dunno," he said – the departing vehicle travelled too slowly to be escaping, and it would be a miracle if the girl found help so far from town and in the dead of night. He looked at the sky, confirming. It was indeed pitch black.

"Nah. I don't think so," he doubted. "She was heading this way so she's bound to be round here somewhere. Either that, or she's still hiding back in there." His eyes however fixed on the red dots way in the distance.

Ben wiped the water from his face then wiped his hand on his sodden shirt. "We gonna keep looking?" He hoped for a negative for he was now bitterly cold and shivering.

"Nah!" Dave decided. "We gotta get back and finish what we started back there before somebody else gets wise. Then we'll come back and follow that track just in case. One way or the other, we'll find her."

Ducking through the scrub, they cut diagonally back to Foxley Road, endeavouring to come out closer to the cars. It was difficult going and in the stormy darkness of night and impenetrable bush, with rain pelting fiercely around them, tracks were few and far between.

Taylor fumed at the wasted time and worried that sitting on a siding track out in the open for anyone to find was a blood red sports car with a body with half a face. Not that it could be linked to them, he mused, but it wasn't in the plan. And Dave liked things to go according to plan.

With that thought, he stepped onto Foxley Road about two hundred yards ahead of the cars. Both vehicles were still there, which eased his mind. For some time he'd toyed with the idea the girl might have double-backed. She could have taken either car seeing both sets of keys were still in the ignitions.

He sighed that she hadn't been that smart, and let the shotgun barrel drape against his leg as he checked out the roadway and wandered down its centre. The battering rain and gusting winds bothered him little – only the job he still had to do was on his mind.

Reaching the olive green Fairlane, he leant inside and riffled through its interior. "Just as I thought," he told Ben. "It's that Cooper girl from Crestwood. We'll come back for her later."

Slamming the door, he left the contents of a woman's purse strewn across the seats.

CHAPTER THIRTY-SEVEN

Spattered with mud and gravel, the truck bounced and tipped along the jagged track, Nick battling the wheel against the pull of the ruts. He cursed each near loss of control and looked back repeatedly. Occasionally he glanced my way before turning his attention forward again. I wondered what he expected to see in the darkness; wondered if we would hear the shot first or just feel its impact ripping through the cab.

"Can't you drive any faster?" I asked, hunkered down on the seat, vivid visions of Pete trying to force their way in. They cramped my stomach, chilled my bones and brought a lump to my throat.

"Sure," Nick shot back without looking down, "and would you like me to crash the truck too? That'll get them here pretty quick."

I tucked back into my silence and said no more.

A short way further up the truck stopped and Nick climbed down from the cab; walked the last few yards to the road barrier and inspected the ground. Glancing back at the truck he cautiously stepped out onto the gravel roadway. I popped my head back down in case he saw me watching, guessing he had also considered our slow travel had given whoever chased me time to reach here first. It was a point that obviously bothered him. But the road was clear and he jogged back to the truck, his rain-soaked hair glistening in the headlights. Reefing open the door, he breathed with relief, shook his head and hands to expel the deluge then swung into the cab. He set the vehicle moving again and turned left onto Brenton Road.

"You can come up now," he said gruffly once he'd made the

turn.

I didn't move: the cramped, curled up position was not only warm and secure, it hid my tears. If I sat up, I would have to tell him about Pete. I would have to recount what happened, and I didn't want to talk about Pete. Saying it would make it real. And I sure as hell didn't want to say anything that would rile Nick Manetti. I pushed all thoughts of Pete away; tried to eradicate the images in my head; tried to dispel the sound of that shot that repeated in my ears over and over.

Nick gripped my arm and drew me up, giving me no choice – I unfolded off the seat, brushed icy tears into the rain that speckled my face and stared out the window into the darkness. My chin quivered, the event in the siding and the images refusing to shift, as if they were burning into my brain forever. How could I tell Nick? How could I explain it ... I didn't know who'd done it, let alone why. The red sticky ooze that had smeared across Pete's window rekindled in the darkened glass, and Pete's face pressed up against the glass, blood pouring over his eyes, hiding them, shielding everything. I'd never see Pete again ... never laugh with him across the grading table ... never rid myself of this horrific image ...

My chin quivered harder, and I shuddered: I was losing it – couldn't hold it together. Tears fell and I shielded my break behind my hand and stared harder out the window, my knees drawing up to my chest to shut out the cold and fight back the trembling.

Nick groped around the seat, his attention still on the road. "Here, put this on," he said, thrusting a woollen coat my way. I shook my head. It was his jacket, he would need it. Yet I noticed with annoyance that he didn't shiver at all, and I was freezing.

"Go on," he ordered, pushing it closer.

I draped it across my shoulders, wrapped the ample excess round me for added warmth; buried my face deep into its collar. I couldn't miss the smell of Old Spice infused in it. "Wh ... where are we going?" I asked, realising I had no idea what Nick intended, and I still had to get to Dayton.

By the hard set line of his jaw in the dash lights I couldn't mistake his anger. I stared back at the road. I'd heard being near Nick Manetti when he was angry wasn't safe. In my peripheral vision I noticed the muscle in his jaw flex; sensed that whatever he was thinking made him more irate. And the news I still had to tell him about Pete was really going to rattle his trolley. And I was in the firing line.

His prolonged silence chilled me for I'd seen him in fights at the Cullan Hotel. Sometimes he forgot his own strength. And I never wanted to be on the end of those angry hands.

"You tell me," he grumped, casting another stern glance my way. His eyes were dark. "I thought you'd gone back to the city with your family."

The fact that he'd heard that surprised me. The fact that it seemed to bother him surprised me more. I matched his tone: "I did, but not by my choice!"

My mind kept pushing ... tell him about Pete – stop pussy-footing around – blurt it out – tell him everything. You have to for your safety, for both your safeties. Indeed I couldn't hold it back much longer – couldn't avoid the news that would make him livid. My heart pounded painfully, the noise of it filling my ears. I inhaled deeply; took control of my nerves again. Breathed out. *Tell him ... tell him now ...*

I opened my mouth to speak but Nick got in first. "Then what the hell are you doing back here?" He cast me a critical glare. "You got away safe, why couldn't you have stayed away? And what's more, why is McCaig chasing you?"

I huddled against the passenger door for his stare had turned to ice – fixed – the truck seemingly left to its own devices to follow the road. My heart thudded louder, his hostility invoking tears. *No, don't you cry! Don't!* But if I opened my mouth to say anything I wouldn't be able to contain them. How could I explain

... Pete's shattered face ... How could I tell him without him going crazy.

I shook my head, Pete's face swamping my mind. "I ... I ..." *Get them out!*

But the words locked in; choked me. I replaced them with others. "I came back for my horses. I wasn't about to leave them here, so I came back."

Those damn tears welled again. The arguments with Dad ... my fears for Jerry ... all rose like a bursting volcano. And it was nightfall again. "Hell, it's been a real shitty day!" I yelled at him, wiping away tears that rolled down my cheeks. I buried my face in my hands to avoid him seeing them.

"I could have done your horses for you!" Nick growled back. He shook his head, his hand thrown up in disbelief. "All you had to do was ask!"

I felt like someone had smacked me over the head with a telephone book. Nick, who had barely spoken a word to me in six months, even when we sidled passed each other in doorways? — Nick, who'd shunned me at the hotel in an electric storm and who didn't even wave when he drove past me on the road. That was ridiculous!

"And McCaig?"

My tears spilled over, the lump in my throat blocking words. "It ... it wasn't McCaig."

His eyes narrowed and he frowned. "It was McCaig's utility," he countered.

"Well it wasn't him. I don't know who they were." My chin quivered again, images flashing into my head. Full technicolour Pete. The rifle raising. The explosive shot.

I gasped and covered my mouth to prevent the words spilling out but they fell out anyway. "They killed Pete, Nick. He drove into the Siding just ahead of me and they shot him. They just shot him. He didn't even get out of his car ..."

Nick's jaw tightened, his expression darkening. "What the

hell are you talking about?"

I shrank back further, clenched my hands around the jacket and drew it closer. I could see Nick picturing it all, understanding but not wanting to hear what I'd said.

"They shot him!" I blurted out, almost shouting to make my point clear. "They blew a bloody hole right through his windscreen." Tears now streamed down my face. There was absolutely no way to control them. "There was blood all over his car. He fell against the steering wheel. He didn't get out ... he didn't ..."

The truck squealed as Nick rammed his foot on the brake, skidding it to a halt and slewing it sideways in the middle of the road. Its nose dipped so sharply I lurched towards the dashboard but Nick's mighty arm thrust out and blocked my forward plunge. He shoved me back to the seat, his grip on my arm so tight a bruise stirred beneath his fingers. I glared back at him, aware of his angst, the way his eyes searched mine for the truth. I met his gaze full on so he could see the goddamned truth.

His breathing heightened.

"Are you being serious, or is this just one of your silly jokes?" His grip tightened and I winced, but he didn't notice.

"Yes, I'm serious!" I grimaced, tears rising from the pain this time. I fought them back for I needed to tell him everything, yet fully aware that he probably wouldn't believe me. Cullan was such a quiet little town ... nothing ever happened here ... that's what everyone said.

"My car was playing up," I rattled on, wincing again as his solid grip persisted. "... so I pulled into Nundajora Siding."

I tried to twist my arm free so he wouldn't break it but it hurt more. "Pete had pulled in ahead of me and I was going to get him to fix it for me.

"There were two men there. One had a rifle. A shotgun, I think. He pointed it at Pete's windscreen, and it went off." Tears blurred my vision again ... "It just went off!" My cheeks felt hotter as they rolled and my stomach churned again. Blood rushed from my face. "There was blood everywhere."

I turned my grief to the window but Nick reached over and turned my face back to him. His grip shifted to my shoulder. "Did you see Pete?"

I looked directly at him, tears rolling, praying he wouldn't make me say any more. His stare fixed on my face, his brow creasing. I didn't have to answer his question.

"Jesus!" he said.

He turned back to the steering wheel, swept a broad hand through his hair.

I rubbed my arm as he thumped the truck back into gear, straightened it up and drove on, his jaw setting tighter. His eyes, now almost black, stared straight ahead. Then he glanced across at me; must have noticed I had pressed myself tightly against the door; must have noticed I was clutching my arm and grimacing. He reached over and rubbed his hand along the point of the bruise.

"Hey ... I'm sorry," he said. "I didn't mean to ..."

I shook my head. It was too late now to take it back. My skin was probably black beneath my shirt. His jaw tightened again, the muscle flexing as he gritted his teeth. He looked back to the roadway.

"You said they saw you?"

I nodded.

"And they fired at you."

I shrugged and nodded.

"There's long gouges right up the front of your car bonnet. Twelve gauge, I'd say. It took out your radiator."

Trembling, I rested my head on the window, stared out into the blackness; drew my knees up higher. *Damn, now my car is wrecked.* Funny that, the things that go through your mind at the most inappropriate times. Maybe I was lucky, seeing it had been that close. But maybe it was only a matter of time before ...

We neared the end of Brenton Road. So far we'd not seen any other vehicles. I huddled deeper into the corner, picturing Pete and praying my life wouldn't end like his. Those men were determined, maybe there was no way of avoiding it. I leapt violently when Nick's hand landed on my shoulder again. He kept it there, his grip firm but not crushing.

"Hey ... why didn't you go straight to Dayton instead of coming this way?"

I continued to gaze out the window, resigned now to feeling so shattered. "Don't know. All I can remember was taking off and passing them, and I was on the road heading home." I heaved a breath, composing myself. "When I realised I was going the wrong way I was too scared to turn around and go back in case they blocked the road. I knew I had to cut back to the highway which would be safe as long as they were behind me — but the damn car gave out. I don't know of any other way to Dayton except along the highway." I looked across at him, realising he probably did.

His lips drew to a thin line, and he nodded and eased out a calm breath of his own. "There isn't one," he said, his voice deep but not gruff, "... not unless you go through Kilcannie — but that's a hundred miles out of the way."

Right then I felt incredibly tired, and a yawn forced its way up, twenty four long hours without sleep suddenly taking its toll. "Where are we going?"

We reached the end of Brenton Road, the highway passing in front of us. Nick held his foot to the brake. "There's nothing behind us," he said flicking a glance at the rear-view mirror; he looked left along the dark length of highway, "... which means there's every chance they might be on the road that way. And I don't have the fuel to get through to Kilcannie tonight." He sighed again, deeply, and leant forward, his big arms hugging the steering wheel.

Frowning, he looked straight at me. "Did you have any ID in

your car?"

I nodded. "My purse is in the glove-box."

Our eyes met for a second and this time I held his gaze. My life was in his hands now, and I waited for his decision.

"Then your place is out. They may have searched your car. And anyway, if they've been around Cullan long they'd know where that big tank of yours belongs ... I guess it's my place then. We can ring Dayton from there and report what you saw." His hand landed back on my shoulder, its strength instilling hope. "You'll be okay," he said. "You'll be okay." And by the look in his eyes I believed him.

Nick let go of my shoulder and thumped the truck into gear. "We'll go in the back way to stay off the highway."

Crossing the Northern Highway, the F100 steadily climbed the rise of Gibson Hill, heading for the western boundary of Northgate.

CHAPTER THIRTY-EIGHT

Nick rolled the truck quietly down towards the house from the top end of the farm. He kept its headlights off – as a safeguard, he said. Steering it deftly in behind the machine shed out of sight, he braked slowly to eliminate its annoying habitual squeak. Rain pelted down on the cab, drowning out all other sounds.

I stared out the window, beyond talking now; beyond explaining anything more. Visions of the murder had played out in my head so many times I felt exhausted; had silently given my life over to Nick for I could not think clearly anymore. Desperately I needed to shut my teary eyes which burned with the need to close. My skin felt frozen. I caught my reflection in the dark window, pushed away mud-matted hair from my face and the wet fringe that hung in stringy tendrils over my eyes. I noted as I did how my hands shook and clenched them to make it stop.

In the darkened glass, Nick watched me, his broad hand ejecting the wet wispy curls that had fallen over his own brow. He'd been awfully silent since Brenton Road.

He reached out, his fingers cupping my chin and turning me to face him. "Hey," he said softly, "you'll be okay."

If only I could wish that was true.

Staring blankly, Pete's face indelibly printed on my brain. I swallowed thickly, the size of the men and their malicious intent morphing over Pete's image. I shuddered more violently.

"You'll be okay," Nick insisted.

I believed that he believed that, and forced a smile. If Nick was on my side, if the stories about him were true, then maybe I did have a chance; maybe he could protect me from whoever killed Pete. *Maybe.* Certainly if he hadn't turned up when he did I'd be dead by now. I shuddered at the thought.

"Come on. Hold it together," Nick ordered. "You're going to be okay. Nothing's going to happen to you."

Hold me! I just need you to hold me! The words flooded my mind, words I so desperately wanted to say, but I merely nodded and fought back the next wave of tremors.

"Now listen," he said firmly, "you're going to stay here while I go out and have a look around. I'll be back for you in a minute, okay?"

Instantly my hand clamped on his arm. *No. Don't leave me! I can't stand being alone right now!*

His hand covered mine. "It's okay. Nobody followed us, I'm sure of that. And I don't think they got a look at the truck either. I just want to check." He smiled fleetingly, which convinced me of nothing. I'd already put two and two together: if they'd been around town long enough to know where my car belonged they would know where his truck came from too. They could indeed be waiting for us. And Nick knew it.

"I'll leave the keys. Lock the doors after me. When I come back, I'll tap on the roof twice. You got that?" He watched for my response, and I nodded. "When I tap, you unlock. If I don't tap, you get yourself behind that wheel and get the hell out of here. You got that?"

I stared at him, shocked that his words confirmed my thoughts. He expected someone to be waiting. He expected they would know where to come. Maybe we were foolish coming here. I wanted to latch a second grip on his arm to stop him – but he would think me such a coward. So I nodded, and pushed back the chill rising in the pit of my stomach.

"Good. You're okay, kiddo," he said. Then he prised my fingers out of his skin, opened the door and slid out into the rain. It soaked him through instantly, and he flinched and pushed down the door lock. "Lock yours," he ordered, and when I had, he softly clicked the door shut.

Rain drummed harder; poured in sheets over the windscreen, concealing me within, the hollow drum-drumming on the roof droning monotonously through the cab.

CHAPTER THIRTY-NINE

Fighting his need to shiver in the icy rain, Nick blinked away the droplets blurring his vision and pressed close to the iron shed. Whoever chased the kid would still be hunting her, and he knew if they knew her car they would probably know his too. He could only pray they hadn't seen it. But then, he never held much store in prayers; and he would never be so gullible as to rely on someone ... something ... to ever protect him. He'd learnt a long time ago he could only rely on himself.

Sidling along the shed wall to the house driveway he scanned the area. Nothing seemed out of place. No cars. No intruders. No lights.

He scooted across the gravel to check the front yard where most people parked, out front of the house, beneath the pepper tree. His eyes swept ...

- the driveway
- the house
- the shadows on the verandah
- behind the glass of the kitchen windows. *Turn.*
- The machine shed
- behind the tractor. *Turn.*
- The side of the house
- the hedge row.

He reached the side of the house where heavy shrubs and clinging vines concealed him; pressed his back hard against the wall. Edging along it, he stopped when he saw the left portion of the front yard. In another step he'd see the tree where Pete parked his car, and his heart pounded with sudden hope that the kid had been wrong. Maybe it was some other red coupe. If

Pete's car was there, his worst fears would be over.

With water trickling off his fingers, his wet shirt transparent, he edged farther forward, wary in case others parked in Pete's place. *Closer.* He passed the Lantana.

And sighed with deep regret.

Nothing! No red car. Not even Sam's blue wagon occupied its usual place.

Nor was McCaig's utility parked farther down in the distance.

He released a breath of relief, and leant back against the wall. *So maybe the kid saw someone else in Pete's car.*

But the facts added up. If Pete had been released from Dayton lock-up he would pass the Siding on his way home. A shiver rippled at the images she'd described, but he didn't dwell on it. Right now he had a problem. Someone was after the kid. But who?

His jaw clenched tighter. *And how much do they know?*

Glancing round in a final check, he crept to the other side of the house, determined to be thorough as he remembered Berinson's yard. Whoever they were, they were good. They were silent, quick, and memorable, and they could strike and be gone before anyone knew. He wondered coldly if that's what would happen to him, or to the kid. Bad feelings were rising.

Relieved that everything appeared normal here, he scanned the Highway below, but nothing stood out there. No lights. No cars sitting idle. No sounds. There was one more possibility: Crestwood!

Moving along the side wall, a little more casually now the need to stay concealed was over, he rested against the wall again. From the tall thicket of Tamarisk hedge, he cast his scrutiny south. From there he could always see the glimmer of lights even though the house was a mile-plus away. On clear days he could sometimes see movement in the yard. But tonight not a thing appeared, not even a light to signify visitors were present, welcomed or otherwise. And that was a good thing.

He headed back to the truck.

CHAPTER FORTY

Staring into the dark space beyond the window, the world distorted by rain, my breath fogged the glass, making it even more eerie. I tried to stay calm. *Nick said I'll be all right, so believe him. God, I have to believe him.* And if the stories I'd heard from Pete and Sam were true, I had nothing to worry about. Anyone would be a fool to tackle Nick. I almost smiled, for Ros had once told me they called Nick 'The Rock' because you couldn't break him. That and because he lacked emotions. They never said it to his face though.

But what if they're out there? What can he do against them? They're armed, kept pressing on my mind. I drew my knees to my chest again, hugged them to shut out the chill washing over me, a chill caused by the distinct possibility that they were indeed out there.

And if they get Nick? ...

He said to take the truck.

I stared at the keys in the ignition; considered sliding into the driver's seat. Just how much time would I get to get away? Pete didn't have time to open his door or wind down his window. And I wouldn't see them coming in the dark.

I looked out the window again. It was so incredibly dark. I wouldn't see it coming either. My heartbeat doubled and I rested my head on the window. *Keep calm, and breathe.*

A face appeared at the window and I almost screamed, my heart leaping violently till I realised it was my own reflection. *Stop it! ... Stop it, stop it, stop it! You're pathetic!* But I'd never in my life been this scared before.

I gazed back at the glass, at my image. I looked absolutely frightful. Then my face paled, my features lost strength as something else appeared at the window. A large hand pressed on the glass over my face. I lost it; screamed horrendously loud. Then I remembered and scrambled for the driver's seat.

Bang! Bang!

"It's okay. It's me. Open up!"

Open up! I flung the door wide and poured out of the cab into Nick's arms.

"It's okay," he said, almost laughing, his giant arms encasing me, drawing me against him. "It's okay, it's okay." He held me tight, turned me, his body blocking the wind as I sheltered in the haven of his arms.

Tin clanged on the shed roof beside us, threatening to sheer off in the next strong gust that blew. Nick glanced up at it, warily. He eased me away, and reached into the truck and removed the keys. "Come on," he said, his arm around my shoulders. "Let's get inside."

Splashing through puddles and rivulets of water, we reached the verandah where Nick pulled open the fly-wire door, wincing as it creaked. Quietly he turned the knob and edged the door open, signalling me to "Ssh. Wait here." with a finger. He stepped silently inside. After pausing a second to listen, he moved further in then disappeared into the darkness of the house. A few moments later he came back looking far more relaxed. "It's okay," he said, ushering me inside and closing the door behind us. "You'll be safe here."

Nevertheless he lowered the shades before flicking on the light, illuminating a cosy cream kitchen. Next he padded through the house, opening doors, checking rooms, lowering blinds where he could to secure our safety. I waited just inside the kitchen door, hunched with cold, my hair trickling constant red streams which spread across Nick's kitchen floor. Then the shivering started again and just wouldn't stop.

Nick appeared in the doorway, stood with his big hands propped on his hips; he heaved a tired sigh, obviously considering we were safe enough for now. Those dark eyes looked me up and down, it seemed for long minutes, then he picked up the phone and dialled a number. The line buzzed and beeped. Busy. Then his gaze returned to where I stood, hugging myself to keep warm, my teeth chattering uncontrollably.

"Come on, Blue Lips, we'd better get you warm," he said, turning and opening a cupboard behind him. He pulled two towels from a stack then strode into the darkness of the room across the way. Gone only a minute, he returned, tossed something white on top of the towels then clasped my hand and pulled me down the passage. Opening a door he ushered me into a small blue bathroom, pastel blue with white tiles. A basin stood beneath the mirrored, wall-mounted medicine chest while a white enamelled bath and shower recess graced another wall. I pictured Nick standing at the basin shaving. Savoured it.

Pulling back the plastic shower curtain, he leant into the recess and turned on taps, waited for steam to rise. "I guess you can handle this yourself?" he presumed tightly, one eyebrow rising.

As tired as I was, I glared at his inference.

"Good. Have a long shower. It'll get your warmth back. Then you can get some rest." He handed me the towels, on top of which was a clean white shirt. By the size of it, one of his.

Stepping from the room, he closed the door but I didn't hear him move away.

CHAPTER FORTY-ONE

Nick stood in the passage listening for movement within the room. The kid hadn't spoken a word since the highway, nothing coming from her mouth except that blood-curdling scream in the car. He hoped she wasn't breaking inwardly as he'd seen soldiers do in the war, delayed shock hitting so severely they developed 'The-Light's-On-But-Nobody's-Home' syndrome. Her pale skin and shaking hands were classic symptoms, and he knew to be careful how he treated her to avoid pushing her over the edge.

He glanced back over his shoulder at the door. The steady stream of water had been interrupted and he knew she'd started showering. Relieved, he headed for the phone.

Dayton Police Station's line was still busy even though he tried the number three more times. Between calls, he noticed his own shivers developing, and became aware the room was growing colder, the wind outside whistling through the eaves and seeping under the door. He moved to the lounge-room, took the box of matches from the high, polished mantel and struck one hard against the roughened strip. It ignited with a hiss and he watched the flame flicker, his face illuminated by the glow in the dark square room. He touched the flame to paper in the grate and other flames sprang up, slowly dancing light and warmth across his face. The paper seared, crinkled, and burned, and finally shared its glow with the kindling, warmly kissing it until the kindling broke into flame. Soon the logs caught, red patterns dancing on the walls, sending glowing embers crackling up the chimney.

Warming his hands over the flame Nick silently thanked Pete — wherever he was — for his fanatical habit. Tonight it was definitely needed, and he hoped his friend would be in to share it. Though he doubted that he would. The kid was spooked right through. Something had definitely happened to make her that way.

In the quietness of those thoughts, the hairs on the back of his neck suddenly stood up, and a sudden cold shudder surged up his back. He knew the feeling well, and it wasn't cold air that caused it. Someone was in the room!

He turned his head slowly, expecting a crushing blow to strike him from behind, and his senses worked overtime to locate where they were. His nerves and reflexes intensified. *The doorway! A shadow!*

Turning swiftly, he prepared to fight, but halted, and released a heavy sigh. *Of course! The kid!* In his mental meanderings he'd forgotten about the kid.

The swift chill subsided just as fast, and he realised his own state of fatigue – he'd barely slept since the night of Sampson's party, and he desperately needed to. But not yet.

Running a hand firmly through his hair, he eased the tension gripping his skull, and stood and faced her.

CHAPTER FORTY-TWO

Dressed in the white robe I'd found hanging on the back of the bathroom door, I stood in the doorway, a towel turbaning my head. I tugged the towel loose, releasing my hair to the warmth of the room, the tumbled disarray swirling wetly down my back. It was good to feel clean again, even though I had felt at a distinct disadvantage showering in a strange man's house with no lock on the bathroom door. I had reminded myself several times that this was Nick Manetti's house so I was perfectly safe – it was more truth than rumour that he hated women.

His eyes swept over me. "Feel better?"

I nodded and lifted the hem of the robe. "I hope you don't mind. It ... covers more."

He smiled – a nice smile, I thought – and he nodded.

"Now, let's get you somewhere warmer."

He crossed the room and turned me around by my shoulders; steered me into the first doorway along the passage, a room almost opposite the kitchen. A wide shaft of light from the kitchen shone across the carpet and the end of a large double bed. Nick drew back the covers and turned me to face him, his sheer size and closeness as he stared down at me electrifying my nerves. His fingers slipped the knot loose on the robe and peeled it from my shoulders before I could reach out and stop him, and I stood feeling vulnerable as he dropped it to the floor.

The sleeveless white shirt which I'd buttoned to the top hung loose, exposing my shoulders, arms and thighs and I was thankful not much else. Nick smiled, and I realised just how silly I looked in his monstrous shirt. I simply stared back at him, thankful his eyes had stopped assailing me.

He pushed me down to the bed, my body willing to follow his command, my brain too exhausted to think of excuses to stay up and stay wake. Warm hands lifted my legs onto the bed, slid them beneath the bedding as casually as if he'd done this a million times. I stretched out along the sheet, and he drew the covers over me. "Get some sleep," he ordered. "I'll be in the next room."

He turned to leave.

"Nick?" My voice sounded panicked even to myself.

"Yeah?"

Don't leave me alone.

His broad outline in the light across the passage almost filled the doorway. So beautiful. So within easy reach. I couldn't remember ever being as close to him as I had been this last hour, and I cherished the memory of his strong heart beating beneath my hand. Had it been only an hour ago? "What are we going to do?"

He propped his shoulder against the door frame. "Well first, you're going to snuggle down and get some rest – and that's an order." I sensed he was used to giving orders. "I'll keep trying to ring Dayton and report what you saw ... if that's okay with you?"

I nodded and sighed, too tired to rise to his cynicism. "Mmm."

He stepped from the room, and I lay listening to him move about the house, the heels of his boots at times clunking on the linoleum in the kitchen, sometimes moving softly down the passage. Finally my eyes closed and darkness swept in from all directions.

In those long moments when my eyelids extinguished the light and let the darkness take over, my thoughts deepened, became potent. The darkness became blacker and blacker, until nothing but blackness filled my mind. Evil closed around me like a cloak, enshrouding every thought. Sent images swirling.

A sleek red car filled the space behind my lids. A young man waited within. Pete smiled as I pulled alongside him. His white, wide, 'life's-a-joke' grin that always invaded his eyes. I smiled back. Waved comically. Clown-at-a-circus stuff. He didn't see it. The inside of his car turned red; glistened and mimicked the duco. Red sprayed round like a spray can in an hourglass, a fountain of fluid filling every nook. Splotches glued like a crazy kindergarten collage to the windows, obscuring vision. Dark, thick and creeping, it oozed out the door's thin cracks; pooled out on the ground, a living thing. It trickled towards me, grotesque devil's fingers groping, crawling after me in the dark. I ran, but the tendrils clutched my legs, snagged my feet, pulled me backwards. I dug my fingers hard into the dirt, long gouges in the soil trailing my path towards that blood red cage. I kicked; screamed as red fingers swarmed me ...

My silent scream ripped me awake, and I bolted upright, gasping for breath. My face dripped cold, cold sweat. I nearly burst into tears then realised the room, the large bed and the widening band of gold through the doorway. I wasn't there – I was here, in Nick Manetti's house, in his bedroom.

I forced my breathing back to normality; lay down; tucked my knees up under the blankets and fought the chill from my skin. *Try again*, I told myself. *Must sleep. Must stop shaking. Think of something else. Think 'beautiful' thoughts.*

Beautiful thoughts meant Jerry. My beautiful, beautiful Jerry.

I settled again tucked beneath the heavy sward of blankets, images of my giant grey companion warming me through. I closed my eyes and savoured the image – his muscles rippling as he stood, ears pricked, mind alert, his milk-white mane flowing in the wind like snow in a blizzard, his velvet softness smooth against my cheek. *Beautiful. Beautiful Jerry.* How magnificent ... How real ... *Yes, override it.*

Sleep came again, and I drifted on clouds watching Jerry on the hill standing beneath the single salmon gum beside the house. Proud and noble, he waited as he always did, a flawless marble statue, his muscles taut and ready to play – our Chasey-Chasey game – where he would gallop around the field, tail high, mane flying and I would dodge his minor attempts to run me down. His mane flew now as he stood ready ... the breeze dancing past ...

My body sunk deeper, totally absorbed in sleep and the scene. My gaze shifted – to a man on the road. To a man watching. A man with a rifle. The rifle raising ...

Every muscle locked as I turned on my cloud. Jerry's nose lifted to the wind, his white mane wafting endless plumes that billowed like smoke. Wafting wisps of grey mingled with his snow white mane. His beautiful head thrown back. His body crumpling. Crashing down. Plummeting. White legs thrashing ...

NOOO-OOO!!!

My eyes flashed open and cold tears spilled to my cheeks. My gasps for air were painful as air blocked my throat. I couldn't breathe. I couldn't sleep. If I did I would only succumb to nightmares and I couldn't bear to see Jerry like that again.

So I lay, forcing off sleep's need, body resting only, not moving as I listened to Nick move about the kitchen. Occasionally he passed by the doorway, and in the silence I waited for his return, remembering how gentle he'd been, how softly he'd put me to bed, how strong his hands felt on my skin. How boldly he'd protected me. My eyes closed with those blissful thoughts of Nick.

CHAPTER FORTY-THREE

Across in the kitchen, Nick glanced at the clock. It was seven-thirty. If the kid was mistaken and Pete was coming home, he would have been in by now, even if he was going out again. He picked up the phone and dialled Dayton Police Station for the sixth time, wondering as he did if the busy line had something to do with what the kid had seen at Nundajora Siding.

This time the phone rang true.

"Dayton Police," the voice answered dully. "This is Senior Constable Willcox."

"Rod, it's Nick." He paused a moment, giving the man a chance to interrupt him with the news but when the line remained quiet he took a deep breath. "We may have a problem."

He paused again, trying to select the right words, feeling decidedly stupid for making such a call. Internally he debated why he should feel that way. "I have reason to believe that Pete may have been killed tonight."

"Killed? Is that what you said?"

Nick's voice deepened. "Yeah ... it's what I said."

"How?"

"Deliberately."

Rod coughed, clearing his throat. "Well I'll fill out a report," he said, "but ... you'll have to pull the other leg first."

Nick gritted his teeth; leant his shoulder against the wall and realised why he'd felt the way he did: it was just so stupid for nothing ever happened in Cullan so who would believe it! It was the very same reason he'd challenged the kid. His silence erased Rod's humour.

"Hey, you're not joking are you?"

Nick nodded that it had had the right effect. "All I know is that on my way out tonight I saw two cars down on Foxley Road, both way back off the highway. One was that big green Ford of Becky Cooper's, half off the road, the driver's door wide open, deep gouges across the bonnet. The other was McCaig's Chrysler pulled in behind it. No occupants, empty rifle cases on the seat. It looked like trouble ..."

He paused, but there was only silence on the other end. "You still there?" he asked dubiously.

"Yeah, mate, I'm here. Go on."

"Anyway, I went down to check it out and found young Becky Cooper with a couple of thugs on her tail. She said she saw Pete – or who she thinks was Pete – shot at the Siding. And they saw her. That's why they were after her."

"Okay. Who's they, Nick?'

Nick's gaze rolled ceiling-ward. "Do you think I'd be standing here talking to you if I knew who they were? ..." He shook his head; mentally calmed himself. "And the kid doesn't know either. Says she's never seen them before. But if it wasn't McCaig ...," – he remembered the voices not sounding familiar and McCaig's uncanny knack of finding concrete alibis – "they've got to be involved. It was his utility."

"What time was all this going on?"

"Dusk." Outside the window, it was now pitch black. He'd completely lost track of time.

For a moment Rod stayed quiet. "Well it would fit," he mused candidly. "We let Pete out of here late this afternoon."

Going instantly colder, Nick ran a hand through his hair, and heaved out a frustrated breath. His gaze centred on the ceiling. There was nothing left to say – except maybe a prayer in the hope they were jumping to conclusions.

"Okay, Nick," Rod said slowly, "what Siding?" Nick told him and pictured Rod writing it down. "Okay. I'll head down there and check it out. Where's the girl now?"

"With me."

"You at home?"

"Yeah."

"Well stay put. I'll ring you back as soon as I can."

Exhaling fully as the familiar click ended the call, Nick hooked the receiver back on its cradle. Outside, a strong wind buffeted the house, the cold draughts seeping under the door making him shiver again. His shoulders sagged at the news, even though he was glad the dreaded call was over. He returned to the lounge and re-stoked the fire, placed the guard across the hearth for safety then went for a shower. It would keep him awake while he waited for Rod's report.

Hot water pelted over him, the force relaxing his aching muscles, its steady spray flushing the mud from his hair and skin. It warmed him through so much he was reluctant to turn it off, but he was expecting a call and didn't want to miss it.

Towelling dry, he pulled on a pair of clean blue jeans he'd found in the laundry and zipped them up then rough-dried his hair, draping the towel around his neck to soak up what was left. Gathering the sodden pile of clothing from the floor, he carried it to the laundry – the kid would undoubtedly need something to wear when she woke and it was already obvious none of his stuff would fit.

The washing machine thumped into action, sloshing and swirling back and forth, back and forth, white froth bubbling over water that quickly turned orange. He smiled at the vision of her standing there, caked with mud, her sleek brown hair thick and redder than ever; her shoulders weighted with clay and slime from the collapsing gully wall. His smile widened – it hadn't seemed to bother her much, not like it would have bothered Marilyn. He hunted for a shirt or wind-cheater in the basket where he'd found the jeans but had no luck and decided he'd have to get something from his wardrobe before he froze to death.

The passage exuded warmth as he padded to his room, the glow from the fire flickering brightly as he dropped his tan boots and Becky's white sneakers, now stained orange, onto the hearth to dry. Then he entered his room quietly so not to wake his sleeping refugee.

From the light beaming from the kitchen, he could see she slept on her back, stretched out, her arms extended above her head. Confidence position. He liked that. Tucked up sleepers were basically insecure, withdrawn into themselves – he'd found that out in the Army, vaguely remembering Stewy Van Kuiper prattling on one night about a thesis he'd written at Uni. God, what a strange mix of intellectuals they'd been. From University students – their Ban the Bomb fanatics – to clerks – Captain Boyce, Salwyn Credo – to farm boys – himself and Sam – and mechanics – Pete and Paul – to a general assortment of layabouts (one of whom they called Mary); the rest seemed to come and go without you really getting to know them – and you deliberately tried not to for obvious reasons. But you had to find out one major thing about each and every one of them – every man, boy and tin soldier in the Unit. Who could be trusted to stand your cover. And who would freeze when dumped in the thick of it. If you didn't learn that in a hurry, your survival rate was minimal. No, worse ... Dead zone. Zero.

But Stewy had been right. Sleeping was the best way to read people. Ignore the conscious – that's what people wanted to be. Go in through the subconscious and see what they really felt. Catch out the phoney brave and cover-up cowboys ... those who curled up tight, an unobtrusive exposé of their inner selves revealed honestly yet without the need for words. And there were many ... those who would have you believe your back was protected, who professed to be in control of their fears, but who couldn't move when you needed them most.

He always trusted Sam. Openly the hot head, Sam admitted fear. And that was a good thing. Those who had no fear did stupid things, never analysing the consequences ... or just not caring. Some even had a death wish – and in Nam those wishes always came true. But Sam was secure. He had a good level head and had rallied when needed.

Pete though was a different story – had been a different story, he corrected, his hands tightly gripping either end of the towel – though he wasn't a phoney either. He was just plain scared. No death wish. No big bullshit. He'd just signed up for an exciting time then found out he didn't want to die. And every day Nam had other plans. So determined was Pete to stay alive, he could barely force himself to move forward into danger, even if that was a safer place to be than where he was. But that was okay too.

Looking at the ceiling, Nick sunk a deep breath through him. He'd known what to expect from Pete, as he'd known when Pete was the only one standing there in his hour of need – that his time was up – he was going to buy it. And he had, the long narrow scars on his side a constant reminder of how ten seconds could be so vitally important, for him as much as for Kennie. The only difference though, was that he didn't blame Pete ... not in the slightest. Pete had never professed to be a hero, and you always knew that if you were going to survive, you had to do for yourself, as he had that day. His lips tightened at the memory of the sharp point that glinted through his side as two VC jumped him. Too frightened to move, Pete had lived with that failing ever since, as *he* had lived with the guilt of Kennie's death. He shook his head, for there was nothing more he could say to Pete to make him feel otherwise. And by God he had tried. He had really tried.

Pulling the towel from his neck he fought back the painful lump in his throat. *Well, you won't have to live with it any more ... if what the kid says is true.*

A few drops of water dropped to his chest and he flinched, and pulled his thoughts back from the past, centred his attention back on the bed, on the kid, on the way her long hair flowed out across his pillow, like a dark tide washing up a pure white shore. *Pretty,* he thought, his eyes adjusting to the dimness. *Real, real pretty.* He liked her hair and the way it spread out over his pillow, just as he liked the sturdy athleticism of her body. She seemed like she wouldn't break too easy.

His next thought bombed in a thunderous boom that suddenly rocked the house as a brilliant streak of light flashed outside the window. It brightened the room to daylight.

He glanced back over his shoulder as lightning cracked again, infusing the air with static as savage forks stabbed earthward.

CHAPTER FORTY-FOUR

My heart jolted at the sudden, violent retort. Breath caught in my chest. *Rifle shot! They're back!* There had been no warning – no voices taunting me. *Too late to run.*

I rolled under the covers and curled up, shivering. This was it.

Then lightning flashed and thunder rolled fiercely, its resonant boom loud, and I realised the cause of the boom, and sighed – there was no imminent danger – yet my thoughts remained on the two men who'd chased me. I stared at the wall, wondering where they'd gone; wondering *if* they'd gone. Where the hell were they right now? I sighed again, my gaze wandering. I remembered where I was … here, in Nick Manetti's house, sleeping in Nick Manetti's bed, nobody knowing where I was, nor, after the morning's quarrels, probably caring. My car was on the road down there, victim to whatever damage they wished to inflict on it and knowing I'd never be able to afford another, or fix it. I prayed in the silence: *Please … please look after my car.*

I felt silly then, praying for some inanimate object, praying for something that didn't have a soul then debated if I really did believe in God. It was only ever in moments like these that I prayed. *And poor Jerry and Millstream, they didn't get fed tonight … Boy will they be pissed. And please, look after Jerry,* I added for good measure. Might as well make the most of it, being like a little kid and saying my night prayers. But it did help take my mind off other things.

God bless Mummy … Long pause. Long, long pause … … … *oh alright! And Daddy. And God bless Nick. We can't forget Nick, can we?*

Lightning streaked earthward again, beautiful, brilliant white.

The room burst into daylight, defining the painting on the wall in that split second – a tree, an old tree standing in a forest, its roots washed by a lazy green river, almost all shades of grey. The wardrobe appeared, dark, solid and wooden. No other impression. And a figure stood at the window ...

My heart stopped. *Someone's outside the window!*

I went to scream. Scream for Nick. But stopped before the sound burst forth as a sudden chill swept over me. My eyes adjusted to the gloom. The someone wasn't outside the window, I trembled, they were much too close. Therefore they were inside the window!

The scream locked in my throat and I lay motionless, begging my eyes to close, wanting to press them shut. How did it go when I was a little girl afraid of the dark? ... What you don't see can't hurt you. Desperately I wanted to pull the covers up over my head just as I'd done back then, but I wasn't little any more, and little girl's games didn't protect you when you grew older. Age forces reality, and right now, reality was a terribly frightening thing. A shudder ripped through me and I remained rigid, watching through slitted eyelids, daring not to relinquish the appearance of sleep. So far that was all that had kept me safe. And, as much as I didn't want to see it coming, I couldn't force myself not to look.

The golden beam of light from the kitchen still played across the end of the bed, fanned out across the end of the room; reflected off smooth golden skin. I frowned at the partial outline. A big man. A tall man. *Pete's killers were big.*

Loud thunder rolled in the sky overhead, the house rocking with its intensity.

Crack! Crack! Boooom ...

More lightning fractured the darkness, and the magnificence of the structure I peered at silhouetted in the flash. My eyes opened. Only one person was built like that!

He turned his head to watch the lightning lash, and I huffed out a breath with relief. More than anything I wanted to sit up and yell at him for scaring me like that, but instead I lay and watched him as he moved around to the wardrobe, appreciating the immense breadth of his shoulders, the enormous size of his biceps, the muscle definition of his chest. This was the beautiful structure I'd so often imagined hidden beneath the crisp white shirt. He "Ssh'-ed" the cupboard to silence as the door grated audibly through the room, followed by a jingling of empty coat-hangers, which he also hushed. I almost laughed at his attempt to move with stealth. The towel plopped on the bed as he turned and moved back into the light, white hovering momentarily as he thrust an arm into his shirt sleeve. How could I not feel safe.

Drawing up the other arm he pulled the shirt on over his shoulders and straightened the garment to lay against his skin then he finger-combed his hair back and looked down at the bed.

"You're supposed to be asleep," he said, catching me by surprise.

I opened my eyes fully. "Doesn't anything escape your attention?" I murmured, rolling to my back.

"No ..." He kept moving towards the door. "... so you'll be sure I'll know if you don't go back to sleep."

"I can't sleep!" I pulled the covers up higher and felt cold as Jerry's dream flashed back to my mind.

"Bad dreams?" he asked less gruffly, looking down at me.

I nodded, and sighed. "I'm just so scared."

Nick nodded. "Do you want to talk about it?" He reached over and flicked on the bed lamp. "A good stiff drink would probably help better but we don't have any, so talking will have to do." He sat on the edge of the bed, waiting, screening my face. "Go on. Tell me what you're scared of. It'll at least bring it out in the open."

I shrugged. "Right now," I admitted softly, "I feel shit scared of everything."

His lips twisted somewhat. "I don't believe that! You can't

be scared of everything."

"Okay, so it just seems like everything!" My throat tightened as Jerry wandering around the home paddock unprotected filled me with dread. No, it actually tore me to pieces. I pictured his rugs slipping and causing him injury, or him writhing with colic because I wasn't there.

"Come on. Be more specific."

"How can I be?" I almost whined. "My damn car is down there somewhere, vulnerable to whatever they want to do to it. My horses, if they're still alive, are at risk of being killed if they go there looking for me. And when they do find me, I know they'll stop at nothing less than making me look like Pete ..."

Heat tore into my eyes, burned in my nose as I looked at Nick, surprise reeling through me I'd actually blurted that out, that I'd mentioned Pete in that vein, for I never wanted to remember how he'd looked. Nick's eyes darkened as he sat there. "Something terrible's going to happen, Nick." His dubious look caused me to add: "I get these feelings. I can sense things before they happen, and something really bad *is* going to happen." I hung my head, realising I might as well get it all out. "And you ... you scare the absolute hell out of me."

His brow creased at my admission, but he quickly suppressed it. "Well you have no need to be scared of any of it," he said deeply. "For one, they wouldn't waste time with your car, not when it's out in the open like that. Secondly, your horses at this point are fine; I saw them both this evening. And you have no need to fear being found because nobody knows you're here."

He stood up and moved back towards the door. "As for me," he shrugged without looking back, "that's something you'll just have to deal with."

He turned back. "Right now, I will be your worst nightmare if you don't go back to sleep."

Tears welled, uncontrollable. "For shit's sake! I can't sleep! I keep seeing it happening every time I close my eyes!"

He came back; sat back on the edge of the bed again, closer this time. "Look," he said, almost begrudgingly, "if it will help I'll sit here with you until you drift off, okay? But you have to get some rest – it'll be a long day tomorrow once they find Pete."

He fluffed the pillows up behind him, swung his legs up onto the bed and leant back against the headboard, sighing as if it was going to be an extremely long night too.

"I've rung Dayton Police and they're checking out the Siding and will ring us back." He yawned, and heaved out another deep breath. I felt like a terrible nuisance to him. "Does that make you feel any better?"

I nodded and looked up at him. Direct eye contact. "Mmm."

"We just have to wait for that phone call then we'll know what they want us to do." He pulled the covers over my arms, and I moved a little closer to the warmth of him. Reaching over, he turned out the lamp.

Silence reigned.

In the light coming from the kitchen, I could see him clearly, propped up on the high bank of pillows, his unbuttoned shirt gaping open, his head tilted back exposing a strong masculine jaw line. He directed his stare out the window while his hands rested on his waist, long, strong fingers touching at their tips. They were nice hands – big hands with neatly trimmed nails, the tip of his thumbs curled back slightly. I wondered how they felt, those hands. I could hear him breathing, slow, calm breaths, and couldn't resist the need to draw my hand up and rest it on top of his. He was pleasantly warm to touch.

"I'm sorry for being such a pain," I murmured. "I really am sorry."

His hand covered mine, his fingers curling to interlock mine with his; he drew my hand to his chest and held it there, over his heartbeat, over the gentle rise and fall of his breathing. "Apology accepted," he said. "Now go to sleep."

Amazingly I did, feeling more at ease with him so close. As

my eyes closed, as total relaxation swept over me, I felt his free hand gently smooth the hair from my cheek. It brushed ever so gently across the line of my jaw, and my heart burst at his touch.

CHAPTER FORTY-FIVE

Rod hung up the phone, his pen tapping pensively on the paper in front of him. He dotted an 'i', crossed a 't', wriggled the pen back and forth in his fingers as he stared at the information in front of him. This had to be a joke, he thought tightly, for nothing ever happened in Cullan. Nothing. The last bit of excitement the town had had was over thirty years ago when Bruce Gordon-Jennings axe-murdered his wife and buried her in a gully on Brixton Downs.

He shook his head. The only thing was, Nick never joked — he was much too solid for that. He smirked at the unintended pun. Scrupulous or stoical might have been a better choice of words. 'No ...' he corrected further, his lips twisting in thought, 'Nick was straight. Straight down the dial.'

But the scrawl on the page glared back at him. He would have expected something like this from Pete or Sam when they'd been on a binge, or from some of the louts in Dayton, and they'd ring back in a minute or two and laugh at his expense. But Nick was different. And with the trouble brewing in Cullan lately ... maybe this was linked.

He checked the clock, the second hand jerking around the face, each click warning him he was wasting time. Rising, he headed for the radio on the far corner cupboard and picked up the desk mike. Then he glanced at the phone again, willing it to ring, and when it didn't his thumb depressed the call button. "Dayton HQ to Dayton One ... Come in."

The radio crackled and buzzed. *Click. Click.* "Roger. Dayton One — what can I do for you, Senior?"

Silence prevailed. The Sarge couldn't be too close or Brett

wouldn't have touched the radio. Rod frowned; pushed the button again. "Is Sarge with you?"

"Yeah," the voice dropped in volume, "but he's pushing his weight with the Elliot bunch at the moment."

"'Roger." Rod pictured the usual group of delinquents, the mouthy but not-so-brave Jarvis Elliot and his roving band of dickheads shrinking back from the Sergeant's mean stare. "Return to Station asap. There's possible trouble in Cullan."

"Will do," Brett said keenly. "Out."

The radio clicked again and Rod settled back to wait. It would take five to ten for them to get back even if they were at the far end of town. He poured coffee into a well-stained cup and leant back against the counter, his gaze flicking over the facts again. Although the stationhouse was bright for that hour of night, someone having flicked on all four banks of fluoros, he felt a shadow of gloom falling over them. This would not look good to their superiors given they'd done little more than make enquiries on this whole issue to date. Maybe they should have dug a whole lot deeper.

He dropped the paper back onto the marble green counter, glanced at the stormy conditions beyond the glass front door. Storms were usually a good deterrent for trouble, he thought, gulping down the steaming brew. He heaved an anxious breath. Apparently, it hadn't had the same effect in Cullan.

Over the rim of his cup he flicked the clock another glance. Seven forty-five. The Sarge wouldn't be too long now, he expected, and hoped young Waddell wouldn't mind doing a stint on the desk for a while. Cullan was his neck of the woods and this was undoubtedly a matter for more seasoned officers.

White luminous shafts spotlighted the wall, swept over the front counter and travelled silently across its length. They came to rest as two white plates on the wood-grain panelling before vanishing, prompting Rod to replace his cup in the sink. He heard the thunk-pause-thunk of car doors slamming and positioned himself at the counter. Footsteps scuttled on the stones outside and a second later the door burst open. Two uniformed officers dashed in and forced the glass door shut behind them, keeping out the blustering wind. The Sergeant was smiling.

A tall, balding, bullish man, Sergeant Owen Cussack could be stern or instantly jovial depending on the moment, and right now having rousted the town's rowdy element, he was grinning. He swiped droplets of rain from his jacket shoulders, tapped the wet white cap firmly against his leg. "What's your problem, Senior?" he asked, good humour still in his eyes.

Brett Waddell headed for the coffee pot, needing a quick mouthful to warm his insides before going out again, and Rod seized his moment. Moving out from behind the counter, he scooped up his cap and flashlight from the shelf and headed for the door. "Man the phones, Waddell," he told the constable before turning to the Sergeant. "We have a suspected murder in Cullan. I'll fill you in on the way."

Cussack's bushy grey eyebrows shot up and his pace quickened towards the white sedan, the rain barely noticed this time as he hurried for the driver's door. Brett stood by the sink, cup in hand, cursing aloud that he'd again missed his chance to be a part of the action.

Nundajora Siding sat seven miles north along the northern highway. Cussack anticipated a ten minute drive, but the heavy sheets of water splattering against the windshield and glistening in the headlights forced his greater caution on the road. The wiper blades clicked and scraped, yet battled to clear the deluge before another wave hit. Soon enough though, the Siding inroad appeared on his left.

Braking, Cussack indicated and eased the vehicle slowly onto the gravel.

The headlights illuminated only part of the stretch ahead, and he braked harder, leant forward over the wheel and peered into night while Rod fumbled with the cord to the spotlight. Unravelling it, Rod plugged it into its socket, directed its face away from him and flicked the switch on and off. It worked. Then he wound down his window just enough to hold the spotter out. Grimacing as the wetness dampened his flesh and shirt cuff, he nodded to his Superior to move on. Cussack let the vehicle roll steadily forward, Rod swinging the light beam from side to side searching like a lighthouse beacon.

It revealed ...

Nothing. There was no car on the track.

They glanced at each other, puzzled, having travelled the three hundred yards that brought them back to the highway. Rod flicked off the light.

Checking for traffic, Cussack swung the vehicle sharply round on the bitumen and re-entered the track from where they'd come. "Try again," he said, "and this time check the bushes."

Holding the light more aloft, Rod swung the beam further afield, water now trickling down his arm, soaking his shirt sleeve through to his elbow and chilling his skin. His bright light however penetrated the scrubby undergrowth to the left and right of the track, revealing only vegetation and glistening silver webs. They reached the end of the track, the wipers still arcing and dropping, the low wind howling and rocking the car in its path. Both men paused, silent, and Cussack scratched his chin, realising its rough stubble caused the itch. "Let's try across the line," he decided, turning the wheel to the right.

The squad car lurched and pitched as it negotiated the high steel tracks, and Rod's nerves jangled. The car would be behind the tall heavy stand of gum trees in front of Carter's fence-line. It had to be for Nick would never make a crank call.

Fidgeting unconsciously, he played the light beam slowly along the boundary fence; watched intensely for any chrome reflection, for glass mirroring light, for glowing fluorescent registration plates. For anything. But only the glimmering richness of gum resin bleeding through tree bark shone back at him.

Cussack's fingers drummed on the steering wheel, his mind sifting through the details he'd been given. He grunted as an idea filtered through. "This Manetti character ...," he said gruffly, "... do you know him?" The fingers stopped drumming though his eyes remained on the blackness outside the window.

"Yeah." Rod nodded. "I've known him for years." He and Nick had indeed spent some time together in their school days, though Nick was three years his junior. They'd been similar then, quiet on the surface yet yearning excitement. They'd both gone looking for it – he'd found the Police force – Nick had joined the Army. Both had eventually found their way home again, Nick taking over the family farm, as he had, mixing it with the Dayton posting. He had married while Nick's plans in that regard had fallen through.

He remembered the Sergeant, still waiting, and looked across at him. "He's straight, if that's what you're thinking."

"Okay. What about the girl?"

"Don't know much about her really." He was careful not to drift again. "She moved into the area a number of months ago. Seems quiet enough – never had any trouble from her."

The fingers drummed again, Cussack's eyes scanning for signs in the darkness while his mind played elsewhere. "I wonder if she was on anything, She could have been on a high maybe, or fabricated the whole thing for attention." His lips pursed with probabilities.

"Don't know, but that wouldn't explain who was chasing her ... and Nick saw them." Rod switched off the light and wound up the window, his arm and sleeve drenched through.

"True."

The Sergeant turned off the engine and reached for his flashlight. Struggling with his portliness behind the wheel, he prised himself out of the vehicle, climbed out into the dismal weather. The rain however had abated for the moment and they trudged through the mud, avoiding deep puddles and cursing when splosh splattered their navy trousers. With flashlights casting brilliant beams both men searched the ground, looking for anything that would indicate a car had been there, that a person had been killed there. After a while with no luck, Rod's gaze slowly lifted from the unrevealing gravel and he turned. The light drizzle had become heavier, and the quiet rumbling was rising to a roar.

"Let's get back to the car!" Cussack yelled above the noise.

Ignoring the pot-holes in his path this time, he sprinted back towards the headlights, his huge paunch swinging in front of him. He made it to the door just as the deluge bucketed over him, filling the soft top of his white cap until it touched his bald spot. He emptied its contents by tilting his head and succeeded in flooding his shoe, setting off another spate of cursing as he squeezed behind the wheel. Rod shivered as the wind whipped wildly through the trees, as it sent the antenna whop-whopping back and forth. Lightning streaked earthward, illuminating the landscape as a blue silhouette, and thunder rolled in its wake.

"No good here," Cussack bellowed above the din. "Any tracks would have been washed out. Even ours are gone." Rod nodded wordlessly. "We'll have another look in the morning." He turned the ignition. "Let's take a run down Foxley and check out where Manetti picked up the girl."

They turned towards Cullan, detouring off the highway and taking the gravel road, retracing Becky's escape route, the car slewing and sliding on the slush. Cussack made no attempt to slow down. Towards the end of Foxley Road, their headlights reflected off chrome – a bumper – then lit up the bright red cat's eyes of a stranded vehicle's tail-lights. Cussack slowed the car and drew slowly alongside; parked across the nose of the abandoned Fairlane. He climbed out, his eyes sweeping over the scene.

The long body of the Ford was in darkness. Empty. The door closed but not locked, the car angled towards the ditch on the left.

Flashlights shone brightly through the blackness, swept around then were held aloft to illuminate the car's interior, checking for anything that might be deemed a clue. Only white vinyl seats and a jumper partly inside the car, partly hanging out through the door glared back.

Cussack opened the driver's door and the overhead light flicked on. Papers fluttered and scurried across the seats and he snatched them up before they escaped the vehicle. A woman's purse lay open on the passenger seat, its contents spilling outward.

"Ah," his eyebrow hiked. He could pinpoint a woman's character by the contents of her purse. But there was nothing derogatory in Miss Rebecca Cooper's. He did however note the absence of powder pack and compulsory mascara tube. Fossicking further, he opened her wallet and perused her driver's licence. Her last address was Cambar, a small town south of Tenderton. Why had she left there? Next to come out was a photo of a girl holding a monstrous white horse. He handed the photo to Rod who leant in through the open passenger door.

"Yeah, that's her," Rod confirmed, nodding. "She's into showjumping or something."

In a very back, rarely used compartment, noted by the stiffness of its support structure, Cussack found another – a shredded photo of the same girl with a man. "Shattered love affair," he predicted casually, angling the pieces for better light. "Probably the reason she left Cambar seeing the torn edges are still pretty clean." He poked them back in place. There was nothing else of interest. "Call in and get Brett to call Tom Wiley out here with the tow-truck, will you? The keys will be inside the front bumper as usual."

Rod moved back towards the squad car. "Where do you want it taken?"

"His yard will do. He can keep it until the Cooper girl

collects it, but tell him he's to check it over. I want to know exactly why she stopped here. And did it have anything to do with those gouges on the bonnet?"

Taking his pen, Cussack poked through the contents of the glove-box. Fossicked through the console between the front seats. Ran a hand along underneath the seat ... anywhere where syringes or joints might be hidden. He found nothing. He locked the car and tucked the keys into the front bumper then returned to the squad car, both men safely back inside it when the rain started again.

"Now," the Sergeant sighed tiredly, "let's go and see Manetti and the girl."

In those long moments of silence visions of Pete Kennedy swept through Rod's mind – a very possible dead Pete Kennedy – a possible dead Pete Kennedy leaving Police custody. This would of course not look good for the Dayton Station. As the engine fired up, he turned to Cussack. "Do you think that's wise at the moment?" he asked somewhat gingerly, not knowing how the Sergeant would react to country policing where they always fed off each other's concerns and opinions. "I mean, if this girl is being chased and Nick got her out safely," he expounded, "wouldn't us turning up there give away where she is? That is, of course, if they're still hanging round looking for her."

Cussack's lips pursed and he nodded thoughtfully. "Go on," he said with genuine interest.

"Well, so far, she's safe where she is," Rod obliged, "and I keep thinking that, if this thing is for real, then we have an eye-witness, in which case, we may have to give her protection ... set up a safe house or something ... wouldn't we?"

"Most probably."

"Well she's pretty safe where she is right now, so I keep thinking, why ruin it? If we can't do anything else till morning, why not leave her where she is?"

Cussack sat silent, his fingers drumming on the wheel again

as it vibrated in his hands. "Will Manetti agree to this?" He turned to Rod, his expression serious. "More importantly, will he keep her safe?"

Rod laughed short and sharp. "It's obvious, Sarge, you don't know Nick. Ex-Nam vet. Three years' service. He just kept going back. He's built like a brick shit-house, and he's lethal. They'd be crazy to take him on!" Rod nodded at his own blunt assessment. "And if Nick let himself get involved in this he'll see it to the end."

The Sergeant remained silent. He didn't like the thought of setting up a safe house – it would reduce his force by at least two men, and he didn't have many to start with, not compared to his city posting. He visualised Manetti – a hulking great oaf in jungle greens; severe crew cut; black nugget streaks across his face; armed to the back teeth, with a heavy commando knife gripped between his teeth. Not to mention the full arsenal of illegal weaponry stashed beneath his bed for backup. He'd seen the type before. Had heard about these so-called Vietnam veterans. Half of them had come home crazy, they'd said, and he wondered if that was what his connie meant: that they'd have to be crazy to take on a 'Crazy'. He smiled at the thought and nodded. Well that would be their problem. Anything was better than being short-staffed.

"Okay, let's head back to the Station," he agreed, "but keep your eyes peeled for anything suspicious."

Rod obeyed and scrutinised the road all the way back to Dayton. Something was definitely amiss – he could feel it all around him. The minor skirmishes in Cullan were fast coming to a head, and maybe, just maybe, this was the breaking point.

Across the highway, atop the hill above Crestwood's driveway, the Taylor brothers sat in the silent darkness. Through the trees they watched the far reaching beams of the Police car's headlights pulling out onto the highway. It headed slowly south, leaving the girl's vehicle behind, and they smiled, for they now covered the two places she would most likely return to – her home and the vehicle.

Climbing out of the utility, Ben turned his collar to the wind and rain and jogged away down the drive, his rifle slung over his shoulder. He didn't look forward to the long silent wait and hoped he could at least find a warm place near the farmhouse to make it far less miserable.

Dave put the car into gear. If the girl was still wandering around out there, he'd find her – it was only a matter of time – though the red tail-lights he'd seen earlier had become a nagging twinge deep in the back of his mind. He tried to remember who in the vicinity owned a Landrover or a largish sized pick-up truck, then realised … who didn't?

CHAPTER FORTY-SIX

Laying back resting, his tired eyes not quite closed, Nick waited for the phone to ring, his patience eroding as time crept on. He squinted as lightning flashed again, its brilliance disturbing the darkness; squinted again as another spear blinded him. He pressed his eyes closed, further shutting out the light; opened them. Still blinded.

An abnormally long lightning strike, he frowned.

Turning his head against the glare, he sat up, and immediately picked up on two orbs radiating like giant white eyes outside the window, their glare penetrating the room.

Headlights!

He released the kid's warm hand, laid it on the pillow and rose slowly enough not to disturb her. Sidling to the window, he took cover behind the heavy navy drapes, watched as the lights grew larger, the rain on the window magnifying their size. Maybe it's Sam, he thought. Or, if his prayers were answered, Pete. He'd know who when they stopped for Pete always parked on the right side of the tree, Sam on the left — the unspoken reservation of rights. It was little things like that which had enabled them to live under one roof in relative harmony — things like never encroaching on another one's space — like respecting each other's time and privacy. In the past three years of sharing, they'd not had an argument — not until the recent scuffle outside the hospital, which didn't really count. He sure hoped it was Pete home now.

Another deluge poured from the sky, throwing a solid grey blanket to the ground, making it difficult to see. But still the lights kept coming, advancing towards the tree ...

– beyond the tree …

– they disappeared up beside the house.

Nick stood transfixed. Nobody ever parked up beside the house … except him!

With the utmost stealth he exited the room, scooted across the passage and kitchen and came to a halt behind the kitchen door, his back pressed hard against the wall. And there he waited.

Car doors closed with an almost imperceptible click. Footsteps squelched on wet gravel then squeaked across the verandah. As yet, only one set. Where the hell was the other? He'd definitely heard two doors closing in unison. Maybe one had headed around to the front of the house.

He tensed at the likelihood; listened harder; heard a whisper. *Male voice.* They were both still there.

The fly-wire door creaked open, slow, hesitation unmistakable. The knob on the solid door turned almost in slow motion. The door opened the barest inch. Deliberately noiseless.

Nick stood poised, taking in slow silent breaths, staying calm. He could see movement through the crack between the hinges but it was too dark to distinguish anything other than movement.

The door eased further open, accommodating the intruder's progress one stealthy footstep at a time, its opening concealing Nick further behind its frame. With each soundless step, they paused, as if listening for sounds from within.

One step.

Nick could hear the intruder's breathing.

Two steps.

A foot and shoulder appeared at the edge of the door.

On the third step Nick lunged, one hand grabbing and wrenching an upper limb up and back while the other reached across the man's throat and locked a hold on his shoulders. His muscles bunched, stretching the intruder's torso back in a body breaking hold, a yield or snap ultimatum. There's no way they'd get through him to the kid. No way. His teeth clenched as he remembered 'two' and spun quickly, placing his first victim between him and whoever stood on the door's other side.

"Christ!"

The word gasped out as the man struggled against the hold, as he tried to tear away the arm that blocked his windpipe. Nick increased the pressure to ensure he didn't succeed. He heard the groan of pain as sinews started to tear, as the intruder buckled with pain and sank. The word, the groan, brought instant recognition and Nick released the hold in an instant. Grabbing the man's arm, he hauled him back to his feet before he crumpled to the floor. His victim wheeled, his fist ready to strike, but he came face to face with Nick, Nick's hands raised in submission.

"What the ...!"

Nick stepped back, giving Sam a chance to disarm the blow. "Hey, I'm sorry," he said, easing out his tension with a deep exhale. *One day*, he chastised inwardly ... *one day you'll act too fast and really hurt someone.*

"What's got you on edge?"

Nick looked around. "Well, you!" he retorted. "Why'd you park up here by the house? You always park out front. Then you come sneaking in here like you're going to roll the place ... how was I supposed to know it was you?"

Wincing, Sam twisted to ease out the kink in his back. "Yeah? Well I happened to have parked up here because, if you hadn't noticed, it's pissing down out there and I have someone with me who'd rather not get wet."

He pushed open the wire door to allow them entry. "And what's more, the lights were on but no cars were here, so I naturally thought we had an intruder."

Nick groaned, and stepped aside to allow Sam's company access to the kitchen, his body tensing immediately when Marilyn crossed the threshold.

"Where's your truck?" Sam asked, looking suddenly remiss for bringing her to Northgate – it was the biggest mistake he'd made since coming here.

"Behind the shed."

Sam frowned then his attention drifted across the room to where Becky Cooper stood in the kitchen doorway, one of Nick's white shirts hanging loosely to her knees. The side scoops revealed a perfect set of bare, tanned thighs, and she was barefoot, her hair loose and ruffled, her blue eyes blinking in the manner of someone who's just woken from a deep and fitful sleep. He scrutinised Nick, who glanced back over his shoulder as Sam's smile flickered. At no time had Nick ever indicated Becky had been on his mind. The smile spread wider as he summed up Nick's open shirt and bare feet.

"Ah," he nodded, "... hiding from Daddy ..."

The muscle in Nick's jaw flexed and a warning finger jabbed into Sam's chest. "Don't go there," Nick replied deeply. "It's not what you think!" He drew taut as Marilyn eyed his state of undress and by the hardness in her eyes knew she'd come to the same conclusion. He glared back at her, challenging her to say nothing.

"Well I wouldn't like trying to explain that it's not what it looks," she defied him. "That could be rather difficult, Nick!"

Nick's lips thinned. She'd have a field day with this. She could really make the moment damaging and embarrassing, and he didn't know which bothered him most. He locked a grip on her arm and hauled her into him. "Just shut up, Marilyn! Just shut the hell up." Deliberately he kept his back to Becky so she didn't see his anger.

Bristling, Marilyn shot a glare across the room but said no more. She certainly hadn't counted on Becky getting in her way. This was something she would definitely have to deal with.

Nick moved her away again; looked over her head to Sam. "There's been more trouble," he said, ignoring Marilyn's closeness, ignoring how brazenly she watched him.

Sam's eyes lifted from Marilyn's perusal of Nick, his

thoughts diverting from the fact they should have stayed together.

"The kid saw someone murdered tonight."

The colour in Sam's face paled. "Oh hell no. Who?"

"She thinks it was Pete," Nick said deeply.

Sam's jaw fell open and Marilyn's knees gave way. Nick gripped her arm and swung her round to the nearest chair before she hit the floor.

"Those who did it are looking for her, and they mean business," he added, releasing Marilyn as she sank onto the seat. He returned to Becky, put his arm around her shoulders and moved her back to the bedroom.

"How certain is it?" Sam asked as he left.

Coming back shortly, Nick flicked on the kettle. "At this point," he answered, "it's not ... as far as I'm concerned. Rod's gone down to check it out. We're still waiting to hear from him."

The kettle whistled and Marilyn rose and made coffees, familiar with the house after their long relationship. Noting her silence, Nick watched her a moment then collected his boots from the lounge room. He pulled them on, eased the trouser legs down over them then buttoned his shirt and tucked it in, feeling less conspicuous in her presence.

His heart skipped a beat when the phone rang beside him, and he quickly snatched it up. "Northgate," he said.

"Nick, it's Rod's. Listen mate, we've been down to the Siding and there's nothing there."

"Nothing?" he scowled deeply.

"Nothing. Not a thing. Zilch," Rod verified. "No car, no body, no traces. Nothing. That girl you got there, she's not on anything, is she? Not been shooting up? Smoking anything?"

Nick bristled. "She's not the type. And even if that was the case,"; he guarded his words carefully in case the kid could hear, "I definitely am not! And there was someone after her!"

Rod sensed his anger. "Okay .., okay. I just had to ask ... for the record ... you understand." Quickly he changed the subject.

"Well it is pelting down out there so we may have missed something in the dark. We'll be going back for another look in the morning, after which we'll want to talk to the girl."

Nick remained silent, a blatant indication of his annoyance, that subtle moment taken to calm his temper.

"Is she still okay with you?" Rod added, trying to break the angst coming down the line.

"Yeah, she's safe," Nick said tautly. If she'd been 'flying high' he'd have known it, and he certainly wouldn't have bothered the cops with it. He exhaled loudly and put his attention back to the phone.

"Well keep it that way," Rod said. "By the way, I don't suppose you got a look at those heavies, did you?"

"No. We didn't hang around for pleasantries. But as I said, I recognised McCaig's ute so why don't you go chase him up?"

"Well, we had a look, but it couldn't have been McCaig's," Rod countered. "We pulled into the roadhouse on the way back and McCaig's ute is up on top of the hoist in the workshop, all locked up."

That news stopped Nick like an anvil hitting concrete. He scratched his head. He was sure it was McCaig's. No, not sure — he was positive! So how could it be on the hoist? His scowl deepened. Maybe he got it out and put it back before Rod got there. There was plenty of time. It was something he would have to look into.

"Anyway, keep that girl protected," Rod ordered lightly. "We can't afford to lose our only witness."

"With my life," Nick answered dryly, his temper beginning to simmer. "Hey, before you go ..."

Rod stayed silent, waiting.

"... how about notifying her folks and keeping them out of the way. They went back to the city last night and her father seems pretty protective. I wouldn't want her drawn out in the open if they grab one of her family. Brian Egan should have their number."

"Yeah. Sure. Good thinking. You should be a cop," Rod prompted, thankful the man's temper had dwindled. He heard a soft huff on the other end of the line.

"I wouldn't have my hands tied like that if you paid me," came the reply.

Rod chuckled. "We'll call you," he said, his mirth suddenly fading. "And ... take care." The line went dead.

Nick hung up and sat back at the table, his hands wrapped around his cup for added warmth. How was the kid going to react to this news? he wondered.

Across the table, he could feel Marilyn watching him and met her gaze full on. If there was anything he had to do right now, it was show her she no longer had an effect on him. Nevertheless he found it hard to forget – so many good things they'd shared in this house, in this room.

Sam grew uneasy as the silence became intolerable. "Well, come on, I'd better get you home," he said to Marilyn, standing and tipping her chair to encourage her to move. He cast an apologetic glance at Nick, but the man glared coldly back. "She had a flat, and no spare, so I offered to run her home," Sam explained. "I only came in to get changed before going into town ..."

Nick looked down at the table, and Sam knew his mistake would take a while to undo. "I'll come straight back," he said, reaching the door.

Nick nodded but didn't look up, an avoidance of Marilyn's pleading eyes asking him to let her stay. He heard the wire door close behind them then the sound of a revving motor, and he sighed that she had gone so quietly. The house though was now too quiet. Quiet without Sam. Quiet without Pete. And that surprised him. He'd always viewed the quiet as preferred, his solitude as bliss.

So why now? Why now is it all so different?

The answer eluded him. All he knew was that he wished Pete would walk through that door right now and prove this whole damn thing a gigantic nightmare, that soon he'd wake up and everything would be normal again. But he knew that wouldn't happen. Not this time. He could feel it deep within. Pete was gone, and the emptiness of loss had filled him.

He blinked heavily. *Death happens sooner or later,* he reminded himself – they'd all learnt that in Nam – and there wasn't a damn thing you could do to stop it. *Your time was up when your time was up.*

And Pete's time was up.

But you'll cope with it, he assured himself, listening to the silence around him. *You didn't get too close.*

He shook his head determinedly. *No, but by God, you will get even!*

CHAPTER FORTY-SEVEN

Sweet, crisp, earthy smells wafted up from the gardens around the house, tingeing the room with scents of wild lavender and honeysuckle. The mauve sky outside the window spread its soft hues to the horizon, mottling where sunlight tried to seep through the tiny holes in the fluffy veil of clouds.

I sighed, and turned beneath the warm swathing of blankets, draped my arms around the deep layer of pillows. Instantly I realised I was in Nick Manetti's bed, that he had lain beside me part of the night holding my hand, but he wasn't there now. I sighed again, more deeply, partly because if being here was real then this wasn't a dream and the whole tragic thing had happened. My sore eyes should have told me that, seeing I had cried for long hours over Pete in the silence. I hugged the pillows tighter, locked them to me to dispel the violent shudder and the tears welling up within. The shudder erupted regardless and I buried my head deep in the spongy softness, holding back the heat that tried to burn back into my eyes. Now it was daylight the whole horrid affair would start all over again.

Some time passed before I dragged my head out of the pillows, the rising tears back under control, the thoughts in my head shifting from what I could do to save myself from a gruesome fate, and realising suffocation by Nick's pillows, while a lateral means of escape, was somewhat drastic. I scanned the room again, taking in the details I'd noticed in the dark. The open door. The forest scene painting on the wall, now vivid with colour. The damp towel lying on the end of the bed. I remembered how I'd clung to Nick in the night; how stupidly I'd admitted my fears and how he'd endured my snivelling insecurities. *God, how stupid of me! What would he think of me? A whimpering little mess who couldn't stand up for herself!* I wondered if my eyes were red and swollen; thought *Probably.*

I wondered where he was. Why was his house so quiet? Something had happened during the night – I'd heard voices and remembered getting up to check, remembered Nick putting me back to bed, but I was too tired to ask what was going on. Maybe something had happened and he'd gone out to be a part of it and simply hadn't woken me.

The bedroom clock ticked over nine. *Something must have happened by now.*

I tossed back the covers, pulled on the bath robe that still lay where Nick had dropped it, and tip-toed to the door. Sam was asleep in the room at the end of the passage, his head tipped back against the back of an armchair. Across the passage Nick slept at the table, his head resting on thick, muscular forearms, his profile soft and approachable.

I crept forward, watching his broad, muscled back expanding and receding with the gentle flow of his breathing. No longer was he the big, powerful man the town feared so much, who at times frightened me. Asleep, he seemed gentler, innocent, almost touchable. I wanted to reach out and touch him, to remember how smooth and warm he'd felt, but pulled those thoughts straight back for Nick's dark eyes had opened and he was taking me in, his blatant perusal sending waves of heat swirling to my cheeks.

He lifted his head, glanced at his wrist watch and pushed himself up from the table.

"Sorry I woke you," I said, annoyed that he was so tuned in to his environment; so tuned in he'd felt my eyes on his back.

"You didn't," he said as he pushed the chair back and rose. "I was only resting." His eyes swept over me, focused a little too long on my face, on my eyes. He heaved out a deep breath, and said nothing.

He looked tired, and I felt suddenly guilty that I'd taken his bed, relegating him to a sleepless night at the table. His hair looked ruffled and a day's dark growth had appeared on his face. Nevertheless my goose-bumps rose and my nipples peaked at the sight of him. I folded my arms to stop the annoying sensation.

Nick bypassed me and went to the passage, emitted a short high whistle through his teeth, stirring Sam, then he gathered and rinsed the cups from the table and flicked on the kettle. "You must be starving," he said, his attention on the sink.

"Not really," I said. "I'm more cold than anything." I kept my arms folded, but couldn't eradicate the cold that prickled my legs, and I wondered how Nick coped in just the light shirt he wore.

"Yeah, it is cold," he said, flicking another glance my way. "Your clothes are on a rack in the lounge. They should be dry now. Why don't you go and get dressed while I make you something to drink."

I nodded at his logic, and I would definitely feel better dressed in his presence where my emotions wouldn't show. And I appreciated that he didn't stare at me even though my eyes were so glued to him.

"What do you have?"

"Coffee," I said, withholding a smile at the old joke that 'he was all that and could make coffee too'.

"Coffee," he repeated with a nod.

"Well that's a good start," Sam said as he came into the room. "According to Professor Nick only fopsies drink tea. And we probably don't have any seeing he threw it all out when Marilyn left and he won't buy any more. You'd have put him on the spot if you'd said tea."

A moment of deadly silence passed during which I took my leave. Though I did notice Nick glanced up as I left. I heard him say to Sam as I padded down the passage: "I've been thinking ... I need you to go to Perth to find Pete's folks," to which Sam groaned.

"Sorry mate. You know I'd go myself but I've got the kid to watch, and I feel the news should come from one of us. But don't tell them anything yet – just be in Perth ready if we get news of the worst."

"Yeah, I see your point. I'll leave straight after breakfast," Sam replied.

By the time I returned to the kitchen Nick had put cups on the table and was just sitting down. He looked up as I came in, his dark eyes doing a slow wander over me, tip to toe then slowly back up again. His lack of expression made me uneasy.

"What plans have you got for today?" Sam asked him, drawing his stare away again.

"First I'm going to hide her out somewhere where they won't find her," he said, speaking as if I wasn't there, yet he pointed to the coffee he had poured me. "Then I'll go into Dayton and see Rod – see if they've found anything yet."

"What do you mean? ..." I frowned. "... found anything?" My eyes narrowed, narrowed a little further at his earlier reference to 'the kid'. That was starting to grate. There was something derogative in the way he said it.

Nick cleared his throat and cast me a wary glance. "They rang last night while you were sleeping," he related almost indifferently. "They'd been to the Siding and there was nothing there."

He must have noticed my jaw drop, my stiff response at the news. "Don't panic!" he warned tightly. "They're going back this morning to have another look ... just in case they missed something."

"You bet they missed something!" *Oh, this looked really good, idiot city kid spooked by storm, sees things in the dark. Great!*

"Are you sure it was Nundajora, and not Burton Siding?"

"Yes, I'm sure! Burton Siding has the wheat silos. I know which is which! And I did see it, Nick!"

"Nobody said you didn't!"

"Well they must have moved everything. They must have gone back afterwards and moved everything. I did see it happen!" Reaching up, he grabbed my arm and dragged me down to the chair in front of my coffee. "The next thing they'll be saying I was flying as high as a kite just to cover their incompetence! Pete was there – I know he was. I saw him."

"Hey," he said firmly, looking straight at me, his expression tight with resolve, "I believe you. And maybe they did go back and move everything, so don't worry. They'll find something today."

I picked up the cup, the steam within me swirling like the fumes rising off the coffee. I flicked a glare at Nick. Maybe he did believe me; maybe he didn't. Pete's absence alone should have proven my story. My gaze followed him as he rose from the table.

"We'd better get you some gear together," he said. "It's going to be a long day."

Fetching a canvas haversack from the hall cupboard, he returned to the kitchen and started stuffing assorted goods into it while Sam fossicked in Pete's room for a relevant address. A half hour later, Nick bent to the driver's window as Sam started the engine.

"If it's late when you're done, stay over somewhere," he said. "Don't try travelling through to here at night."

Sam nodded. "I'll probably look in on Ros while I'm down there anyway," he said, glancing across at me. He gave a finger salute. "See ya, Beck," he called as he reversed the car in an arc. He stopped; looked back at Nick who stood with his thumbs jammed into his pockets. "And take care, mate. I'd like to have something to come back to," he added, his smile fleeting.

"Yeah sure," Nick replied. "Didn't know you cared." He tapped on the car's roof twice and received a thumbs up as Sam pulled away. Nick watched until he'd reached the highway then slowly returned to the verandah.

Back in the house, he went to his room and came back with two jackets; he tossed one to me. "Come on," he said as he pulled a black nylon wind-breaker up over his shoulders, "it's time to make a move." He picked up the haversack as I pushed my arms into the heavy woollen jacket and hoisted it onto my shoulders. It was incredibly warm but I grinned that more of it hung off me than on, and I flapped the loose sleeves hanging below my hands, like Dopey-the-Seventh-Dwarf. Nick smiled as he ushered me out the door. "Come on, you'll need it where you're going."

"Why can't I just stay here?" I asked, looking up at him. "You said yourself nobody knows I'm here."

'Because it's different now. Marilyn knows you're here and she's got a dangerously big mouth."

I smiled at the way that sounded. No love lost there apparently. "Where to then?" I asked as he followed me out the door.

"To somewhere not far from here."

He signalled me to stay on the verandah while he stepped into the growing sunlight and checked that the driveway was clear. Then he beckoned me to follow. "We'd better hurry and get you out of sight," he impressed, taking my hand and hauling me along the track after him. It was the same steep track we'd arrived on the night before, both sides of it bordered by a thick belt of trees that stopped the wind bludgeoning the main farm buildings. Many times Nick turned back, checking we weren't being watched, his nerves taut like newly strung fence wire. As soon as we passed the machine shed, he left the track and led the way into the scrub, disturbing two great grey kangaroos, which bounded away up the slope ahead of us.

Nick moved lithely, extremely light and pliant for his size, and he moved in total silence, picking a path through scrubby brush and parrot bush without breaking a single twig. For the first time since I'd seen him he looked relaxed, totally at home in the terrain and not overly bothered by the disruption to his day.

Once or twice as we climbed I caught him watching me, a smile barely stirring his lips that I'd turned and noticed.

Once amongst the trees, the slope became more gradual, though in places it rose quite steeply and required a fair bit of scrambling up. Here Nick pushed me ahead of him, his hands stabilising my climb; hoisting me a little higher on sharper inclines that posed a slight problem. "Up there," he kept pointing, always directing me towards the highest point of the land. When the ground became rockier, he linked one arm through the shoulder strap of the haversack, supporting it behind him with one hand while he used the other to climb.

I stayed ahead of him, picking my way over the best going, though occasionally glancing back to see where he was, only to find him standing, watching me again, or waiting for me to clear the way. Finally I scrambled up the last part of the rise where the ground levelled out, and rose to my feet. Nick completed the last few yards effortlessly and came to stand beside me.

"We're here," he said, pointing to a small wooden shack barely noticeable through a tangle of fallen branches, bridal creeper and dead or dying bushes. "You'll be safe here."

We crossed through the thinner bush to the shack, where he put his shoulder to the door and bumped it partly open. Spider webs stretched, snapped and sagged as the gap widened, and I shuddered at the thought of spending a day with spiders.

"What is this place?" I asked, the cold darkness of the bush and the distance from the house making it a senseless place to build anything.

"Just a place," he replied. "It used to be the old homestead, then we used it to store seed." His tone deepened as he put more strength to the door and forced the gap even wider. "I haven't been up here in a long time ... and to my knowledge, very few people know it's still here, so you'll be safe."

Finally the door gave to his insistence and swung fully inwards. "I used to stay up here sometimes as a kid. We just use it for storage now."

I nodded that the explanation sufficed as he stepped inside the shack, and drew aside a multitude of webs. The open doorway cast enough light to illuminate the one small room. Stacked in one corner was a pile of boxes filled with old books and papers. A table and several old chairs were pushed against one wall while several old mattresses were propped up or partly fallen over against another. The room smelt musty, and was layered in an age of accumulated dust. A more extensive network of spider webs hung higher up the walls, thickened by years of falling dirt, making the place look creepy. Nick looked around, picked up a small dormant goanna and deposited it out the door. He dragged the table out to the centre of the room and dropped the haversack on it.

"There's a kerosene lamp up there, and you'll find some matches in one of those boxes," he told me, thumbing towards the corner. "There's kerosene for it in the bag, but close the door before you light up. We don't want your light giving away your location. You've got plenty of food here so you won't starve while I'm gone."

He headed for the door but turned back in the opening. "I'll be back before dark, but whatever you do, don't leave here. You got that?"

I nodded.

"For any reason!"

"Okay! I'm not going to do anything stupid."

"Good! And don't set fire to the place either. I'll see you later."

I followed him to the door and stood watching as he scrambled and slid lightly down the slope, a denizen of the jungle that surrounded him. Lithe. Sure-footed. Totally in control. *A demi-God.* And I sighed that he was the epitome of perfection. My idea of the perfect man. A jarful of candy in the lolly shop window and I didn't have a single dime to spend.

He looked back once before disappearing behind a broad stand of trees. After that, I didn't see him again.

The shack was about a mile north-east of the house and he'd headed south-west. Already it was a quarter to noon. I settled back to spend the day alone in the cold dark shack above Northgate, and to constantly wonder what Nick was doing with his time.

CHAPTER FORTY-EIGHT

Nick arrived back at the house refreshed by the early morning exercise and feeling good. For the first time in a long time he'd actually felt needed, a feeling he hadn't had since Vietnam. He showered and shaved, backed out the truck and was in Dayton before the stroke of two.

Rod was still at the stationhouse, his eyes bleary, a full day's shadow on his chin; he was scratching at its roughness when Nick pushed open the door.

There was no more news even in daylight, Rod told him. No car. No body. No evidence. Not a sign a murder had been committed.

"What now?" Nick asked, frowning at the total absence of evidence. Whatever they had failed to find still didn't explain Pete's disappearance.

Rod propped his elbows on the front counter and leant forward. "Sarge wants to speak to your girl," he said quietly, casting a glance past Nick in case anyone else entered or in case he'd brought her with him. "By the way, where is she?"

"Stashed safely," came the reticent reply.

"Can you bring her in?"

Nick's attention drifted out the glass-panelled door to the busy roadway. "When?"

"Whenever."

"Okay." Nick turned back to the counter. "Tonight. That way there'll be less eyes on the road."

Rod nodded. "I'll let Sarge know you'll be coming."

"Did you get a line on her folks?"

Rod nodded, and smiled somewhat grimly. "Ted Cooper

wasn't too happy about my call though. Apparently the girl's a hot-head. He pulled the family out of Cullan for their own safety and the two of them had a big row over it – something about a couple of valuable horses they got out there on Crestwood. Anyhow, the girl up and left – walked out; said she was going to get the horses off the place and move out altogether."

Nick's insides gripped with sudden cold and his lips thinned to a fine line. He turned to see if the door had opened and let in a cold blast of air, but it hadn't.

"He'd like to be kept informed however," Rod continued, "but he won't be coming back for her. Says he has no control over her anyhow."

Nick half grinned, and nodded. And changed tack. "I sent Sam down to see Pete's folks, just to make sure he hasn't turned up elsewhere."

"Yeah. Well we've got an A.P.B. out on him too," Rod added dryly, "and are checking with the Richardsons at the hospital just in case."

"Yeah. Well let's hope one of those avenues turns up something," Nick wished aloud, the memory of the previous night in the gully however telling him it was a waste of time.

As he drove back through Cullan there was no sign of McCaig's team in town, neither at the hotel, nor at the roadhouse so he turned the truck around and parked up at the hotel. While things were quiet, it was a good time to visit Sheila. The kid was safe enough where she was for a while, and he needed to know if Sheila's grapevine had grown any news.

She came around the bar and locked her arms round his waist in a warm, consoling hug. "Sam was in this morning and told me about Pete," she said, her voice almost breaking. "Have you heard anything more? Is it true?"

Nick prolonged the hug. To Sheila, losing anyone in Cullan was like losing one of her family. "Nothing's definite yet," he told her honestly, without mentioning Becky. He hoped above all hopes Sam had the sense to keep his mouth shut on that score. If he hadn't, the whole town would soon know where she was. He needed to find out if Sheila knew, without giving her reason to suspect he had news she didn't know. "How about a coffee?" he suggested, glancing at the eternally steaming pot behind the bar. If he stayed long enough she would eventually mention all the news she had.

He swung his leg over a bar stool, rested his elbow on the counter and looked about him. Only one table was occupied, one in a corner by the window – city-ites by the style of their clothing. Probably stopped for a short break before pushing on for the coast – the fishing rods on the rack of the sedan out front a dead giveaway. He sighed, remembering the last time he'd gone fishing ... in a gentle running stream that wound down between two mountains, the stream shielded by an endless wall of bamboo. He'd sat and watched a few of the boys paddle their bootless feet while trying to snatch silver fish from the water with their hands. The laughter of village children filled his ears as Pete snared one and tossed it high on the bank, the young man's smile as wide and white as the gleeful dark-faced native's. *Yeah, that was the last time he'd gone fishing,* he sighed. And he felt rued that it was so-so long ago.

"You look tired, love," Sheila noted as she passed him the brew.

"Am a bit," he admitted, rubbing his head. He fought back the desperate need to yawn. "Where's McCaig's bunch today?"

"Shearing. Brian's crew is almost nonexistent now. Pete's gone. Young Carla's in hospital, poor thing. The Cooper family's gone back to the city ..."

Nick waited tensely but no comment about the kid came, which meant Sam hadn't slipped up. Sheila moved away down the bar, replenished another jug for the travellers then came back again. "... It's not a good state of affairs, love," she added, picking up exactly where she'd left off. "This new bunch is having a field day out there."

"Well they won't be getting mine," Nick promised her, his anger prodded by the thought. Draining his cup he stood, his mood now pushing the urgency back on him to move. "Anyway, I gotta go," he said.

"Nick," Sheila's hand gripped his arm, "be careful ... please."

He gave her a tight smile and nodded. "And you stop worrying."

Outside, he stood for a moment on the top verandah step, his dark eyes panning the town. It looked like Cullan on any ordinary day, not an inkling of the deadly current rippling beneath the surface.

Jack Pollitt sat on his usual drum at the opening of the workshop across the street, reading and smoking a crudely made rolly. Jack was as observant of the town's goings-on as Sheila, and there wasn't much gossip missed by one that wasn't gleaned by the other so Nick by-passed the F100 and ambled over. He had questions needing answers, questions that would only worry Sheila. Maybe old Jack was the one to give him those answers. He would need to be careful though for Jack liked to think he was a hard old bastard.

The old man lowered his paper as Nick approached. "'llo young'un," he greeted, surprised that Nick had approached him outright. Most of the young folk in town didn't give him the time of day – nor him them. He liked young Manetti though even if he wasn't a hundred per cent Australian. Hell, it wasn't his fault his father was a bad-tempered philandering foreigner. He was sorry too the relationship with his grand-daughter hadn't worked out for the girl wouldn't do much better.

"Jack," Nick returned the greeting. Shooting a quick glance around to make sure they were alone, Nick crouched to save the old man craning his neck, and Jack tipped the tattered peaked cap higher on his head, obviously glad of the visit and undoubtedly willing to talk. Nick appreciated the sign – if the peak had remained lowered, the man wouldn't have been as receptive to the company nor likely to indulge in conversation. It was like Army ranking – the higher the rank, the lower dipped the peak. The lower the peak, the more aloof they stood from the men. He was thankful Captain Boyce had shown a lot of brow; it had made him easy to work with. And Jack showed a lot of brow now, age-creased and weathered as it was.

"Looks like you've got something on your mind," the old man perceived, knowing the young man was usually short on words, so whatever was up had to be pretty important.

"Yeah, I have," Nick nodded, sounding deliberately perplexed to capture the old man's interest. Stroking his chin, he flashed a sideways glance at Jack.

"Well, spill it out! I can't help ya if I dunno what it is now, can I?"

"Okay, well it's like this," Nick started, catching the old man's eyebrows dipping as he concentrated on the forthcoming facts, "I reckon this new shearing crowd is tied up in all the trouble we're having here in town but I can't prove it."

The old man made no comment so Nick played out a bit more. "Each time something happens, they benefit, but I can't work out how they're doing it and still have alibis."

Jack started sucking on the end of his smoke. Still no help. "I don't suppose you've seen anything," Nick hinted strongly. "Maybe they've been using threats to get people to vouch for them. You know ... to say they were here when they weren't." His eyebrows hiked in anticipation, but Jack shook his head.

"Wrong track, sonny." The smoke, now out of his mouth, twirled in Jack's fingers as he talked. "It's just the opposite in fact." He talked so slowly Nick's leg started numbing, the pull of his jeans cutting in behind his right knee. "They actually go out of their way to be seen. You know ... stay together ... be in public. I don't mind saying they scared the hell outta me the other night though."

Nick leant forward with interest.

"A couple of them grabbed me and invited me to their poker game; real friendly like they were. Over friendly, if you know what I mean. Now I didn't want to play no bloody poker, son, but I'll tell you, I was too bloody scared not to. Now they didn't say anything to make me feel that way, mind," he pointed a withered finger to discourage Nick from jumping to conclusions. "I just felt it wasn't safe to say no. I had to stay there till two in the bloody morning. Nearly hit a cow on the way home." He put the smoke back in his mouth.

Nick's heart pounded more rapidly. "What night was that, Jack?"

"Er ... Thursdee, I think."

"The night Carla Richardson was raped?"

"Yeah, that'd be right."

"And their cars, Jack. Where were their cars?"

"Outside. All night. I could see 'em through the window."

Nick's enthusiasm died with a huff. "What about last night? Was McCaig's car gone last night?" he asked more pointedly.

"Well yeah, sorta. After your mate's little prank they all needed some major restorin'," he smiled wryly, the smoke stub now ducking and diving in the corner of his mouth, "so Tom locked 'em up in the workshop for the night."

Nick's lips twisted in thought. "And that's where I keep getting stumped."

"Sorry I couldn't help, but if it means anything to ya, I think ya right! They're tied into it somehow."

Nick nodded and stood up, thankful to get some feeling back in his leg. He thanked the old man for his time, and Jack nodded back, very tempted to ask him to give Marilyn another chance — she needed someone to sort her out, and young Manetti was just the bloke to do it. The words poised for seconds on his lips then he thought better of it. It really wasn't any of his business, so he merely watched as Nick returned to the truck, hobbling slightly now where he hadn't hobbled before.

Nick pulled open the driver's door, pins and needles pricking his leg painfully. One more stop then it was back to the kid.

CHAPTER FORTY-NINE

Hoskins' farm was awash, rivulets still seeping away after the night's torrential rain. The soil around the circular rose garden out front of the red-brick home was strewn with multi-coloured petals, leaving on many stems a green-black node where the flower had once bloomed. Nick looked at them despondently for they'd been real pretty once. *But,* he shrugged inwardly, *nothing's ever permanent.*

He found Geoff at the side of the house, trying to remove a hefty branch that had come down in the storm, the man's face crimson as he struggled to dislodge the limb's precarious lean against the wall. He stopped battling when he heard Nick's voice. "I should have cut this damn thing down years ago," he complained, silently cursing that he'd postponed it once too often.

Nick signalled for Geoff to get on one end of the limb, and together they hoisted it clear of the building, Nick bearing the main weight through his shoulders, back and legs. They dropped it aside on a clear strip of lawn, ready for chopping.

"Thanks," Hoskins puffed, rubbing a sore spot in his back. Then he looked suddenly wary. "Now what brings you out to this neck of the woods?"

"I'd like to see Bruce if that's okay. I need to ask him about his accident."

Hoskins' lips pursed. "That's fine," he agreed, "but I don't see how he can be of any help. He's told all he knows to the Police."

Nevertheless, he tapped on the side window and beckoned Bruce to come out.

Moments later the boy appeared at the edge of the front verandah, his arm still encased in the sling. "Nick wants to ask you some questions, son. I want you to tell him whatever you can."

The boy nodded and stepped down to the lawn to join them, his lesser height making Nick stoop to make eye contact. "I want you to think in particular about the car that hit you," Nick said, placing an encouraging hand on the boy's good shoulder. Bruce nodded that he would. "Did you see who was driving?"

He watched the boy's face as memories started to flow. "Take your time. Really think," he prompted.

The boy's eyes narrowed as he stared into space, his eyes moving slightly as he delved back into the past, as he sifted through the details. Finally he shook his head. "No. I didn't see who was driving. The car pulled up a little further down the road, but nobody got out. When I called for help and tried to get up, it just took off."

Nick let it go. "Okay ... the car then. Can you remember the car?"

Bruce went silent again, his thoughts deepening. "It was white, I remember that. I think it was a ute ... But it went by so fast and parked far enough away I can't be sure." He looked up at Nick and shrugged apologetically.

"That's okay. You're doing fine." Indeed, Nick's satisfaction reigned, the pictures were coming through to his minor questions. He posed the big one. "Did you get a look at the number plate?"

A long silence ensued as the boy's eyes narrowed again, then narrowed further. Bruce's brow furrowed, and his head began to shake very slightly in negation. After a moment his eyes widened a little, and an eyebrow hiked. He looked up at Nick in surprise. "I can remember. I did look!" he declared excitedly. "I did like you do, Dad, and looked to get the number plate."

"What colour was it?" Nick coaxed. "White and black? White and green? What can you remember?" Nick shot Hoskins a glance and mentally crossed his fingers.

"That's just it! There wasn't one!" Bruce exclaimed. "That's why I couldn't remember it. I did look, but there wasn't a number plate!"

Nick punched the air. *Bingo!* He patted Bruce on the shoulder, straightened and pushed the kink out of his back. "That's what I'd hoped for."

Hoskins looked cagey. "Are you onto something, Nick?" he asked, his eyes narrowing. "If you are, I want to get involved." More so, he wanted to get even.

"Maybe. I don't rightly know just yet, but Bruce has helped." Without committing himself further, he returned to his truck, smiling broadly. It was definitely time to get back.

It was warm in the cab and he threw off his wind-breaker before climbing in. Straight home, he told himself. At least now something was falling into place. Somehow, but as yet he didn't know how, McCaig's utility was involved in both Bruce's accident and Becky's close call. He just had to work out how.

CHAPTER FIFTY

Pulling into Northgate's driveway, Nick drove towards the house, wondering what the kid was doing with her time; he smiled that she was probably bored out of her brain. Looking up at the slope he felt pleased – the shack was indeed totally concealed by scrub, and he hoped she'd done as told and stayed there.

Rounding the gentle curve in the track, he followed it upward, the house coming into sight ahead. His focus immediately shifted. He had visitors. A car was parked out front and, even from that distance he could tell it wasn't Sam's. And it wasn't Pete's. And he hoped even stronger that Becky had stayed there.

He drove closer. It was definitely a white utility.

And closer.

No number plate. McCaig's utility!

So, is this him checking to see if I've changed my mind? Or is he here to gloat that Brian's team is lacking? Either way it would make no difference. In fact, this was better. His knuckles tightened over the steering wheel. He had a score to settle.

He pulled onto the turning verge that ran beside the driveway, parked well away from the house and stepped down from the cab. It was the best way he could think of to draw the men away from his home. Two men sat in the car ahead, waiting, and he went forward with callous intent. Nothing would please him more than to throw McCaig and his scrawny son off his goddamned farm.

He was halfway to the utility when the car doors swung open and two strangers stepped out. *Big mother-fuckers,* Nick thought.

Damn big. The closest thing he'd ever seen to a goon. Certainly not McCaig ... nor his scrawny son. He slowed his steps as the men straightened and faced him then he stopped and waited in the open, quickly assessing them. They were built like tree trunks, one maybe slightly broader and heavier than the other, maybe due to age – one was certainly the more powerful looking. While both carried weight, it was bulk not muscle, so hopefully they carried less strength than him. Both had boxy square jaws – *fist breakers* – close cropped tawny hair, all indicating a strong family tie. Together they looked awesome. He focused on their eyes, pure green meanness, and the muscle in his jaw locked tight. He had no doubts they weren't here to sell him insurance, and knew this was going to hurt.

Steadying his nerves, he held his ground, trying to remember if he'd seen these guys before. He didn't think so. But why then did they have McCaig's utility? He could only hope he'd misjudged the intent of their visit.

Both men moved to the back of the car, and by their stance Nick knew straight off he'd read it right: very soon he was going to have the shit kicked out of him.

He breathed deeply, loosening muscles that had tightened at this instant revelation. *Easy, Nick. Just take it easy.* Deep inside him fear slowly rose and he breathed in and out again, slowly, deeply, deliberately ... eradicating it, pushing it away, his dark eyes not daring to leave them.

"You must be Manetti," the taller goon presumed, his voice raspy like an old saw on green wood.

Nick watched his cold, calculating eyes. "And if I am?"

"Well we've just popped by to help you change your mind." It was the other man this time, a slight, ugly smile indicating he would enjoy his mission. And they didn't waste time giving him further options. With a simultaneous glance at each other, they moved slowly apart. *Practised manoeuvre.*

Nick glanced about for something to use as a weapon, but

out in the open there was nothing, the paddocks always clean. If he'd parked up by the house he could have grabbed a bar or tyre lever from the shed, but here he was vulnerable, and their attack would come from two sides.

Coldness washed over him and his stomach quickly knotted. That they were also weaponless was completely uninspiring. It would be hand-to-hand combat, his two to their four – and he noted the size of their paws. Huge! *Nick, you're gonna die.*

He moved back to keep them both in sight. "Fuck you!" he rebuked, stalling the inevitable. "You and whose Army?"

"We don't need no fuckin' army," the smaller goon laughed.

Nick faked a grin. "Well at least you had the good sense to come in pairs ... otherwise I'd think you were stupid. What are you two anyway ... Siamese Twins?"

A sneer started on the smaller man's face.

Good. Take him. You might take him. You definitely won't take the other. But do it now before you lose the chance.

Nick raised his hands, beckoned with his fingers for the smaller man to approach. He had two tactics: fend off whatever came at him, and rile the man enough to slow his thinking. "Come on, fat boy, if you think you can do it."

"He's mine. All mine!" Ben snarled.

Nick glanced back at the larger hulk who was working his way to his back.

"Go for it!" the man grated, raising his hands and stepping back.

Nick breathed with relief. *Good, one on one. Now stay cool.*

He back-stepped to keep both men in front of him as Ben Taylor moved in boldly, and badly feigned a left jab Nick's way. Nick barely bothered to lean back from its reach, but ducked below the arc of a hefty right cross that followed. His own fists ready, he shot two sharp jabs under the man's fleshy rib-cage, the impact doubling the man over. He followed up with a slamming left cross that spun the man up and around and pummelled him face-first into the ground.

The man lay stunned, gasping and groaning.

"Come on," Nick cajoled with fake disappointment. He worried though that the second man was drawing in from behind, and half turned to guard his back. The man on the ground struggled slowly to his feet, blood staining his bottom lip. He wiped it away on his hand, examined the stickiness and almost bull-roared.

"No!" he yelled abrasively as the other man closed in. "I said he's mine!"

The bigger man stopped moving. "Well get him then! Get in there and get him!"

Nick glanced again at the nearness of the voice, and was caught off guard as his rival lurched forward and landed a powerless blow to his chest, its delivery too far away to reach full potential. He moved back with the punch, further disarming the blow. What he didn't see was the left hand coming and its full force crunched his jaw, the blow sending him reeling. He fell hard up against the side of the utility as his opponent closed in.

Staggering a few steps to regain his feet, Nick felt his jaw, checking it was still in the right place. He watched the man's fists closely, for another one like that wouldn't do him much good. The ache in his jaw was already more noticeable than he wanted to admit. The man surged forward again, crowding him in near the vehicle, a right upper cut aimed solidly at Nick's mid-section. The fist was in flight and Nick instantly put his whole strength to tensing the muscles there, noticing at the same time the left cross being structured. His body stopped the first punch like a double brick wall, its deliverer looking down in total surprise at its lack of effect. Nick's right arm blocked the left cross and followed it up with a strong left fist to the nose which sent his opponent sprawling to the ground a second time.

Seething, Nick closed in and stood over him, waiting, fighting to control his breathing; fighting to hold down his anger.

Intent on subduing his target, he forgot the other player until a pair of thick arms locked under his own and wrenched his arms upward. Two massive hands locked behind his neck and shoved forward, the force wrenching Nick's shoulders further back, crushing them. With his arms so totally locked above his head, the powerful body behind him stretching him mercilessly, he was completely opened for the next assault. He went cold as the order bellowed past his ear: "Get up! Get up and finish him!"

He twisted against the hold, trying to pull free; he tried to drop his body forward to pull his assailant over his shoulder, and tensed to gain more strength to break the hold but he couldn't writhe clear of the vice-like arms and he couldn't drag him forward. He tried to breathe in, muster more strength, but the structured hold strained his lungs, stretched them beyond inflation. He was immobilised. Vulnerable. And he went even colder. *This is it! Say goodnight, Nick* ... He breathed in what little air he could.

Taking his advantage, his attacker planted two solid punches under Nick's ribcage, forcing the rest of the air from his lungs. Even though he tensed to lessen the impact, he couldn't dull the force of the blow, all the pressure in his body drawn to his shoulders, exposing him completely to whatever they chose to deliver.

As the man advanced again, Nick arched further back, his body opened further for the kill, and it crossed his mind they made a good team. His feet lifted slightly off the ground, his assailant too exuberant, and adrenalin suddenly surged through him. His mind bellowed: *Yes, do it!*

As the man forged in, Nick sank his weight, making the man restraining him carry it. Bringing his knees up, he kicked out at just the right time, his feet hitting his target's chest full on. The sudden thrust forced the thug off balance, knocking him backwards, the backlash taking his captor by surprise and knocking him over backwards as well. The mighty grip released as they all thumped heavily to the ground.

Nick rolled quickly and lunged back again, delivering all the damage he could in the short time he had. Straddling the man, he landed a bevy of powerful blows to the face before the man could gain his senses, the force splitting the skin on his knuckles. It was his only chance to save himself – get in what he could when he could. He certainly wouldn't out-do them on strength alone.

Rising to his feet, Ben stumbled forward. "You bastard!" he roared, his teeth gnashing as he snatched a metal bar from the back of the ute tray. Advancing, he brought it forcefully down across Nick's shoulder blades.

The blow shocked Nick upright, his hand shooting back to contain the pain as the impact knocked the breath from him. As stars danced around his eyes, huge hands reached for his throat, and he knew they had him and would crush the life from him. But he never felt the hands lock on as another whack smashed against his skull, knocking him to the ground. The earth, the sky, all objects around him started tumbling, spinning out of control. Every ounce of strength he had left drained out into the ground. His head pounded mercilessly, almost matching the blows that thumped into him, heavy boots thudding into his flesh, jerking him with the force of each vicious kick. A sharp jolt smashed his ribs, shot searing pain up into his chest, equalling the pain in his head. He groaned: *You're dead, Nick* – and he slumped and felt no more.

CHAPTER FIFTY-ONE

In the cold timber shack above Northgate I sat flicking through a newspaper Nick had shoved in the rucksack, paying more attention to a large spider that crawled around in the far corner than to the headlines on the page. If the spider headed my way I'd be out of there, and I'd already drawn my feet up off the floor to avoid whatever wandered there. Eventually, the spider's hairy legs scratchily disappeared into a crack in the wall, and I only kept a half eye on it, and one eye on the paper. Not that I'd had much interest to start with — newspapers were always depressing — and my thoughts were still fixed heavily to the men who'd chased me and where they might be right now.

Constantly I forced those thoughts away for Nick had said I'd be okay. Bored with the paper, my interest eventually fell on the stack of cardboard boxes in the corner. They'd been annoying me most of the day, and I soon found they contained letters and memorabilia, and all sorts of other stuff that had been loosely tossed inside. Nick's memorabilia, I realised, dearly hoping he would give me ample warning before flinging the door open on his return. I didn't have to be Einstein to know he wouldn't appreciate anyone snooping through his stuff.

In a tattered shoe box deep amongst the stack I found a pile of letters, some to his mother — sensitively written letters scribed in a youngish hand — some to his father, postmarked Vietnam. These letters caused a frown. In one letter Nick had written about the war, the harshness, the brutality, the sheer futility, yet, by the tone of his words he didn't sound too unhappy being there. In another, he explained his reasons for staying, for signing for a second Tour, reasons that gave him a purpose in life. And there was one that followed, from his father, a letter that slated Marilyn Perry something chronic. I'd heard gossip of Nick's relationship with Marilyn. Obviously Nick's dad hadn't liked her much, and this letter was cruel; was undoubtedly meant to hurt. I wondered if it was deliberate retaliation for Nick's decision to stay overseas.

Beneath the letters were photos, mainly ones of the Army, some of a Unit of young guys grouped together, laughing, smiling, lined up by a row of tents to capture a memory. Some boys looked no older than I was now. There was one of Nick standing alone, his rifle shouldered as he stared into the distance, sombre, deep in thought, a cigarette hanging from his mouth. I'd never seen Nick smoke; and thought I would have noticed if he did. He looked miles away in thought, obviously caught unawares. I liked that one best for it revealed another side of Nick, the unexposed side I wanted to explore. There were several of him with Marilyn, arm in arm, looking young and very happy. I pushed those to the bottom of the stack. Marilyn was someone to whom I couldn't warm, and I didn't want to. My perception of Nick however had been right: there was indeed another side to this intriguing Man of Steel, a side he didn't show, a side he covered with his heart of stone.

I flicked a glance at the door. It was getting late. Nick said he'd be back before dark, so I packed the boxes away, carefully covering my delving. The last thing I wanted was to be caught poking through his stuff.

Reopening the newspaper, I sat and waited.

Another hour passed, the room dimming with the time. I looked up as a shuffling noise came from outside, and rose and went to the door; listened harder, hoping it was Nick coming back. But the sounds were loud and heavy, and that wasn't Nick, and the rustling came from two sides of the shack.

An evil chill crept over my skin and I opened the door a crack and peered out; pulled back as two long shadows stretched towards the door. The sudden creak of timber pierced the scrub and startled two great grey kangaroos, the noise sending them bounding away and crashing through the scrub till they disappeared in the darkness.

CHAPTER FIFTY-TWO

Dim light slowly filtered in, a grey cloudy light that brightened as Nick's eyes opened. He winced and pressed them closed again, trying to alleviate the pain the light magnified. He tried to move but felt greater agony. *Keep out the light! And breathe,* he told himself. *Just breathe.* But even breathing hurt.

He forced his eyes to open again, needing to see where he was, needing to gain some sense of the situation; he realised he was lying face down, in the open. He couldn't remember why. His shirt and chest were wet from the ground's dampness, and his head throbbed; exploded with every single move. He concentrated on breathing; took slow, shallow breaths; tried to lessen the rise and fall of his chest; limit moving. He dreaded doing anything more than breathe. Yet knew it was unavoidable. Mustering the nerve, he rolled to his back.

Searing pain ripped through every fibre of his being, and he knew his mistake. The hammer in his head smashed double-time, and he gulped air, which set up a fit of coughing which further racked his body. He groaned, and lay for long silent minutes, not yet ready to suffer another onslaught.

He became aware of a wet patch that spread across his neck and shoulder, and raised a hand to contain it; raised his hand to his sight. *Blood!* He closed his eyes again, dreary, the light still too bright. The hammer on the anvil beat more aggressive tunes. "Well at least you're alive," he muttered, feeling unlucky to be so.

Still concentrating on his breathing, he raised one knee, alleviating the gnawing ache in his back. All around him seemed silent.

Come on Nick, up you get! The day's a-wasting.

He heaved a sigh. But that was all.

Come on! So it's going to hurt. What are you going to do ... lie here all day and bleed?

He heaved another breath and rolled back to his stomach, groaning as the pain shifted to new unaffected places. Gritting his teeth, he pulled one knee up underneath him and raised himself to an elbow. Another knee up, the other hand down, and like that, he pushed himself to his knees. Explosions rocked his head and he pressed his hands to his skull to contain them; to stop the slow rotations of the world spinning him round.

Long minutes passed.

He took the last step and rose to his feet, feeling immediately that the world was out of kilter. Staggering, he reached out for support, and found metal. Cold, cold metal. He grabbed it; clung to it; forced his eyes to stay open; forced away the grey, grey cloud. Focusing, he realised he was holding onto the bull bar of the truck. By the greyness overhead, it was either late evening or rain was going to fall. The trickle of blood oozing down his neck annoyed him and he wiped it away on his hand and looked around again, things becoming clearer. His lips drew to a tight line. The windshield of the truck was shattered, shards of cloudy blue-green glass crystallised over the bonnet. The truck was a long way from the house. *Why?*

Then he remembered – there'd been a fight.

Dispirited, he leant over the bonnet of the truck, gaining balance. His Ford had been trashed. The wide, heavy tyres were flat, large rips in the side walls, and he remembered the men who'd done it. Big bastards. Fucked up freaks of nature.

He shivered as a thought crossed his mind, and he turned cautiously, his nerves jangling at the thought of being grabbed again from behind. He fell against the truck with resurging pain and relief. The men ... the utility ... were gone.

But where?

He scanned the surrounds.

— the house?

Mentally, he shook his head. It looked the same.

— the farm?

He turned slowly, holding the gash at the base of his skull to contain the blood that poured as he moved.

No. Farm seems okay.

His eyes stopped at the tree covered slope, his vision starting to swirl. *The shelter belt.*

He stared at it. *Something about the shelter belt …*

He'd been there recently. But …

His breath left him. *Shit, the kid!* Then he panicked. *Did they get the kid?*

Pushing away from the truck, he scrambled for the slope, the pain in his ribs restricting his breathing, the splitting thumps in his head drifting him in and out of conscious thought. At times he climbed with purpose, knowing where he was heading and why, then a section he'd scramble up unsure of anything except his desperate need to reach the shack on the rise. Once, he stopped altogether, leant against a tree to catch his breath and forgot what he was doing until panic forced him on again. The pounding in his head became questions. *What if she's not there? — where will I look? Who the bloody hell are they? And how do they tie in with McCaig?*

He reached the shack.

All about was silent, total, deathly silence, the incredible hush broken only by his own laboured breathing. He tried to block it out, tried to listen further afield, but no other sounds came to him. And now it was totally dark.

Staggering forward, the tight knot in his stomach making him nauseous, he reached the shack and fell against the door. It crashed open on its hinges.

Inside, the lamp was lit, the room bathed in a warm yellow glow. The kid was by the table, fear sweeping over her beautiful face. *Why so frightened?*

He took a step towards her then the room went suddenly dark.

CHAPTER FIFTY-THREE

Silver coins dropped into the roadhouse till as Marilyn bid the last two truckers goodnight. With them now pulling out on the long haul north, the cafe sat empty – no more truckies due until just before dawn. She strolled outside to serve a southbound sedan, noticing as she crossed to the pump that the hotel was just closing up, lights flicking off one by one. Only the Public bar, Sheila's favourite haunt, still glowed.

She shoved the nozzle into the Datsun's fuel tank, her gaze remaining on the distant figure of Sheila wiping down the counter. She used to like Sheila once, a long time ago, but that had all changed when she'd come between her and Nick. If Sheila hadn't told Nick where she and Gary had gone that night nothing would have happened. She huffed an angry sigh. Sheila was jealous that Nick spent his time with her instead of at the pub, that's why she'd interfered. If she'd just kept her mouth shut Nick wouldn't have caught her and Gary Peters together; Nick wouldn't have torn the door off its hinges and wouldn't have put Gary in hospital.

She remembered how out of control he'd been; how gorgeous he'd looked when incensed. She remembered too that Gary had left town after that and returned only occasionally, and then spent the best part of his time looking over his shoulder.

She withdrew the nozzle as the last light in the hotel went out; only the lights on the verandah now on for whoever occupied the rooms above.

A dark scowl marred Marilyn's face. She didn't care what Sheila McKenzie thought, she was going to get Nick back, any way she could. There was just the small matter of Becky Cooper to deal with first, for not for one minute did she believe Nick's excuses when they'd been caught together. He'd been far too protective of her. She shoved the nozzle back in the side of the pump and replaced the petrol cap, wondering where Nick was at that moment. She wondered if he was still with Becky. The thought bit deep as the driver reached out and paid for the fuel, orange eddies whirling along the highway as he spun the wheels through the gravel on leaving. The dust choked Marilyn and forced her back inside.

Returning to the counter she dropped the cash in the till, and looked up as the shearers from the motel came in for a meal. They dragged out chairs at two tables, the scraping of steel legs on the tiled floor bringing Kate out from the kitchen. With a bored expression, she took their orders, ignoring their crude suggestions with "Only what's on the menu" as she moved around the tables. Her face showed that her patience had worn thin, and she'd already complained to Tom that the Queenslanders made the burly truckers look like proper gentlemen. She stood well back, keeping her long braided ponytail from their reach as she jotted down their preference, promising herself one of them would wear a hot cup of coffee before the meal was done. And Tom wouldn't chide her if she did.

Marilyn cleared the table where the last trucker had dined, also avoiding their tables. She felt their eyes roving over her curves, mentally undressing her and she escaped outside to serve another customer. Lacey's gaze followed her.

More cash landed in the till, freeing her to assist Kate with serving the meals. She slid the oval white plates piled high with food down onto the tables, half listening to their talk of head counts and arguments over who was the better shearer. The haggard old one complained about his back and said he'd be glad when the job was over. Pete Lacey, he of the sexy blue-blue eyes, leant back to make more room for her, and she flashed him a smile and went on to the next table where the podgy contractor's voice dominated.

"It's a puzzle," he said, shaking his bald, beanied head. "There's been no sign of the Cooper girl at all, and her car was towed into the wrecker's yard last night, but nobody's been in to claim it."

He glanced up as Marilyn placed Madden's meal down before him. "When the coppers came round asking, I told them none of us have seen her. Maybe she's ended up like the Richardson girl and is lying out there in the bush somewhere."

His eyes lingered on Marilyn's breasts, a long, open appraisal, and he didn't move his head back as she lowered his meal, ensuring his mouth came very close to her assets. "I told 'em that too, but they didn't listen," he went on. "They're so bloody arrogant they wouldn't know if they're coming or going. They're just flittin' back and forward from here to Dayton like a mob of blue-arsed flies wasting our time. You'd have thought they'd have a search party out there by now."

Leaning back from his face, Marilyn shoved his plate down with a clatter. "Why should they?" she cut in over him. "They know where she is!"

McCaig's scowl was instant, and his mouth fell open, but he quickly recovered. He glanced up at her. "Ha!" he scoffed loudly. "I don't believe that!" He picked up his fork to avoid looking interested.

Marilyn slid the last plate down and glared back at him. "It's true. She's out at Northgate."

"Oh go on! Pull the other leg!" McCaig chided, sliding his hand onto her thigh to distract her.

Marilyn lurched back, almost knocked over a chair, but the distance removed his hand. She swore she'd slap him if he tried that again. "It's true!" she retaliated. "I saw her there last night."

Flouncing her golden hair back, she thumped a pair of salt and pepper shakers down in the centre of the table then retreated to the kitchen to complain to Tom about the inappropriate touch.

CHAPTER FIFTY-FOUR

Hours passed.

Nick lay silent, his head inside a big bass drum. It was the middle of a concert finale, all instruments blaring. Between his shoulder blades, a dull ache gnawed deep into the tissues, and pain shot to his elbows and hands each time he tried to move. The pain behind his left eye was so horrendous he avoided opening it. He drew breath thinly, wincing as his lungs expanded, and wondered why he felt so broken. Equally, he wondered where he was for, right then, he simply couldn't remember. All he knew was he was hurting. The pain in his hip and back alluded that something was broken but he loathed moving to find out. Only once he remembered feeling like this ... *and nobody walks away feeling too healthy after a grenade throws you eighty feet.*

A cold chill washed over him.

Fuck! Nam! Am I still in Nam?!

His nerves tightened, and his breathing sharpened.

No. ... No. You can remember more than that!

Snatching a breath, he let the recent events seep in; pieced together images, remembered two big sons-of-bitches ... *oh yeah ...* they'd fought ... and by the feel of it, he'd lost.

His head started spinning again. *Stop thinking!*

His throat and mouth felt parched yet he was shaking. From fear or cold he didn't know. He just knew he didn't feel well. And he didn't know where he was. Hell, he didn't even know if they were there, just hovering over him, waiting for him to rise, or whether they'd gone. Without opening his eyes, he had no way of knowing.

He lay listening for clues, heard the wind whistling through branches in the distance, and the gentle creak of timber – he was obviously amongst the trees ... and ever so slightly beside him he heard a breath being drawn. *They're still here!* Now he was disadvantaged. He drew a deeper breathe, preparing to move, mustering his strength to do whatever he could to survive. A hand landed on his chest and he momentarily froze. *Time to move!*

Staving off the pain, he grabbed the assailant's hand, his other hand powering up and connecting with pliant flesh as he sat bolt upright. He had only one shot at survival before pain overtook him and he heard with satisfaction the heavy thud of a body hitting the floor. He followed the flow of his energy and was up and on top of his assailant in a second. Straddling him, he drew back his fist, armed it with all the power he could draw ... One punch was all he'd get. His shoulder muscles bunched to send every ounce of strength into his fist, and he opened his eyes to make sure his aim was true. Everything in front of him was a grey hazy blur. He took his chance; heard a high pitched squeal. The mass beneath him squirmed, and he locked a hand tight to its throat to pin it down. *Keep still, you bastard!*

"Nick!!"

The blow was on its way but he stopped its arc half way; pulled back. *The voice.* He knew the voice; that familiar scream. Pain wracked his body but he forced his vision to clear, his right eye yielding to his will and focusing slightly. The left eye screamed to close.

Through the haze, the floor came into focus, and then the body beneath him. He realised the horrified look; the captivating face that stared back at him; the halo of dark flowing hair. *Beautiful hair.* He stared down at her, accepting the fear that was now turning to rage.

CHAPTER FIFTY-FIVE

I writhed to escape Nick's next onslaught, but couldn't move. All I could do was turn my face so he wouldn't break my nose. My jaw already pounded where his fist had connected.

Closing my eyes, I preparing myself for the pain, screamed at the thought of impact for his punch would smash my face.

But nothing happened. Then the hand released my throat, and I looked up as Nick sat back on his calves, lowered his fist, and sat looking down at me. He coughed, the pain taking his breath again. He looked around, scanning the dark confines of the shack then looked back at me. I guess I must have looked in as much pain as him because he kept staring at my face; kept sitting, making it impossible to move.

"Would you mind getting off?" I insisted, those few words sending sharp stabs of pain through my jaw. Was this what it felt like to be dislocated? I'd seen riders with dislocated jaws, especially when they'd been rocketed into a wing or landed face first in the dirt. I tried to hold the explosion from breaking out further. "Owww! Jesus! Whose side are you on?"

He shook his head; heaved another breath and swung his knee clear of my thighs. I rolled away and rose to my knees, somewhat groggy from the pounding. Stars still spun in my head.

"Hey ... I'm sorry," he said, slowly rising to his feet. He looked less balanced than I and locked a grip on the table, stared at the floor as if staring down lessened the effects of the revolving room. I gained my feet as he almost toppled, the table sliding under his weight so I moved in to provide stability, my hands resisting his slow decline sideways.

"What happened to you anyway?" I asked, noting the dark

swellings spreading into bruises. He heaved another breath, short and laboured, and looked around the shack again. He was shivering. I hadn't seen Nick shiver before.

"I was hit by a fast moving truck," he muttered drily.

"Oh, really!"

He stared straight at me and I suspected he wasn't going to be on his feet much longer. "What really happened, Nick? You were gone so long."

He eased in another breath. "I met your friends," he said huskily. "They like to party ... "

I rubbed the back of my head, my own egg rising where my head had hit the floor. "So do you."

"Yeah," he trembled harder, "but I say I'm sorry." His dark eyes locked on the corner of the room. "And that's all I'm up for right now. ... Go and flip that mattress down, will you," he changed the subject. "I think we'd better rest up a while before we head back to the house."

I did as he said and flipped one of the old kapok mattresses over and dragged it across to him. The way he looked right then he wasn't going anywhere but down. His bruised face was puffy, especially the left cheek, and his knuckles were swollen and split in places. Blood stained his hand, and a fresh trickle oozed down his neck and over the back of his shoulder. He put his hand up to contain it, the move gaping open his torn white shirt. Angry scrapes and bruises marred his ribs and chest.

"Just for a while," he said as he lowered to the mattress, the shivers getting stronger, "then I'll get you into Dayton."

Nodding, I sank down next to him; pulled a handkerchief from my pocket and placed it over the gash on his neck. He closed his eyes, and I suddenly realised I was on my own again. With Nick barely conscious, I felt vulnerable, and wondered what the hell I would do if someone should burst through that rickety doorway.

❧

CHAPTER FIFTY-SIX

Outside the roadhouse, Bill McCaig paced back and forth near the telephone box, hunched-backed and muttering as he willed the thing to ring. Nine o'clock had already passed and Taylors were late, which bothered him. He returned to the car, intending to use the radio, but the phone started ringing as he opened the door. His enormous frame rippling as he jogged back to the booth, he snatched up the receiver, pulled the spiral cord until it stretched to the corner of the building, guarding his privacy. From the corner of the building he covered both sides of the roadhouse car park.

Taylor's voice grated down the wire. "McCaig?"

"Yeah it's me! What the hell are you two playing at out there?"

"What are you talking about? We're doing exactly what you tell us to do, so watch your bloody tone!"

McCaig ignored Taylor's demand. "Yeah? Well where's the Cooper girl then?" he hissed. "You found her yet?"

"No. But we've got a few ideas where she is."

McCaig looked in both directions then whispered: "Does one of them have anything to do with Northgate?"

"What? What are you talking about?" Dave sounded slightly amused. "Actually we took a little walk over Manetti this evening." He poked at the swelling around his eye and cheek, at his fat lower lip, and grinned. He'd made Manetti suffer extra for each of them; had put a good boot hard into the bastard's rib-cage. "He'll be lying up for a good few days," he said with glowing confidence.

"Yeah? Well he'll be laying up with company. Manetti's got

the girl!"

"What?" Taylor listened harder.

"I said ... Manetti's ... got ... the girl! Now you two get your fat fucking arses back there and take care of 'em both. And when you do, make it final, then get the hell out of the State. We can't afford to be linked to you two anymore, not this trip."

"You worry too much," Taylor replied. "Nobody can prove a damn thing, and you know that!"

"Well I ain't so sure any more. Since you messed up things are boiling over round here. Now you've got an eye-witness roamin' round loose again and I bet Manetti can give a pretty good description of you two."

"I think he'd think twice about that."

"Yeah? Well I don't think he would," McCaig countered deeply. "And I'll tell you another thing, smart arse ... if he or that girl make it to the cops, we're history, pal. *History*! You hear that? All it will take is for someone to check into our travels and the whole lot of us are gonna end up in the shit-hole! And what if they find that kid's body before we're outta here? Have you thought about that?"

Taylor snuffed smugly. "As I said, you worry too much. Where we parked him nobody'll find him, at least not until late summer! Same as before – no body – no case."

But McCaig shook his head. "As I said, we got a lot to lose, so you get back and finish the job ... before they talk to the cops ... because I'm warning you mister ... if we go down, you go down!"

Taylor's back stiffened. "You keep your threats to yourself, old man," he warned. "And what you better remember is ... we're taking all the risks, all the time, so you lot had better damn well be ready to take on some heat if we need back-up, or you will be going down."

"You don't need to worry about that. Now get back and finish what you started. Phone me when it's done. I'll wait here for your call."

The line went dead.

Ben wrung his hands together as Dave relayed the message. Wincing as he poked his bruised ribs, he relished a second chance at Manetti. Revenge would be so sweet.

CHAPTER FIFTY-SEVEN

The night was moonless as they drove back into Northgate and heavy clouds still rolled in from the west. The wind gusted strongly down the hill, buffeting the ute as they drove at snail's pace along the gravel track, neither the night nor their headlights betraying their arrival. Ahead, the house was also in darkness.

They cruised level with the yellow truck that now listed towards the track. "Keep your eyes peeled," Taylor hissed a warning. "That bastard's out here somewhere!"

"Can't see him," came the whispered reply. "We left him over there."

"And we knocked him pretty senseless, so he won't have gone far."

Ben looked across to his brother. "Unless the girl helped him."

"In which case, they could have reached the house ..."

Ben looked ahead again. "There's no lights on up there," he shrugged.

"Jesus!" Dave pulled a 'you-moron' face. "You don't think they'd be silly enough to advertise the fact they're home, do you?"

Ben didn't answer.

Parking beside the damaged F100, Taylor slid from behind the wheel, stripped the leather sheath from the 12-gauge shotgun and slipped two cartridges into the chambers. Ben unsheathed his Enfield 303 while Dave scouted the area; shouldered it as they moved towards the house. Travelling across the open easy green Taylor kept his eyes glued to the building, intent on picking up the slightest movement within. But nothing showed. Nothing that he noticed. The darkness and silence were one.

Reaching the house, they ducked below the window beside the back verandah, Taylor panting with excitement. Sweat beaded on his skin though he'd not yet expended any energy. An adrenalin rush surged to his core, stirred by the thrill of the hunt, the anticipation of the kill. He felt an erection starting, and realised just how much he got off doing this sort of thing – pitting his skills against the unknown – making the kill.

"Cover the front door," he whispered to Ben. "Get them if they come out!"

Like an obedient puppy, Ben scampered around the house and, positioning himself below the front porch railing, levelled his rifle at the ripple-glassed door. Dave waited a few moments then stepped up onto the verandah, using the sides of his feet so his rubber soles didn't squeak on the gritty red concrete. He wanted nothing to alert his prey to their surprise, that element of the hunt an even greater reward – seeing the shocked look on their face before he pulled the trigger.

A sudden snarling hiss erupted from the shadows, and he scuttled back, froze for barely a second then whipped around with his rifle aimed and ready.

The audacious hiss came again and he breathed with instant relief; swung a kick at the cat that had bunched itself and spat at him from the darkness. The cat hunkered down further but didn't move, and he was tempted to lower the barrel and pull the trigger just for the sake of it. Cut short its feline arrogance. But there were things more important this night that required silence.

Stooping low, he pulled the outer door open, and winced as its creak amplified in the night. He reached up and tried the handle, almost laughed as the door slid softly open then sighed inwardly, his hopes deteriorating. Rising, he stepped cautiously through the opening, doubting he would find anyone inside. No fool would hide out in an unsecured house, the noise of someone breaking through the barriers would be the perfect warning to run.

But his eyes narrowed with the thought that Manetti was smart, and tactical. An unlocked door could be just the ploy he'd pull to catch them off guard.

He regenerated caution, pressed his back against the wall and stole along the passage, silent as a prowling panther. In each doorway he raised, levelled and aimed the shotgun, swept the room with its barrel, ready to fire at the slightest sign of movement, at any infinitesimal sound. At a breathe. Room by room, he cleared the house, visions of Army days priming his steps, his tension growing at the expectation of ambush, for Manetti would likely strike that way.

He scanned the Lounge, the last room, his body sagging with disappointment. The quarry had escaped out of range, too far now to be followed. He turned the small knob on the front door lock and opened the door a crack. Ben leapt up in that instant, his rifle raised and sighted, his finger already locked on, pressuring its trigger. He could blow a hole right through the door and get one of them if he had to, and Dave would be so pleased if he did. He pressed the trigger further, his nerves twitching eagerly.

"Nothing here," Dave called through the slit. "House is empty."

Ben retracted the rifle's aim, relieved he hadn't squeezed off the shot. Dave wouldn't have been happy at that. The door opened wider.

"What do we do now?" he asked as his brother stepped onto the high front verandah.

"We wait. It's gonna be bloody cold out there tonight, and wherever Manetti is it's my bet he'll be back. Go get the car and hide it up amongst those trees at the back of the house." He thumbed roughly towards the heavy thicket of Tamarisk.

CHAPTER FIFTY-EIGHT

Rod Willcox paced back and forth inside the stationhouse, trying to look busy, his night shift already into its second hour. The clock had just clicked over midnight, and he worried that Nick hadn't shown.

"So what had he meant by 'tonight'?" Cussack had asked him. "Before twelve? Twelve? Early morning? Just how dark does dark have to be?"

Rod had merely shrugged.

Across the room, Cussack drummed his fingers on the desk, and glanced at the clock again; he had mentioned a while ago the investigation was becoming too drawn out, and Rod had agreed. Yet they'd given Nick another hour. If he hadn't appeared by then they would go after him.

Indeed, Cussack wasn't willing to sit on the case any longer. Already he should have made contact with the CIB, but so far there'd been nothing to corroborate the story. And it was a hell of a long way to be calling them in if this was a wild goose chase. Maybe, just maybe, it was a fabrication, he'd thought several times. Pete Kennedy had been known to abscond before. Maybe he'd done it again. He would decide what he thought of that when he finally confronted the girl. He nodded to himself. Indeed, if it was a hoax, he'd get to the bottom of it. He'd pick holes in her story so fast he'd make her head spin. At the end of it, he'd get the truth. The only problem was ... if it wasn't a hoax ... where the hell was Peter Kennedy?

He poured a coffee, walked to the front door and looked out at the empty street; checked his wrist watch again then glanced at the constable standing behind the counter. Willcox shook his head, the creases in his brow deepening.

"Try ringing again," Cussack told him.

Rod picked up the phone for the fifth time. There had been no answer before, and each time they'd rung they'd presumed Nick was on his way. But now, the nearly half hour trip had taken two hours. He shook his head again as the telephone rang out.

"I've got a bad feeling, Rod," Cussack said, putting the cup down and pulling his cap from the shelf. "Let's go."

Rod grabbed his cap, relief flooding in. "You've got bad feelings?" he mused. "Mine are worse!"

In the doorway, the Sergeant suddenly turned half back. "I'll warn you though ... if this friend of yours is playing us a fool, he's in for a heap of trouble!" A cold wall of air chilled him the moment he opened the door. "Bloody hell it's cold out here. Why does everything have to happen on nights like this?"

He strode to the car. "You drive," he said as he opened the passenger door, "seeing you know where you're going."

They pulled into Northgate some time later, the headlights casting wide beams of light to chase away the darkness. "How far now?" Cussack asked as he peered out the side window and caught his own reflection in the glass.

"Just around the next bend we should see the house."

The bend curved right and the track rose slowly up. But still darkness prevailed.

"No lights on at the house," Rod pointed out.

Shielded by the night, the Taylor brothers scuttled silently out the back door and into the dense cover of Tamarisk hedge, pulling branches deftly back to conceal their presence. The shotgun remained ready, its wielder watching closely. Two cartridges filled the chambers – one each was all he'd need.

The headlights drew closer.

Inside the approaching vehicle, Cussack strained his eyes as he tried to imagine where the farmhouse was in the blackness.

"No, no lights on," he agreed, "but look over there." He thumbed to the side of the track ahead, his keen eyes catching a glint of light reflecting off the Ford's side mirror. Rod saw it too and swung the car towards it, directing the headlights onto the disabled pick-up. Both officers stepped from the car.

"It's Nick's truck all right," Rod confirmed. "But Jesus Christ! what the hell has happened here?"

"Don't touch anything," Cussack ordered as he reached back into the vehicle. Pulling clear a flashlight, he stepped closer to the truck and shone the light-beam through the interior. No-one was inside. He examined the tyres, the concentrated light exposing six inch long rips through the side walls. Only the two on the right side were damaged, the effect causing the body to list severely. He swung the light over the windscreen, glass glittering back like crystal gems from the bonnet.

"Look at this!" Cussack said, examining the hood closer. A smear of red streaked the yellow paint-work. Rod leant over to inspect the damage and paled at its appearance.

"Blood," he said, looking up at the Sergeant.

Cussack nodded. "I'll be damn surprised if it's not." He swung the light beam around and across the ground near the vehicle. The surface was disturbed; scuff marks in the soil; grass uprooted in one or two places. He looked across at Rod, rubbed his chin with firm fingers as visions dallied forth. "I dare say there was a damn good reason why your friend didn't show."

Stepping into the light, Rod stooped down, a glittering of gold attracting his attention. He picked up the object, examined it and handed it across to the Sergeant.

"Manetti's?"

"I think so," Rod answered. "I can't be positive, but if it's not, it's very much like it." He blew out a hard breath.

Cussack examined the watch, the broken band dangling out through the palm of his hand; he dropped it into his shirt pocket. "I hope I get to give it back," he murmured, searching further with the torch. Then he moaned with despondence. "Ah ... but I don't think I will." Walking forward, he crouched down, touched the grass and rubbed the residue he'd found between his fingertips. "Hit the spotlight, Rod."

Returning to the car, Rod plugged in the cord, turned the key and fed the cord out through the open door. Something was terribly wrong: the Sergeant's voice was strained.

The long-ranging beacon flooded the area with light, touching Cussack crouched in its path. The man examined his fingers closely then examined the ground.

"It's blood all right," he confirmed, and the bottom dropped out of Rod's stomach. "Not much, but sure's the bet somebody's not feeling too healthy right now ... or just not feeling at all," he covered all possibilities. He looked up at Rod, and stood up. "I don't like jumping to conclusions but my guess is your friend's in a spot of bother. Better cast that light around a bit,"; he pointed at the darkness, "... make sure there's not a body or two out there anywhere."

"Shit!" Rod went colder than the chilly wind permeating him. But the ground proved clear in all directions, and the fear that gnawed with each moving foot of the light beam abated. Several minutes passed before Cussack was satisfied.

"Okay, we'll check out the house. He's got to be somewhere, and we've got to find the girl. At least now it's obvious that something is amiss." He climbed back into the car. "I just hope we're not too late!"

Driving up, they parked beside the house, level with the verandah, opened their doors and stepped out. Dave Taylor's finger curled eagerly around the metal trigger, his thick lips twisting sardonically. They need only take a step or two in his direction and that was all he'd need to empty both barrels.

But they didn't. Their sweeping flashlights illuminated the path heading to the house. Cussack opened the fly-wire door and rapped loudly on the solid wooden barrier, waited a moment then rapped again. When there was no answer, he tested the door knob. The door swung easily open.

"Doesn't he lock up?" Cussack asked, surprised.

Rod pursed his lips and shook his head. "He figures he hasn't got much worth stealing — says if they want to get in they'll only break in, so he's avoiding damage."

"Crazy," Cussack replied, entering the kitchen.

"Country," came the prompt contradiction.

The torch beam located the light switch and Cussack flipped it on. A neat cream kitchen appeared, with rinsed coffee cups in the sink. He felt the kettle. Cold. Together they searched the rest of the house, but it was void of life. Cussack used the phone and rang the station, but Manetti hadn't shown in his absence — but after what they'd found he'd kind of expected that. He drummed his fingers absently on the bench top.

"What are you thinking?" Rod risked asking, accustomed now to the new Sergeant's mannerisms.

"Well I can't figure it yet, but it doesn't look good for Manetti either way," the man frowned. He looked straight at Rod. "You say he's big ... a powerhouse, right?" The drumming slowed.

Rod nodded acquiescently.

"So he wouldn't be taken easily."

Rod shook his head.

"So it would mean for anyone to overpower him, there would need to be at least two, maybe three of them."

Rod nodded again, visualising the sort of men it would take to bring Nick down. It would have been one hell of a fight, and he swallowed hard.

"... or to kill him ... one rifle," Cussack compounded the theory, conjuring further unpleasant images for his subordinate. The drumming stopped. He tapped the bench top, punctuating his thoughts. "As I said ... either way, it doesn't look good. And I wouldn't mind guessing that it ties in with whoever is after the

Cooper girl."

He tipped his hat further back on his head. "Now, before we go any further, we have to find out what happened to the girl. Was she with him when they got him? ... if they got him ...," he corrected, pacifying the remorse that crossed Rod's face, "... or was he alone?"

"Well, he said he'd stashed her somewhere."

"Where?"

Rod shook his head. "He didn't say. He just said he'd stashed her safely, and I figured if he wanted me to know he'd have told me where. He didn't, and I guessed he wouldn't have even if I'd asked."

"Well that's great Police work, Rod!" Cussack chided, but this wasn't the time or place for snippiness so he let it go. "Okay then," he continued a little more gruffly, "maybe he left her with someone. Who does he associate with?"

Rod thought carefully. "No-one really. Pete and Sam mostly, but they live here. Marilyn Perry at one point, but that's been dead a long time. And Sheila McKenzie at the hotel. Apart from that, he keeps pretty much to himself."

"No girlfriend?"

Rod shook his head.

"Mistress? ... Lover? ... Anything?" Cussack quizzed, but Rod kept shaking his head and smiling.

"Not that he's said anything about, and he probably wouldn't. He keeps his life fairly private," Rod reflected. "...actually, he's fairly detached from everything, and everyone really. It's like, if he talks to you or has a drink with you, you're a friend, but he doesn't say much. But he'd be the first to stand at your back when you need it. You know the type."

Cussack nodded. "Had a friend like that myself once. Special Forces bloke. Only he'd rather kill for you than have a drink with you. Got a bit risky keeping him around." He grunted a short, deep laugh at the memory then let it go. "So, ... there's no-one special."

Rod pursed his lips and shook his head again. "The closest person to him I suppose is Sheila at the Hotel. She's sort of the town's adopted mother."

"Would he go there? Maybe dump the girl there?"

"Maybe. I wouldn't know of anywhere else."

"Let's ring her and find out," Cussack said, picking up the phone.

Rod looked wary. "Why not go there on our way back," he suggested. "The hotel is closed, and the only phone is in the bar. Sheila lives in the house next door and only has a connecting bell. It would take her a while to answer."

Looking about the kitchen, Rod hoped above all hopes Cussack was wrong. As much as Nick was a loner, he would be sadly missed. "Besides," he continued, "as much as she is all Nick has, the same goes for her. If there's any bad news to be given I'd like it to be given face to face."

Agreeing to the request, Cussack turned off the light and shut the door behind them. "We'll take care of this first, then, depending on what happens there, I think it's time to call in the boys from Homicide. This thing has gone too far."

"I just hope we find them alive," Rod replied as he pulled open the car door.

The Taylor brothers smiled at each other across the darkness: Luck was still with them.

Disappearing into the night, only a slight glow of red lights remaining, the Police sedan rounded the bend in the track. The Taylor brothers crept back to the house and settled in for the long wait.

McCaig received his phone call and was happy with the news: Manetti and the girl were still both at large, and as yet had not made contact with the Law. They would have to come home soon, Taylor assured him. It was bitterly cold outside and wherever Manetti was, he was on foot. They didn't have a vehicle between them, and they'd desperately be needing shelter.

"Maybe they went to her place," Ben suggested as he peered out the window.

"I doubt he could walk that far," Taylor half-laughed at the suggestion, then shrugged, "but take the car and go check it out."

A half hour later, Ben returned. There was no sign of them at Crestwood. The place was deserted, locked up tight. The only vehicle was a trail bike chained securely to a beam in the shed, signifying Coopers intended to be away a long time.

The waiting continued.

CHAPTER FIFTY-NINE

Several hours later.

I stirred as the scent of wattle and eucalypt drifted through the room, and shuffled closer to Nick, using his body to keep the chill from my back. His hand fell from his ribcage, draped along my thigh, his fingers squeezing momentarily to assess what had moved. I rolled towards him, his fleeting glance surveying his surroundings. His other hand clamped to the back of his neck and he groaned as pain erupted.

Propped up on an elbow, I watched him force off sleep, his eyelids seeming reluctant to stay open. "You sleep like the living dead," I said, admiring how handsome he was even with bruises.

He winced and slowly sat up. "Good, 'cose that's about how I feel." Balancing himself a little better he glanced at his wrist, but there was no watch there, only the small pale impression of where it had been. "What's the time?" he asked.

"Two o'clock."

One eyebrow rose. "Morning or afternoon?"

I laughed. "Morning."

"Mmmm," he sighed deeply. "Then we're not too late to get you into Dayton."

My cold bumps rose higher at his intention, and I could see the same prickled texture on his chest when he moved. The wind outside gusted fiercely, as it had most of the night, and branches creaked more frequently as they buckled to its will. Already I could feel the coldness in my throat.

Nick slid to the edge of the mattress, and slowly, with difficulty, pushed himself to his feet. The removal of his body made me even colder. "Come on," he said, "it's time we made a move."

Straightening to his superior height, he groaned loudly as pain, deep and unexpected, doubled him over. His hand locked to his ribs.

I rose, ready to follow him though logic pulled at my will. "I don't think you'll be going anywhere for a while," I aired my thoughts. "I don't think you'll get very far at all."

His dark eyes warned me not to question him. "We have no choice," he said, his voice strained. "For one, you're expected in Dayton, tonight." He attempted to straighten again, slower this time. "Secondly, if we don't make a move, we'll freeze up here." Already he was shivering visibly.

Consequence and Action tore through my brain: the cold would be worse outside, and what would happen once we were out there and he couldn't continue? One of us had to maintain some sense of sanity.

"Well the cold is just something we'll have to put up with," I contended, "because you aren't capable of reaching Dayton."

His fingers probed his left rib-cage, looking for broken bones, the dark look in his eyes telling me he might already have considered my statement. He half shrugged; breathed deeply to replace the air the pain had stolen. "Fair enough on that one, but we at least have to reach the house. We can phone Dayton and let them know you're safe."

"God'll love you for trying, but I bet you can't walk as far as the door," I scoffed.

His eyes hardened at my challenge. "I bet you're wrong!" His hand clamped tighter to his side, and he started moving. "... and when I get there," he said, sucking in another breath, "you'd better be ready to follow."

Coldness gripped my stomach. *Point to Learn: Never challenge Nick Manetti.* "Shit, Nick! At what point do you ever concede defeat?"

His eyebrow rose again as he looked back at me. Then he

smiled. "What's that?"

I stepped across the mattress, keeping up with him. "Look at you. You can't climb down like that! You won't make it down those drops."

He drew taut, combatting the pain of moving. "I got up here, didn't I? ... and I was ... worse than this." Even talking now was becoming an effort. "The pain in my head's gone, I can breathe easier ... and I promised to have you in Dayton tonight, and you're going to be there."

He reached the door; stabilised his balance on its framework. I caught him up, nudged him back against the wall to stabilise him further. Obviously it was going to take more than words to stop him getting out the door, so I pressed my hand against his damaged ribcage, a pseudo attempt to support him. He tilted over as his pain tripled. "Look at you! You can't!"

He moved my hand higher and forced another breath in. "Take a look around you, kid," he said breathlessly. "There's no fire, no heater, no blankets. It's cold enough now ... In another two hours it's going to be unbearable. Then what are you going to do? If we make our way down now thirty minutes of cold wind and you'll have all those comforts and a bed to sleep in. ... we don't have any alternative."

I shook my head. "The name's Becky!" For some reason, the way he said "Kid" really grated on me. "And the way I see it, you'll get part way down, flake out on the slope and freeze to death. And there won't be a damn thing I can do to stop it. You're too damn big for me to carry!"

I fought off a shudder, the cold already tightening my muscles and making them ache. "Why can't we stay here and go down in the morning. I can cope with the cold for one night. I'm not a baby! Besides, what are you going to do if they're down there waiting for us? You're not going to be much help to me then, are you?" I threw in the last round of ammunition: Logic.

His face hardened at the thought. Obviously he hadn't

considered that. Sighing deeply, he glanced around the shack then sighed with resignation. "Point taken," he conceded, and I sighed with the deepest relief. "Okay, we stay."

His gaze settled on the kapok mattress in the corner and he nodded. Removing my hand from his body, he moved slowly back across the room.

"What are you doing?"

"Making our bed. Take off that jacket," he ordered.

My jaw dropped open. That was a sudden change of behaviour! "That's not what I had in mind!" I frowned.

He grinned widely, and proceeded to drag the mattress already on the floor over to the corner where a second one stood propped against the wall. Together we pulled the second one to curve around the two walls and lapped it over the top of the first. Two brown field mice scurried out from behind the mattress and scuttled across the floor, and I couldn't miss Nick's eyes flicking up to gauge my reaction. Mice were mice, sometimes cute, sometimes annoying when they chewed into my bags of horse feed. I'd move them along but never kill them. I watched them now as they skittered across to the farther wall and ran down its length to disappear out through the crack in the door. I looked back at him unperturbed, more important things now swirling through my mind: like, how could I avoid lying down with Nick Manetti; how could I lie down next to Nick Manetti without wanting to hold him; without revealing my very desperate need to be with him in more ways than he intended. Already my skin was heating.

I folded my arms to quell the annoying sensation in my breasts. *Damn him.* It was so annoying how he could produce these reactions over which I had no control.

The kapok windbreak completed, Nick lowered himself gingerly into its curve and leant back against it; he looked pleased that the wind seeping through the walls had been blocked. "I said, take off the jacket," he ordered again.

Huffing my annoyance, for without the jacket my body's reactions would be more visible, I shucked it from my shoulders and tossed it down to him. He caught it and put it aside then patted the mattress beside him, his extended arm inviting me to lie beside him. "Come on. We can keep each other warm."

Manic rabbits tore up my spine, and the butterflies fluttering across my breasts made my face heat. My heart flipped crazy loop the loops just at the thought of his touch then bolted out of control, taking my breath away. I shook my head. It was one thing to lie down beside him while he was sleeping, it was totally another to lie beside him while he was awake. I was bound to do something indelibly stupid. And my rapid heartbeat would undoubtedly give my thoughts away.

I stared down at him, and shook my head. *Keep your distance, keep your pride.* And I certainly didn't need a reoccurrence of clinging to him in the night, as wonderful as it had been. Regardless of what he thought, I wasn't a cry baby.

"Oh hey!" he said, suddenly realising my thoughts. "It's not what you think. For one, I don't touch kids, and sec ..."

That did it! "Okay, you whoa there, Nick Manetti!' I flounced. "I've had about as much of that as I can take. I'll have you know I haven't been a 'kid' for a bloody long time."

His eyes smiled, and an eyebrow rose in contradiction. No words necessary.

My glare burned him, the heat on my face equatorial. "Huh! Well if I'm a kid you must be an old man."

Giant arms folded across his chest as he stared back at me, his eyes exuding that annoying glimmer that inflamed my temper. "Compared to you, I guess I am," he said.

My jaw dropped. "Humph! Well, Grandpop, I bet there's not more than ... what? ... four, maybe five years between us. What are you? Twenty-six? Twenty-seven?"

His eyebrow rose in query of where this was going. "Twenty-eight," he answered frankly.

"Yeah, well that's really old, Grandpop!" Every single time he'd used 'kid' came boiling back to the surface. "And seeing there's only what?... seven years between us ... that doesn't make me a kid!"

His eyebrow hiked again, just slightly, and quandary crossed his face. Then his smile flickered, but he pulled it back almost before I'd noticed. "Well good for you," he retorted, "you can count! But it still doesn't change things." He shifted to get more comfortable, worked to place his ribs in a position that hurt less, which meant bending more over the injured side.

"I also don't complicate my life with women and rash affairs so come down here so we can keep each other warm."

His words cut like a knife, dulled my heartbeat, stopped it in that instant. Nick doesn't complicate his life with women. There it was in a nutshell.

"And neither do I," I snapped, realising I should have expected it. Nick didn't complicate his life with women, and whether he looked at me as a woman, or as a kid, I came into that female category. I stared down at him, wondering what life would be like for him given he was only a shell of a man, and I sighed heavily. He scowled, and his lips thinned at my reluctance to do as told. My own lips tightened in response.

Before I could answer his boot hooked in behind my left knee and pulled forward, toppling me off balance and dropping me forward to the mattress. I landed on top of him, my hand unwittingly striking his chest as I fell.

"I don't ask a third time!" he rebuked, rubbing at the pain I'd caused. His other arm opened to receive me, drew me in beside him.

Blood rushed through my veins as I shuffled into the fold of his arm, as he drew me closer into the curve of his shoulder. I curled up tight, my hand on his skin, his chest feeling like smooth hard stone, cold and solid, his muscles moving warily beneath the subtle layer of goose-bumped skin. His arm curved around to contain me, his hand resting on my hip having great effect in boiling my blood. If he wanted to get warm, I was now generating enough heat for us both.

"And I promise, I won't touch," he said deeply.

"I know. You're practising to be a monk," I retorted.

I glanced up, hoping he would get as angry as I was, but he smiled, a broad grin I would cherish forever. "Yeah, and with you around I'll get a lot of practice."

He pulled the woollen jacket across our torsos, closing out the cold, increasing the body heat below, and he shuffled a little closer. He raised one knee to get more comfortable, and his big arm draped over me, pulling me into the breadth of him until my head rested on his chest. I could hear his big heart thumping deep within, his strength tripling my warmth.

"So why does everyone call you 'kid'?" he asked softly when I'd settled in against him.

It was nice that he'd asked. "It's a nickname. I've been the youngest rider on the senior jumping circuit for so long," I explained, "they forgot over the years that I grew up! And with Granddad always entering me under the nickname, the name sort of stuck."

His arms wrapped around me tighter and I lay enjoying our closeness, hoping my quivering would be blamed on the cold.

CHAPTER SIXTY

Startled from her sleep by loud banging, Sheila sat bolt upright. "My Lord, what on earth's going on?" she spluttered. She peered at the luminous figures of the clock face. "Two-thirty!"

Pulling her floral gown on over her nightdress, she hurried to the front door.

"Heavy sleeper," Cussack commented to Rod as he rapped his knuckles hard against the wood a third time.

A meek voice came from behind the barrier. "Who is it?"

Rod told her, and the latches clicked and the verandah light went on. A crack appeared in the doorway and a face peered out through the slit, one eye showing first.

The door opened fully.

"What's the problem, Rod? And whatever are you boys doing out so late?" She blinked wearily then focused on the second man, his unfamiliar face taking seconds to calculate. "You must be the new Sergeant!" Cussack nodded, and she turned back to Rod. "Now, what's up then?"

"Sheila, we need to know ..." Even though Rod had rehearsed his words carefully on the way over he faltered, fumbling for the right phrase that would cause her the least alarm. She was onto him in a flash.

"It's Nick ... isn't it?" she said, the tiredness instantly falling from her face. "Well?" Her grey eyes darted from one to the other. "Isn't it!"

"Well, maybe," Rod hedged, subduing her panic. "We don't rightly know yet, Sheila." He fidgeted with his hat. "Can we come in a moment?"

She pulled the door open and led the way down the passage,

Cussack's eyes roving deftly room by room as they followed her. By the time he'd reached the lounge-room, he was sure the house was otherwise unoccupied.

Halfway across the room, Sheila turned back. "What's happened?" But Rod countered it with a question of his own.

"Sheila, did Nick leave someone with you? Someone to hide? It's urgent for us to know, and okay for you to tell us, regardless of what Nick might have said."

Sheila shook her head.

"... Did he tell you anything? ... maybe where he's hidden her?'"

"Hidden who? What are you talking about?" she snapped. "And where is Nick?"

Cussack intervened. "Nick was hiding someone for us, Mrs McKenzie ..." His roving eyes centred on a photograph of a young soldier on the side table, "... keeping them safe ... only now he didn't show when he was supposed to, and the girl is missing too."

Immediately Sheila looked less frightened, and rubbed the worry from her brow. "Oh, is that all it is?" she sighed. "You needn't worry, Sergeant. Nick will show up when he's ready. He doesn't pay much attention to time, you know."

"It's not that simple, Sheila," Rod intervened. "We've been out to his place. There's been trouble. His truck is wrecked ..."

The lady's face turned ashen again and she stood a moment as the details registered, as she linked it to the severity of the town's problems. Her knees weakening, she plopped down into a chair.

"... and there's been evidence of fighting."

Cussack pulled the broken watch from his pocket and held it in his open hand.

Sheila's hand went to her throat and tears welled in her eyes. "Oh my God!"

"We were hoping the girl might be here," Rod said softly.

Sheila shook her head then looked up. "But he'll come here," she said. "He'll come here."

'If he can, Mrs McKenzie." Cussack looked down at her. "I don't suppose you'd know of any other place he might go, do you? Somewhere safe?"

Sheila shook her head again and wiped away a tear. "Wherever Nick is, is safe," she murmured, the words more a whisper to herself than to them.

Maybe not any more, Cussack thought as he stared down at her. "Well, if he shows up, get him to ring us, urgently," he said, leaving her a little hope. He laid a printed contact card on the settee beside her.

Sheila nodded but didn't look up, nor did she rise to see them out, her legs too weak to support her. She heard the door click shut, the motor start up and the car pull onto the highway. The sound of its motor faded quickly, and she was alone again. Maybe permanently.

CHAPTER SIXTY-ONE

I woke as a thin strip of grey peered under the wooden door, the kerosene lamp having burned itself out in the pre-dawn hours. Outside, birds chortled and whistled, a peaceful orchestra that melded with the fragrances assailing my senses, making me forget all but the blissful moment of waking in the country so early in the morning. I inhaled deeply, savouring it. Yawned. In the headiness of smells I picked up another scent, more pleasant than the wattle; snuggled deeper into the warm blankets around me and sighed again.

Another yawn as I stretched and turned to find more space as that other scent stirred me; became familiar. *Old Spice!* I stopped moving, realising the warmth of my pillow, which had a strong and vibrant heartbeat. Nick's arms were wrapped around me, their weight trapping me against him as I lay along his length. Chilling, I prayed he wasn't awake; wondered how I could extract myself without disturbing him. His steady breathing seemed more rhythmic than the night before, which proved that staying had been the right decision, and, if that was the case, then the longer he slept the better.

I winced that my thigh lay across his thigh, my lower leg lying between his calves. It would be damn difficult to extract myself without disturbing him. Yet I had to for, if he woke, this position would be embarrassing. I had to move.

Quietly I eased my hand from behind his neck; felt the woollen jacket pull up higher and press in around my shoulders, his hand gently pushing it there. Cringing, I cursed silently that he was already awake, and looked up.

He looked down at me, smiling that confounded smile he

used when amused by someone else's discomfort. "Sleep well?" he asked.

My face flushed with colour and I moved away from him, pushed myself to my knees. Before I moved too far he gripped my arm, twisted it to read the time on my watch. It was eleven o'clock. We'd slept the morning away.

Groaning, Nick sat up and stretched the tightness from his muscles, clicked the bones free in his neck and shoulders then climbed, grimacing, to his feet. "We'd better make a move," he said, pulling me up after him. Urgency seemed the order of the day now we had woken. I caught the jacket he tossed me and watched as he gathered the knapsack. "We'll stop at the truck first," he said, stowing the items back into it. "If it isn't too bad, I'll get you straight into Dayton."

Travelling downhill was easier than going up, except for a few slippery drops Nick helped me over. We headed slightly more east than before, the line intended to bring us out close to the truck. Eventually its yellow body dappled through the trees, growing larger and larger as the bush thinned out.

Nick's truck sat in the open, leaning to the right, a crippled victim of a lost battle. He groaned when he saw it, and pulled me close beside him as he stood concealed behind the broad scarred trunk of a jarrah tree. His eyes darkened as he stared at the slashed tyres.

"No point even going out there," he said with a dejected sigh. "I only have one spare ..." His fist thumped hard against the tree trunk. "Shit!"

As the deepening hue overtook his eyes I looked elsewhere to avoid his anger. Above us, rolling clouds tried to fill the sky and rain would soon be on us. "What do we do now?" I asked, drawing Nick's attention away from the truck.

"We go up to the house as planned and phone Rod to come and get you."

He pointed the direction to travel, a line along the slope but still within the scrub. He started moving, following the belt line and staying within its cover. Occasionally he stopped to listen; and it was not hard to pick the edginess growing within him as if he expected something was about to happen. I felt it too.

At the point where the track crossed over to the house, we stood for a long time, Nick watching, studying the surroundings, listening to everything around him. His big hand pressed me close in behind him, making sure I didn't move from where he'd placed me.

"I don't know," he murmured deeply. "Something just feels wrong." He raked a hand slowly through his hair, his dark eyes now intense.

"Looks clear enough to me," I whispered, shrugging that indeed everything looked exactly as we'd left it.

"I know. I just have this feeling."

"Maybe it's just that we're getting so close ..."

"Maybe," he nodded. "Yeah, maybe."

When he stepped out onto the gravel track I again became his shadow.

CHAPTER SIXTY-TWO

Inside Northgate's cosy kitchen, Ben Taylor slept, his head on the table, his loud open-mouthed breathing reverberating through the room. His rifle rested lightly against the table leg, always at the ready. Even in his sleep he could snatch and fire and probably hit his target.

Annoyed by the raspy droning, Dave swung his thick solid legs down from the kitchen bench where he'd stretched out, his back pressed against the wall. It was a great view out the window – one window looked west towards the track wending up to Northgate's upper pastures, the larger northern window overlooked the drive and Manetti's immobilised truck. He gave the table leg a sharp kick, the jolt rebounding onto Ben who bolted upright, his big hand snatching up the rifle in that instant. Dave stretched exuberantly, his back to the window as he let out a muscle-waking yawn.

"It's your turn to watch a while," he said as Ben retracted the aim. "And keep an eye on the road. We don't want to be caught by the coppers coming back. It'll be harder to get outta here now it's daylight."

Ben swung onto the bench. "I don't think Manetti's coming here at all," he griped, frustrated with the long hours of waiting. "They're out there somewhere wandering around, and we should be out there looking."

"Nah!" Dave shook his head, more accustomed to waiting than Ben. "You're too hasty," he laughed. "You'd never have lasted in our Unit, boy. We'd sit for days not moving an inch, just waiting for something to happen. If you moved as much as an inch, you'd be on remand. Compared to us, you're Unit was a pussy brigade.'

"Yeah? Well compared to anything, this is just plain boring."

"So? Just think what comes at the end of it. Death comes at the end of it. Manetti's, and the girl's."

But that wasn't enough for Dave. Some key element was missing from the task, something that should have kept his nerves on edge: the risk factor. He'd fathomed some time during the night it was that undeniable element that kept him waiting and watching. In the war, if you fouled up on watch, the risk was death. But here, that didn't apply. For one, he shared the watch, which made it lose its intensity, and secondly, Manetti was going to walk right smack-dab into the point of his gun. He needed more intensity!

He raided the fridge, found a few cold beers to replace intensity's absence and tossed one over to Ben. Flipping the lid, he cured the dry patch in his throat. "They'll be here," he said confidently. "I can feel it."

Indeed he could feel it. His bones vibrated with anticipation, stirring him deep to the core. He would feel like this just before a prey appeared; like a sudden premonition; a quivering hunch. His prey was close now ... so very, very close. "They must have held up overnight somewhere, but they'll be here ..." he added, "maybe when it gets warmer."

"Yeah? Well I don't think it's going to. Look at that cloud bank coming in over there."

Through the west window, large black clouds boiled threateningly over the coast, bubbling downward, and a strong wind churned them to the ground. "There's a lot of rain in those babies," he added as he settled in to watch their growing mass.

CHAPTER SIXTY-THREE

Before Nick had taken two steps onto the red gravel track, he grabbed my arm and hauled me back to the trees. His massive back pinned against the trunk we'd just left as he pulled me hard against him. His head tipped back as he caught the breath he'd lost in the sudden sharp move and his heart thumped hard against my hand.

"We're not alone," he answered my unspoken question.

Leaning around the tree trunk, he checked again, and nodded that he was right. "The thicket's been disturbed, and there's something white amongst it. And the kitchen blinds are up – we left them down." He inhaled deeply; let it out again, settling his nerves. "Well, that option's out. I think we have visitors."

He looked down at me. "I don't suppose you have a spare set of wheels at your place."

I shook my head. "Dad's got his car with him, and mine's on the road down there ... Do you think we could make it to mine? It'll be safe enough seeing they're here."

Nick shook his head. "Yours is in the towing yard in Cullan. Rod sent it in to get it off the road."

"Shit! Doesn't anything go in our favour?"

Nick smiled grimly then stole another look at the thicket. When he looked down at me again, possibilities danced in his eyes. They weren't nice possibilities.

"Maybe I could nick down and steal their car," he said. "I can pick you up here once I have it."

I knew by the look in his eyes the risk he'd be taking, and shook my head.

"We don't have any choice." He turned and scanned the

bushes behind the house again, sizing up his chances. Then I remembered ...

"What about a bike?" I said, tapping his chest till he turned. "My brother has a trail-bike. Would that do?"

His face brightened, a look I would cherish. He nodded and said: "Let's go!"

Pushing me ahead of him, we cut a path directly uphill again, stooping low and sneaking through denser scrub. Nick said we would cross the track higher over the crest where we could move from one tree belt to the next without being seen. While it was a longer route to take, it was the safest one. He picked the direction, carefully manoeuvring his way through prickly parrot bush as he sought the easiest path to take. I kept pace with him, most of the time, and he kept glancing back to make sure I didn't lag behind. Tiring as it was, I pushed on relentlessly, remembering Sam's words as the need for my morning coffee started to rise ... tea was a fopsy's drink, and Marilyn drank tea. That made Marilyn a fopsy in Nick's eyes. I never wanted to be seen as a fopsy so pushed on harder, and made sure I stayed with him.

Ignoring the rocky ground that repeatedly slid away and almost turned my ankles, I prised back the nettles constantly stinging my legs. If Nick could ignore them, so could I. But the distance seemed interminable, even though he made it as easy as he could.

Over the crest, we stooped and scuttled across the gravel track, stayed crouched low until concealed again in the heavy jarrah shelter belt that joined Crestwood and Northgate. In time, the wires of the boundary fence appeared, and we climbed through and continued walking, now on Crestwood soil. Some time passed before the brush thinned out again.

Nick slowed his pace as our bungalow-style homestead came into sight, the building looming larger and whiter the nearer we drew. It was a compact home set amid a well-kept border of green lawns and colourful gardens, my mother having restored them from their previous droughty state. She had maintained the pioneer practice of no large trees near the house, reducing the risk of losing all to fire.

I gathered Nick noticed that too for his jaw muscle flexed as he screened the open ground between us and the house. We would have to cross open paddocks and would risk being seen. He sank down behind a tree, rubbed his ribcage and winced as I arrived beside him, puffing from the effort I'd made to keep him in sight.

He looked up. "I knew it had been too easy," he complained, stealing another look around the tree. I dropped down beside him. *Easy!* I was nearly spent.

He scanned the long corrugated-iron shed to the right of the house, a shed that also sat well within the vast expanse of open space. "The bike?" he asked, thumbing towards it.

I nodded. "But the keys are in the house."

"That's not the problem," he replied. "Getting across there is."

He looked back through the trees to Northgate. Even from where we sat the sheds were visible, the white utility even more apparent on the southern edge of the hedge. They would only have to come out to the car while we were dashing across the paddock and we were thwarted.

But I had more important things on my mind right then, and found what I was looking for. My heart soared above Cloud 9 for Jerry and Millstream grazed peacefully by the wind-belt, safe.

My scent must have carried on the wind because Millstream lifted his head and nickered, a short whuffling sound that said 'you haven't fed me yet'. *I know, I know.* He ambled across the field towards me.

I rose to meet him as Nick took another long look at the house. When Millstream blocked my view of Northgate I edged away from the scrub and swung over the top wire into the paddock. It was so good to touch his velvet coat, to feel the life in his veins when I'd been so scared they would both have been dead. My fingers curled gently over his nose to contain him.

When Nick turned back to check Northgate again, he cursed and scrambled to his feet. "Get the hell back here!" he growled, his dark eyes darting from me to Northgate. "Come on!"

"No, you come on," I beckoned. "You want to get across there, well come on. I'll show you how."

Staying below Millstream's back, I gripped his mane and, with one hand guiding his nose, moved him closer to the fence. "Come on, baby. Come on, come on." I soothed. "He misses all the pampering," I smiled at Nick as I stroked Millstream's long warm face. "Come on," I beckoned Nick again, "it's an old Indian trick … you're the back end."

Reluctantly Nick scaled the wire, crouched low and made the distance between me and the fence then ducked below the height of Millstream's rump. Clicking the bay on, I guided him towards where I kept the feed, making it an easy steerage towards the house, our legs concealed by Millstream's legs, our bodies hunched below the height of his back. "I used to avoid Dad like this when he was mad at me," I admitted. "It's quite effective."

At the boundary fence, we climbed through the next set of wires, and, being careful to keep Millstream between us and Northgate, we ran stooped the last few yards up the lawn to the house where the garden concealed us.

Nick tried the back door and looked annoyed. "Do you lock up everything?" he said.

"Always."

He huffed and shook his head then moved round to the western side of the house, but the windows there were also well secured. "Give me your jacket," he ordered. I slipped off his jacket and handed it over; frowned as he wrapped it several times around his elbow.

"What are you doing?"

"Breaking in." He caught my dissension. "Don't worry, I'll

repair the damage!"

"I'll hold you to that," I scoffed. "This is my room."

Positioning himself in front of the window, he struck the glass with a sharp rap of his elbow. The pane cracked and fell apart, leaving a hole in the lower right corner. Unravelling the jacket, Nick gave it a good shake and handed it back to me then slipped his arm carefully through the opening and reached up and snicked the catch. The frame slid silently up.

"Now that really worries me. You do that so well."

He drew me across in front of him and legged me up to the sill; waited till I'd shinnied inside before pulling himself up over the ledge.

"Get the key," he told me.

Obligingly I disappeared down the passage and turned in at Jason's room, Nick following me part of the way; he stopped to open the drapes in the front room the merest crack and peer out, but all outside was quiet and still.

By the time I'd found the key and returned, he'd picked up the phone and had dialled a number, which was quickly answered.

"Is Rod there?" he said. From his expression, I gleaned he wasn't. "I don't know when I can get to a phone again so just tell Rod Nick is on his way in," he said. His eyes lifted and focused on me. "Tell him I'll be coming in the long way – there's some not so friendly people on our tail. He'll know what I mean."

He hung up and I held the keys aloft.

He hurried me back to my room, a room dominated by a double bed quilted with frilly pink lace, Mum's idea not mine. Nick stood staring down at the bed, and I wondered as I reefed open the wardrobe and yanked out a warm size 10 jacket if he was needing to rest up again. He looked back at me as I shucked off his jacket and tossed it across to him, his torn bloodied shirt providing him little warmth. "Here, you'll need this. It's still pretty cold outside."

He caught the coat and put it on then took another long look out the window. When everything remained perfectly still, he said it was time to move.

Dumping the knapsack inside my wardrobe, he slipped back out the window, caught me by the waist as I followed and hoisted me to the ground. Then he pulled the window shut.

Jason's bright green trail bike leant against an upright in the shed, well maintained and heavily chained. Nick nodded as he looked at it, and smiled, the look in his eye indicating he thought we had a chance.

Clasping my hand, he pulled me after him as he crossed the open space. He unlocked the padlock, and unravelled the chain from the wheels, dropped it into a rattling pile on the floor. He removed the petrol cap and checked the fuel. The tank was about half full, which he said was plenty to get to Dayton.

He pushed the cycle out and swung his leg over the seat. "Come on. Hop on," he ordered when he'd successfully started it. I swung up behind him, my hands light on his waist, like when I rode with Jason. But Nick took my hands and hauled them around in front of him, shouting above the now high-whining two-stroke. "Where we're going you're going to have to do better than that!"

So I leant further forward, locked my arms tightly around him, pressed my head in against his back and held on like my life depended on it. Satisfied, he turned the cycle in a tight arc, opened the throttle and headed away up the hill to the shelter of the highest tree belt. We were on our way to Dayton.

CHAPTER SIXTY-FOUR

Ben hummed absently as he stared out over the driveway, his head bobbing in time with his hands which tapped a recurring beat on the kitchen bench. "Bom bom bom bom – tap tap tap – bom bom bom bom – tap tap tap – bom bom bom ..."

"Will you shut that crap up!" Dave finally erupted.

The passing, unproductive hours had slowly impressed on Dave the futility of the cause. Furthermore, the vibrations of his prey's impending arrival had left him some time ago, and doubt had filled its place.

"What's wrong with you?" Ben whined. "Nothing wrong with a good bit of music. Great day, huh? Music, and beer – only thing missing is a little bit of hot sexuality ... now that would make a really great song title, wouldn't it? Music, beer and a little bit of hot ..."

"Shut up!"

"You sound like you need a bit too," Ben persisted, deciding being annoying was better than being bored.

Far off, the ming-ming-ming of a high whining engine broke through Ben's prattle. Dave listened intently as it competed with the screeching cacophony of black cockatoos fleeing the trees.

"Chain saw," Ben predicated slowly.

Dave shook his head. "That engine's fading. Didn't you say there was a trail bike over at Crestwood?"

"Yeah, locked in the shed." He swung down off the bench.

"A two-stroke? ... Jap bike?"

"How'd you know?"

"Did you disable it?"

"No."

"Well I bet it's not there now." He snatched up his shotgun. "Get the bloody car!"

Minutes later, they reached Crestwood and found the shed that had held the cycle empty, a length of chain piled on the floor, the open padlock through its last link for easy finding. Dave picked up the hand mike from the dashboard and made several urgent calls until McCaig finally answered.

"I read you," the tired voice replied.

Taylor chose his words and tone carefully. "Get the boys on the road, Boss. Our good friends are heading your way ... destination Dayton. Make contact will you. We're following up."

McCaig copied his cheerfulness. "We're moving at this end. Will look forward to meeting them on the road. Keep in touch."

"Will do. Out."

Smiling, Taylor tossed the mike back onto the seat and examined the tyre tracks in the dirt. They headed northwest which surprised him. Dayton was due south, and he wondered what Manetti was playing at.

Standing for long seconds, he stared at the northbound track, trying to understand his rival's logic. Finally he got back in the ute. "Follow him," he told Ben. "I don't know what he's doing, but it's not going to help. We'll just keep moving along behind them and push them down to McCaig."

Grinning, Ben accelerated along the gravel that skirted the tree belt, the sound of the whining engine no longer audible. It was almost two-thirty. It was Monday afternoon.

CHAPTER SIXTY-FIVE

Elated at hearing Manetti's voice, Brett Waddell picked up the two-way's microphone. The news was bound to cure the depressed atmosphere that had spread throughout the station, that had spread over Rod Willcox in particular. The Senior Connie had sat silent for hours after their late night visit to Northgate, refusing to go home in case news arrived; he'd even taken an extra shift to be around if news came through. He was now out of the office, the Sergeant requiring all available officers at a road crash near Kaljani. It was obviously a bad one for already he'd put a call through to Nanadine and Dayton for ambulances, and both Police vehicles from Dayton attended the scene. He cursed himself for being the youngest and most subordinate constable for again it meant he had to fly the desk. Maybe, he considered glumly, if he took a city posting, this wouldn't happen so often.

He depressed the button on the hand-piece. "Patrol One. Patrol One. Come in, Patrol." He waited, resisting the urge to repeat the call when a response was a long time coming. Then he did repeat, for this was important too.

A crackling came over the speaker: "This is Patrol One, HQ."

It sounded like Willcox. Or maybe Ray Smedley. Both sounded alike. "Is the Sergeant available? Over." He stuck to protocol in case he was. New Sergeants could be arseholes when it came to correct procedure.

"Not at present. There's a lot of action here right now and he's pretty tied up. Can I pass anything on?"

Ah, Smedley. He could tell by the phraseology. "Affirmative.

Tell the Sarge ... and Rod," he almost whispered the latter, "that Manetti is still with us and is on his way in. Over."

Cussack stood up as the voices carried to him on the wind. He signalled for Carter to take over his task and headed for the radio, tapping Rod on the shoulder as he passed. Taking the microphone from Smedley he leant in through the car window to reduce wind distortion. "This is Cussack. I heard the message. How did he sound?"

Brett paused a moment. "Okay, I guess, but he said he'd be taking the long way in to avoid his unfriendlies. Over."

Cussack looked at Rod, his brow furrowing deeply. "Anything else?"

"No sir ..."

"Well good job. Keep us informed if there is, and ... lighten up on the radio, son." The Sergeant tossed the mike down, smiled subtly as life returned to Willcox's face. "I'm looking forward to meeting this friend of yours. I like what he's made of," he said. "He should be a cop."

Rod chuckled. "He said he's not that stupid," to which came no response.

Cussack surveyed the scene in front of him. Bodies were strewn everywhere. Some human, the rest sheep. Ambulances wailed eerily as they arrived to tend the humans while members from Dayton's Volunteer Emergency Service darted back and forth, lugging equipment to prise apart the vehicles in an effort to clear the road. Every so often the retort of a rifle ruptured conversation as another animal's suffering was healed. The roadway remained blocked by the over-turned Semi and the mangled wreckage of what had once been a family sedan, the vehicle still partly embedded in the steep embankment. A child's teddy lay on the roadside bathed in a puddle of fuel.

"I'd like to send a car to escort them in," Cussack finally admitted, his eyes settling on the teddy and realising that he really wasn't as hardened by experience as he'd thought. Accidents with kids always did this to him. Shaking his head, he looked away, the severity of the present situation forming his decision, "... but I really can't spare one just yet."

Rod shrugged in consolation. "You'd probably be wasting your time. Nick's long way could be any way ... by Kilcannie, by the coastal road, or even along farmer's back roads. He knows this country like the back of his hand and if necessary could take hours to shake off whoever's after them."

"I just want to make sure he makes it in this time."

Rod worried only slightly. "Mmmm, but he's careful. If he can survive three years in Nam, he'll survive a short trip to Dayton." A smile flickered in his eyes. "My bet is he'll lead them on a merry chase."

"Well I hope so. You lot make him sound invincible."

Rod laughed and moved back to his task. "Well I guess in a way he is."

"Yeah, well I sure hope so. I'd like to give him back his watch."

The wailing sirens wound down as ambulances drew to a halt, the red flashing spinners still arcing and pulsing across the scene. Orange lights approached noiselessly in the distance. It would be a long while before the highway was clear, and Cussack cursed the time. Again he'd missed his coffee break.

Part Four

The Chase

CHAPTER SIXTY-SIX

Nick made a direct run along the gravel to the top of our farm and braked in front of the boundary gate to Northgate. Dropping his foot to the ground, he looked back over his shoulder. "You're on gate duty, kiddo," he yelled, so I swung from the pillion and ran ahead to swing the gate wide open. Nick rode through, and waited on the other side, wincing slightly as the sharp kwak-kwak-kwak retorted in his ears. He was rubbing his neck below the cut when I swung back up behind him.

"If you were a horse, that's about three stitches worth," I said, leaning forward again, "so leave it alone or you'll make it bleed again."

He nodded and I wrapped my arms around him again, much firmer this time, my arms running vertically up his chest for better purchase.

We sped along the track that ran across the top of Northgate, making good time even though we were heading away from Dayton. Nick's muscles rolled and bunched as he avoided deep puddles on either side of the track, as he skirted wider pools without slowing down. He handled the cycle so well I felt safe, much safer than I'd ever felt with Jason, and I had something more substantial to hold onto. On the next braking however Nick skidded the bike. I almost toppled off and I realised I had better stay focused. I swung down and ran ahead to the gate that opened to the road.

Nick crawled the cycle through, turned left and waited, his expression this time deep and broody as I worked the gate latch. A strange look had crossed his face when I turned, and I wondered what he was thinking; wondered if he'd suddenly realised the danger he was in; wondered if he thought me an absolute pain and that he should ditch me as soon as he could. That's what I'd been thinking he should do, so why not him?

My eyes locking with his made him aware he was staring and he lowered his gaze. I swung back onto the bike and resumed my vertical embrace only this time my hand inadvertently slipped inside his open jacket and rested on smooth skin. He looked down then opened the throttle wider, his chest seeming to expand beneath my hand.

We were now on looser gravel where one wrong move would send us scooting down the road without a bike, but Nick kept it steady. Under full throttle the motor squealed louder as we created a muddy wake all along the top of Weldon Road.

The Taylor brothers had just climbed the first slope towards the trees on Crestwood.

CHAPTER SIXTY-SEVEN

At the next road junction, Nick stopped again to check the roads for options. Roads went north and south. Traffic was nil.

"We'll take the scenic route," he yelled, to which I nodded. Scenic sounded good. In fact, any way to Dayton was fine by me.

He crossed the road and entered the long red driveway of Schuman's farm. All the while a low ceiling of heavy black clouds rolled further inland, the cold, relentless wind chilling my hands and making Nick shiver.

Veering onto a left curving track, he steered the bike between rock and scrub, accelerated over a ridge and down the other side. We crossed a creek, which splattered mud and water up our legs, and passed through two open gateways. Another road appeared, and another gate. I scrambled off, and Nick took the opportunity to zip up the jacket to stop the wind freezing him. A slight drizzle had now started to fall.

"Cold?" I noted as I came back to the bike. He nodded as I used his body to swing back aboard.

The next stretch took us across Perry's land, and out onto the highway, and a mile later we shot up another driveway to skirt through Marsh's Fields. We shot across another side road then back in through a gate into Carter's, Nick steering a course ever southward, running along the western side of a ridge that stretched the length of *Dam'ard*.

Crossing the main bitumen drive that linked the Carter homestead to the Northern Highway, he pumped the farm bike to the top of the ridge, its high bouncing wheel almost dislodging me from the pillion. My grip pulling against him reminded Nick I was there. At the top of the hill, he stopped to survey the land, to check how much farther we could go across the farmlands. He pointed out two more gateways, after which a series of gullies at the floodway would make it difficult going. But they were not impassable, he said. He'd ridden them before.

"Look, we're level with Nundajora!" I realised, looking east.

Nick must have felt my shudder for his hand dropped to my thigh – he seemed to know what was running through my mind. He pushed on, steering the cycle down across the ridge, cutting a path toward the first southern gateway. The slight annoying drizzle intensified, became angled by occasional gusts of wind. We skirted a dam, its vast surface crinkling as it caught the winter offerings and I realised as we skirted it, Pete was right – it was the largest in the district, more a small lake than a dam.

Partway across the valley Nick stopped the cycle again, and stared back at where we'd been; stared back at two long furrows in particular that fed water into the dam. More gouges than furrows, I thought. Nick stared at the dam, a frown creasing his brow. He turned the bike and rode back up the hill. From there he scanned the dam again and I clearly saw the furrows starting from the bitumen driveway. Nick's heart beat started thudding beneath his jacket. He cut the engine and started to lay the bike down before I was even off it.

"What is it?" I asked, swinging clear before it pinned my leg to the ground. "What's wrong?"

He laid the bike against the lean of the hill and walked long strides back down the slope, and I had to jog at times to keep up with him. All the while his eyes scanned the water's surface. He circled round the dam wall, shaking his head, but still said nothing.

At the top of the highest bank he stopped, and his jaw set firm as he studied the water. Wordlessly he stripped his jacket and handed it to me then pulled off his boots.

"What the hell are you doing?"

"Going swimming," he said, his voice unusually deep.

"You're crazy, Nick! You're plumb downright crazy!"

"Yeah, I hope so," he said dully. The solemnness of his expression doused further words. I stood staring as he slipped down the steep embankment into the crinkled water.

The icy chill took his breath away, and he gulped a breath to replace it. Drawing in two more full deep breaths, he ducked beneath the surface of the dam.

CHAPTER SIXTY-EIGHT

Below, the water appeared as it was on top, a bright bluish-green, slightly shadowed brown around the edges where recent rains had rushed soil over the sides of its banks. The brown however was even more prevalent at a point below the furrows — a reddish-brown more constant in the sediment.

Nick dragged himself down into the water's depths hoping above all hopes his line of thinking was wrong, but he couldn't betray his instincts. He couldn't betray what his trained eye had told him.

Gritting his teeth as the water froze him from outside to in, he forced himself to keep going, forced himself to not to think of it. He looked back to the surface, the dim filtering of light above now struggling to penetrate the deep.

Swirling water aside with his hands, he propelled himself down to the murky stain which loomed redder and redder in front of him. He pushed deeper, his next stroke hitting hard. Not bottom! He knew that. Metal. A plate of wide red metal. The shadow had been real.

The wide sheet spread out before him and although he'd expected it, the shock expelled half the air from his lungs. Inwardly he wanted to release it so he could take another breath, so he could rest the tension gripping his insides, but to do that he'd have to surface ... *So do it! Do it now!*

No! You just want to prolong the inevitable. You aren't even straining yet! So get it over with!

He groped for a handhold, for anything to help pull himself lower, to keep himself down. He found the rim of the roof and locked his grip on, pain instantly biting into his hand, shooting up his arm like a glowing hot poker. A cry tore from his mouth, expelling more of his air before he could stop it. But still he held his grip. His blood mixed with the water as he lowered himself further, as he lowered himself level with the fragmented windscreen. His lungs straining and threatening to implode, his eyes stinging in the murky haze, he peered through the gaping hole in the driver's front window.

And found Pete.

The rest of the air gushed from his mouth in one violent breath, the vile taste rising from his stomach almost choking him. He coughed, gulped air but took in water, and could only imagine what else floated in with it. That made him want to vomit more. He stole another look, to be sure – it was definitely Pete – or what was left of Pete. Only the right side of his face existed, the left side was as fragmented as the windshield, bits of skin hanging outwards in the water, battling to stay attached, some with hair attached, most without. Blonde strands floated in a swaying dance while the body itself bobbed gently in its seat, not enough hole anywhere to let it out.

More than ever Nick wanted to vomit, and his lungs screamed to fill again. He released his hold, more pain jolting upward through his palm and into his upper arm. He gulped again at the severity as whatever had grabbed him snagged deeper into his skin. He coughed out the water blocking his throat, wrenched his hand free, and used the top of the car to kick himself back to the surface.

CHAPTER SIXTY-NINE

I paced around the rim of the dam, debating what to do for Nick had been down an awfully long time. Something had to be wrong. I stripped my jacket but air bubbles appeared on the water's surface, so I knew he must be surfacing. And I waited. And waited. It seemed like minutes passed. But still nothing happened. So I positioned myself to dive, almost kicked off the dam wall when the water erupted and Nick burst to the surface, coughing violently. He shook his head, dispelling water from his hair and eyes.

Turning, he located me on the bank; gulped down more full breaths of air, and trod water. By the look on his face I knew something was wrong.

"What is it?" I called. "What's down there?"

He answered with one deep word. "Pete." My knees almost buckled.

Coughing several more times, Nick kicked himself towards the shallow end of the dam and started to swim, his strong arms and shoulders pulling him swiftly forward while I stood, shocked by the news, and stunned by my own reaction. I felt ... nothing. I couldn't believe I felt absolutely nothing. Initially I thought when Pete was found I'd finally grieve, that the horror and pointlessness of it all would overwhelm me. But all I felt was relief. Why? What was so wrong with me that couldn't mourn his death; fall apart. Christ, he'd been a friend of mine. I fought to be normal, to find a reason for my lack of empathy. Was it because I'd fully accepted that it had happened – I'd had visions of Pete and the car every hour, every quiet moment since I'd seen it happen ... how else could I not accept it?

Nick reached shallow water, and I met him on the lower bank as he rose from the dam. "We now have the car, and the body," he said, standing knee deep in swirling murk. I could see his remorse in the way he stood, slightly hunched, some of the light gone from his eyes. He looked down and opened his hand, watched blood pour down staining the water around him; he closed his fist again and stepped onto drier land, his clothes and hair still pouring a torrent. He walked straight by me, blood still dripping, but I reached out and grabbed his wrist, stopping him. He turned and I prised open his fingers, viewed the long gaping slice across his palm and the heel of his hand. Whatever he'd done, it was deep. He clenched his hand again, looked down at me, a mixture of resignation, acceptance and futility on his face. His eyes hooded and he shrugged.

The coursing wind swirled around him making him shiver and he peeled the torn wet shirt from his skin, took the jacket I returned to him and pulled it on. I re-donned my jacket and picked up the discarded shirt. Rinsing it in the dam, I tore several large strips from it as I followed Nick back along the bank. When he turned to cast a long look back at the water, I caught him up and shoved a thick folded cloth into his hand to cover the gash, tightly wrapped the strips of cloth around it to restrict the bleeding. Our eyes met briefly as I made the last wrap and I noticed his eyes had fully lost their shine, lost even their darkness. I didn't know what to say or do to console him. Without warning, his big arms wrapped around me and pulled me into him, and for a long while we just stood hugging, his body tight, his arms overwhelmingly possessive. I felt him heave a breath; felt his body draw tighter, his muscles bunching. When he slowly eased me away again I didn't like the look marring his face.

Turning, he collected his boots, pulled them back on and pushed me up the slope ahead of him. We reached the bike and he pulled it back onto its wheels, pushed it to more level ground and straddled it. Then he reached out and pulled me closer.

Wordlessly I swung aboard, and we sat for long moments staring down at the dam, Nick's anger building. His knuckles had turned white on the handle grips, and the air around me felt ominous. I averted my gaze to avoid the vengeful look in his eyes.

"Nick! Look!" The words poured from my mouth with alarm.

Turning abruptly, his gaze followed my finger-line to the ribbon of highway below. Parked there was a white utility. Even across the distance I picked the distinctive shape of McCaig standing beside it. He was looking straight at us, and we watched as he scurried to the driver's door and climbed in. In the next instant the car was moving, turning at high speed amid a haze of smoking rubber, its wheels straightening as it reached the bitumen driveway. Then he came straight at us.

"If you weren't holding tight before, babe," Nick bellowed over his shoulder, "you'd better hold on now. The scenic tour is over!"

I locked my arms around him as he opened the throttle wide and we raced down the slope towards the southern gates. At the first gateway, Nick glanced back – McCaig's car was on the crest, leaving the bitumen drive; he was travelling slow over the wet and slippery pasture but following just the same. We pushed on, the bike's front wheel lifting and bouncing over uneven ground, Nick cursing its lightness as he pitched his body forward in an effort to keep it down. I followed his every move.

At the second gateway, the utility had reached the first and Nick throttled back. We had reached the gullies and would need to find a crossing, one firm enough to carry our combined weight. Already the wash was starting to fill with water, brown liquid trickling along its base, though the undisturbed ground still looked solid enough.

"We have the advantage," Nick assured me. "The bike will get across here, but McCaig won't."

Scanning the high ground, he looked for the access back

onto the highway from where we would make a clear run for Dayton. The time to stay concealed was over. He eased the bike along the gully's edge, looking left, looking right, looking around, searching for the gateway to the south, but he couldn't find it.

He turned and rode back again, his gaze skimming the western rim.

"Shit!" he cursed long and loud.

Above us, new fence posts stuck upward all along the rise, new wire tightly strung above the gullies on all three sides. The gate no longer existed.

Nick shot a look over his shoulder. The white utility now blocked the northern gateway, and the high wire fencing surrounding the gullies south and west was taut and viciously barbed. To the east the highway broke the pasture land, also fenced, rows of loosely strung wire tangled like a war zone barricade. And there sat a green windowless mini-bus, parked on the south side of the gully.

We were trapped!

Nick's eyes danced with options, of which I couldn't see many. We could surrender and die, or we could ... surrender and die.

Nick turned the bike in a circle, and yelled to me: "Hold on tight as you can and shut your eyes!" then he opened the throttle wider and tipped the cycle's wheel down the steep embankment. Riding into the wash, we picked up speed along its outer edges, picked up more and more as we hurtled beside the bank towards the highway. Faster and faster Nick sent the bike, its whining engine loud and piercing. To our left, the white utility turned and raced back across the farmland towards the farm's main entrance.

Regardless of what Nick said, I kept my eyes open, pressed my head hard against his back. Beneath the jacket, I could feel him moving smoothly, perfectly controlled, giving me every confidence we'd come out of this okay. Bushes and undergrowth on the gully's tip however streaked by, ablur.

As we neared the highway I snuck a look ... the tangled fence growing clearer ... each individual strand identifiable ... no chance of stopping before propelling through its lethal barbs. The men by the mini-bus stared open-mouthed as we hurtled towards them. When I peered forward over Nick's shoulder I knew he'd gone insane.

A few short yards from the wire Nick suddenly changed direction, steering the bike higher onto the right bank then quickly dropping down and across to the left. The slope increased our speed; improved our angle. The engine screamed louder as he opened the throttle to its fullest and sent the bike climbing up the farther bank. Up the steep embankment to the road we flew. Up, up, and up. I felt the urge to give an aid – *Jerry, tuck up your legs.* We ascended and soared, became almost vertical, yet still the bike climbed higher. Nick leant well forward to reduce the vertical lift, and I, his shadow, followed. *A Grade jumping. Pillion Prix Caprilli. Stupid thoughts! Concentrate!*

Higher and higher, above the fence we flew, propelled forward and ever upward by the unassailable speed. We were fully airborne. Lightning flashed, a brilliant blinding fork that filled the air with static, silhouetting us in the skyline above the road. My fingers dug deep into Nick's flesh at the thought of the crushing landing. And I held on tighter.

Soon we were coming down, the back wheel dropping quickly, the cycle staying angled skyward. My position locked in against Nick's became difficult to hold and I started slipping back on the pillion.

Time seemed eternal as we slipped from the sky, to land back wheel first, the jolt jarring our backs as we crunched onto the bitumen. The tyre squealed short and sharp as it grabbed on solid ground then wobbled for several long seconds. Already insecure, I almost slipped sideways off the pillion as the bike found traction on the tar. Then the front wheel lowered, much too fast, throwing me forward, the impact with the road making it bounce exuberantly, which flung me backward again. We were bucking down the road, the bike threatening to become airborne again, threatening to tip right over backwards.

Nick threw his weight forward, dragging me with him, the move forcing the front wheel back to earth. The wheel bounced twice more but lesser so before it levelled out, our speed increasing as we raced away to the north. Nick glanced back to see where we'd landed, to see if our pursuers followed. He bellowed over his shoulder: "Are you okay?"

I bellowed back. "No. I want to get off!"

Ahead, the white utility streaked out from the Siding, its brakes screeching, smoke billowing as its solid frame suddenly blocked the road. Our sight filled with the solid wall of white sliding from road verge to road verge. Nick hit the brake and the back wheel locked and slid sideways on the wet road, the move almost dropping the bike onto the bitumen. "Hold on!" he yelled as he fought to hold the front wheel true. He let the bike lay over; let its speed reduce in that flat sliding line, his muscles bunching as he tried to keep it under control. I heard him growl as his left ribs bore the agonizing pressure. But hold it true he did for he couldn't afford not to.

Saunders' place was fast approaching on the right, just before McCaig's white barricade. Nick glanced at the entrance, waited till we drew level with it then straightened the bike up again. He touched the brake sharply so the back wheel spun around, lining it up with Saunders' gateway then he accelerated, the move pulling the bike up smartly, almost tossing me off. He opened the throttle and we tore away again.

"You're bloody crazy!" I yelled, terrified yet still clinging to him. "You're ... *Jesus!*"

We'd made it into Saunders' place, but were now heading northeast. I clung tightly to Nick, not daring to imagine what he'd try next but not daring to be anywhere else.

The rain started in earnest, at first only sparse heavy drops then thicker and heavier until a wall of water dumped from the sky. Clouds swirled dark and oppressive and opened heaven's floodgates. Nick took to the cover of a vast belt of trees. Slowing the bike he picked his way carefully in through the scrub and a short way in, stopped. Keeping the bike in idle, he lifted my arm and read the time on my watch. His other hand rubbed his chest where my nails had dug through his jacket.

It was four o'clock.

Nick's head spun to the sound of fast approaching cars, and he winced as the high pitched motor gave our position away; he opened the throttle and we moved on again.

Breaking through the brush at high speed, we shot across an open field; skirted the top of a dam and hurtled headlong towards another belt of timber, the move taking McCaig and his crew by surprise. Ahead, a narrow path entered the scrub, wide enough for the trail bike but not for a car. Nick took it, and, as the purpling sky pulsed daylight and white streaks of brilliance bolted earthward, we reached the path. Thunder rolled in the distance, boomed loudly, its peal echoing and diminishing as we disappeared amongst the trees. Spiny parrot bush and spiky Grevilleas slapped about the bike, pricking our hands and thighs. Nick dropped his head, protecting his face from low hanging branches while I cowered below his back completely at his mercy. He didn't slow down, and bushes streaked past my face unrecognisable, yet I thanked small mercies the belt was densely timbered for McCaig's men were unable to follow. I wondered what Nick intended next for we would soon have to break from our cover and head back towards Dayton.

With the motor cranked open we broke through stinging nettles into a bit of a clearing. I felt his body tighten and he shouted a warning. I peered over his shoulder. *Shit!* A sapling lay across the track ahead of us, blocking our way, and I knew what Nick meant. At this speed we wouldn't stop in time to avoid it. In another second the bike jerked round as Nick hit the brake, the effort thrusting me heftily against his back. Then he reconsidered and went back to the throttle and yelled: "Hold on!" But it was too late. The sudden surge flung me back to the pillion and, as the front wheel lifted from the ground, I completely left the seat. I noted feeling weightless – Nick's bandaged hand reaching back to grab me – the ground rushing up to meet me. Then a crushing blow pounded against my hips. The ground streaked past my face even closer, everything happening so vividly it moved almost in slow motion. If Nick's grip did lock on I didn't feel it, but the next bounce seemed less crushing than the first. I was used to taking a tumble and instinctively tucked in my limbs and rolled as I skidded along the slippery, rocky surface. Maybe even the pain developed in slow motion ... Nevertheless, I slammed, back first, into the fallen tree trunk. The ground stopped streaking past my face. I heard Nick groan as he landed with a thud on the sapling's other side, the bike doing a slow aerial dance as it pitched with a less than perfect parabola over the leafy trunk. Its nose tipped into the branches as it ended its life in a theatrical somersault. *Eight faults for the fall! Ten for the pain!*

I lay for long minutes staring up at the sky, which now bordered on charcoal grey and black, and I felt rain spattering on my face. I heard the bike's motor cough and die; heard the whirring thrum-thrum-thrum of the wheel spinning on its axle. And that was all. Raindrops touched my mouth, eradicating the dryness that now assailed my throat.

Get up, Becky, I ordered, trying to draw a breath.

I wriggled to find a less painful position; tried to raise a knee but greater pain tore through me, stealing every ounce of air. I tried to suck it back, but failed, no air willing to enter my lungs. I started to panic; tried to convince myself I was only winded; told myself to relax. But here I was, pinned against the tree bark and feeling ... feeling .... nothing. Feeling nothing where I should have felt branches, texture, small pebbles, rocks pressing into my back, gravel rash even. But there was nothing. The pain was in my lungs, and nowhere else. I concentrated on feeling my arms — couldn't — not even a tingle in my fingers. *Can I move my fingers?* Coldness flooded me and the blood rushed from my face. I couldn't feel where it went. The horror of the damage I'd suffered bore in. I tried to call to Nick, but words without air were words without sound, so I lay gasping, feeling colder and colder as each gasp failed. The world started dimming, going grey.

Then Nick bent over me, his breadth shielding me from the rain. "N... ... Nick ..." I fought back a flood of tears, fearing Dad's premonition had won out, only it wasn't caused by Jerry.

Nick smoothed the hair from my face. "It's okay, kiddo. You're gonna be okay. Just stay still."

"I ca ... I ... can't ... breathe ..." *Is that a symptom of a broken back?* I couldn't remember, but the thought chilled me further.

"I know. Just stay still. Don't try to move yet."

I doubted I could have even if I'd wanted to. Even my lungs weren't working. Nick's dark eyes swept over me, and I felt his hand tip my head back, his hands trembling when he touched me. "Is anything broken?"

"I ... don't ... know ... I ... can't ... ... feel ..."

Nick's rugged jaw set at my words, tightened his whole expression. His eyes for a split second focused on something a long way off, his breathing seeming to stop in that brief moment. He shook his head, almost indiscernibly, as he crouched closer. "Jesus, kiddo ... don't let McCaig win now."

His hands slid beneath me, his fingers probing along the back of my neck. "Tell me if anything hurts," he said. The look on his face said 'tell me if you feel this.'

He pressured my shoulders, my back, my legs. Probed firmly around my hips, his big hands firm but gentle. Nothing crunched, and nothing jarred. More pointedly, nothing shot searing heat further down a limb to make me scream. "Did you feel that?" he asked, looking hopeful.

I nodded, and drew breath.

"Can you move your fingers?"

I concentrated on my hand and warily gained a wriggle from my fingers. And found more air, the flow coming easier.

"Toes?"

I had to think harder, fully expecting it to hurt. And found relief when it didn't. My toes wriggled inside my joggers right beneath Nick's fingers. I breathed deeper.

He smiled. "You can feel that?"

I nodded, also aware now that I trembled uncontrollably.

The tightness in Nick's jaw eased and his expression lost its tension. "I think you're okay. Probably just stunned and winded." He heaved out a hard deep breath. "Come on, let's try and get you up."

Offering me his good hand, he pulled me up with one arm; and supported my weight against him. His dark eyes had gone to scanning the bush. "... and we've stayed here far too long."

I noticed then his left arm locked to his side. "Are you all right?" I hadn't once thought how he had fared.

His lips pressed to a grim line. "Never better," he said, but I felt his sharp intake of air when he moved. "Well," he huffed it out again, "we're alive ... but I think our transport's dead."

He appraised the bike, the rain starting to fall harder as he cursed the buckled wheels and twisted forks. Thunder rolled again, louder and closer than before, and he checked the menacing sky as clouds released their fury. Pulling me back against the trunk of a stout, well canopied red gum, he drew me into him, his arms and shoulders curving around me lessening the downpour as his back bore the pounding force of the rain.

"Not having much luck, are we?" I noted, looking up at him.

He looked down, and half smiled. "I've had worse." And he covered me further. The rain increased, his chin resting on my crown as he drew in closer, and I wished we were doing this for totally different reasons.

Heavy sheets of rain drenched all around us, the trees

eventually providing little shelter. When it eased a little, Nick decided to move. Someone was waiting for us and he didn't want to give them time to change the game plan.

Easing me away from him, he said, "Come on. We've got a long walk ahead of us."

I wiped the raindrops dripping from my nose onto the back of my hand; looked up at him. "I know this sounds a repetitive question ... but ... where to now?"

Nick paused; cast his gaze north then south. "Back to town," he answered decisively. "It's eight or nine miles from here — Dayton is thirteen."

I baulked as the pain in my right hip became more noticeable. "Oh no, you've got to be kidding!" But Nick's eyes hardened and one eyebrow hiked. I knew that look. "Why can't we go up to the house here?"

He gripped my wrist and, ignoring the rain and my resistance, set out northward. "It's empty; the Saunders live two farms away, and it'll be the first place they look."

We walked into the storm, dark skies prevailing as we used the trees for cover, our sodden clothes icy on our skin, our hair channelling steady trickles down our necks and backs. Nick looked back frequently, happier now we had lost the noise of the cycle, for, he said, he could now hear things happening behind us. After a short way he stopped and turned swiftly.

To the right of us, headlights swung into the scrub, wide beams penetrating the trees, trying to locate us, as yet too far back. We breathed more freely and kept moving, our relief short-lived as shouts echoed in the night. Torch lights flickered through the brush and loud shouts erupted in unison. Shouts of celebration. They'd found the bike!

Spreading out, the torch lights came faster, glimmering, and another bright set of headlights swept in from the left.

"Shit!" Nick cursed. "They're pushing us out in the open."

Behind us, the torch lights danced as they started jogging.

Then running. Heavy crashing came from the left as McCaig's men swept around to close off our escape.

"Go!" Nick ordered. "Go on, run." He pointed in the direction I had to go, and stopped as I put distance between us. I glanced back. He was moving again, but slower, and I tried to fathom his plan. I kept going, hobbling, gaining more distance but when I next looked back, Nick had stopped and turned round. Rain pelted down all around him and I could see his silhouette in the headlights shining across the field.

Then he turned and started running, catching me up. I ran on, limping more now as cold and fatigue hit my nerves. I knew he would catch me quickly, and shouldered my way out of the thinning underbrush until it was no more. I stood on open ground, pasture all around me. I was out of the shelter belt, and had no idea which way to go.

Through a blanket of heavy rain Nick reached me, still sprinting, headlights, torch-lights, swinging this way and that behind him. He powered along, still behind the trees but coming fast. Voices shouted, and jeers rose in their frenzied chase.

Then he reached me, stopped, and turned back. He must have seen my exhaustion, realised I was too spent to run any more. They were so close now. There was nothing else to do but stand and fight.

"Keep going," he ordered sharply.

I took a few painful steps, tears filling my eyes at Nick's intentions: he was going to stand his ground; he was going to slow them down, and sacrifice himself in the bargain.

"Nick?" My tears mixed with the rain.

He shot a glance over his shoulder and shook his head, flinched as lightning flashed a silver aura almost over his head. Its electric whip struck a tree a short way over, exploding it, sending shards and chunks of timber whizzing across the ground, making us duck further. Flames spurted upward, sizzled in the rain. The whole landscape lit to daylight for a second split, like someone had turned on a light; it revealed us standing apart, looking at each other, on the rim of a silver dam.

As the wide scanning light-beams reached out from the bush, missing Nick by inches, he shot forward, stretched out his arm and gathered me up in the darkness. Another moment of airlessness as we hauled out from the bank and dived into nothingness. Thunder rocked the ground, its loud rumble covering our sounds as we hit the icy water with a splash. Liquid folded over us like heavy batter, and I cursed its bitterness as I instantly froze.

Kicking himself back to the dam wall, Nick found a handhold on a piece of protruding rock. Reaching out, he dragged me back to him.

Shivering, I tread water beside him, watching him in absolute awe, wondering what lengths he'd go to to survive, wondering what had sparked such an insane sense of bravado, and how he could be so self-assured in this deathly situation.

Voices came closer. Angry voices. Nick pulled me closer, whispered: "When I say, you take a deep breath and hold it. This is our last chance so I hope you've got good lungs."

I nodded as the voices became more audible, and watched Nick for his signal.

"They have to be here somewhere!" McCaig's voice rasped above the rest. "I know we haven't missed them."

Lights glowed over the bank higher up, flickered over the shallow end of the dam.

"Now!" Nick signalled.

I barely had time to gulp a breath before he pushed my head beneath the water, his hand on the dam wall pushing himself down as well. Restructuring his hold, he pushed us deeper; kept me pushed down beneath him and I watched through the blackness of the water the light sweeping the surface, back and forth, skirting the dirty brown edges. They searched so intensely my lungs started to burn. I was running run out of air. I began to struggle, signalled Nick that I needed to breathe. He let me up, but only a little, the light still shining wide across the water. The colour in my face was changing to blue, and I had to take a breath. Even though I would only take in water I had to take in something.

I started to thrash, my eyes feeling ready to burst from their sockets – tried to tear Nick's hand away to free myself, but he pushed me deep again. When air burst from my lungs and water gushed in to replace it the water went black again, an eerie void of blackness. The torches had swung further north. As a deeper blackness washed over me Nick hauled me up, but before I could gasp or cough his hand clamped over my mouth, silencing all sound. I started to choke on the water trickling down my airway, but Nick's hand remained fixed until I'd controlled my need, and only then did he let go.

As the voices faded away to the north he edged forward along the dam's shale wall to watch the movement of their lights. Above, the clouds still sent their blessing which seemed to please him, the rain having destroyed our tracks. Promising to find us drier shelter when McCaig had given up, he pushed me back into deep water. In or out of the dam, we'd be wet, he said, and although the water was cold here we were protected from the wind.

I shivered violently and my lips had turned blue, but I said nothing for that would make me a fopsy.

CHAPTER SEVENTY

McCaig turned a circle, and rubbed his chin as he scanned the space around him. Manetti had to be out there somewhere. He and the girl. And, seeing the fan of his men had channelled their escape route out onto open ground and they weren't behind them, they had to still be ahead of them. He swung his light erratically into the blackness. Found nothing. The only thing pleasing him was the wrecked trail bike – its absence would slow them down. He pressed on, sent his men forward, for the Taylor brothers were lying in wait ahead and soon the prize would arrive in front of their guns.

Twenty minutes later they stepped back onto open pasture – no wild shouts of excitement – no rifle shots to indicate their prey had been captured and disposed of.

McCaig swung his powerful torchlight back over the scrub, back over the open paddock, up over the white utility where Dave Taylor stood waiting, his back against the closed car door, his rifle cradled like a baby.

"Well? Where are they?" the man grumbled openly.

McCaig looked round in disbelief. "You tell me!" he huffed. He wiped his mouth with a cold, hard hand, his concern growing as disgruntled mutterings rose along the search line.

"You must have had your bloody eyes closed!" Taylor barked, stirring the fat man further.

The rain had stopped now and the wind whipping across the stubbled earth was a cruel and painful replacement, prompting a call of "What now?" from the darkness.

"We go back!" McCaig ordered, not relishing the thought of another long walk.

"That's pretty pointless." Taylor countered as he slung the rifle barrel over his shoulder in an undisciplined shouldering of arms. "Somewhere you missed them, and you don't think Manetti would hang around waiting for you to come back for him, do you? He's probably long gone."

"He can't be! He's got no transport!'"

"Just my point. He's on foot and he's silent. Maybe they ditched the bike for that reason — and what's more he knows the country. We don't. He could run us round in circles all bloody night."

"So what do you propose to do about it, Mr Great White Hunter?"

"Pack it up for now," Taylor growled the order, letting the sarcasm go over his head. "Let it be obvious we've given up and my bet is, give them enough time, we'll pick them up on the road somewhere."

He signalled the men to come in closer, and, as they huddled against the cold air that whistled through the underbrush, he issued new orders.

"Bill, you go back to Cullan. Keep an eye on trucks and cars coming into town. They may try to get a lift in. Lacey, you and your mate go back to Dayton. Watch all movement of the cops. If you get a chance, immobilise them, but do it quietly. I don't want them getting out to pick Manetti up if he makes contact. Then wait on the highway somewhere. Keep an eye on traffic coming in just in case they try to get through that way. Ben and I will check out the farmhouse here in case he tries to get to a phone then we'll patrol the roads. My bet is he'll be walking back to Cullan, at least until he can hitch a ride to Dayton. The thing most in our favour now is that the girl will slow him down."

He swung the rifle down again and tapped it against his leg then took a long look at the crew before him. They weren't the greatest fighting force he'd seen but at least they now had good reason to do a proper job — keeping their freedom depended on stopping Manetti.

"Okay, let's get going before we get caught for trespass. And keep in radio contact, half hourly."

A string of vehicles pulled away from Saunders' farm, skirting the dam on exit. Two engines faded along the gravel track, heading west toward the highway while the third streaked east towards the farmhouse.

CHAPTER SEVENTY-ONE

We waited in water up to our chins, Nick's handhold on the dam wall supporting us as we stayed as immersed as we could. I clung to Nick's arm and he stared at me constantly in the darkness, as if reading my whole life story in my face. I tried to ignore his scrutiny, but my heart raced, making it hard to breathe.

Sounds of motors and men's voices carried on the wind – distorted sounds – but it was enough to announce their return. Nick steeled as the engines approached and pushed me further back in the water. I prayed I wouldn't have to endure another spate of breath-holding for I just couldn't do it this time. The cold night air had already chilled my lungs.

Headlights appeared on the track ahead, motors racing east and west, the lights soon disappearing.

Sighing, I let go of Nick's arm and headed towards the shallow end but he grabbed me back. "Not yet," he warned. "They've only gone to the house. They'll be back in a minute." He gave a tight-lipped smile that said he knew how I was feeling and that everything was okay for the moment, but I'd stopped believing his lies.

Minutes later though the lights returned, travelling slower on a last long search through the night then they too headed west. Nick kept listening as the motor quietened before revving up and roaring away.

He waited a moment longer then kicked himself along the dam wall to the shallow end, dragging me with him. Rising to his feet, he hauled me up until I stood beside him, looking like a bedraggled rag doll that had been left out in the rain. This was becoming a habit. Water poured from our clothes and pooled into the puddles already spreading around us. He smiled and looked slowly round, I guess checking that the departures weren't a ploy. He looked pleased with the silence, and took a moment to empty the water from his boots; indicated for me to do the same. Then he clutched my hand tightly.

"Come on," he said, pulling me after him, "we've still got a long walk ahead."

A cruel, biting wind gnawed at our legs and backs and I cursed openly as my shivers tripled, no space now between each one to give me a chance to control them.

"Keep moving!" Nick ordered. "Keep your body heat up!"

"I can't. I left it back in the dam."

"Then pretend," he hissed.

His grip increased and he hauled me up alongside him, forcing me to move, forcing me to keep moving, yet his hand felt just as cold as mine – like a slab of meat from the freezer. Nick kept saying things like:

"Keep moving."

"Exercise will keep your mind off it."

"Think warm!"

He chanted that one often, whether for his benefit or mine I didn't care – none of it worked.

"Come on! Mind over matter! You don't feel it."

He powered on, occasionally flexing his back to release the cramping muscles that had bunched against the wind.

Relief came in short bouts as we meandered through dense scrub, low shrubby natives and towering timbers, each breaking the wind's intensity, but the time was too short before we were back in the open again. For four torturous miles that seemed more like twenty I kept pace with him, walking silently, intent on not slowing him down. Then a fence blocked our way. Nick pulled the wires apart, opening a gap for me to climb through. As he followed me under the wire I stopped and turned abruptly.

"Nick, I've had it! I have to rest." I stood limp, unable to stretch my cramped muscles to stand upright. "I can't go another step."

"Okay," he nodded, heaving out a breath. "... we'll rest, but only for a while." Looking round, he found a well-sheltered grove a short way over. "In there," he pointed.

His compassion surprised me, but he too had started looking tired, only muscularly though for his eyes remained alert and not trusting the darkness. Finding a suitable tree stump, I plopped down and hunched over to keep the cold from my chest, pressed my head down on my knees. After a while, my lungs filled fully with slightly warmer air.

Nick stood watching from a distance, his thoughts obviously churning as his back pressed against the wet stripping bark of a red gum. He unfolded his arms and turned, stared at the highway, quandary dancing in his eyes. By his altered level of breathing I knew he was planning something, something that bothered him. He turned back; watched me a moment longer; watched me watching him.

"I'm ready," I lied, not wanting to force him into a decision he didn't want to make.

He moved away from his resting place, and looked pleased; looked further pleased that the rain had stopped again. "Okay," he said. "We're nearly halfway there. It won't take us long now."

We strode on again in silence, side by side at first, only the squeak of my sneakers and the occasional clunk of boot heel on rock tapping out in the night. Thick clouds raced across the moon, creating greater pitch, the shelter belts becoming more difficult to negotiate in the darkness. Eventually we had to walk on colder, open ground to avoid injury. The rain came again, heavy and relentless, and I started to suffer beyond my mind's negotiation skills. Never in my life had I been so frigging cold. I hunched against the pounding rain on my back; used my shoulders to keep the water from running down my chest. But every so often a trickle escaped and dribbled down my breast, and

I cursed and shuddered until I wiped it away. The water in my hair grew heavy so I stopped, twisted it like a rope to wring it dry so it wouldn't weigh me down. It felt lighter and less cold and I moved on again. We covered another mile, each footfall requiring more and more effort, and all the while the storm remained unyielding.

Nick strode ahead, finding easier, more sheltered tracks to walk, but they never seemed easy enough. My breath seemed constantly diminished, the pain in my hip nagged and increased with the distance. Soon thunder rolled again, long and low, each peal louder than the last. Squally gusts whipped up from the west; billowed around us to blow us off course. But still Nick forged on. I cursed him silently and frequently for his lack of feeling, for his machine-like stamina, for his absolute unwillingness to give in. But I refused to lag too far behind. When I did, I forced myself to jog and catch him up.

"You really like doing this sort of thing, don't you?" I puffed as I again arrived beside him.

He smiled as he wiped the rain from his face and chest and looked down at me. "What makes you think that?"

"'cose you're so damn good at it." The look I shot him was none-the-less derogatory. "Don't you ever get tired?"

"Don't you?"

"Funny, funny." I stopped and heaved in more air but Nick continued walking, which made me run again. "Tell me, you must have had to practice to get this good at something. ... So, where did you practise? Vietnam?"

"Maybe."

"It's either that, or you're a masochist."

He almost laughed. "You know me so well," and shot me a manufactured grin.

"What? – so you're a masochist?"

He smiled wider.

"You look nice when you smile."

"Has anyone ever told you you talk too much?"

"To someone as miserly on words as you, I probably do. How much further do we have to go?"

"About four miles."

"You said that earlier."

"Do you want me to carry you?"

"Don't be ridiculous!" I heaved in more air. "If you can do this, I can do this." No way would I fail in front of him. Those words became the new chant as I fell behind and followed him a while. *Don't give up. Don't give up. Nick's the sort who deplores weakness.* I snatched another breath and pushed on again; caught him up again, but I was tiring more quickly than I liked, and it was getting harder and harder to breathe. I forced my mind to other things. "How long ago did you split with Marilyn?" I asked, drawing alongside him again.

He tensed at the question. "How do you know about that?"

"Town talks."

"Oh, yeah." He accepted the words like old news he'd temporarily forgotten. "Like it talks about your broken love affair with what's-his-name."

"Tony," I filled the gap then looked surprised. In the darkness I gathered Nick's eyes hadn't left the track. "I guess everyone is entitled to one mistake."

"Dead right," he agreed though his voice had deepened slightly. He looked down at me; never missed a step. "Only a fool does it twice though."

At that, I shut up. And the chants became more important in my bid to keep him in sight. I started singing beneath my breath, anything than risk another put down. Eventually I couldn't think of any words to sing so recited nursery rhymes, my mind-play keeping out the thoughts of the cold, the rain and exhaustion.

Another half hour, another fence. Nick had the wires apart before I got there, having already checked the road that paralleled it. He stood on the outer perimeter, his foot on the lower wire to widen the gap. I clambered through, weary, barely able to lift a foot. My lungs burned, and the cramp in my back was almost unbearable. At least the raindrops masked my tears.

As Nick released the wires my foot caught on a rock on the roadside and I stumbled, no energy left to throw out my arms to save myself. He stepped across my path, his body blocking my fall, his strength still untapped. He scooped me back to my feet and at that point I gave in and admitted there was no goddamned way I could ever keep up with him.

Worse, he laughed as he took my weight against him. "Steady on. No need to hurry." My icy body trembled, and he realised now I was crying.

'I hate you, Nick Manetti," I murmured as my head fell against him. "I really really hate you."

"That's nice," he said, looking down at the pain on my face. "Hey, it's okay. You just need another rest."

"Leave me alone. I can do this." But he wrapped his cold arms around me. "... it's so ... so damn cold ..."; and rubbed his hands up and down my spine, warming me with friction; trying to ease the tightness in my back. Then he scooped me into his arms, no strain, no warning.

"Only three crow miles to travel," he said striding across Brenton Road.

I squirmed in his arms. "No ... I can walk! Please, put me down. Put me down!!"

But his grip tightened. "No. Now stay still ... and keep shivering – it'll keep you warm." Hoisting me higher, he started north again, his step shortened slightly by the weight against his damaged rib-cage. And while he walked I gave up to the night.

CHAPTER SEVENTY-TWO

Only three miles to go. Only three miles, Nick chanted as he strode on carrying his waif.

He'd endured similar tasks in the Army, carrying loads greater than this over much longer distances, sometimes carrying so long he'd thought his arms would drop off; sometimes he'd falter, stumble, the load almost falling, but he'd never drop the load: he never dared, the penalty being another five mile. At first, he'd simply ignored the discomfort and when the agony set in he would block the pain with bitter thoughts and endure.

Looking down at the package he now cradled he realised the unfair comparison. This weight was well proportioned, not too heavy, her shape fitting comfortably against him. He liked the feel of her, hoped the closeness of their bodies would increase her warmth, increase his warmth, but she felt very cold in his arms. The added exertion of carrying her had encouraged his own sweat to rise, hard to distinguish though from the rain pelting through his jacket.

Some time passed before he realised Becky had stopped shivering, her body no longer fighting to keep out the chill. She'd given in to the wind, and it was freezing her from within. He jostled her in his arms. "Hey Bec ... Becky, rouse kiddo. Hey, are you still with me?" His voice was deep with concern.

"Pat-a-cake, pat-a-cake ..." came the mumbled reply.

He jostled her again. "Come on, babe! Don't give up on me now!"

Her head lolled against him, loose and uncontrolled, causing him to seek out shelter. Ahead, the lights of Cullan twinkled through the trees and he thanked God, for Becky had not responded lucidly to his words for some time and she'd become heavier, further draining his shoulders.

Warm! He had to get her warm.

He reached the road, the first road of Cullan. Only a block to go and he'd be at Sheila's, his only hope of a haven. *Come on*, he urged himself. *You don't have much time.*

His energy almost depleted, he pushed the pace again, but words ripped to his brain. *Don't let your guard down. People are still hunting you.*

He looked down at Becky, her beautiful face now pale, and his jaw set as the urgency to get her warm prodded him again. But his logic pushed over it. *You'll both get a lot colder if you slip up now.*

He slowed his pace again; resumed his caution.

Checking the road, he crossed over and took cover beneath the low-canopied verandah of the row of old shops on the backstreet. Doorway by dark doorway, he moved along the walk, avoiding the heavy rain and remaining obscure. From the Co-op's frontage, he could see the back of Sheila's house and the lights glinting through the high side windows of the hotel. He crossed over and stopped, pressed his back up against the cold metal wall of the Farm Supply shed.

A light was on at Sheila's house! He frowned. That was unusual. The hotel was still open so it wasn't all that late. Therefore, Sheila would be behind the bar.

So who's in the house? Sheila never left lights on. In all the miles of walking he hadn't expected this, and his nerves grated. Something was wrong. Had to be. And damn! that was all he needed right now!

Restructuring his hold on Becky, he crossed the shadowed alley between the cream house and the Supply Yard; edged along the side of the kitchen wall. Avoiding shrubbery that Sheila had given a little attention to he peered through the window. The room was empty, and he wondered if Sheila had simply forgotten to turn out the lights. His brow creased deeper with the risk he was going to take.

As he started to turn away a light flicked on further down the passage and Sheila stepped into the hall. Nick's deep sigh was instant. He slipped around to the back of the house again, stood beneath the metal canopy as the rain beat a noisy tattoo on the roof. His arm muscles cramping with the weight of his waif, he elbow knocked on the door, the dull thud echoing through the room within. He looked around to see who else might have heard it. Lights appeared on the road along which they'd come, and his nerves ripped taut as the new problem confronted him. He looked back to the closed, solid door, which remained obstinately shut. He knocked again, harder, his elbow bruising with the force. A second later a light flicked on and the door opened the merest crack.

The lights on the road drew closer, travelling slow.

"What's going on?" The voice inside sounded timid, but he'd expected Sheila's caution for no-one ever came to the back door.

"Turn out the light!" he urged in a whisper as the car drew almost level with the back of the house. He wondered if it travelled so slowly because they were searching ...

"What?"

"It's me. Nick."

The door flung open, and the overhead light extinguished.

The headlights cruised slowly by as Nick slipped inside.

"Oh thank God!" the woman cried. "For the love of mercy, I knew you'd come," but the free-flowing tears wetting her cheeks contradicted her words.

"Sssh," Nick tried to console her. He wanted to put his arms around her, but both were fully occupied, so he moved further in and kicked the door shut behind him. "Pull down the blind," he said softly.

Sheila did as told, covering the window. "They thought you were dead," she told him, raising his grim smile.

"Close, but not yet," he tried to make light of it. He gave her a worried glance. "Why aren't you at the hotel?"

Sheila's gaze lowered and her lips pressed together. "I couldn't bring myself to go in, not aft ... not with the way things are," she said, "... so Margaret's filling in." Her gaze fell to the bundle in his arms. "Rebecca Cooper?" she mouthed in surprise. She looked up at Nick. "I thought she'd gone back to the city."

Nick's lips thinned as he nodded. "She did – it's a long story. Right now, we need somewhere to hold up."

"You know you don't need to ask, love." Her hand on his arm reaffirmed her commitment. "Now tell me, what's happened, and what can I do to help?"

Nick appraised the bundle in his arms. "She's frozen through – we'll need to get her warm." He headed down the passage to the room Sheila called his. "Can I have some extra blankets?"

Reaching the bedroom door he nudged it open, his voice dropping in tone. "... and I need to ring Rod Willcox ... we found Pete."

"Oh no, love ..." Sheila's chin quivered. She stood at the end of the hall, new tears clouding her eyes.

Nick nodded solemnly. "He's in his car in Carter's dam."

She opened the cupboard, still watching him and the way the girl's hair swayed as he moved. "Keep it hush," Nick added, "... and for God's sake be careful. McCaig *is* involved."

Sheila nodded as Nick entered the bedroom then pulled out several blankets and a pile of fluffy towels. She followed him into the room and dumped them on the bed then drew the curtains and pulled the cord, activating the wall heater.

Nick lowered Becky to the brocade chair in the corner and crouched, checking her condition. She was barely conscious. When Sheila's hand rested on his shoulder he glanced up, his face tight with worry. He rose and collected a towel from the stack.

"What can I do, love? I want to help."

"You can make that call to Dayton," he told her, "... it's real important."

She stood appraising him, shocked at how drawn he looked. "Go on. Make the call. We'll be okay here."

She reached up and wiped the raindrops from his face, his iciness transferring to herself. "All right, but you get yourself dry too, love ... and try and get some rest. You look all spent."

She backed out of the room and shut the door behind her, and Nick was glad she didn't know just how spent he felt. He turned back to Becky, leant over and towel-dabbed the wetness from her face. Instantly she turned her head to avoid him, her hand gripping to his arm as she tried to pull herself up. He helped her forward, supported her against him as she fought to stay upright.

"I ... I can walk from here," she said, but her head fell against him and he realised she wasn't in the same place he was.

He laughed as his arms encircled her. "Like hell you can," then he frowned as she started trembling again, trembling uncontrollably, but that was a good sign. Drawing her to her feet, he wrapped the blankets around her; held her against him, body warming body, though there wasn't much warmth left in his. *Warm slowly, kiddo. Warm slowly.*

CHAPTER SEVENTY-THREE

Inside the hotel, Margaret wiped over the bar as the last patron left. Sheila bid her an early goodnight, locked the front door behind her and dimmed the lights then headed for the recess behind the bar where sat the phone.

In Dayton, Cussack picked up the receiver to stop the incessant ringing. The phone had run hot all afternoon on what had proved to be an incredibly long and miserable day. Now it rankled his nerves. The collision at the Bindibar turn off had been a bad one – two were dead, three seriously injured, at least two hundred sheep had been destroyed, and it had taken most of the day to clear the wreckage and remains. Then Manetti had failed to show again, a point that concerned and angered him. It was now very late, and waiting was not his forte.

"Dayton Police, Cussack speaking," he snapped down the line. Immediately he recognised the female voice, and picked the fear in it. "... I have a message from Nick," she said.

Looking around the corner of the recess, Sheila made sure the bar was still empty for she realised she'd left the back door unlocked. Her uncertainty dwindled Cussack's anger.

"Yes, Mrs McKenzie, I'm listening," he prompted.

"Nick's at my place, Sergeant." Her voice was shaky and barely audible. "He says you'll find Peter's body in his car in Carter's dam."

Cussack put his hand over the mouthpiece and signalled Rod. "Your friend's made contact, and he's found Kennedy." He took his hand off again. "How is Nick, Mrs McKenzie? And is the girl with him?"

"He's fine, Sergeant, and yes, Rebecca's with him. Oh ... and

"

Nick said to tell you McCaig is definitely involved. He was adamant about that, Sergeant. Very adamant."

Cussack bit into the side of his mouth, his subconscious taking over the details. "Thank you for ringing, Mrs McKenzie. You can let Nick know we are sending a car."

Agreeing, she cradled the receiver then checked the bar again. She was still alone, but across the road, parked beneath the lights of the roadhouse, she could see McCaig's utility casting a long reaching shadow towards the hotel. Its aloneness looked sinister.

Cussack sighed deeply. At least something was going right for a change! "Get the car, Senior," he ordered curtly. "We'll go out and pick up your friend then we'll set up a full investigation. Your mate's found the body."

Grabbing the keys off the hook, Rod strode out to the squad car, bothered little now by the rain. It could piss down all it wanted as far as he was concerned, he thought smiling, his hand rubbing his brow to release the throbbing there. He reached the vehicle, and stopped, scrunched the keys in his fist and swore beneath his breath. Turning, he strode back to the stationhouse for another set of keys. While he was out, someone else would have to fix the flat back tyre – he would simply take the other vehicle.

He cast his eyes over it as he walked. And stopped. The oppressive drizzle no longer registered. Scowling, he strode back and circled the car; counted ... one, two ... three, four. Then back to the first vehicle. One, two, three, four. He pushed open the glass front door and yelled across the office. "Hey, Sarge, we've got a problem!"

Following him out, Cussack stared at the damage. "Damn! Jesus! That does it!" he ranted. He looked around. "Rod, get a message back to Manetti. He can hold out for one more night ... I'm calling in the city boys."

He stormed back into the station, pointing as he barked orders at his shift. "Get a tow truck on call, then ring Bob at the garage and tell him we need two cars fitted with tyres ... tonight! ... and I do mean tonight! Don't take any of his shit about how late it is. This is an emergency. And I want that mobile crane that's down in the hire yard." His blood pumped with life that he hadn't felt in a long time. "Waddell, get on the phone and call in the volunteers. We'll need every available man out here tonight. Tell them to bring floodlights, power ... whatever the hell else they've got hidden in that shed over there – and I need them ready by the time Homicide gets up here from the city. You got that?"

Brett grabbed the receiver off the hook as the stationhouse bustled to life. Within minutes, lights in Dayton flicked on all over town as it responded to the call.

CHAPTER SEVENTY-FOUR

As Sheila reached the back door of the hotel the phone rang again. She hesitated a moment, wanting to get back to Nick and pass on the message but something warned her to go back and answer it. It was Sam and he sounded frantic.

"I've been trying to ring Nick all day," he huffed with frustration, "but there's been no answer so I drove on back." His voice deepened. "Jesus, Sheila, what's been happening here? His truck is wrecked ... there's no sign of Nick anywhere ... nor Becky Cooper for that matter. Ros came back with me and we're both going crazy with worry."

"It's all right, Sam. It's all right. They're both here." She heard Sam sigh; heard him relay the news to Rosalind. He sounded less perturbed when next he spoke.

"Well, what's been happening? You don't know what's been going through our minds when we got back to find this. Ros came back to stop Becky leaving and found the horses and trailer still here so we knew she hadn't left but we couldn't find her – we didn't know what to think."

"Don't worry, love. They're both safe for the moment, just as long as McCaig doesn't find them. And the Police are on their way here now."

"McCaig? So Nick was right. Well, I guess it's time we do something about McCaig!"

"Oh no, Sam, no!" A chill surged through Sheila at the prospect of more violence. "You keep Rosalind safe where you are, and leave this to the Police. They'll be here shortly. Do you hear me, Sam Chapman? Don't you dare do anything that will make things worse for Nick!"

A long period of silence followed while Rosalind spoke in the background then Sam sighed aloud. "All right, but just for tonight! Tomorrow will be different, I promise you!"

"What are you planning, Sam Chapman?" Sheila demanded. "You're only going to ..."

"Don't worry, Sheila, it's not what you think. I just feel it's time this damn town starts to stand up for itself! Every time there's a bit of trouble, Nick carries the weight of it while everyone else hangs back. Well it's damn well time they give him a hand for once. Let some of the others find a do-or-die attitude. Let them fight for their own damn peace for a change. Personally, I think it's time Nick stopped letting them all be cowards."

Silence fell between them as their thoughts followed different lines. Then he said: "Can we use the front bar in the morning? Just for a meeting ... one we don't want to hide this time."

Sheila could say nothing to dissuade him – he would hold the meeting in town regardless, either at the hotel or in the roadhouse car-park – either place would suffice. So she agreed to open the doors early. At seven-thirty, she promised. At least then she could keep an eye on the situation. With that, she hung up, but the phone rang again before her hand had left the receiver. She snatched it up, expecting Sam again.

It was Rod at Dayton Police. They'd been detained and Nick would have to wait, which elated her for Nick could do with the rest, and she told them so. The house was a safe place, and no-one would suspect them being there.

Relieved, she hung up and went back to the door, which now stood wide open. Someone stood in the shadows of its framework, the silhouette impossible to miss. Her blood ran cold.

"You closed early tonight," McCaig complained, his piggy blue eyes narrowing at her.

She paled. Had he heard the conversation? "It's the storm," she said, fighting to keep the tremor from her voice. "Nobody ever comes in when it's like this ..."

"Well how's a man to get his beer if he does come in?" the man snapped back, stepping further into the room.

Sheila backed away. "That's not a problem ..."; she wheeled quickly to keep distance between them and returned to the bar. What if he'd heard? "I can get what you want."

She tried to sound brighter, to sound normal, but all she could think of was Nick in the house a few short steps across the darkened alley. What if he came over because she was taking too long?

She flicked the light on so Nick would be able to see who was there before he came too close. "What'll it be?"

McCaig looked around, his eyes narrowing as they settled on the phone. "Half a dozen," he said bluntly, turning to look out the window at his car across the road. "Not much activity at all in town tonight, is there?" he noted as Sheila went to the cool-room.

She came out again. "Most sensible people are safely tucked up at home, I guess," she answered matter-of-factly.

"All except you." McCaig flicked a finger at the phone.

Sheila glanced around at the object of his interest, and smiled grimly. "Family problems in the city," she lied. "The only chance we really get to talk is when the hotel's closed."

McCaig put his money on the counter and picked up his night's supply. "We all have our problems, I s'pose." Rubbing his chin, his eyes still on the phone, he turned to go.

"You can go out the front way," Sheila told him, following him across the room and quickly unlocking the doors – anything to keep him away from her house. When he stepped onto the verandah, she locked the doors behind him and watched as he wandered back to the roadhouse. She turned off the lights again, locked the back doors, and jogged through the easing rain to her own back verandah. The storm was finally breaking.

CHAPTER SEVENTY-FIVE

My senses cleared slowly. I stood in a dimly lit, red-hued room, Nick holding me tightly against him. Blankets covered my back, heavy and damp now as the moisture from my clothing seeped through them. I shivered strongly even though the warmth of the room had touched my face.

Nick shifted his hold, stripped the sodden jacket from his shoulders. It dropped to the floor with a splosh. Then my swaddling of blankets dropped to the chair behind me, letting in the cold again.

"Sorry, kiddo, this is for your own good," Nick whispered.

He unzipped my waterlogged coat and pushed it down my arms, its sheer weight sliding it to the floor. Then Nick fumbled with the tiny pink buttons I always had trouble with, prising them open with one hand. *Oh shit!*

I started to fight him.

He ignored me; used his strength to peel the shirt away. I was left standing in my jeans and a pink lace bra. *Embarrassing.* I squirmed away from his hold so I could cover myself, but he pulled me in against him again, pressed my icy flesh against his warm bare skin. He felt divine. Contoured. Safe. I fell against him, moved in closer to gain more warmth. His arms encircled me again, and he eased the blankets back around me, this time containing his own body within. I felt so absolutely, incredibly safe.

"Warm slowly, kiddo," he whispered, his words close to my ear. "Warm slowly." His skin felt even warmer beneath the glow of the wall heater, beneath the layers of blanket, and my flesh sought his for the same.

A long time passed before Nick eased me away again, his unbandaged hand pressing against my cheek. I still shivered violently, not even the blankets eradicating them. "What's happening?" I murmured as a fresh set of shudders coursed up my spine. "What are we doing?"

Nick kept me close as I opened my eyes, and took in our surroundings, the room and Nick's tight embrace. *How the hell did this happen?* Then I remembered, and knew how he would hate it. *Fopsy!* I pushed against him then realised I was nearly naked.

"No, stay here," he said, his arms increasing pressure, their size covering more of me, pulling me back to him. "You're not out of the woods yet. You still need a lot more warmth before you're through this."

I forced the gap wider, not wanting him burdened by this human contact. "I'm not a fopsy!" I snapped, twisting away from him. "I can do this ..."

"Okay, okay, I won't force you," he said, releasing his hold, "but I warn you, you're only half-thawed." He reached across the space between us, and pulled the blanket closer to me. I retreated from his touch, conscious of my state of undress, and almost toppled into the armchair behind me. He made an attempt to grab me.

"Don't! I'll be fine!" I insisted, pushing his hands away.

He swept a hand through his hair and heaved a breath. "Okay, have it your way," he replied, watching as I gathered the blankets around me, as I wrapped them as tight as a baby's swaddling around my shoulders. Another fit of shivers ripped through me, and my teeth chattered. *Damn this!*

"... I want you to go in there, get out of those wet clothes and have a warm shower," he added, tossing some towels from the pile at me. "Wrap yourself up in these and get into that bed, and I don't want any nonsense! Your body heat has to come up a hell of a lot higher before we go out there again. But don't have the water too hot."

He gripped my shoulder and steered me to the bathroom, his own body goose-bumping from the loss of the blankets. Then he pushed me into the room and closed the door behind me. The thought of warm water drew me to the taps. When I turned them on Nick called through the door that he was going to check on Sheila, and moved away.

When he returned a short while later I had snuggled down beneath the heavy blankets, a towel turban keeping my head warm. I still shivered profusely as I drifted towards deep sleep.

CHAPTER SEVENTY-SIX

Nick stood in the warm room looking down as Becky snuggled down beneath the blankets. He was glad she was resting, but was concerned she hadn't been in the shower nearly long enough to raise her core temperature to where it needed to be. Nevertheless, he took his turn in the bathroom to raise his own body heat. Steaming hot water jetted from the nozzles and he reduced the temperature, aware too quick a change in body heat could pose greater problems, a point he'd learnt in the Army.

He stripped his sodden clothing, stepped into the shower recess and pulled the curtain across, images of Becky taking his thoughts. He hoped she'd spent enough time to at least raise her core heat a little, and sighed as he remembered how she'd clung to him, how she'd sought his warmth in those long silent moments. He thought about how soft she'd felt even as cold as she was. These thoughts sent warmth coursing through him, a warmth he hadn't felt in a long, long time.

Leaning back against the cold tiles, he let the water pour over him, the spray thrumming his skin, stinging the abrasions, smarting on the bruises, soothing everywhere else. He closed his eyes and soaked it in as he listened to her moving in the bed in the room beyond the door. He stayed longer in the shower than he'd planned, deliberately giving her more time to settle, for she'd been on the brink of sleep when he'd last checked on her. Finally, when all had been quiet for some time, he shut off the water and wrapped a towel round his waist.

At the basin, he swiped away the steam on the mirror and realised what Sheila had meant — he indeed looked rough, his face drawn and drained, and shadowed by a day's heavy growth. He shaved, gingerly around the tender jaw-line, hoping to reduce her worry. Then he stepped into the bedroom where Becky lay silent and still, and he nodded that that was good.

Gathering the pile of wet clothing, he carried it to the laundry, trying to avoid splattering muddy trails over Sheila's beige carpet; already a large stain had appeared where their coats had lain. More important though, they would need dry clothes when Rod arrived, and he relished the thought of Sheila's closet dryer. He entered the laundry as the back door handle dropped down, and the door edged warily open.

Nick tensed. No time to think. No time to act. No time to do anything as the gap cautiously widened. He steeled, dread flowing through him, the bundle of clothing locked tightly in his grasp.

Sheila slipped in through the opening as he stood tautly drawn, ready to toss the clothing, ready to use his hands on whatever came his way. His eyes turned ominous.

Sheila closed the door behind her. "It's okay, ducky – it's only me," she said, turning and taking the bundle from his arms. "How's Rebecca?"

"Sleeping," he answered, leaning his shoulder against the door-frame as she sorted the garments, "but I'll watch her through until the Police get here."

Sheila's eyes cast over him, over the cleanness of his body, over the scrapes and bruises on his arms and chest, over the tightly wrapped towel. He looked better now that he'd shaved, she thought, her eyes catching the rag encasing his hand. She turned and pulled the medical kit from the cupboard. "They won't be here for a long while yet," she told him, taking his hand and unwrapping the frayed strips of fabric. Nick submitted wordlessly. "Rod says for you to sit tight."

She winced at the length and depth of the gash and shook her head; covered the wound with fresh gauze and strapped it firmly. Reaching up, she turned his head to the light, peeled open an adhesive covering and sealed shut the cut on the back of his neck. "That will hold you until you can get to a doctor, pet. Now, why don't you go and get some rest yourself."

Nick nodded. He needed time to let his wounds heal, to let the tenderness diminish and the aches subside, and he still needed to replace the dreadful cold in his bones. Sheila pulled more blankets from the closet and tossed them across to him.

"Go on. You go and take it easy, and keep warm. I'll get these things ready and shut the house down. It'll look rather odd if the house is lit all night."

Agreeing, Nick padded back to the red-tinged bedroom where Becky had curled up tight, the bedding pulled up about her neck. He closed the door to keep in the heat then noiselessly moved the brocade chair over under the heater, closer to her. Wrapping a layer of blankets around him, he sat and made himself comfortable. He could see Becky clearly in the red glow of the heater, and damn, she was shivering again.

CHAPTER SEVENTY-SEVEN

In Dayton, lights all over town flicked on, twinkling like bright stars in a cruel dark sky. The north end of town blazed with yellow glow as men bustled under floodlights, preparing tools and machinery for the grim task ahead. Cars lined the curb opposite the Police Station, yet keeping clear of the access to both buildings as civilians scurried to load the gear, equipment jingling and clanging on the metal floors of truck trays.

Above the general banter of conversation, a voice shouted instructions, intermingling orders with a constant flow of praise to lift the men's morale. Conditions were dismal. All about, rain drizzled over them making their yellow weather-proofs glisten under streetlights.

In the office across the road, Owen Cussack coordinated the operation and, if waiting was his worst forte, this was his best: controlling a force of men. He thrived on organisation, on structuring the manpower available to expedite the task. With the weather so changeable, with two civilians still at risk, the extraction at Carter's dam would have to run like clock-work. He'd accept nothing less, and hoped the Emergency Service volunteers knew their stuff.

Sitting in his high-backed chair, he glanced out the window as yellow coats darted in and out of the shed opposite. They certainly looked an able crew, he thought, and they had certainly proved their worth only hours earlier; he wondered if they were annoyed at being called twice in one day, then mused: 'Ho-hum, it never rains but it pours!'

Running a pencil through his scant crop of hair, he intercepted an itch and yawned then realised the same applied to him. In his months at Dayton there had been little excitement, apart from the odd pub brawl or minor car accident. Maybe he detected a momentary surge of apprehension on Tuesdays, the one day of the week when the local louts could sit their driving tests – a time he called *fear-of-the-unknown*. 'Well, there'll be no tests tomorrow', he sighed, and that was good. The last week had provided him and the town with enough excitement to last the next thirty years.

A smile teased his lips. Maybe too, after all this was over, he would go back to the city for he felt rather comfortable now, and suddenly realised he actually liked sorting out the horrors people committed on each other; realised too that maybe somewhere over the last six months he had quietly come to terms with the mayhem that had pushed his escape to a dead little country town, surrounded by deader little country towns. Maybe somewhere over the last six months he'd learned to accept the death of his son, a young man at the start of his career, stabbed to death on a busy city street, watched but unaided by a crowd of gawking prats ... not one ounce of compassion in the whole goddamned bunch of them! ...

The tow truck pulled up outside his window.

'Well, at least these people have compassion.' His jaw set tightly. 'These people care!'

He watched as the shed across the road was locked up. The trucks were ready. The volunteers were ready. He still had to get ready. He looked back to his office, to where the uniformed constables bunched around the wide polished desk. He tallied the force in front of him – they were all there.

The itch had now travelled to his chin and he scratched it, realising the stubble was back – he would have to shave before going out, before fronting up to his superiors, but for now, he had to start the clock ticking. He cleared his throat.

"Okay," he said, grabbing their full attention, "we have two D's and a diver coming up from Central, and they're dragging the

Coroner with them. Apparently the man's not too happy about that so I'll warn you not to get in his way. They'll be arriving by light aircraft ... ETA zero one hundred hours. Bob will have the vehicles ready by then.

"Ray, you'll take one of the vehicles and go out and pick them up at the airstrip. Transport them straight to site.

"I've called for back-up from Stansville and Mount Lawson, and they're sending a couple of men from each. They'll be here in about two hours. Rod, you'll be in charge of them when they front. Direct them up to site, and I want you to take care of the Media as well. Keep them the hell away from there. Hopefully, we're so far out they won't even hear about this till it's over."

He tapped his pencil incessantly on the desk, turning it over and pushing it through his fingers at each tap, his mind racing. "I also want you to get a line on this Queensland crowd. Get me more information. Find out where they've come from, and see if there's a file on this McCaig fella. William T. is how he signed the roadhouse register."

Rod scrawled the information on a notepad.

"Brett, you man the phones and radio." He ignored the officer's groan. "Ken, you take the volunteers and get them up on site. If you go now, you'll be all set up when the D's arrive. Nobody is to enter the water until the diver gets here." He laid the pencil down and pushed his chair back. "Go to it!" he ordered, the sweep of his hand emptying his office with a murmur of voices. He rose, slouched his tension away as he took another long look out the window.

At that exact moment Lacey and Beattie pulled out from the kerb and headed north out of town, the interior of the camper-bus whistling noisily as the wind and rain poured in.

CHAPTER SEVENTY-EIGHT

Ron McCaig stood up and stretched, loosening joints stiffened by the cold night air. He wandered to the utility, slapping and rubbing his arms, his annoyance deepening as the night blew colder. The snoring came louder from behind the car's steering wheel, mixing with the voices and static crackling over the radio.

He pulled open the car door, glared at his father as he reached for the microphone.

"Poppa, this is Goose!" the voice came again.

"Yeah Goose ... what's up?"

"Well it's about bloody time. Listen ... there's a whole lot of activity going on down here in Dayton. The whole town's out tonight ..."

The older McCaig slowly stirred.

"... too many for us to keep in. Hell, they've even got a crane going out."

Suddenly alert, McCaig snatched the mike. "Come a little way home. You-know-who might try to make it through with all that diversion."

"Gotcha Boss, but it's getting rather hot down here."

"Just do it," he barked, and tossed the hand-piece back on the seat. He turned to Ron. "Get over to the rooms. Tell Jim to start loadin' our stuff ... everybody's ... everything. We're pulling out tomorrow. Tell him to put it all on the truck."

Ron looked hopeful. "Are you calling the boys in? We're going home?"

McCaig shook his head. "Soon. We still gotta stop the girl, and there's a small matter of some cheques to collect or all this hoo-ha's been for nothin'. We're gonna go home with somethin', even if the Taylors have finished us in this town.

CHAPTER SEVENTY-NINE

I woke slowly, noting a glowing red room and that a warm layer of blankets covered me, and no wind. No wind at all. I lay, my eyes barely open, confused as to why I still trembled, why I felt so much pain. I watched Nick breathing in the warm air and letting it out again. He looked magnificent, barely clad, a layer of blankets draped around his broad shoulders, his chest muscles tight as he sat leaning forward. His brow wrinkled as another fit of shivers attacked me, the blankets vibrating with their force. I groaned as my back cramped up against them, the move chilling me again.

Nick rubbed his face tiredly and his lips pressed together, thoughts dancing in his eyes. I pulled the blankets closer but nothing seemed to eradicate the cold.

Nick shook his head. "You still cold?" he whispered.

"I'm freezing," I whispered the reply. "Why the hell am I so damn cold?"

"I told you, you had to raise your body heat much higher; you should have stayed in the shower longer than you did."

"It's so painful ... I promise I'll listen to you next time." My words muffled against the pillows as the shivering started again, and I tucked my legs up further, curving my back to stretch out the cramp. "... my back hurts so ..."

"Yeah, I know," Nick nodded. A moment passed before he moved closer. "Turn over," he said.

I rolled to my other side, buried myself back into the bank of pillows, the move doing little to alleviate the pain. I felt the blankets lift, my back exposed to the cold for a second as Nick slid in beside me. He reached over, pulled me back against him, my whole body exploding with warmth as his massive arm encased me and drew me in to the taut breadth of him. "I'm just going to keep you warm," he said, his arm tightening as if to enforce his will. "Trust me."

My core throbbed at his touch, and I closed my eyes, revelled in the feel of him. I could feel the power of his body even though he lay in quiet repose; his strength evident even in his idleness. My heart raced till I thought it would burst from my chest. I fought the sensation back; killed the butterflies rising on mass, stilled the fluttering motion of my heartbeat, for he was merely keeping me warm. And with Nick Manetti, I could expect nothing more. "Oh I trust you," I muttered, snuggling further into the warmth of him, my skin burning where his flesh touched mine. "Who wouldn't trust Nick Manetti?"

Silence reigned a moment then he said, "And what's that supposed to mean?"

"Oh nothing ..." I sighed and stretched out to find more warmth along the length of him. "... just a comment."

"I bet." His face felt close to mine, his lips almost resting against my ear. I could feel the warmth of his breath against my cheek. "And I bet it has nothing to do with Nick being a monk." I felt his chest tighten against my shoulder blades, and his biceps felt a little heavier. "Nor with rocks having no emotions."

I lay silent, suddenly intimidated; pulled the sheet up higher to cover myself; turned in his arms. He lay on his side, his head now propped on his hand as he gazed down at me. "You know all about that?"

"I don't miss much," he answered, his voice soft and deep.

Another fit of shivers coursed through me and his face turned more sombre. He pulled me closer, keeping me warmer.

"You play the game very well you know," I said, picking up the sadness in his eyes. My fingers couldn't resist exploring the sensuous tanned hollow at his throat. I wanted to kiss it. The thought tingled through me and heat tore to my core, but I pushed the urge away.

He smiled, slightly amused at my observation, but it faded. "And what makes you think it's a game?"

His eyes hardened, as if daring me to make further comment. I met the look full on. "Because nobody who is so unfeeling would do so much for people. And you do, Nick, you're there for everyone."

A moment of silence passed before he started to laugh, almost aloud. "What the hell have you been listening to?"

I stiffened at his jibe. "I haven't been listening to anything!" I shuddered violently, the shakes returning. "I've ... seen it – you're there for Sheila McKenzie – you're there for Sam and Pete; you came after ... me ... without the slightest ... concern for your own life." My hand, which I'd squeezed in between us to keep our bodies apart, now rested on his chest, directly over the pounding force within. "Nobody would do all that if they didn't have a giant heart in there."

Indeed, the power of it thudded against my hand.

Nick's lips thinned again and his eyes darkened with thought then turned derisive. "I wouldn't put too much store in that," he warned.

"I would, but I just keep wondering ... was it Marilyn who hurt you so much you hide so deep within?"

His next move surprised me for I half-expected him to push me away, dump me out the other side of the bed, or turn over. Instead he pulled me a little closer, secured his arm further beneath me, crushing my arm between us. I trembled at our closeness now, at the thought of all the places our bodies made contact, at the way Nick looked at me, maybe also aware. He smiled thinly. "Well, Miss Freud, seeing you are well enough to analysis my problems, why don't you try and get back to sleep and get even better."

My arm, trapped between us, went numb so I wriggled it clear; moved it higher. Up over his shoulder was the only place it could go without posing any embarrassment. "One day Nick," I told him softly, "you'll learn to ..."

"Goodnight," he said tersely.

And that was that. I huffed out a deep breath, said a dismal "Goodnight," and rolled over in his arms; buried my back into the hard wall of his stomach. As I heaved out a disappointed breath and closed my eyes, as I tried hard to control the pounding of my heart, he pulled the blankets up around my neck and lowered his head to the pillow.

Long minutes passed as we lay, his breath soft and warm against my neck.

"And what brought you to the conclusion that I'm such a tortured soul?" he suddenly asked.

There was only one answer to that. "Because I know how it feels."

"You don't look very tortured to me."

"That's because I took one look at you and decided to snap out of it."

Another moment of quiet passed before he said, "So, what is it that this Tony ...?"

"Goodnight, Nick."

I felt a smile broaden his face as his arm tightened around me again, one hand now cupped beneath my breast, accidentally or deliberately I couldn't tell, but it sent my heart crashing through my ribs. I lay about as far removed from sleep as a naked nymphomaniac lying beside a magnificent naked demi-god could get.

CHAPTER EIGHTY

Cruising along a dark empty back-road between Cullan and where they'd lost Manetti, Dave Taylor peered intently through the windscreen; squinted through the raindrops that glued themselves to the glass. His thoughts dwelt on their tactics, on what they'd done since the trail had gone cold. So far they'd covered all the back-roads, crawled at snail's pace back and forth along the busy highway – they'd even toured the block several times in Cullan, all without results. He stared harder at the rain, the windscreen fogging in front of his face leaving streaks of condensation, making it more difficult to see through.

"Where the hell can he be?" he griped, his hand wresting a grip on the rifle barrel leaning against his leg. The rifle was primed and ready, its chambers loaded, and he willed a certain party to step into its path.

His jaw set as Lacey's voice came across the two-way. "Sounds like they're getting ready to pull up our poor friend," he said, scowling at Ben. "Things are getting just a bit too lively down there."

"You reckon we should pull out?"

Dave's eyes narrowed at the thought. "Not until I get Manetti," he replied, stroking the rifle affectionately.

Ben's gaze shot sideways. "Why bother? Let's just go. Let McCaig take the brunt of it!"

But Dave's jaw clenched and his next words breathed out harshly. "Because I want Manetti!" His body tightened at the thought, tightened because it was personal now. Never before had it taken so long to bring down his prey and he needed the kill to prove that he was smarter. While Manetti had been cunning, he would soon show him he wasn't cunning enough.

A smile crept over Ben's face. "I'd like a go at the girl myself," he said with a wry grin. It took the edge off, and Dave laughed. "You're demented!"

"Yeah, I know. It must run in the family."

Ben flicked the indicator and turned left towards Dayton.

"No, wait," Dave said, rubbing his chin again. "Pull over." A whole series of calculations skipped through his mind as the engine died. "Look, Manetti's got the girl, right?"

Ben nodded.

"And it's pouring cats and dogs, and blowing a gale out there."

Ben looked out the window to see just how heavy the rain was, and again nodded.

"My bet is that, by now, Manetti's taken cover somewhere. If he's got any sense, and I think he has, he'll wait till morning then make a run for it. I say we do the same and hold up till dawn. Then we'll watch for him to come out."

"How do you know he's not already in Dayton?" the notion suddenly struck Ben.

"Because McCaig would be behind bars by now, or at least hauled in for questioning, and he's not. And I don't think Manetti would try to walk to Dayton in this weather. They'd both be hypothermic before they got there." He shook his head slowly. "No ... he's nicely tucked up somewhere with that little piece.

Ben sighed with despondence. "Yeah, well you said he was smart."

"Yeah ... and I think we'll play it smart too. But let's head back to Cullan first, I want to check something out." His eyes narrowed with the possibility that Manetti had put up at the hotel. "If nothing comes of it, we'll find a quiet place to wait it out, and let Manetti come to us."

ॐ

CHAPTER EIGHTY-ONE

Several hours passed in darkness. Suddenly Nick tensed, his skin chilling. High above him a slender silver blade glinted in the blackness, the sudden brilliant flash of light on shiny steel jolting him awake. He tried to reach up to stop its downward strike but was heavily weighed down, too restricted to do anything but flinch as the knife arced towards him. His muscles locked tighter in pre-knowledge of the agonizing penetration and his dark eyes flicked open. He looked down, waiting ... waiting for the protrusion of the blood-smeared point to appear through his side. He saw only blankets.

Gulping a breath, he blinked quickly, fighting off the bleariness; fought to steady his breathing. Quickly he assessed his surroundings.

The red glow radiating from the wall was now a red glow radiating from the wall, not coloured smoke. The weight restricting him was not the two VC who'd jumped him. Movement against his skin stirred another tremor and he glanced down again, heaved a more contented breath. He was lying on his back, with Becky asleep beside him. Her head nestled in the crook of his shoulder and her arm draped across him; his own arms folded possessively around her, keeping her there. He knew then what had woken him – her fingers rested on the scar on his side, her fingertips in the small depression that trailed down from his ribs. Immediately it all came back ... the silence of the trail ahead – too quiet – the soft steady footfalls of his mates behind him. Still too quiet. No bird song. No thrumming insects. He'd raised his fist and thrust it down, sending them to cover. The silence deafened him. He'd half-turned, unsure of what had spooked him, unsure that it was nothing more than instinct. Premonition. They were on him when he turned back – three puny VC. Two charged from the front, from nowhere, and tried to pin his arms, trying to keep his rifle from rising. A third latched an arm round his throat. He rose fully, lifting the little man off the ground, used his shoulders to evict those dragging at his limbs, tossing them like hay stukes. They'd tumbled to the grass, but were up again and at him before he'd raised his weapon, the man at his back still clinging on by an arm. He heard a shout go up, from Stewy; heard Sam bellow something as he sprinted forward; saw Pete between them, standing pale and motionless, confused, looking to both directions. He used his shoulders again to clear the two puny attackers, flung them off towards Sam and Co. But the man behind him had gained a footing on higher ground, on the bank of the dry riverbed. He doubled him back as his tiny feet found leverage. Then something sliced through his side, searing heat coursing to his chest. He'd looked down as the shiny pointed blade appeared through his skin, blood stained and dripping, glinting in places where the sun struck unstained steel. It disappeared, and he glanced behind him, saw it striking again. He could hear his bellow of pain as he raised his arms and grappled upward, trying to claim the knife. He'd found the man's arms on its downswing, the strike aiming for his chest. He'd locked his grip on, his hands still above his head. Unable to stop the downward arc, he'd increased its momentum, drew both hands sharply down and arced out of its way at the last moment. The knife arc kept flying, found its mark deep in his enemy's gut. He'd never forgotten the look of horror that crossed the man's brown face, the shock and stunned surprise, the blood that trickled first then spurted from his mouth. He'd let the man fall forward on his face. Turning, he'd looked back at Pete, who still hadn't moved; saw Sam, Stewy and Credo pulverising the other two on the ground, and he'd sank to his knees, pain over-riding him as blood started gushing through his fingers.

That knife point had set his life on a huge turn-around, sent everything from then spiralling downward. The war had finished before he'd recovered – his father had died soon after, leaving him to run the farm – Marilyn, well he'd learnt the hard way about her. Then the boredom of living had set in. Absolute and total boredom. His life just shuffled along, one day drifting into another. Then The Kid had come along.

He'd seen her the day she'd arrived in Cullan, towing that big fancy horse float with two big horses aboard. Showjumpers, he'd eventually heard. Then she'd shown up one night at the hotel weeks later. He'd liked her in a general sort of way, from the moment he'd stood behind her at the bar, the top of her brunette head just below his shoulders. She'd worn work jeans, jeans that fitted comfortably to her frame, and short polished riding boots – no make-up – her hair had been loose, flowing down her back as it most times did, and most times it was wind-blown from driving with the window down. He liked the way she felt comfortable with her looks, the way she didn't care what people thought. He'd picked that by the way she looked at them – straight up, head on, chin up at times, or at times she looked straight through them, as if she didn't care, like she did to him sometimes.

He inhaled deeply, lifted her hand clear of the scar and locked it higher on his side; pinned it there with his arm. He realised now as he looked at her how much he liked watching her, whether she was at the hotel, or riding in Crestwood's lower pasture, or even when she drove the gutsy Ford into town and parked. He'd found himself looking for her, at times made sure he was near where she was, going into the Store when she shopped, pulling in for fuel at Barney's when she was fuelling up even if he had nearly a full tank. He remembered once he'd tried to talk to her on the hotel verandah but couldn't think of anything to say except lame-brain stuff about the weather, which seemed so damn pointless, and she hadn't taken the topic any further for it to lead to other things. He'd caught himself that night; realised what was happening; realised not too late that it was best not complicate his life, or hers.

Then this had happened – with Pete – and she'd spent the night in his bed. The moment he'd laid eyes on her standing in his shirt she'd turned his guts to fire. And every moment since. She intrigued him, made him laugh, but more, he admired the way she stood up to him and spoke her crazy mind. He liked the way she looked at him direct and calculating. She wasn't afraid of him, even if she said she was. And he liked the way she trusted him enough to do exactly as he said.

Now, as she lay almost naked beside him, warding off her hypothermic state, his guts had gone volcanic. They'd raged with heat for the past few hours for he wanted so much to touch her – touch her in a way he wanted no other man to touch her. But he couldn't. She trusted him to keep his word. So he lay, his heart pounding hard in his chest as he stared up at the ceiling, as he wondered about her past – about her broken relationship with what's-his-face.

He looked down at her, tossing more logs on his fire. Gently he pulled her closer, kissed the top of her head – it was safe while she slept – then he lay his head back down, stared harder at the ceiling and started the process of talking the feeling away till he'd regained full control of his body. In the red glowing silence he decided it would end when he got her safely to Dayton, that there would be no point pursuing what he wanted – it was obvious she had her life mapped out. She was going places, had dreams to fill. She was going to be something.

He thought then about Dayton and what might avail when he tried to get her through. McCaig and his mates were pretty desperate, and the thought of the two big men who'd mangled him sent his blood coursing again. His heart re-fired with strong vibrant beats but for a different reason.

CHAPTER EIGHTY-TWO

Something disturbed me and I woke suddenly. Nick had moved, and I immediately became aware of his strong, rapid heartbeat. "What is it?" I hissed, scanning the room with sudden fear.

"Nothing," he said. "Go back to sleep."

He eased my head down against him, his other hand stroking my side, soothing my growing alarm. I submitted to the pressure and lay against him, still incredibly tired.

"There you go again," I murmured, "locking it all inside." I closed my eyes, and snuggled closer, half yawned. "You can't go keeping everything to yourself, you know. Sometimes it's better to get it off your chest."

"It's not anything you would understand."

"And of course you won't let anyone get close enough to understand."

He gazed down at me. "Getting close to me isn't an experience you'd enjoy," he quipped honestly.

I looked up, my smile mocking him. "Is that so? Well I personally don't think you'd give anybody the chance." I lay my head down again, not wishing to witness the staid expression on his face, wishing to fall victim to the sleep bug again. "You must get pretty lonely, Nick."

He smirked. "You think you have me all summed up, don't you?"

"Nope. I don't think that's possible." I didn't look at him. "But I can't help thinking it would be interesting trying."

"So what's that mean? ... you're into playing games? Stick around just long enough to sort me out?" He glanced down at me, his eyes and jaw hardening. He shifted to his side, the move subtly dumping me back to the sheets.

So Marilyn played games. I realised in that moment I'd struck a raw nerve, just as he'd struck one with me. I recoiled at his insult. "Nobody has the right to play with somebody's emotions, Nick," I said sharply, all of Tony's lies or lack of the truth coming back to haunt me. "Nobody!"

My eyes moistened that he could accuse me of that and a lump rose in my throat. He was too far gone to even try reaching him. And if you did try he lashed out in defense. *Arms distance by cruelty. Stone heart.* I rolled away from him. "That's the cruellest acc..."

"Shit!" he cussed gruffly before his hand clamped a grip on my arm and pulled me back, his mouth claiming mine the moment I turned to face him. His kiss, that sweet tasting kiss, stifled the rest of my words, his big hands pinning me to the hard wall of him, locking me against him so tightly I couldn't resist.

I pushed him away — *how dare he accuse me of that!* — I shoved against his shoulders; tried to put space between us. What was he playing at? Why was he doing this? His sudden change of tack took me completely by surprise.

His kiss persisted, burning my lips, his arms holding me so tight I thought he'd break my ribs. But his lips remedied the cruelty of his words, and when his tongue set a fire raging through my core I realised I was kissing him back, seeking more of the sweet taste of him, revelling in the manliness of him, knowing that his body sought mine as much as mine sought his. My head screamed *No!* — *wrong* — *wrong* — *wrong* — and roiled with every reason why I shouldn't submit. But my heart would stop beating if I denied him that pleasure.

Savouring his kisses, I let those gentle hands sweep away the fabric that separated our flesh. I allowed him to lie hard and warm against me, my skin heating beneath his touch. Kisses laid a trail over my neck, over the curve of my shoulder, over my breasts, fire raging deep within when his thumb strayed boldly over a peaking nipple. His lips followed, tracing the line of his hand, smothering my neck, brushing warmly over the curve of my shoulder, along the curve of my breasts, igniting my womanhood as he teased each nipple. I was beyond stopping anything he wanted and rode the peak of intense pleasure and pain over and over, clinging to him, my face buried into his shoulder, stifling my sounds. When he'd reached his own height of ecstasy, I buried my head deeper in his shoulder and murmured from my heart: "Oh God, I love you."

CHAPTER EIGHTY-THREE

A yellow dawn dappled the eastern hills as the gathering at Carter's dam began to dwindle. Cussack stood back yawning as his eyes panned the scene. Behind him, water still trickled from the red coupe that perched atop the dam's high wall, a startling monument to the tragedy soon to shock Cullan. The driver's door was open, the body that had floated within it now confined in a black vinyl body bag and on its way back to Dayton. He stared at the vehicle, remembering his last words as the young man departed. I don't want to see you again.

Don't worry, you won't.

And he sighed with remorse that Pete Kennedy had been right on that score.

Looking around, his gaze fell on the group of orange-clad figures huddled on the ground beside the muddy Police car. They'd done a good job and he was relieved things had gone according to plan.

Amid the cluster however sat two young men, farm lads from *Colinda*, and he shook his head. They'd been too enthusiastic, those two. Too keen to get involved. They'd defied all warnings to stay back and let the Police handle certain aspects of the extraction. They'd ignored the downpour of water escaping the vehicle as it was lifted high on heavy chains and swung across to land. They'd crowded in, their hands on the wheels to assist its gentle descent. As the vehicle's suspension lowered to its maximum, they'd peered inside, a first-hand look at a corpse — and they'd both turned and puked all over the ground. It had been their first rescue, one which Cussack considered might well be their last. He remembered his own stomach lurching as he'd viewed Pete Kennedy's body, the gruesome killing made worse by days of immersion. He wondered if his face had shown the same pallid texture still worn by the young volunteers.

He turned away as the radio called his attention. "Cussack here," he said, leaning into the car to eradicate the wind. He watched as the tall, most senior detective wandered over to listen.

"Willcox here, Sarge. I just got word from Central. Following up on the information you wanted on the Queenslanders, apparently there was an incident a while back ... in Wilcannia ... New South Wales," Rod added briefly. "It happened four or five weeks ago, and they tried to link the disturbance to McCaig's crew but there wasn't enough evidence to substantiate a case so they had to let them go."

"What sort of trouble?" Cussack inquired, looking directly at Marcus Platt, who now butt-rested against the vehicle's front fender.

"Same as this, Sarge. Scare tactics mainly ... a couple of minor accidents. Problem was, there was this one eye-witness who seemed willing to come forward but she suddenly disappeared before they could get her story. They haven't been able to trace her since despite lengthy ground searches and APBs."

"Maybe they should try checking the dams," Cussack commented, not caring if anyone heard. "Anything else?"

"No. That's it so far," Rod answered. "I haven't heard back from anyone else yet.

"Okay. Keep on it though." He hooked the hand-piece back on the holder and waited for Platt to make comment, seeing this whole case was now his jurisdiction.

The man simply nodded as he finished jotting notes on his clip file. "You've got enough for a warrant as far as I'm concerned," he said without looking up. "Let's get back to town and organise one then we'll go and pull this crowd in for questioning."

Cussack smiled smugly – he'd handled his end well enough. "Well," he said confidently, "what's in our favour is that we still have our eye-witness."

CHAPTER EIGHTY-FOUR

The storm outside had broken when I next awoke. I turned over wanting Nick's warm arms around me, wanting his gentle kisses, his hunger. But the bed was empty, the covers tucked in around me, and I had to be content with the memory of the night. I blushed in my solitude for he'd stirred sensations in me I'd never experienced before, sensations I couldn't control. I warmed further at the thought of him, adored how he'd held me for hours afterwards, caressing me, keeping me pulled in against him, making me feel so safe.

But where is he now? And why did he go without waking me?

Then a cold wave washed through me. Maybe he regretted the night. Maybe he preferred it hadn't happened. Nick was a loner. He didn't like people getting close to him. *He doesn't complicate his life with women.* He'd told me that. Yet my whole being told me I wanted the opposite. Nick was all I'd dreamed of since the first time I'd seen him. I wanted to spend the rest of my days pleasing him. But that would never happen. I told myself that over and over, just as Ros had told me over and over.

"Don't do it this time, Becca. I know you, you always go after what you can't have."

"No, I don't," I'd corrected her emphatically. "I go after what I need. There's a difference."

Well, maybe I needed Nick Manetti. But maybe the night had simply been a crack in his hard exterior. Maybe I shouldn't have let it happen; maybe I shouldn't have incited it. And I had incited it, hadn't I?

Fighting the heat in my eyes I sat up. *God, what he must think of me!* After all this was over I'd hoped we might have been friends, at least then he might have talked to me on the odd occasion – it would have been enough. But not now. I'd just ruined everything. I'd stirred him with my taunts, with my subtle touches in the darkness – and in my deliriously happy state I'd told him that I loved him. Now that would have been a whammy to his freedom; that alone would have hammered a huge irremovable wedge in the friendship.

Maybe he didn't hear you. You can only hope he didn't. God how stupid of me!

Looking at the window, I cursed the daylight beyond the curtains ... daylight always brought back reality; always destroyed the glorious illusions dreams created. And my worst nightmare was now about to start: Nick would treat me with the same contempt he bestowed on Marilyn Perry. And I couldn't live with that.

My attention shifted to the room as I forced back visions of the treatment to expect. This was not Nick's room, nor was this his bed, and I wondered who he would call on in his hour of need. He certainly never seemed particularly friendly with anyone but Sam and Pete.

The pastel blue room was neat and masculine, beige curtains matching the cotton bedspread. A no-frills room yet neat and tidy, everything having a purpose. The solid-framed brocade armchair was now in the corner under the large front window and I remembered Nick's deep expression as he'd sat bent forward under blankets, much closer to the bed than it was now. I noticed my clothes piled neatly on the end of the bed, and wondered if Nick had put them there. Or had some-one else?

The bedroom door was closed so I dressed quickly, and, though I wanted to hide away in shame, I fought the discomfort back and walked softly to the end of the passage, worrying that Nick might not be in the room at the end of the hall. I wondered what I would do if that was the case. How would I respond to whoever was there? Maybe they had even heard us in the night, though Nick had stifled my cries with his hand or his lips, looking delighted at my irrepressible responses. Then I worried how I would respond if Nick *was* there.

Voices came from the room at the end of the hall, Nick's one of them. My heart thudding dully, I drew a steadying breath to prepare for whatever response he would give me, straightened my back and walked into a kitchen of warm creams and golds, walked in ready to show him I expected nothing from him for that was the only way we could go forward from here. What had happened had happened. It was done and over. I would force myself to pretend it never happened – as long as he didn't repel me. That was all that mattered.

Nick sat at the end of the table, facing me, his elbows resting on the table's cool surface, a cup of steaming coffee in his hands. He wore a crisp white shirt, by the size of it one of his, and I wondered, if so, how did he come to have one here. It took seconds to dawn that he may have spent other nights here, and felt somewhat more apprehensive, for who else was he in the habit of spending nights with?

Warmth surged through me as he looked up, the night's sensations returning to my face in that instant. A nervous tremor fluttered through my stomach and into my breasts, petered out through my fingers and thighs. I wanted to touch him, wanted to be held by him. *Will I always feel like this when he looks at me?* I fought the sensations back and pushed my gaze to the other occupant in the room. *Sheila McKenzie.*

Sheila sat opposite Nick, and smiled a meek Hello.

Immediately my jealousy abated as I realised what I'd witnessed between them at the Hotel. Nick and the woman were close, and that was good for it meant he wasn't totally alone. He at least had someone to care about.

Sheila turned as I entered the room. "Oh, she does look better, Nick," she remarked. "It's just as well you stayed over."

My gaze fell back on Nick; found his returning look hard and dark. I lowered my eyes as remorse flooded in. He would think so ill of me, being so willing; having a past with Tony. I'd be so cheap in his eyes. I cursed myself again for not stopping him, for not having control of my body. I wanted to tell him so, but certainly could say nothing in front of Sheila.

Avoiding his gaze, I turned to the woman. "Thank you for taking us in."

"You're welcome, love, and I'm glad you feel much better."

Nick rose from the table, his dark eyes briefly scanning my face as he moved. I didn't look at him; couldn't bear to see the derision in his eyes.

"Sit down," he told me. I glanced at him for the merest second, his profile hard as he turned towards the sink. "I'll get you something to drink."

Lowering to a chair, I stared after him, my eyes and throat starting to burn as I wondered if this was how it was to be from now on: admiring him only while his back was turned, always remembering how wonderfully close we'd been but knowing it would never happen again. This treatment was worse than none at all, and I forced back the rising pain in my throat and looked away.

Over at the sink, Nick stirred the cup loudly, and I noticed Sheila's eyes rove from me to him in the silence, her grey eyes narrowing as she looked at Nick with concern. Rising, she said: "I'll go and open the yard then, but I do wish you'd wait, love."

He shook his head, his jaw set firm. "We've waited long enough."

Without further argument, she clicked the back door shut. It was obvious whatever Nick had planned his mind was made up.

Returning to the table, he placed a cup before me and sat down again; watched me openly. The steam from my coffee rose in shimmers, its haze as good a place as any to centre my thoughts, anything but meet that dark, critical stare; anything to avoid the rejection in his eyes. As I reached for the sugar, his hand caught mine half way and stopped its reach, his long, broad fingers filling my vision for long moments before I shifted my gaze to his face.

"Are you okay?" he asked deeply, his eyes searching mine for the truth.

In what way? My health? Or my pride? I could only nod, to which he briefly smiled.

"Drink up then." he said. "I'm going to get you into Dayton once and for all, before things get too hot around here."

CHAPTER EIGHTY-FIVE

Sheila's footsteps scrunched on loose stones as she scurried on tiptoe across the asphalt drive, shooshing herself to silence as the wide enclosure gates squeaked open. The sound pierced the town's early morning peace and she looked around, her nerves raw for she didn't want to draw attention to her business. With the gates now open, the Supply Yard returned to quiet – deathly quiet. It sat misty, like a cemetery just before dark, or as now, just after dawn. Droplets of rain glistened in the eerie hue, plopped silently from stands of dormant machinery into sleeping puddles. Ripples forged across their surface, waking them, distorting faint reflections. There was barely any wind, not the slightest moan of air to cover her movements, and the low hanging sun did little to eradicate the chill.

Crossing the yard, she fumbled for the small silver key that unlocked the shed door, a key hidden among many that jingled on the key-ring. Nick had warned her many times to split the bunch. "Lose one, lose them all," he'd say, and for the noise value now she wished she had listened. Her sounds reverberated across the yard, seeming amplified by the intensity of silence, and added to by her own worried mutterings.

After much fiddling, she had the shed door open. Another clattering of keys resounded within the building as she searched for the bronze one that released the padlock on the next latch. It thankfully came to her hand more easily. The roller door clattered up, scraping and grating metallically as she jerked the circle of chain like a priest tolling steeple bells on Sunday. The door went up in stages and she winced as the sounds of her doings echoed again through the town.

When the door was raised to half its height, she left it, the clearance adequate and turned to undertake the next of Nick's instructions.

At the back of the shed between the rows of pump parts and flexible hoses sat a cream Toyota Hilux. Kennie's truck. His favourite toy. Although it was now rarely used, she hadn't had the heart to sell it. It was her last link to Kennie, apart from, of course, Nick. She was glad now she'd let Nick maintain it, that he occasionally drove it to Dayton for light supplies, but a long time had passed since that had happened. She hoped it was still functional for he was determined to make Dayton, and the rising bad feelings he'd expressed had transferred to her.

Taking the keys from the office, she poked them into the ignition switch. She'd never learnt how to drive, but Nick had told her what to do and she turned the key until needles swung up on the gauges and a light went on in the dash. She found what she was looking for – it had a good half tank of diesel.

Stepping back into the yard, she gazed around. The town looked deserted, not a movement anywhere, so she hurried back to the house.

CHAPTER EIGHTY-SIX

Across at the roadhouse, on the concrete kerb that skirted the garden bed, Ron McCaig sat rubbing the heels of his hands into his tired eyes. He blinked rapidly to alleviate their soreness; squinted as the sun's early rays tipped over the distant hill and burned them red. His butt had gone numb from the hours he had waited, and it now felt like a dead weight he had no control of. So he stayed, watching the tip of his discarded cigarette die slowly on the asphalt, appreciating the solidness of a forty-four gallon drum that blocked the night's annoying breeze.

Pulling his coat collar high up his neck, he looked across at the green truck laden with cases and bedding. It was ready to roll, and soon they'd be heading home ... soon they'd be getting out of this crappy little town. He'd considered several times over the last few hours of just getting in it and driving away, driving back to Kerry and leaving them all behind. He shoved his hands deep in his pockets, shook his head, and scanned the empty road. Hell was going to go down here and he didn't want any part of it. Maybe he should, he considered again, just get up and go.

His shoulders hunched in his sullenness for he hadn't wanted to be involved in any of this, but he was in too deep now and there was nothing he could do. His Dad, big Bill McCaig, had denied all involvement in this, and in the incident back east, until he was in so deep in the shit there was no getting out. He couldn't prove he had no involvement, and he cursed his stupidity for being so gullible, for not demanding the truth, for not having the guts to just get up and walk away. Kerry would need him soon ... very soon ... and all he wanted was to get home and be there for her. He would do anything he had to now to achieve that. And when he got there he would get as far away from his father as he possibly could.

His thoughts turned to Rosie. Her misery would start all over once his Dad returned, but that was something Rosie had to sort out.

A long squeak broke his thoughts and he leant forward to peer around the wall of green metal. The fat lady from the pub was tiptoeing across the puddles on her way to the shed. He almost snickered for she looked like the dancing Hippopotamus from Disney's television ads. But what was the old biddy doing opening up so early?

He checked the time. It was not quite seven o'clock.

He held his position, and watched with growing interest; watched the roller door jerk up to half its height, much too low for the delivery truck he'd seen on the road. More scrunching came as she ballet-danced back across the water pools, back towards the house, the shed doors and gates left wide open. He leant back against the wall, frowning, and noted again how pleasant the sun's radiance felt without the chill of the morning breeze. He closed his eyes to enjoy it.

Click. Crunch. Crunch. Crunch crunch crunch crunch.

He opened his eyes and leant forward again, his brow furrowing as he wondered what the silly old fart was up to now, as he tried to locate her on the short stretch between the house and shed. It took a while to register. There were two people now ... hand in hand ... running across the yard ... splashing through the puddles. A guy and a girl ... *Oh Jesus fucking Christ!*

He bolted upright so fast he almost lost his balance, almost up-ended the green drum in his haste. It was Manetti and the girl!

Grabbing the drum before it toppled over, he swung it back on its base as the pair disappeared inside the Farm Supply shed then he dashed around the corner to the white utility and wrenched open the door.

"Hey, wake up!" he bellowed into the cab. He pounded a fist

against the fat leg that stretched along the seat. "It's Manetti and the girl!"

McCaig grunted mid snore. "Mmmm. What?"

"Come on!" Ron pressed, spasms of panic leaping through him. "Come on! It's Manetti and the girl! They're across the road!" All thoughts of Kerry had flown.

McCaig woke and swung upright, his gigantic belly wedging against the steering wheel. Wriggling, he strained to free himself as he snapped back at Ron, "Where?"

"The fencing supply yard," Ron pointed urgently. "They ran into the shed."

"Well go after them!"

Ron slammed the door shut as Nick turned the key, the green pre-ignition light now off. The Toyota's motor whined, laboured several times then failed. Taking a deep breath, he tried again, but it whirred, coughed, and died a second time, the battery failing. As he feared, the truck had been sitting too long. He cursed, turned the key on and off in quick successions till the motor finally whirred and suddenly fired. He exhaled with relief, dropped the gear lever into first, and eased the Toyota out beneath the door.

Ron McCaig raced around the corner as the cream Hilux passed through the tall mesh gates, two occupants clearly visible in the cab.

McCaig slid to hasty halt beside him. "Come on! Get in! They're heading for Dayton!"

Ducking his height into the vehicle, Ron ripped the microphone from the dash and had it to his mouth before the force of take-off slammed his door shut. "Big brother! Goose! Come in fellas! Come in."

A slight pause which seemed like minutes passed, then: "Goose copies," the voice crackled.

"Yeah. We copy." Taylor's voice was super calm.

"Your friends are coming, fellas, in a small cream pick-up.

Southbound from town. We're following. Where the hell are you?"

Click click. "Just south of Burton Siding," said Lacey.

Taylor's voice followed. "Just north of Burton Siding ... and now heading south. We'll be ready. Show him the way in and we'll organise a party." *Click click.*

McCaig stamped on the accelerator and the white utility skidded on the loose gravel before finding traction on the solid earth below. The engine laboured then quickly gathered momentum, tyres squealing and smoking as they spun onto the bitumen.

CHAPTER EIGHTY-SEVEN

Sheila unlocked the door to the Public bar, wishing Nick had waited. In another twenty minutes he would have had all the help he needed, but he wouldn't wait, and now she trembled. Her knotted stomach made her nauseous, and she prayed that whoever Sam had mustered would arrive soon. It was much too quiet, the street deserted, devoid of all noise, and the grey sky dared not to breathe.

She shivered at the idiom: the calm before the storm.

At the bar, she poured herself a Scotch, straight — by no means her normal behaviour. It did little to ease the cold that gripped her insides. She placed on the bar the long brassy bullet she had found that morning on the hotel's back verandah, and walked to the open door.

Looking out, she listened for the sound of approaching motors. But it was still much too early.

CHAPTER EIGHTY-EIGHT

Beside me, Nick gripped the wheel, worry etched on his face. He glanced across at me and flashed me a quick reassuring smile before looking back to the road. "Keep your eyes open," he warned. "We don't want any surprises ..."

I stared out the window, noting how taut he was drawn, his smile not fooling me for a second. There was a very real chance we would not make it to Dayton.

Eventually Brenton Road flashed by. Five more driveways on the left joined the highway between Brenton Road and Burton Siding, the Siding on the right about another four miles down. The road ahead stayed clear, but any one of those driveways could conceal a car. My nerves bunched as each one drew nearer, for each one passed narrowed down the odds. The scathing tone of Nick's voice soon pulled my eyes from the road.

"Damn it! We've got company. You'd better hold on." His foot went down, demanding more from the vehicle.

I turned in my seat. Indeed, the car behind was gaining on us, and I noted not much else than its whiteness. "Are you sure it's after us?" I frowned.

Nick nodded. "It's McCaig all right! I'd know that loose number plate anywhere."

He pressed his foot down further but the utility drew closer and closer, the outline of McCaig and his son becoming clearer through their windshield.

Nick glanced across at me, his jaw muscle flexing as he steered the Toyota over the broken white line and travelled the centre of the road. Beside us, the sloping road shoulders were soggy and unusable and I knew he intended to stop McCaig from passing. I held on tight to the door handle.

Nick checked the rear view mirror often but the utility remained behind, hounding us but not threatening to pass. The registration plate vibrated on its single screw as the wind whipped the metal to a furious, incessant shuddering. Nick looked ahead again, scowling; looked back again. Something obviously bothered him.

"They're not even trying to overtake," he finally noted aloud, "and that's odd."

Beside him, I screamed, "Look out!" and braced myself hard against the dashboard. Nick sucked in a breath, for shooting across the width of road ahead was the apple-green mini-bus. The route to Dayton was blocked, its length and the steep, muddy shoulders either side of the road just as impassable for us as they were for McCaig.

Nick hit the brakes, locking the Toyota's wheels, and a thick pall of smoke and grey acrid stench billowed out behind us. The squeal of tyres pierced the air as the pickup's rear-end slid around, Nick fighting to keep it under his control as he quickly gauged the surroundings.

"Burton Siding," he said. "We can reach Burton Siding."

The grey rippled iron of the pig-pen silos was visible through the trees, the red gravel track on our right ushering the way in. Nick breathed out. "We're okay," he yelled above the screech of rubber.

My face felt cold, my hand now clutching Nick's arm as well as the door handle.

"Once around the silo and back ...," he shouted further.

"What if they wait here on the road and don't follow?" I panicked.

Nick spun the wheel clockwise, his other hand smoothly shifting the gears. Pedals dipped and rose, the wheels unlocked; the front of the cab now slid sideways, and the brakes locked on again. "Well, you keep an eye out ..."

My eyes widened in horror as the wheels along Nick's side of the car lifted from the road, the flat-top tipping precariously my way. I could see the excited faces of those in the bus beside me waiting anxiously for it to tip right over. Nick groaned, his muscles tightening as he leant his weight to counteract the listing.

"No you don't!" he muttered through tightly clenched teeth.

Balanced precariously on two wheels and veering slightly with the lack of steerage, the Hilux threatened to crash right over. At our speed it would roll several times and probably collide with the bus. But it teetered dangerously, wavering on its line before crashing down again, its metal structures creaking as the suspension thudded hard. The cab rocked vigorously, and Nick exhaled, the gears and pedals sliding and gliding in unison as the Toyota found all four wheels again and surged ahead.

"... and tell me if they come," he finished. He flicked a glance in the rear view mirror. "There's another track out behind the silo. We'll just come out on the back road and skirt around them."

He sent the Hilux hurtling, mud and slush splattering outward from the depressions of recent rainfall like the bow wash of a speed boat in a choppy sea. I kept watch out the back window.

"Just the ute so far," I shouted, "and they're catching up."

Nick flicked another glance in the mirror. McCaig was far enough behind that we still had a good chance of making it and he smiled at me that everything was fine. He looked forward again.

And hit the brakes.

"Fuck!" he drawled long and hard.

We were half way round the silo, the wooden triangular supports streaking by uncountable. I turned forward, and my mouth dropped open. The Hilux slid a short way on the slimy ground then slewed around on the loose stony surface. The sudden stop thumped my shoulder hard against the door and launched me forward but Nick's arm swung out and pinned me back to the seat, saving my head from smashing on the windscreen.

Everything stopped.

Blocking the way about eighty feet ahead of us was the white Chrysler ute. Nick's face fell straight and he glanced up at the mirror.

Behind us, about eighty feet distant, was the white Chrysler ute. His fists clenched on the wheel and his eyes took on a deeper hue. "Shit! The number plates! Those damn stupid number plates!" He thumped his fist on the steering wheel.

I looked ahead then behind. Indeed the number plates were both from Queensland, one squared and fully attached while McCaig's had lost a screw. I shrugged.

"They're both the same. Identical cars, shared plates. That's how they could do things while McCaig's car was still in town."

His teeth clenched, and he heaved in a breath; let it out again. His eyes however still burned at the vehicle ahead for its doors had started to open. He clutched my hand and squeezed it. "Okay Kid, the party's about to begin," he said. "I want you to do exactly as I say."

I went to speak but he shook his head, silencing me. "We're going to get out of the car, and we're going to keep apart. You got that? Don't come near me ... under any circumstances ... Do you hear me?"

I nodded, my eyes fixed on his anger. The colour left my face as I realised what he intended.

"When I yell 'Run', you run ... that way." He flicked a glance towards the front of the vehicle, the direction we'd been heading. "Don't look back and don't stop for anything. Head for the highway." He conjured that infernal, reassuring smile. "I'll be right behind you."

I nodded and he patted my hand. "Let's go then."

We opened the car doors in unison.

The two giant men I'd seen kill Pete had already climbed from their car. Rifles hung down against their thick, solid legs. My heart stopped at the sight of them, and Carla flashed to my mind ... Then Pete.

Straightening, Nick stepped forward and moved away from the Hilux; moved away from me as the bigger man approached and raised the shotgun. A smile flooded his face. He'd only have to pull off a shot and Nick would look like Pete.

I shuddered and fought the image away.

Nick's face straightened, his dark gaze drifting across to the other man, the smaller thug who was watching me back away. The distance widened between us yet my eyes remained on Nick.

As my line of escape came closer the smaller man lifted his rifle, slowly, as if he had lots of time. Nick stepped closer to it, seeming complacent as he came across its line. "Well, if it isn't the Siamese Twins," he jibed. "Now, this is more like it. I see you brought some protection."

He stepped closer to the smaller man. "I like your bruise," he added.

I forced myself not to look for the man's bruise and moved further away, giving Nick every opportunity to keep his distance from them. He took another step forward, and I saw his shoulders roll subtly back as his muscles loosened for action.

I eyed the rifle. A 303. Tony had had a 303. It'll make a big hole, he'd said.

"Didn't your mother ever tell you ...," Nick started, taking another step across the man's aim, "...that guns aren't meant for .... *RUN!!*"

On his word, I turned and bolted, no thoughts other than doing as he said.

CHAPTER EIGHTY-NINE

The shotgun barrel levelled off as Nick sprinted forward, Dave Taylor's finger squeezing off a shot as Nick leapt upward. Turning in mid-air he knocked bodily into Ben Taylor, his foot lashing out and kicking upward, striking the twin barrels of the rifle. A loud blast ripped skyward as two bodies crashed to the ground.

Recoiling from the onslaught, Dave Taylor snatched another cartridge from his pocket and filled the empty chamber, snapped the barrels shut. His finger floated over the trigger but he couldn't squeeze off the shot for Ben was in its range – if he took a shot at Manetti, the impact would also get Ben. So he hovered, waiting for his chance.

Looking up, he saw Becky running, heading away from them and raised the barrel again, his finger ready to stop her flight. As he pressured the trigger Ben stumbled to his feet and inadvertently blocked his line again. Instantly he retracted the aim and shouted, "Ben, get out of the way! Get out of the bloody way!"

As Nick lay sprawled he threw his head up, caught a glimpse of Becky running, heading around the wall of the silo. The skinny McCaig had set out after her, his long gangly legs looking hard to control as he sprinted. The fat man, puffing and panting, battled his obesity as he joined the chase, both of them quickly leaving him behind. Becky had a good lead on them.

Nick took comfort in knowing she was fit and they wouldn't catch her. *Just keep her out of the line of fire a second more and she'll be clear*, he wiled. *Keep running*, he prayed silently then looked around.

The smaller goon was back on his feet now and stood

between him and the loaded shotgun. Nick rose stealthily from the ground, his elbows smarting from a long gravel rash. This was it. This was his last chance. He used it for Becky.

As the man turned to gain his bearings and locate him, Nick bore forward and upward, connecting head first with the man's bulky ribcage. Powering on, he took the man reeling back; ploughed him heftily into his brother and sent all three of them crashing back to the ground. This time Nick scrambled quickly, hurled a bevy of well-aimed punches before needing to retreat.

Taylor was the first to break free of the tangle of arms and legs and came to his feet at the same time as Nick. The shotgun lay several yards to his right, and he made a sideways dive for it, but Nick reached it first and kicked it further afield.

"Come on, big man. What? ... not capable of anything without it?" he taunted. He caught a glimpse of Ben Taylor coming to his knees, blood smearing his face, and silently despaired. *Here we go again.*

Taylor reacted instantly, his mighty fist swinging in from the left. Nick let it connect, the blow crunching his jaw even though he followed its impact sideways. He hit the ground hard with his shoulder, his hand scooping up the rifle stock and gathering it into his grasp as he rolled. He came back to his feet in the same smooth move and raised the shotgun level with intent.

"'llo fellas," he smiled. Pain however erupted in his jaw. In his neck. In his left ribcage. All had taken a pounding over the past few days. "Looks like it's my turn now." He plopped a shot into the ground at their feet, stopping their coordinated approach.

Both men paled significantly.

CHAPTER NINETY

My joggers pattered on the hard wet ground, each step strategically placed to avoid slippery patches. I'd never been a great one for running, my only practice Jerry's games of Chase-Me, but this time I didn't have an option.

Sprinting round the side of the silo, the curved wall seeming endless, I headed for the highway as Nick had instructed, and I didn't look back. I'd already gained enough distance I could no longer hear him but was consoled that I also hadn't heard another shot. My hopes soared. Nick said he would be behind me and I had to believe him.

After a short distance though a small twinge snagged at my side; nagged worse the further I ran. Eventually it demanded I stop, my hand failing to suppress it. The stitch slowed me down.

Then I heard footsteps ... running ... catching me up ... *Nick!* I found another burst of will and pushed on again. He would reach me quickly.

The wall continued its interminable curve.

Rounding it a little further, I skidded to a halt, slid precariously on the loose round stones.

Ahead of me sat the apple-green mini-bus that had earlier blocked the road, two men leaning with their arms folded against it. They were younger than the others, not a great deal older than myself, but their meanness was unhidden. Unshaven and ill-kempt, smug looks marred their faces as they blocked my way.

Staying back from their reach, I waited – Nick would be with me soon. Turning, almost smiling as footsteps arrived behind me, I shuddered coldly as Ron McCaig appeared, looking ridiculous and awkward, his lanky legs swaying as he reached me.

Where's Nick?

My hopes grew as more footsteps approached and I glanced back as Ron McCaig and the one I knew as Beattie slowly closed in. A second later the fat shearing contractor closed in from the right, red-faced and gasping for air. He was the second set of footsteps. There were no others.

The semi-circle complete, I was trapped against the grey silo wall.

Keep each one in sight, my mind reeled. *Where's Nick?* I almost screamed out his name. *He said he'd be behind me! So why isn't he?*

Then I heard a shot and flinched, the loud reverberating blast bringing my heart to a standstill. Ugly images flew into my head, ugly-ugly images and I hugged myself with despair. My eyes widened, and filled with tears, which made McCaig laugh, a girlish titter as he jiggled about like a spoilt child receiving a gift he'd demanded. I wanted to hit him with a brick.

Doubling over, the pain in my heart and throat so great I couldn't breathe, I watched as the arc closed in. Fighting was useless. Totally and utterly useless ... and I realised Nick had known that all along. When he'd said he'd be behind me he had lied.

Tears rolled down my face now, hot and salty, and I knew they had won. All Nick's effort in saving us, all his pain, had been for nothing. His death had been for nothing. I imagined him lying disfigured, my throat burning even hotter at the image, choking me. Nick was gone – he'd gone down fighting.

A deep breath flooded through me as more visions ran. Of Nick. Of Pete. Of all the events of recent days. Of what a tragic waste it was. My anger rose for these thugs had no right to do any of this. They had no right to come here to Cullan and destroy its peace. My teeth clenched. If Nick had gone down fighting, so would I!

Scanning the ring of men I noted the gaps were almost equal in the arc of the circle, maybe slightly wider between Beattie and the fat man's son, but they were all closing in, the openings getting smaller.

"Come on, honey. Come to Poppa," Beattie teased, his fingers beckoning me to move his way.

I turned, feeling like a trapped gazelle in a lion pack as I further assessed the ring. Nick had said to run, so, without warning, I took off towards the widest gap, leaping and ducking a barrage of grappling hands. I set off in a flat out sprint, and swept through the closing gap. But Beattie was closer than I thought and swooped in, his arms scooping round my waist, reeling me back to him. I spun, struck a double-fisted blow straight to the bridge of his nose. He yelped in pain and dropped me and immediately I was back on my chosen line.

But Beattie didn't let up. His fingers groped for my clothing as I passed; hooked on my jeans belt tags and reeled me back. His hands slid over me, but I twisted, avoiding them again, and I heard him curse as I eluded him. I was clear and running again.

Then a severe jolt jarred me. His hand caught onto the waistband of my jeans, the sudden tug almost pulling me over. An arm wrapped around my waist, the hold crushing my ribs as I was wrenched from the ground. I spun to hit him again, but he was ready this time and quickly crunched my hands in his fist. He tossed me over his hip, rolled me and dropped me across his shoulder, and like that he carried me back. With nothing left to lose I screamed as loud as I could; pounded vicious blows upon his back, but nothing made a difference.

McCaig followed behind us, chuckling at my efforts, smug in the knowledge their job was almost done.

CHAPTER NINETY-ONE

The group stopped abruptly, and McCaig's laughter cut out mid chuckle. He moved to the front of the men and I wriggled and caught a glimpse through Beattie's elbow of Nick standing with a rifle in his hands. He raised the barrel a little higher at the two big men's heads.

"Put her down," he ordered, raising the barrel higher, "or these two are finished." By the look on his face he wouldn't think twice about firing into their midst.

Ever so slowly Beattie lowered me down, my feet touching soil, his hand however kept a crushing hold on my wrists. He turned me round to face Nick.

"Let her go!" Nick repeated, his finger moving over the cold metal trigger.

"Uh-uh!" Beattie shook his head. He grabbed a fistful of hair at the back of my neck and pulled down sharply, wrenching my head back. I screamed as the unexpected movement strained the muscles in my neck. "Put the gun down, farm boy, or I'll snap her neck like a chicken."

Nick didn't move, the shotgun still on his targets. "I'll warn you again ... let her go or I'll take them both out! *Now!*"

"Go ahead. Who gives a shit!" Beattie retorted. He tugged down harder, and I screamed louder. My eyes filled with tears. I tried not to cry, but couldn't stop. "Last chance, mate!" he warned, keeping the pressure on. Nick didn't move and he twisted my neck further. I cried out as neck muscles started to tear.

Nick's jaw locked, and his body tightened. I could see the quandary in his eyes. Would they do it? Wouldn't they do it? I had no doubt they would, and I knew it was going to hurt more than this, and tried to tense against it.

Then a strange look crossed Nick's face. A look of hard resolve. A look that said we were both at our ends. He shifted the angle of the barrel, aimed directly at my brow. He could be merciful and make it quick. He could end it now. Save me from enduring any more.

Then uncertainty crossed his face and he looked straight at me, beyond the sight of the rifle. He raised it a little higher, held it steadier. Restructured his grip on the stock. Found dead centre. Lowered it again.

"Nick, no!" I yelled as he faltered. "Do it!" Without a hostage to consider he would have a chance to fight.

But Beattie wrenched my hair down even more, the force yanking me over. I screamed and hit the ground; lay sobbing, tucked up in a ball, clutching my neck with both hands. I was sure the muscles had torn that time.

When Nick lowered the rifle, defeated, McCaig yelled sharply: "Get him!"

Spinning round, the biggest man's hand swiftly claimed the rifle, his other hand laying a sharp backhand hard across the side of Nick's head. Nick's head snapped round with the blow, but he stayed on his feet and glared back at the man. Blood soon seeped from a split in his skin above his left eye, trickled down his face, but he kept his hands down. Knowing Nick, he wouldn't give them the benefit of knowing ...

Then the big man lifted the rifle, caressed the stock theatrically as he glared at Nick, the corner of his mouth twitching upward with satisfaction. Raising the rifle high, he jabbed the stock butt hard into Nick's left rib-cage, doubling Nick over. He dropped to one knee, gasping for air, his pain evident. I screamed. He called my name, but shook his head and lowered his face from view. We were beaten.

"Go on, take him, Taylor," someone yelled from beside me.

The big man's name was Taylor. And Taylor was going to kill the love of my life.

I watched through tears as he circled round behind Nick and locked massive hands around Nick's wrists, wrenching them back behind him, then he wrenched them up, forcing Nick to his feet. Totally breathless, Nick was powerless to prevent anything that happened.

"Not so smart now, are you Manetti?" the smaller one jeered, his words hissed close to Nick's face, his huge mitt crushing Nick's jaw. I'll never forget the intense look in the man's eyes – they were a madman's eyes – and Nick stared back with equal intensity. He gave no reply, just drew a hard, deep breath.

The man glared at him then stepped back as though gauging Nick's chances of freeing himself. Striding forward he landed two sharp blows to Nick's side.

Nick arched away as the blows landed, his shoulders pulling excruciatingly tight, the stretch of his body tearing the buttons from his shirt. He groaned; shot a glance at where I lay, crying now at the punishment they gave him. He shook his head again and I sensed he was saying: *Don't watch, kiddo.*

The smaller man's gaze followed Nick's. "Hey, I've got a better idea," he suddenly changed his mind. "Hold him, Dave, and watch this!"

Backing away, he turned and strode to Beattie. A scuffed brown boot rolled me onto my back, and the ugly freak stood looking down at me. What was he going to do? What ...?

He glanced back at Nick, noticed Nick's resigned expression change to one of panic. Bending over, his huge hand gripped my throat, almost encircling my neck with one hand. He checked Nick again, and grinned when Nick struggled against Taylor's grasp. I squirmed as he ran a hand down my shirt, as he lingered over the swell of my breasts. He laughed as Nick's face twisted with rage and intensified his struggle.

"Sweet Lordy, she's mine!" he bellowed across the space.

I was now in for the fight of my life. Repulsed, I writhed as he grabbed my shirt; aimed a kick at his groin as he came closer but connected with his thigh just above his knee. I tried again before three others converged and pinned my legs to the ground. To one side, McCaig bounced excitedly as he loosened his belt, urging my attacker on, and I realised the fullness of their intentions. It wouldn't just be one. I kicked myself along the dirt in desperation to escape, but the man pinned me with his knee, and my shoulders were forced to the ground by the others. Only the tall, skinny one stood back, yanking at his father's arm, trying to be heard.

"No, Dad. This isn't right," he growled. But the man ripped his arm free and ignored him.

"She's nicer than the Richardson girl," the brother shouted loud enough to be heard across the gravel. He popped the stud of his jeans and pushed down the zip.

"Oh God no! ... Please no," I pleaded, staring up at him, hoping above all hopes some shred of humanity would suddenly sweep over him.

"Oh God yes, little girl," he retorted, his smile now ugly. "And you can thank your boyfriend over there for his interest."

He spoke deliberately loud so Nick would hear as he reached for my waistband. "Now I get to have you first, see ..." His face twisted in a sneer as he straddled me and thumped my hips to the ground. My skin crawled beneath his hand and I turned my head from the sight of him; saw Nick, his body contorted from the pressure, his muscles bulging, great knotted cords standing proud in his neck and chest as he battled against Taylor's hold. I felt his pain, and pleaded again, for us both. "Please don't ... don't do this ..." I would rather die than let them do this to me in front of Nick.

The stud of my jeans snapped open and hands grappled with the zip, fingers digging into me. "No! ... NO!" I screamed. "Nick, help me!"

CHAPTER NINETY-TWO

Nick's eyes darkened and his face drained of colour as he twisted with rage. He tried to wrench his wrists free of the big man's hands but the freak laughed at his efforts and dragged him further back. Still chuckling, Taylor propped himself against the bonnet of the ute to watch; planted a boot firmly in the small of Nick's back and pushed forward, further crushing Nick's shoulder-blades and placing exorbitant pressure on his shoulders. So stretched, Nick's joints came close to popping as he was stretched to breaking point. He groaned loudly as agony tore through him. The force on his shoulders unbearable, he fought to drag air in through his teeth; fought to alleviate the heat of sinews tearing in his chest. He had to do something. Anything. And to do it he had to blot out the pain.

He set his mind to it, blocking out everything, concentrating on moving slowly. Carefully he lowered one shoulder while inch by inch he lifted the other up. Like this he lightened the pressure on his joints all along one side. By increasing the pain in one limb he slightly freed the other, quietly but surely making adjustments he needed, suffering the greater torture in one area until he could make his move. One more inch would give him the strength he needed to achieve it; one more inch without the big man sensing his strategy. Dave Taylor laughed as he felt Nick shift, and repositioned his boot in the hollow of Nick's back. It was time.

Bellowing with rage, Nick stretched to breaking point. As the boot almost re-established its presence, he twisted suddenly and snapped his right arm free, jerking it away from Taylor's mighty grip. Keeping his arm extended, he let the pressure of the man's boot kick him further round, providing enough impetus to land a solid straight armed blow across the big man's ear. The impact unbalanced him, toppled the hefty body from the car. Nick's left arm jarred then unlocked from the man's solid hold. Regaining his balance, Nick grabbed up the shotgun, jabbed the butt sharply into Taylor's chest, and Taylor hit the ground writhing. Checking the breech, Nick stalked forward.

CHAPTER NINETY-THREE

I screamed and fought against the hands, fought to keep them away from me, but they were so strong, and too many. My jeans were partly torn down, exposing my hips, but still I kicked to prevent them grasping more. "Nick ...!"

McCaig hovered over me. "Slap her," he ordered, shoving the small goon forward as his patience dwindled. "Knock her silly." His encouragement ceased as a cold metal barrel prodded his podgy cheek, the click of the safety catch releasing stealing his pleasure.

"Party's over, boys," Nick said, his voice strained and raspy. His dark eyes cast over me, his relief obvious that he'd been in time.

All but Ben Taylor heard him. All but Ben stepped back, his hands busy forcing my thighs apart. Nick panned the gathering with a steady barrel, sending them back several steps. Then he rapped the man's skull with a heavy clunk of the barrel and brought it to rest in his ear.

"Touch her again and I'll blow your fucking brains out." The look on his face revealed his desire to do so. His finger shifted over the trigger, itching for some provocation. Blood still trickled down his face, the swelling above his eye hindering vision.

The hands stopped groping me, and raised clear.

"Now get up!" Nick ordered, "... slowly and carefully."

The man obeyed, making sure he made no move to cause a sudden blast.

"Over there," Nick indicated, directing them to the curved tin wall with the shotgun. When they all started moving, he offered me his hand. "Come on, babe, we're getting out of here."

He pulled me to my feet and released me, needing one hand for the rifle, the other to clutch the pain in his ribs. "Get to the car." He struggled to breathe as he shepherded me across the gravel.

I half walked, half ran, pulling my clothes back around me. Nick kept the rifle aimed at the men, and kept himself between us. He opened the cab door and pushed me into the cab, noticing Taylor stumbling to his feet further over.

Sliding onto the seat beside me, he transferred the rifle to his left hand, its aim directed out the open window. He turned the key and dropped the car into gear; pushed it straight into second and sent the Hilux tearing away. A muddy wash sprayed from its wide spinning wheels as we continued on our original course round the silo.

Immediately we passed them, the shearers bolted.

Stooped over, Taylor raced across the gravel, his eyes scanning the ground. As the flat-top slewed passed, he grabbed up the discarded 303 and got off one quick shot. The retort echoed loud but was too far to the left and punched a hole in a raised corrugation of the grey iron wall. No score.

The two McCaigs reached their vehicle first, Taylors not far behind them. Lacey and Beattie sprinted the length of the wall towards the hidden mini-bus as Taylor signalled for McCaig to take the left curve. He signalled the two runners to pile into the back of the ute.

Nick put all his attention to driving, his lips thin with concentration, his breathing irregular. As the grey wall streaked by the green camper-bus appeared before us. He discharged a barrel into its petrol tank, the second shot sparking off metal igniting the fumes from the fuel. Flames erupted on the ground, licked up the side of the paintwork and he smiled thinly at his score.

We were on the track to the highway, so far nothing in sight. How far we'd get towards Dayton before being stopped we didn't know, but anything was better than the torture we'd suffered at

Burton Siding. Blood still trickled from the cut above Nick's eye, the swelling obscuring his sight. With his hands committed to the wheel, he wiped the stream away on his arm, the motion allowing him a glimpse in the side mirror. Behind us, the twin utilities skewed sideways as they raced onto the track, and a large ball of flame ripped skyward.

The highway was a hundred yards ahead.

Rocking, bouncing and creaking, the Toyota leapt the railway line, but traffic ahead whizzed past a-blur. Nick braked hard to avoid a collision. His breathing heightened with the waiting as cars and trucks continually sped by, and he bashed a fist on the door ledge. "How come when you bloody well need help, nobody's ever around," he snapped. "Just when we don't want it, we get a fucking procession!"

Revving the engine, he kept it primed for take-off as both utilities gained ground. In the lane heading to Dayton two road-trains hurtled along in convoy, fast approaching the Siding and too close to attempt a claim on the lane. Two more were northbound but much further back. As a white utility slewed in behind us, men leaping from the tray before it had stopped, Nick stepped on the pedal, pulled hard to the left as the southbound convoy rumbled by. Tyres squealed and smoke billowed as we hit the bitumen northbound, showering the smaller Taylor with rocks, slop and debris. Horns blurted as trucks signalled trucks, as the mighty Kenworth gave mechanical abuse at the suicidal tactics on the road in front of it. The little flat-top lurched forward, the heavy metal grill of the barrelling Semi quickly filling its mirror.

Slowly Nick widened the gap, but only marginally, and he breathed with relief that well back the utilities were blocked by the congestion.

He wiped a fresh flow of blood onto his arm. "Tell me something ..." he said, glancing at me. I looked back at him, my face still pale from the close call we'd had. "Just how often do you go to Church? It's gotta be you getting help 'cose it's certainly not me."

"What ...?"

The Kenworth hauled rapidly on, pushing the Toyota ahead of it. Nick appreciated its cover as he planned his next move. We both knew it would have to be a good one.

CHAPTER NINETY-FOUR

We entered Cullan, the Semi behind us backing off to meet the town limits. Nick kept his foot down. As we neared the turn off, he picked the left gradient and spun the wheel sharply, swinging the Toyota onto it. Spinning the wheel again, he slewed it sideways across the gravel and spun it halfway round, dust and stones spraying across the verge. He flinched as the thundering Kenworth rumbled by creating its own wave of dirt, its horn blurting as its gears reowwed down in quick succession for the turn-off. The next Semi barrelled through, showering more mud and stones across the cab.

Nick reached over and pushed me onto the seat. "Lie down, and stay down!" he ordered. He lay over me, pressing me to the seat, staying below the dashboard, and like that we waited, listening. Nick wished in undertones that luck was still with us.

"When they shoot past we'll take off back to Dayton before they realise we were here," he whispered.

"And if they don't ...?"

"We'll play that by ear."

Brian Egan stood at the window of the Public bar staring out at the street, the rest of the team milling about him. They'd been talking for a while, most of it snaky, some of it crude, and some had left a bad taste in his mouth. The meeting had just finished and Sam had stirred in a potful of home truths that had made them all bubble. As far as he was concerned, the lid was about to blow and McCaig was the fuel on the fire – McCaig, and the constabulary's reluctance to help them. Maybe Sam was right, he thought deeply as he looked back to where Sam stood; maybe they had all taken the back seat too often, watching bemused as Nick stepped up and took on the town's brawlers and nut-jobs. He heaved a deep breath. Okay, maybe they had even backed away at times, but risk had never been a question in the past. Nick was a trained fighting machine.

This time though it was different. Lives had been lost, others destroyed. They had to make a stand; it was time to confront the intruders and send them packing.

He shot another glance at the group, and nodded. Yeah, they should have done this from the beginning.

His interest drew back out the window as a small cream Hilux slid onto the verge across the road and spun about-face. He frowned. In those few brief seconds, it had looked like Nick at the wheel. And unless he was badly mistaken, he had a passenger. But what the hell were they doing?

"Hey Sam, come over here and look at this," he called across the room.

Two trucks whining down for the intersection hid all as Sam reached him. When they were gone, the Toyota was left spattered with mud and grime, but now empty.

Brian scanned the roadway, wondering where the two had gone, wondered if he had somehow been mistaken. "I thought Nick was driving that pickup," he explained, scratching his head.

"Nah," Sam said. "Sheila said he's well on his way to Dayton. In fact, he should be there by now. But it does look like Kennie's ..."

He looked across the bar to where Sheila was still on the phone trying to verify their arrival. He saw her shake her head, her face slightly paler than before. He turned back to the window as two utilities roared into town, one braking to a dramatic halt in the centre of the road just before the hotel, the other veering towards the left verge, taking the same line as the Toyota. McCaig was at the wheel of one; two men he'd never seen before in the other.

Brian scratched his head again as McCaig hollered something out the window and pointed to the Toyota, the words shouted in anger. He didn't wait any longer.

"Something's going down," he roared, rousing his crew as he headed for the verandah. He arrived in time to hear the fat man yell: "Come on, let's finish it!"

Taylor eyed the Toyota with rising suspicion, his instincts gnawing at the scene before him. Manetti wouldn't leave his only means of escape, and he wouldn't so easily allow himself to be cornered. He eyed the hotel, deciding. Of the two most likely places, he felt drawn to the small parked truck, and his foot pressed down to block its intended run.

But another yell from McCaig turned his head.

On the verandah of the Cullan Hotel stood the local shearing team, a handful of locals behind them. Taylor cut the engine, considering that maybe for once he was wrong. Maybe Manetti had sought shelter in the hotel, and now had reinforcements. He shut the motor down and stepped to the roadway as Beattie and Lacey swung down from the tray. Sorting through the back of the ute, Taylor located a long iron bar and pulled it out, tested its impact several times on the palm of his hand as he willed his target to appear.

Ben found a length of heavy chain and wrapped it into his fist, its excess falling with a clatter to the ground.

McCaig accelerated past the hotel and pulled in at the motel, his fat fist pounding on the horn as he braked. His signal brought those inside out to check out the noise.

Stooped with nagging back pain, Jim Sweeney stepped around the corner of the building. "What's your hurry, Bill?" he moaned, looking around perplexed. He spied the force of men assembling on the roadside and slowly understood.

"It's going down," McCaig yelled as Todd, Merv and Madden approached the car. McCaig climbed out, thumbed towards the hotel and headed in that direction. "Come on," he roused. "We've got a job to finish!"

Madden turned suddenly white. "Oh shit! No way, man," he drawled and started backing away. "I didn't sign on for none of this shit!"

"You're in this as much as we are, Madden!" the fat man jawed, grabbing a fistful of his hair to stop his departure. He hurled the young man forward.

Maddern staggered, tried to regain his footing but McCaig kept thrusting him closer and closer to Egan's waiting crew. He saw the Taylor brothers stalking in from the far side and, as much as he feared the fight, their presence raised his courage. He straightened and fell into a shuffling step beside Beattie, worried now only at his lack of a suitable weapon. His eyes danced keen to find one.

Taylor's malice swept the crowd.

CHAPTER NINETY-FIVE

Sam pushed Rosalind back inside the doorway and ordered her to stay there then he stepped down off the verandah and joined the line. Todd snatched a jack handle from the roadhouse workshop as he passed, Ron McCaig a wrench from the back of the ute. Beattie was already well equipped with the sharp slender blade he always carried, and like this the rival groups spread out across the roadway.

Raising his head slightly, Nick wiped away another stream of blood that oozed down his face as he peered over the dashboard. "It's too quiet," he said. "Something should have happened by now." Then he groaned and sat up, freeing Becky to also rise from the seat.

Across the road, Dave Taylor worked his way around to come at Brian from behind, his weapon held high for the strike. Roger Baird turned side on, trying to cover both sides of the line, which wasn't going to be easy. It had all happened so fast, and so silently after McCaig had shouted his threat – the war was on.

Nick pushed Becky back to the seat and pinned her there with his hand. "You stay exactly where you are," he ordered, his dark glare warning her of the trouble she'd be in if she didn't. He opened the car door and stepped out, one hand immediately clamping over his left rib as he moved.

He scanned the street. Nearly every man was armed – solid bars of metal, stout wooden beams, other weapons of potential fatality. He had nothing, the back of the flat-top bare. Steeling at that thought, he stepped around the back of the Toyota and reached the road, his immediate target the larger Taylor. He had a score to settle, and he didn't need any goddamned stick to achieve it!

At the door of the roadhouse old Jack Pollitt stood wary and shaking, keeping Marilyn pushed inside. Hesitant, he knew he was too old to fight, but was too proud not to. Gingerly he let the door go and strode on bandy legs towards the melee for Brian's crew were three down on advantage.

He looked up, his eyes reaching the tall, impressive figure coming from the roadway. One down, he corrected. Young Nick counted for two. He pursed his lips.

Nick's keen eyes found Jack the instant he moved and he shook his head. One haphazard blow would kill the old man outright. Making a fist, he raised it to his ear then tilted his head for Jack to go. The old man obliged and retreated, pushed open the glass panelled door and headed for the phone. He wondered if anyone else had thought to ring Dayton for assistance. By Christ they were going to need it!

Marilyn stayed in the doorway, leaning out. She spotted Nick as a sudden gust of wind swirled across the road, ruffling his hair and clothing and chilling the blood of those who stood in its way. So far no-one had moved, no-one prepared to strike the first crucial blow. Nick's attention shot back to Taylor. The man was hungry enough for trouble to start the blood-bath, and he wasn't wrong: Taylor's arm rose higher, drawing the metal bar above his head, his aim towards Egan's back.

"*TAYLOR!*" Nick bellowed, a distraction to the attacker and a warning to the victim. He stepped into the intersection, diverting Taylor his way, for Brian's crew were no match for these trained killers nor for the hostile Queenslanders. If this thing went down it would be a pitiful finish. He caught sight of Sheila and someone else he didn't have time to determine standing behind the glass then turned his eyes to Taylor. He wished Sheila didn't witness this.

Then the melee started.

Taylor's eyes caught Nick's as his arm reached its zenith.

"Fuck you, Manetti! You're next!" he roared as he swung the bar with force.

Nudging Brian aside, Roger Baird took the blow on his forearm, and howled in agony as the bone snapped with a sickening crack. White points protruded from his lower limb then disappeared again, the ivory replaced by a flood of scarlet red. He dropped the wooden plank he carried and grabbed the hanging appendage, supporting it tight against him. He doubled over, vulnerable.

Taylor raised the bar again, ready for the kill, but Nick was on the move, covering the ground in a rush. He intercepted the bar on its downswing, his arm muscles bulging against Taylor's weight.

The roadside erupted amid shouts and snarls of anger as metal clashed metal, as metal thunked wood, as both found their target and thudded against pliant flesh. Watching in horror from behind the multi-paned window, Sheila grabbed Ros and silenced her terrified scream; turned her head from the brawl. Metal glinted in the subdued sunlight as bodies fell to the ground. Some got up again. Some didn't. Egan's weapon connected with McCaig's thick shoulder, the short verandah cross-rail plopping hard against fat, causing the old man to drop to one knee. Brian swung his free arm, his fist striking a fleshy jaw and McCaig's neck snapped back and dropped him to his back.

Hearing Nick's challenge, I sat up and stared out the window just as he grabbed the metal bar. With Taylor's big hands on the weapon and Nick's strength opposing, it remained immovable. I scrambled from the car as Nick directed the full force of his thrust into his left hand. He spun round, the blow he delivered with the point of his elbow jerking the big man sideways and toppling him over. The bar chinked to the ground several feet away.

"It's just you and me now!" Nick growled, his jaw setting

tightly.

He towered over Taylor's fallen form, waiting for him to rise, staying out of range. He didn't see the smaller thug approaching from behind nor did he hear my warning yell.

Ben Taylor swung the heavy chain, the chinking *whack* arcing across Nick's back, shocking him completely. He whipped around and caught the chain on its second flight, wrapped it swiftly around his wrist and reeled its wielder in. The smaller goon jerked towards him and he struck a well-aimed blow to the chin and sent the body sprawling. In the same swift move he hurled the chain away.

Around him, John Casson swung a bevy of punches, bloodying the face and breaking Beattie's nose. Beside the petrol pump across the road, Jack Pollitt lay motionless, blood pooling around him as if coming from the hose nozzle dangling loosely beside him. Marilyn stood over him screaming: "Pop, get up! Get up, Pop. Help me! *Somebody help me!*"

Jeff Madden backed away from the body, his hands raised in submission. He hadn't meant to hit the old man; he'd simply turned and lashed out at the unfamiliar face behind him and the old man had gone down, and lay unmoving.

Stepping over the body, he ducked behind the bowser and searched for a line of escape, his gaze settling on McCaig's utility. He ran for it, reefed open the door and slid in, the keys jingling as he reached down and turned the ignition. When the engine roared, Ron McCaig spun on his heels and cursed as the utility shot backwards across the gravel.

Back across Devlin Street Nick held his ground as Taylor rose unsteadily, the man rising to a wobbly crouch, his head low. He flicked a glance at the fleeing utility and snarled, distracting Nick. Then, with a sudden surge belying his groggy state, Taylor lurched forward, his crown hitting Nick in the rib-cage, knocking the wind from him. But Nick locked his arms beneath Taylor's as they collided, ensuring they would both end up on the ground. As his shoulders pounded the bitumen he kicked his legs up and tossed Taylor up over his head then somersaulted away from him, breathless as pain tore through his side.

Along the highway, blue beacons pulsed, the accompanying sirens evident but still so far away.

Madden's foot stomped on the accelerator, the vehicle scattering gravel and dirt far across the road, leaving ruts in the earth as it skidded and swayed onto the roadway. Stony pellets flicked up and showered the smaller Taylor brother as he retrieved the chain. Ben coiled the chain's length back around his hand, turned his back to deflect the dust and slop as he went in search of Nick.

Rolling to regain their feet Nick and Taylor dove back at each other, the big man's powerful forearms locking front and back of Nick's neck, his big arms crushing inwards, his massive body bearing Nick down. It was a solid neck-breaker, and Nick knew it.

Ben advanced towards them, the clinking chain dragging behind him.

CHAPTER NINETY-SIX

I screamed. *"No! No!"* Nick wouldn't stand a chance against two of them.

Bolting forward, I launched myself at the chain bearer; vaulted onto his back, my arms locking around his neck to keep me there. Flinging myself sideways I tried to throw him off-balance, trying anything to stop him reaching Nick. He writhed to toss me off, but I'd been on bigger mounts than this that couldn't get me off; my legs wrapped around his waist to get a better purchase. Before I could dig my heels in to lock myself on board he reached back and tried to drag me from his back. But I clung on tighter to his neck.

Ahead of me, Nick worked hard to free himself, twisting into the hold rather than against it. He swung half round; dropped to one knee, arched his back and pushed deep into the bigger man's stomach. Drawing both hands behind him, he locked them behind the man's thick neck then dropped his body forward and hauled his assailant up and over his back. He bellowed at the strength and pain he'd endured to achieve it, and kept the hold locked on. In another second he'd restructured his grip, duplicating the hold Taylor had had on him, the change performed so fast I barely saw him move. His forearms now folded front and back of the big man's throat and crushed inwards.

The man lashed out with a leg to kick Nick off balance, but he avoided it. Avoided it twice.

Horror filled Taylor's face as he realised he was in trouble, the hold Nick had on him fatal if he followed through with it. Nick pulled the big man upright, his legs braced, one between the man's legs, the other well back to stabilise his stance, keeping out of reach of Taylor's leg strikes. Moving again, he drew his knee up into the man's back and pushed forward, his arms dragging the hulking frame backwards. The man's neck stretched, labouring his breathing as his spine crushed inwards.

Beneath me, the chain bearer screamed: *"NO! NO! DON'T!"*

Hurling the chain away, he reached back and dragged me from his back, hurled me aside as he rushed to dislodge Nick. I'd been tossed before, but this toss launched me out onto the road just as the utility powered through. I saw a flash of white; tried to regain my balance and land on my feet to avoid it but the left front fender struck me as I straightened; the impact crushed so fast I didn't have time to scream. All the "survive-this-if-you-can' training came back in that split second, and things started rolling in slow motion; things I'd learnt the hard way shot into my head. Save yourself stuff: clear the horse – don't get tossed under foot – flip yourself higher so you have more time to plan how to land. *Flip yourself higher than the buck.* I didn't want those wheels to go over me – I'd seen a dog run over once and the way it was rolled and twisted and broken in half underneath the car had haunted my sleep ever since, so I flipped. Flipped myself higher, like stunt men when they show you how they do it in the movies. For a moment I was flying. Weightless. I crunched onto the bonnet, slid up along it, smashed against the windscreen. My back hit the glass with a resounding whack – *definitely get some bruises out of that.* Still in slow motion. My legs took control and splayed out like a cartwheel. Then my back was on the roof and my feet to the sky – those infernal gym class warm ups. Stretch to the left. Over, and stretch to the right … only I went one way. And over I went, rolling across the top of the car, my hair arcing twice the distance in a dark silky halo looking like it had just been brushed, every strand individual. Then I was airborne, turning in the air, dropping to the road. *Land on the fattest part!* But I had no fat on me so that didn't help. In that split moment I realised this was going to hurt.

Unbelievable pain ripped through me as I smacked down onto the bitumen. Slow motion started speeding up. *Roll. Roll. Tuck up and roll.* Heat seared my skin from every little rock on the road as it embedded in my flesh, minute little grazes from each and every one that scored up my arms and hips and penetrated my clothing. I rolled to a stop and lay wondering how badly I was damaged, but only for a second as my head bashed against something solid. Stars scattered across my eyes, and my world rolled in circles. The last thing I saw was the white utility flashing by and disappearing into a great black hole.

CHAPTER NINETY-SEVEN

Nick's heart leapt as Becky screamed, Ben tossing her onto the roadway as the ute powered through. He saw her land on her feet slightly off-balance, the ute coming at her, hitting her as she straightened, the speed flicking her up onto the bonnet, slamming her hard against the windshield, tossing her onto the roof. She was still spinning when she hit the roadway.

His heart stopped as she rolled to a halt and lay motionless. He needed to get to her; needed to get to her now – and he didn't need any hindrance.

Changing his grip, he locked his mighty hands beneath Taylor's boxy jaw, the man's chest widening as he bent him further back. Taylor's neck reached its limit and in that brief second Taylor realised his opponent was carrying it through: he was breaking him in half. His big hands groped behind him. "No! No!" he cried, but his voice was muffled beneath those powerful hands.

Crack crack. His body bent abnormally back as his neck was ripped sideways. Dave Taylor felt no more.

Discarding the body like a useless rag doll, Nick turned to the roadway, heading to where Becky lay. His head shook, his body draining of air and strength as an invisible force squeezed his heart in his chest.

He moved slowly at first, not wanting to see what he knew he would find, his whole body chilling internally, externally. Desperately he wanted Becky to move; he wanted her to sit up and give him that cheeky smile that sometimes spread across her face, or give him that inconsequential glare that only she dared give him when she blamed him for something he might or might not have done. His throat tightened, a lump blocking his airway for he knew that wasn't going to happen. And his heart grew more pained that the rest of him.

Screaming like a wounded beast, Ben Taylor stood over his brother's lifeless form, and for the first time in his life he cried. Tears streamed down his face unchecked. He swung around ignorant of the sirens and blue pulsing lights entering Cullan as he headed for the car.

Nick slipped his arm under Becky and gently rolled her over, her body limp in his arms. Vaguely he heard far away someone calling his name, but it didn't matter. Nothing mattered now. He smoothed the hair from her face, wiped away the blood seeping from a long scrape in her cheek then lifted her into his arms. The sticky warmth of fresh blood trailed down his arm, dripped from his elbow. He tried to reposition his arm to contain the flow; tried to seal the gaping wound in her flesh and will the life back into her. Cradling her against him, he carried her from the roadside; carried her towards the hotel. Her eyes opened briefly and she looked up at him, those beautiful dark blue pools glazed and pale. He didn't think she saw him. But he did feel her breathing. *There's still time.*

He passed the body of Dave Taylor ...

– but didn't see it ...

– he passed Rosalind, standing frozen, her hands clamped over her mouth, silencing her scream ...

– he didn't see her.

Sheila stood on the verandah, crying, calling his name, the horror of what she'd witnessed painted across her face.

"Get an ambulance. There's still time," he told her.

Reaching in through the car window, Ben Taylor grasped the wooden stock and pulled his rifle cleanly through the opening. In one swift move he threw it to his shoulder, took aim and fired. Even though tears blurred his vision his aim was true, and white smoke and the heavy smell of cordite wafted on the breeze.

"That's for Dave!" he said, pulling back the bolt. He rammed it back in again and squeezed off a second shot as Manetti turned his way. "And that's for me!"

Rod Willcox stepped from the Police car, stunned by the bodies strewn across the roadway. It had been a massacre, a senseless bloody massacre. He watched as Ben Taylor pulled the trigger the first time, and snatched his weapon from inside the vehicle.

"Police! Drop your weapon!" he bellowed, raising the pistol and taking aim. Another shot tore from the barrel, and Rod made it a third, hitting the gunman just off line of the temple, a little hole spurting blood as the giant body lifted from the ground and crumpled back to earth.

Nick's eyes remained on Sheila. "Get help," he said hoarsely, his voice barely audible. Suddenly he was jolted forward, a violent force bowling him almost off his feet, almost making him lose his grip on Becky. *Don't drop the load! Never drop the load! Shit, what was that?*

Pain ripped through him like a knife, burning and tearing simultaneously through his side. Blood sprayed out in front of him. He frowned as the realisation took place, as he fought to catch his breath and fight back the agony fast overtaking him.

Clutching Becky tighter, he looked up at Sheila, and frowned deeper. Then he turned, needing to know what had hit him. The second bullet embedded deep in his chest, driving him backwards into the side of a grey van parked in the Hotel car park, his body buckling the panels.

He looked down; saw the sticky red stain oozing through his shirt, oozing through a burning hole in his skin. *Too much*, he shook his head. *Too much.*

His legs buckled beneath him and he slid down the panel,

blood smearing the paint-work as he sank. Still he held Becky tight.

Sheila swung down from the verandah, tears blurring her vision. She knelt beside him as his dark eyes lowered, as he came to terms with what had happened. He glanced up at her then lowered his gaze to Becky, but still she didn't see him.

"Help her," he begged. Then he coughed, the pain stealing his air. "There's still time ..."

Sheila cried openly. "Nick ..."

His head tilted back against the car as he tried to blot out the pain, as he tried to force air in, but nothing seemed to work. "Jesus," he coughed. He gasped a breath, tried to swallow it down but his body tightened against his will, blocking it; and he trembled as the cold swept over him.

He groaned as Becky's lashes lowered, her eyes closing fully. *Jesus no*. He closed his own eyes, pressed them tight, not wanting to see anything more, not wanting the moisture rising in his eyes to fall. He felt them take her from him, clutched tightly to her to stop them.

"You've got to let her go, Nick," someone said as they prised his fingers open, and then she was gone. He felt something press hard against his chest and opened his eyes again. Rod knelt beside him, his hand pushing hard over the hole in his chest. "Funny," he said, coughing again, "I knew it would be like this." He closed his eyes, and concentrated on breathing; just the tiniest breath. He heard Rod's voice shouting: "You hang on, Nick. You hang on there. Just hold on, you hear me? Somebody help me here! Somebody get me a ... ...! Somebody ..."

Sheila's arms wrapped around him; he could smell her lavender perfume. "Oh my boy ... my poor boy. You'll be all right, Nick. Please, you'll be all right." She rocked him, her voice soothing as he started to shiver.

"I'm sorry about Kennie," he murmured, wanting more than anything to tell her the truth right then – it wasn't right that he hadn't told her. But his head fell heavy against her, no strength left to say anything at all. *No feeling, no pain.*

Epilogue

CHAPTER NINETY-EIGHT

Looking out at the roadway Cussack shook his head: the slaughter on Devlin Street was a sight Cullan residents would never forget. The damp red earth around the hotel was spattered a deeper hue as splotches of blood trailed towards the hotel. In and out the solid brown door his officers trudged, parading in a procession of injured men and highly emotional women. Blue revolving lights mixed with red ones, both marbling a pattern on the cream hotel walls, the colours penetrating the windows and reflecting off the mirror behind the bar. They turned the room an eerie pulsing mauve.

Cussack's huge frame sagged as he turned. He looked down at the Publican, Manetti still cradled in her arms. Tears misted his vision. The man resembled his son; was about his boy's age too, and he realised maybe he wasn't as over his loss as he'd thought. He remembered the watch in his pocket. Looking towards Dayton, he blinked to clear his eyes, so many memories flooding in.

The second ambulance was arriving and he sighed. They would need a lot more yet.

Under the morning sun vehicles dotted the roadway, the town more like a Saturday evening than a bleak Tuesday morning. Two white utilities remained as left, one on the verge, the other stopped in the road's centre where its escape had been thwarted. Farther off, a mud spattered Hilux sat alone, a grim reminder of a last desperate bid to reach safety. Further down, a fleet of squad cars lined the highway opposite – two from Dayton, one each from Stansville and Mount Lawson.

Leaning against the front of one sedan, Rod Willcox hunched over, his body shaking with cold and grief. It was understandable, for this was his town; these were his friends. The shock of his action in the line of duty hadn't yet warranted his focus. He stared blankly at the body of Ben Taylor which lay beside the utility, its face now covered with a Police jacket, and, while he felt unusually cold, his iciness had little to do with his state of undress. He heard Ken Carter on the radio making urgent requests for more ambulances from surrounding towns, but didn't look up. It was just too late for some.

Strewn across the gravel, grey blankets hid death's ugliness from passers-by. 'Not that anyone could get by with the melee's aftermath blocking the road,' the Coroner thought as he stood among the mounds. He read from a clipboard, mildly grateful the Police Sergeant had been thorough, for in front of him, in scrawled but legible print, was the death list. Names. Possible causes of death. Witnesses. All the information he would need for the moment. He stood turning, surveying the scene with casual disregard as he wondered where to start for not since the random bombing of a Saigon cafe during the war had he seen so much human suffering in one small place. He shook his head at the likeness.

Parked below the Hotel steps, two ambulances prepared to make the dash to Dayton, lives depending on their speed. He hoped they would make it for it would make his job a hell of a lot easier. His attention swung to a slender blonde being escorted from the scene, her arms flailing in her resistance to move away. She kept screaming for someone called Nick. He turned his back on her, shook his head, and wondered which of the poor unfortunates that was. An ambulance pulled out, its siren wailing its urgency. The second one was closing up, almost ready to follow. It would be some time before any more arrived.

His gaze fell back on the paper and he put his mind to work, matching mounds with names. Daresay he would get to 'Nick' soon enough. But for now, he had a constable ready to assist him.

Ray Smedley peeled back the first blanket.

The name on top of the list was POLLITT: Jack Earnest. Age – approximately 80. Most obvious cause of death: Head injuries. Witness: Marilyn Perry, and in parentheses the warning: 'Grand-daughter'.

'Poor kid,' he thought, looking up as he tried to pick who Marilyn was, if she was even still here. It could become quite a game putting names to faces, but the total waste of life tended to make it a rather sinister past-time, and he imagined himself yelling excitedly "Six. Six out of ten!" and chastised himself for his callousness. It really wasn't funny. He turned back to his job, more subdued.

The pallid face of the withered old man beneath the blanket was stained with blood yet somehow he looked strangely peaceful. He'd seen that before on the aged, and wasn't surprised that the small head wound had bled so profusely. But, he shrugged, there wasn't much he hadn't seen over the years.

He examined the old man closer, making notation that he would first examine the bridge of the nose to verify its shattering as the main cause of death. He let the officer lower the cover and looked around to keep his thoughts clear.

To his right across the intersection he noticed the Police officer who had drawn and fired, and the rather bulky Police Sergeant, both butt-reclining against the front of a Police sedan.

Staring at the ground, Rod shook his head and exhaled loudly; he still rocked slightly.

"How are you feeling now?" Cussack inquired.

Willcox shot a harsh glance at the corpse lying on the roadside. "You know," he said with dull surprise, "... I don't regret it." He looked back at the Sergeant, his emotions more staid with the time he'd been given to compose himself. He glanced across to the other officers who were making order from chaos.

Cussack put his hand on the man's shoulder and sighed, remembering Manetti's resemblance to his son. Then his own eyes flicked down at the body by the ute. "With scum like that I don't think I would either," he admitted. He heaved a deep breath, and let it out. "Well it's done now, so try and keep busy," he suggested, "and besides, you've still got some mates in there that might need a hand."

Nodding, Rod pushed away from the car and slowly crossed the Hotel parking bay. He paused on reaching where Nick and the Cooper girl had lay, swallowed hard on seeing the pools of blood and the long smear of red on the shiny grey duco. Inhaling, he set his jaw and walked on up the steps to where Sheila sat on the stairhead. Her face was ashen, her teary eyes red from crying. He eased her to her feet and hugged her tightly. She really needed a friend to help her through this.

Taking a last long look over the top of her head at the blanketed bodies, he guided her back inside. Cullan, from this day, would never be the same.

The Coroner's eyes dropped back to the paper, to the second name on the list.

"TAYLOR: David Lester," he told Smedley. He followed him across the road and read silently as the blanket was lifted. Approximately 35. Broken neck ... with a big question mark and a scrawled note saying 'YOU'RE THE CORONER'. He looked up at Cussack who now stood at the foot of the hotel steps, and wondered if the man was trying to be funny – he'd heard the Sergeant had a warped sense of humour ... or maybe he was being facetious. It didn't matter. He read on. Witness: Peter Lacey.

Bending over, he inspected the body and shook his head in awe. The neck was broken all right, and he'd be interested to find out how. The guy had a neck like a Northwest bull, and he wouldn't like to meet whoever broke it. Out of interest, he looked around, trying to find someone bigger than Taylor. But couldn't. He indicated to Smedley to re-cover the body.

"McCAIG: William T.," he said.

Only ten strides away. As the grey cover lifted, a pale grey face stared back, contorted with fear and pain. He glanced back to his paper. "Age: Late 50's. That looks about right. Head injuries."

He frowned for nothing was obvious. He took a punt and scribbled on the page 'Suspected coronary'. That he could picture, in which case a witness would be an asset.

"Ron McCaig," he read the name aloud.

"His son," Smedley offered briefly.

"Hasn't been a good day here for anyone, has it?" he said, glancing around. "Grand-daughters. Sons."

Smedley shook his head and pursed his lips. "That one's brother is over there," he offered further, indicating Dave Taylor and the corpse beside the utility.

"A real family affair." The Coroner wandered across the road, crouched and lifted the jacket himself.

"Ben Taylor," Smedley said, coming up behind him.

The scrawl on the paper said TAYLOR: Benjamin Lewis. Age: 30 plus. The words 'Head injuries'. This time he laughed. If Cussack was trying to be funny, he'd done it. The neat hole had penetrated the temple and the bullet probably rattled around inside the skull and brain. As good a way to go as any, he considered. "He probably didn't feel a thing," he muttered, replacing the coat.

"Shame. After what he did we'd liked him to have felt the most," Smedley snapped, his face drawn to a harsh profile.

The Coroner rose to his full height, reminding himself to be mindful of what he said. For all the distance between towns these people were closely linked. He nodded to the officer beside him, noting that he had heard his comment. If he wanted to take it as agreement, he could – it didn't matter much.

Stepping back as the second ambulance pulled out of Cullan, he scanned the battlefield then lifted the page on the folder and added Peter Kennedy to the list, a reminder that the circumstances were linked. Looking about again, he turned to his assistant. "Chalk the outlines, then we'll organise getting this lot moved," he said.

He headed across to the two city detectives. So much for the quick country flight these boys had promised when they'd dragged him from his bed. He couldn't see himself getting clear of Dayton for days. Then a thought drifted in – if he could find a phone he'd ring home. Seeing this sort of loss always made him miss his wife for no-one ever knew what tomorrow might bring.

CHAPTER NINETY-NINE

At first, the room seemed dark then cleared to a hazy opaque grey. Hands moved about him – soft, warm hands. His mouth felt dry, his throat parched and sore, and his head swum in slow disorientating circles. Breathing in caused pain, so much so he resisted it then found he couldn't. He felt like he was drowning, sinking in a senseless stupor that wouldn't let him surface; each time he tried something pulled him down again. Heaviness weighed over him, the solidness of his own limbs restricting every movement. But he kept trying, kept pushing upward, drawing closer and closer to the light. Then all became brilliant though his lungs hurt. He coughed as air burned a long trail upward.

Desperate to rise from the deep place he was at, he swept the haziness from his mind. Saw colour. Brown. Brown hair. Soft fingers touched him again; stroked his wrist.

"Bec?" The word sounded slurred even to his own ears.

"Mr Manetti?" The voice was soft, unfamiliar. "You can wake up now, Mr Manetti."

Mr? Nobody calls me Mr. He blinked heavily. Drew in more air. *Uniforms. White uniforms.* White pillows caressed his back. He tried to lift his head but couldn't. It felt dull and heavy. All he could do was turn it slightly and look.

Nurses! ... Hospital ...

– another spate of the proverbial squeaky shoes.

Plastic bottles and tubes hung above him. His left side felt numb, and his head now swam in a tumult of thoughts that rose and fell and churned. He raised his right hand to stop the swirling, noted that his breathing evened out.

"Becky?" he said more determinedly. *Answer me!*

From the right, another white coat leant over him and a bright light shone into one eye then the other. His right eye blinked rapidly in response, the other barely registered a flicker. Cold fingers took his pulse. He couldn't feel his heartbeat and wondered for a moment if he had one. *Or is this how it is at the end? Transition.* His vision became less ghosted.

"You are in hospital, Mr Manetti," a male voice said through the swirl in his mind. "I'm Doctor Wilson ..."

With the thick glasses and greying hair, the name fit, but Nick didn't comment. He was trying to form other words.

"You're a very lucky man," the medic added as he wrote on the chart at the end of the bed. "The Flying Doctors had their work cut out keeping you alive." Nick stared at the ceiling; forced his eyes to focus. That didn't matter. He needed more information.

"Do you remember anything that happened?"

He mustered a word with difficulty. "Enough." And felt breathless again.

"You suffered two gunshot wounds ... one to your chest, and another which tore a path through an old wound in your left side."

Not important! He shook his head. He had to force out the words he wanted.

"... This will take a while to heal and will be fairly painful until it does, so I'm afraid you're in for a long period of bed rest. Other than that there was no long term damage to vital organs." The man played with the dial on one of the tubes, increased its flow, and warmth flowed through him. "We also found a couple of cracked ribs in there so you just lay still and take it easy. Don't move around too much."

"The Kid ..." Nick breathed out.

The Doctor leant closer. "Pardon?"

Nick drew more air, summoned more strength. "Becky ... how is she?"

The Doctor raised an eyebrow at the nurse who shrugged. "I'll find out for you," she said, squeezing his hand. It was a dull touch. Had his hand gone completely dead? He lay back, closed his eyes, and waited for news.

The room was much lighter when next he opened his eyes. Cream curtains hung across a window, and he knew he had slept a long time by the simple fact he could breathe, and where once he had felt numb he now felt pain. He opened his eyes fully, no longer drunken in senses. A brown-haired nurse at his side adjusted the dial on one of the tubes, compared its flow to her wrist watch. She smiled down at him.

"Did you have a good sleep?"

He didn't answer for he had a question of his own. "How long have I been here?"

"Three days."

"Three days!"

He scanned the room but no-one was there. No-one sat waiting in the chair beside his bed as had sometimes been the case when he'd woken in the Army Hospital. He did note however that his watch was on the cabinet to his right. He thought he'd lost it.

"Becky ... How is she?" he asked, wary of his own question. Maybe she'd put it there.

The nurse shook her head. "I'm sorry, Mr Manetti ..."

He closed his eyes tight, not wanting to hear.

Turning from straightening the covers, she checked the tape that held the tubes to his arm. "... she wasn't admitted to this hospital so I haven't been able to get that information for you. We're still trying to find out and I'll let you know as soon as we hear something."

Nick's optimism sagged. She wasn't admitted. Why wasn't she? He ran a nervous hand over his face, felt cold sweat emitting from his pores. *You know why! You saw it happen ... She's gone. Accept it!* His throat tightened, invisible hands of despair clamping around it, squeezing hard. *No.* He couldn't accept it. He inhaled deeply, wishing the hands would tighten, and just keep tightening. He'd dreamt of her living in his house; pictured waking up beside her every morning. He'd seen the emptiness of his life plummeting ... made plans again.

Come on. You've accepted it before! Death is death. Remember? It all happens sooner or later.

But his mind screamed. *No. Not this time! This time it matters!*

Blinking faster, he stared at the ceiling, the throbbing above his eye annoying. But it couldn't match the tightness in his chest or the hollow feeling in his gut.

Block it out! It doesn't matter. You're just back where you started, that's all, only now minus a friend. Then he remembered Pete. *Minus two friends*, and the hollow space within him deepened. He exhaled, his chest aching, the pain in his throat burning hotter as the vision in his good eye blurred. He fingered the moisture away.

Completing the chart, the nurse inserted the clipboard back into the holder. "Can I get you something for the pain, Mr Manetti?"

He shook his head. It wasn't that pain that bothered him. "No. It helps break the boredom," he sighed and turned his face to the wall.

She smiled. "Well I can see you're going to be a bundle of laughs to look after. Just try and get some rest. I won't be far away if you need me."

Nick stared back at the ceiling and, closing his eyes; concentrated more on the pain. It was better than feeling the nothingness that now tore him apart.

Sometime later, he slept again, the faces hovering over him taunting.

Dozing lightly, more resting his eyes than sleeping, Nick heard the click of the door as it opened. Then silence. *No squeaky shoes*. No click to signify the door had closed again. He heard a faint whisper: "Go on ..."

He opened his eyes and turned his head to the door, which stood ajar. Through the brightness of the corridor beyond he saw a silhouette. Two silhouettes, one obviously Ros's hourglass frame. Her voice. His breath left him for the other shape was broader, sturdier, athletic. *Unbreakable*. He prayed.

His heart pounded life back into him and he blinked to clear the haziness in his eyes. If this was a dream, these dreams were worse than Nam.

CHAPTER ONE HUNDRED

I froze in the doorway, wondering if I could carry out what I'd come to do. For days I'd wanted to come here, but I hadn't been able to stand, the lacerations in my back and arms and concussion keeping me in Dayton Hospital longer than I wanted. Finally I'd been so determined to leave they'd let me go.

Ros nudged my shoulder and I went forward, intending to stay only a few short moments. I just needed to know that Nick was okay then I'd leave. He'd probably be too polite to tell me to go, and he couldn't exactly get up and leave himself from what I'd heard.

Nick Manetti doesn't get involved with women. Those words had drummed through my head all those days in Dayton Hospital. And even though we'd shared something wonderful, something I would carry with me the rest of my life, I didn't expect him to be 'involved' just because it had happened. And that alone had cemented my decision. Coming to Cullan had been one giant mistake. Meeting Nick had been the only good thing that had come of it; he had given me memories I would treasure forever.

I drew closer, fighting to hold back tears that rose at the damage he'd suffered, mostly from protecting me.

He was propped up on a high bank of pillows, the bronze toning of his skin a far contrast to the crisp whiteness of the linen. They made him seem more golden, but highlighted the bruises too. His face was bruised and swollen, the split above his left eye now stitched and yellow, his eye barely able to open. A thick wad of dressing covered his left shoulder and chest, his rib-cage encased in heavier tape that disappeared beneath the covers. I knew now what Sergeant Cussack had meant when he'd said

Nick looked like he'd gone three rounds with Muhammad Ali, with both hands tied behind his back. His right hand was bandaged to the fingers, and the gash on the back of his neck was covered with a narrow strip of gauze.

I shook my head, for even when they'd warned me he was pretty messed up I hadn't expected this. This was Nick ... the 'Rock'.

He looked straight at me. No expression. *Here goes.*

I reached his bedside trying to muster the words I'd practiced for days. "You look awful," just tumbled out. Not the words I'd practised.

"Yeah? Well it's nice to see you too," he smiled slightly.

I love that smile. "I ... I didn't mean ..." My eyes started to moisten. *No. Don't cry. I won't cry.*

Nick reached out. "Hey, come here."

I moved closer, and his hand found mine and closed over it. He drew me closer, his fingers reaching the loose flowing ends of my hair, which he gathered in his fingertips. Gently he pulled down and I submitted to the pressure, following his direction until our lips were close. *This is confusing. What does he want?*

Don't confuse me, Nick. You don't complicate your life with women.

He started to lift his head the rest of the way then said: "I'm a bit laid up. You'll have to come down here."

Still in a quandary I let my lips touch his. It was a warm, lasting kiss, totally unexpected, totally instigated by him. The night we'd spent together tumbled through my mind, the pictures tightening my breasts and making my heart flutter. *Don't play games, Nick!* How I needed to say those words out loud. I fought not to respond to him. I wouldn't make that mistake a second time.

He let go of my hair, let me up again then noticed Rosalind backing out the door. She gave him the 'Ssh' sign with her finger and finger waved. "I'm off downstairs to see Sam," she said softly.

Nick's face straightened and he tried to sit up.

"It's okay ... he's doing fine," she told him. "Someone in the fight had a knife. They sent you both down on the same plane. Sam's been pretty worried about you and wants to know how you are. Apparently it was touch and go with you all the way ..."

Nick's expression hardened, and Ros put her hands up. "I'm going ... I'm going."

"Say Hello for me," he told her as she slipped out of the room. His gaze turned to me, and he raised a hand and gently lifted my jaw, turning my bruises and grazes to the light. "Are you okay?" he asked, his concern genuine. He tried to roll to his side to see me better but the pain thwarted the attempt. Nevertheless he seemed pleased that I nodded. Then he looked worried as tears rose in my eyes.

"Just a few stitches and one hell of a headache," I shrugged, trying to shake off my sadness. "It looked worse than it was."

He looked further concerned. "Are the horses okay?"

I nodded and almost smiled. It was an odd question for him to ask, odd that he would even think of my boys – no-one else ever did – and it was sweet of him to think of them. I scanned his face to place it indelibly in my mind, to burn him into my memory forever. *It's time.*

I squeezed his hand, held it a moment then let it go. Catching my breath, I pushed back the tears that burned a path to my eyes. "Well, I gotta go, Nick. I just came to see that you were okay, and to say goodbye ... and to say thanks for everything you did for me, and everyone else. I'm really sorry it happened. I'm really sorry you ended up like this." My tears became a furnace, but I fought them back, straightened my back to win the war.

He huffed a laugh – that old 'what the hell are you talking about' scoff. "It wasn't your fault ..."

I smiled grimly then turned and moved towards the door.

"Hey," he called after me, "what's all this about? Where are you going?"

I shrugged; couldn't turn back. "I just gotta go," I said, the finality of it cutting deep. I started walking.

"Becky, come back here!"

I shook my head, the tears winning the battle. I looked at the ceiling, fighting harder to keep control, my heart thudding like a sledgehammer pounding on a tree trunk.

"Why, Kid? Tell me, what's going on?"

I drew breath, hoping it would extinguish the fire. "The folks are coming home and I want to have my horses out and be gone by then. I go where ..."

Nick raised himself on an elbow; started coughing. "There's a gate in the boundary fence at the bottom of your lower paddock. Let them through into Northgate," he said before I'd finished.

My tears rolled. "No, Nick. I ..."

"Why not? The paddock's clean ... safe."

"It's not that."

His voice softened as if he'd suddenly gained insight. "Ah. You don't like living in Cullan?"

I turned back to him. "Of course I do."

"Then why not?"

I stared at him wordlessly. *Because you don't get involved with women! And it's just too hard seeing you. And it's just too painful if you ever treat me like Marilyn.* "I just can't!"

"Come over here."

I shook my head, not daring to get close to him ever again. And I would never make him feel he had to commit to me because of what I'd let happen, for what I'd instigated.

He tried to sit up but pain forced him down again. "Becky, come back here ... please ... come back here."

I didn't move, my tears reaching the threshold of my lids.

"I don't ask a third time," he warned, his teeth clenched against the pain. "If I have to I'll rip all these tubes out and come over and get you?"

My jaw dropped open. By the tone of his voice he'd do it. Slowly I returned to his bedside, his hand claiming mine as soon as I came in reach. The simple warmth of it poured life back into my soul. The strength of his grip impressed his words and increased my strength.

"I want you to move into Northgate. I'll be laid up here for a while yet, and it'll give you time to think about what you really want. But I at least want you to be there when I come home 'cose, kiddo, we gotta talk."

I shook my head again, my hair swaying down my back near where his fingers twined amongst the ends.

"Why not?" he asked again, sounding a little bored.

I drew a frustrated breath. "I just can't. Look I'm sorry for what happened the other night, I really am sorry, and I have no intention of complicat ..."

"Hey ..."; his fingers on my lips stopped my words, "what happened the other night I've wanted to happen since the first time I saw you. And have you thought maybe I might want to complicate my life with you." He half smiled. "I could certainly complicate yours." He reached up and caressed my cheek, tenderly around the blue patchy bruise. "Please, don't go yet. I need you to be there."

My heart somersaulted, and I leant into him, a single tear rolling that he considered me worth changing for. Still I shook my head. I'd already looked at this from every angle. "No. You don't need ..."

His eyes darkened. "*I* don't need ... What makes you think I don't need? Because I'm a rock? Well I'll tell you, kiddo, rocks shatter like everything else, and you're shattering me more than those damn bullets." He fixed his stare on the ceiling and drew a deep resigning breathe. That was that then. He was beyond fighting. A long moment passed before he flicked a glance my way.

My tears rolled fully and I bent down and pressed my lips to his, and he pulled me down further, the slight tasting of his lips not enough. His lips, his tongue, rekindled the fires he'd stirred in me before, as if needing to convince me of so many reasons to stay. "You said something to me the other night," he whispered against my cheek, "and I'd really like the chance to find out if it's true."

I drew back from him, my cheeks flushing that he'd heard my murmured confession.

"Do you remember?"

I nodded.

"Is it?"

I nodded again and a single tear rolled. I wiped it away.

"So it's yes?"

I smiled warmly, happy tears falling as my heart burst with the need of him. "Oh yes. Every single bit yes."

The door clicked open then and a nurse stopped in the opening. "Just checking, Mr Manetti ... do you need anything before I go off duty?"

Nick smiled broadly and squeezed my hand. "No. I've got everything I need right here," he said. "And hey! ..." he called as the door almost shut again.

The nurse's head reappeared.

"... the name's Nick." God how he hated superfluity!

ABOUT THE AUTHOR

Western Australian born author Helen Iles writes in all genres. Her love of the State's Northwest and particularly the northern wheatbelt region stirred the idea for this novel. Her strong background in training horses and emergency service work also features throughout the adventure.

A Creative Writing tutor, Helen writes adult and children's fiction, text books and poetry, and provides manuscript assessment and editing services. She conducts writing workshops between penning the chapters of her next intriguing novel.

Other titles by this author:

Penny's Silver Dragon – (Young Readers)
The Horse Keepers – (Fiction Novel)
Ride a Crock Horse (Poetry)
Of Bushmen and Brumbies (Poetry)
Writing Poetry - Simplified (Non-fiction)
We Are Different, You and I (Children's Picture Book)